Burn Down
Bloody Twilight

A Novel
by
Jeff Holland

Threat Quality Press
1299 New Gulph Road
Gulph Mills, PA 19428

The characters and events in this book are fictitious. Any similarity to real persons, living or dead, is coincidental and not intended by the author.

ISBN 978-0-9828884-0-7

For my family and friends.

PART ONE: BEFORE BLOODY TWILIGHT'S END

1. Captain Mene's Final Assessment

It took him over an hour of fighting, but Victor Mene, captain of the Royal Guard of Western Sun, had finally made his way to the edge of the kingdom. His armor was spattered in blood. The blood was more gray than red.

One of his soldiers stepped before him.

Mene greeted him formally. "Sergeant Colby. Good to see you." He firmed his grip on his sword. "I'm sorry."

And then Victor Mene swiped his sword and took off the man's head, as another soldier came up to him.

"Corporal Howell. I'm sorry." And then Victor Mene smashed his shield into the man's face. Crushing it completely.

A feeling he would almost categorize as shame had been creeping up on Victor Mene throughout the last hour. Maybe longer than that. A rare feeling, if he was being honest with himself. Up until recently, he had felt nothing but pride for the entirety of his military service. Shame...he hardly had a context for it.

It wasn't for leading his men into a total slaughter. An entire battalion of Western Sun's finest, coming back to their homeland dead on carts in waves. Though he would always keep that loss with him, as he believed no leader should ever forget his failures.   But this is the nature of warfare. Good men die. One of life's simple truths, no matter how abhorrent it may be.

It wasn't for keeping quiet when the Orphan – the Queen in Waiting, he corrected himself – listened to Grolev, her advisor. Mene had spoken his piece when the decision to invade the southlands had been made. He had explained to the best of his ability his doubts that they could annex that savage land. But in the end, Victor Mene was a soldier, not an advisor. He would not accept the blame for the poor judgment of the Queen in Waiting's cabinet, or the manipulations of her mystical advisor.

And it wasn't because he did not foresee Grolev's manipulations resulting in the current state of his kingdom. But Grolev's suggestion to raise the dead sons of the kingdom, and that the Queen in Waiting, in her grief over one young private, would agree to this course of action - who could possibly have foreseen that?

If the feeling in his gut was indeed shame, as he was starting to suspect, then he placed it squarely on the fact that he had apparently trained his men so poorly that they would rise up from death with no memory of his battle tactics. No fighting skills at all, really, other than frantic rushing and a sloppy desire to spill blood.

"Peter Mink. You too, eh? No more than a schoolboy. I should have drummed you out when I first saw you. I'm sorry." And his sword dropped again.

Victor Mene believed himself to be without fear. He came from a long line of guardsmen. Victor honored the guard and everything it stood for. It was the family business, after all. His mother had died in childbirth, and he had no siblings. He was raised by guardsmen. He had learned to fight - learned to win - from the moment he could stand.

Atticus Shore shambled up to attack him next. "Corporal Shore. Well. You were a waste. I'm not sorry." He split the man's skull with his blade, then gutted him with the shield, and moved on his way.

Victor Mene's major failing, as far as he could fathom it, lay in what he could only see as his piss-poor training of the men under his command. That they would return from the dead was both disgusting and regrettable - but not his fault. That they would be such easy prey for a lone guardsman, that this mass of angry, pathetic retches that he had once called soldiers, would let him leave the kingdom grounds this easily, on the other hand....

Mene once again felt shame in his gut. He accepted that his own failures had been a part of this travesty, as well he should have.

He blamed other people more.

And he knew exactly who to deal with, in order to take the vengeance he felt he had earned. She had reached out to him, offered him a means to exact that revenge.

She had also mentioned that Nathan Cord would be instrumental to his goal. Cord. The disgrace of Western Sun. Indisputably Mene's greatest failure before this day.

After dispatching a few more of his former charges, he finally, for the first time, let himself feel fear. The very real fear that he would not be able to restrain himself from killing Nathan Cord before he had outlived his usefulness.

Captain Victor Mene let the fear feed his anger, and hacked his way through a dozen more dead shambling things that were once his soldiers before passing the barrier that kept them within the kingdom's walls.

There was bloody, miserable work to do.

2. The Glory Road to Admiral Mudd's Lament

Quinn Kind had taken a horse and rode it for most of her journey, but when she got close enough, she slapped its ass and sent it hustling back to its home at the edge of the Pic Forest a few miles back. She hoped to reach her destination without drawing any unwanted attention that might fall on a short woman riding a tall horse.

Moving through the fields, nothing but swift and silent, she had time to wonder what kind of mood the chief would be in. It would probably depend on the amount of people in his bar. More than three and he would grumble something abou feeling crowded, and in that case his mood would probably make "foul" seem sunny and conversational.

She reached the end of the fields, the last bit of cover she would get. Now staring at the long, flat expanse of empty plains ahead of her, she surveyed the rest of her journey. Open space. Nothing but. She squinted. She didn't need to; it was purely for effect. Her eyes could make out detail from two miles ahead if necessary, but she'd spent a lot of time around humans and managed to pick up a few mannerisms as a result.

Not that she minded, really. She always liked how humans would squint, and then frown, and say something simple and obvious yet authoritative like, "Here they come," or "We've got to take that hill." That tendency of theirs always cracked her up.

There was a lot about human behavior that amused her. Like the behavior they called "brave" and "courageous," but which the Pics, and indeed most other woodlander clans, would dub "suicidal." If things went according to her admittedly harebrained plan, she noted, she might get to compare "brave" and "suicidal" firsthand.

Quinn Kind eyed the next few miles of flat land, of green green grass and springtime wildflowers practically glowing in the late afternoon of the sun.

And totally devoid of decent cover. A Pic in the woods is a ghost, as invisible as air. A Pic in the open, acting without serious caution, is a moving target.

She made her squint-face, because she saw what she was hoping to avoid, right between her and her destination. Wolves. Lots of them. Maybe two hundred feet ahead. Pretty much exactly where she didn't need them to be. She processed the situation calmly, then mustered up her own human-ism. That thing to say when they see something they don't like, but know they'll have to deal with all the same.

In a low, calm, quiet voice, she muttered, "Ah, crap."

Wolves are a cranky lot any day of the week. But they take special glee in hating Pics. "Pixies," as the humans referred to her people – usually in the pejorative. Wolves held particular contempt – she always assumed, anyway – for "pixies" with six-inch curved blades strapped to their calves and pressing business on their minds.

Quinn rolled it around in her mouth again, then dropped it out a little more carefully: "Caaaa-raaaaaap. Cra-papa-pa-pap."

There was pretty much only one course of action she could take, and she wasn't pleased at all to be so limited in her options. A Pic trick. Sink into the ground. She'd gone to such lengths to blend in, camouflaging herself with a woodland greens, grays and browns in her clothing. After making the effort to cloak herself, sinking into the ground just felt like cheating. And going underground for that long always made her feel a bit wobbly and disoriented when she finally came out on the other side.

Being chomped on by wolves will probably feel a lot worse, she reasoned. So she melted into the grass, slithering along with the green blades, invisible to anything outside her own kind. Then she headed further down. Invisible to everything but the earth itself.

A great deal of concentration and several miles later, Quinn Kind became a gentle eruption in a garden three doors down from her destination.
Her head careened wildly about, unable to situate itself. She bent down to focus her eyes on a stationary object. Namely, her own trembling feet. It only made her vomit. It could have been worse.

After letting the shock make its way through her, accepting the rough receipt of transition from earth back to being, she worked on getting her bearings. Perked her nose up to sniff out the lay of the land.

Sawdust.

Mud.

Pigshit.

"Close, at least," she whispered to herself, cracking a slight smile. Something brushed past her ankle. She looked down. A pig oinked back pleasantly. It was then that Quinn knew what she was standing in.

"Ah. Crap," she muttered, realizing she might have to request a shower when she got to the chief's place.

Walking up the road of what could be referred to by judgmental types as a shanty-town, Quinn rehearsed the pitch she would use when she put her proposal to the chief. Revision one? Stop referring to him as "chief." If there was one thing that would piss Nathan Cord off, it would be the mention of his former title. No matter how well deserved it was, it would only serve as a lousy reminder of the circumstances by which he had lost it.

He would see through flattery. And he wouldn't respond to the "For the good of the people" argument. He didn't *like* people as a general rule. And in particular, considering the people of Bloody Twilight would demand his head on a pike if they knew for sure he was still alive, he probably wouldn't be able to muster up much patriotic love for them.

Quinn was having a hard time figuring out exactly what tactic he *would* respond to. No, that wasn't quite right. There was one. She just hated it. And it wasn't so much a tactic as it was extortion, but she knew Cord would have to meet her request if she went through with it.

No real downside, except for the coin-flip of two scenarios: the best-case, wherein Cord would never speak to Quinn again, or the worst-case, which entailed him cutting her up into tiny little pieces the moment she opened her mouth to explain things.

It was hard to tell with him some days. Hard to judge for sure just how far gone he was from the man she had called a friend. And a man she had once referred to as the best humankind had to offer.

She hoped it was a good day, and marched up to Admiral Mudd's Lament, a hole in the ground – literally – that Cord saw fit to call a bar. From the outside, it was nothing special or unusual. Bricks, mortar, and a hastily-painted sign, hung four feet high. On the inside, after marching down six steps, pretty much the same, without the sign. A fireplace in the center of the room. Small windows, barely the width of her own petite shoulders, situated along the ground outside, letting in little creaks of light. Less a bar so much as a very inviting cave, atmospherically speaking.

After making her way down the uneven steps and slipping through the door, she scanned the room. A couple of tables manned by the area pig farmers, a few neighborhood regulars perched by the counter. Udo, the best bartender in the Cabrea region, refilling their glasses. And in one dark corner sat the one-eyed king-killer himself, the infamous and disgraced former chief of Coal Brigade, Nathan James Cord.

Quinn never really understood what special body chemistry allowed the Pics to move undetectably to human eyes. Then again, she never questioned it either, since it was one of her favorite species differences. Not even the northern

Tree-bob clan, who were more common to this area, was as naturally gifted as the Pics when it came to…well, she could only think of it as psychic camoflage.

She stepped stealthily through a shadow or two until she was at the bar, her small frame hidden behind two burly farmers drinking a reward for their hard day. When she smiled, Udo suddenly saw her. It was rare that Quinn visited the Admiral's Lament, and Udo knew it, so he connected the dots and didn't bother to give Cord any kind of signal.

Clever man, Udo, Quinn reminded herself.

Udo was actually sharper than a lot of people ever gave him credit for. It might have been his size – he was a thick, tall man. Imposing without showing signs that he knew it. Head shaved bald, save for three long black ponytails jutting out of the back of his skull, down past his shoulders, and more metal than flesh visible on his ears – all pirate stylings. His eyes were small, black stones, impossible to read. And he wore a thick goatee that hid his mouth when deigned he spoke.

Aside from an occasional conversation with Quinn those few times they ran into each other at the marketplace, she wasn't sure he spoke much at all, really. His reticence, combined with his lumbering physique, was likely what had given people the impression that he was a bit on the slow side. And he certainly didn't speak much about himself. But though he never said much regarding his past, lots of people had heard whispers of rumors about from whence the big man had come.

The prevailing rumor tagged him as a pirate under the command of Admiral Jonas Mudd, the renegade privateer and general bastard of legend.

If that were the case, people assumed – if he had indeed sailed with Mudd – then obviously, there must be the blood of some unfortunate sailors on Udo's hands. And what else could a man like this have been, to arrive out of nowhere with a heavy sack full of gold, enough to pay the local farmers to help him build this cave-bar, plank by plank and stone by stone?

The best tale told – Quinn's favorite, at least – entwined Udo and Mudd with the disgraced, fugitive ex-chief of Coal Brigade, Nathan Cord. The story went that the crew of Admiral Mudd's ship, the Royal Hell, had found Cord on a piece of driftwood out at sea, dehydrated, nearly dead, and stark raving mad. They put him to work on the Hell, but upon regaining his strength, Cord had attempted a mutiny, and, for whatever reason, Udo had sided with him.

The mutiny failed, but before they were tossed overboard, Cord and Udo had stuffed chunks of the admiral's plundered fortune in their boots. It sunk them to the bottom of the ocean. And they started running. Udo reached the shore first, and when Cord couldn't make it any further, Udo, waiting diligently on the shoreline for his seafaring brother, marched into the water and dragged him the rest of the way back to land.

In thanks, the story went, the ex-chief gave him his share of the gold with one simple caveat: build a bar. And then Nathan Cord disappeared from the world for the better part of two years.

When the former chief of Coal Brigade returned, wild-eyed and heavy-bearded, he found that Udo, quiet fellow that he was, had neglected to name the tavern he'd been running all that time. Learning this, Cord, in a fury, grabbed a bucket of paint, a piece of wood, a saw, and a length of chain. Ten minutes later, a hastily-scrawled sign announced to the town the bar's official name: Admiral Mudd's Lament.

The sign has hung outside the door ever since.

It should be noted that no one has heard from Jonas Mudd since the bar opened.

3. A Proposition on Dead Ears

Quinn liked that story a lot. She was biased, of course, since she had helped tell a substantial portion of it, making sure it spread out like a plague among the people. And as she'd hoped, the bar got something of a reputation for danger and daring.

Of course, there were some embellishments in the telling. And some outright lies. But the essence of the story was true, and its fearsome, ludicrously epic quality kept people from digging too deeply into it. By making their journey into a tall tale, something no one in their right mind would believe entirely, she had helped relieve Cord and Udo of deeper scrutiny. So she truly loved that story.

She liked the version where they fought off sharks more, but….

"My dear ol' Quinn. How are we today?" Udo asked her. "Been far too long." Fortunately, Quinn had eyes sharp enough to detect Udo's smile, under all that beard.

She returned it with a beaming, flirty grin of her own. "I'm lovely now that I see your ugly mug."

"Speaking of ugly mugs," he chuckled, and plopped a tall pint of beer in front of her. She gazed at the glass in hidden terror. Given her stature, the damn thing was nearly the size of her head.

"You know I appreciate it, but do you have anything more…uh, my size?" She batted her eyelashes. She didn't need to.

Udo looked her over jokingly, like he was measuring her up. "Hmmm…lemme see what we have down below…" He ducked behind the counter, came back up with a shot glass filled with whiskey.

"Perfect. How'd you get so good at this, Udo?"

The big man shrugged. "Some men are made for the sea. Some are made to send men swimming."

"Got a real poetry to it."

The slight tilt of his mustache meant Udo had smiled again. "I've been told."

Quinn rested her arms against the bar and smiled warmly. "Tell me the girls are all over you, Udo."

He rolled his head back slightly, like he was probing his memory. "Oh, I do okay…"

One of the pig farmers raised his mug. "Get another here, Udo?"

Udo nodded thoughtfully, and when he had found the proper response, answered, "Yep."

With an appreciative nod to Quinn, he wandered over to his patron to refill the glass.

Quinn took her shot. A human might belch, or cough, but she blew out a little blue flame, and steeled herself for a far more unpleasant conversation with Cord.

Cord was sitting at his usual corner table, in a comfortable looking chair, reading a leatherbound book. She reasoned that it was either a historical work, or a cheap action yarn.

Quinn, knowing she was still just out of his line of sight, used the moment to take the man in. He was wearing a black knit shirt that clung tightly enough to his body to let her know he hadn't taken his exile as an excuse to let himself go.

Above the shoulders, it was a different story. His hair was shaggier than the last time she had seen him, which she realized must have been a good six months ago. And he'd let the beard out again.

Huge mistake, in her opinion, because it grew out in three different colors: the reddish brown that matched that wild mane, along with some stray blonde and black hairs, lord knows where they came from. And she could swear there were more than a few grays spitting out the sides of his mustache. She reminded herself that she had known the man for twenty years, give or take, and was as such surprised that there weren't more.

The ill-advised beard might have been his attempt to draw attention away from the crooked scar that ran down the left side of his face, from forehead to jaw. It was already broken up by the eyepatch, but neither beard nor patch was really up to the job.

When Quinn was ready to talk to him, she tilted her body out of the shadows, and saw Cord's right eye light up. And half an instant later, her magnificent eyes caught the glint of a short blade presenting itself under the table. He saw her and smiled.

There was only one woman who ever found that smile truly comforting, and she was seven years dead.

"Hey there, Quinn."

She shrugged off the discomfort that came with the smile, and matched his dangerously casual tone. "How've you been, Nate?"

Gesturing at the book, he answered, "I was a little better before you interrupted my reading. I'm in the middle of a paragraph. Just getting good, too, but I think you might've killed the momentum."

"You'll work your way back." Quinn moved closer to the table, grabbed the chair opposite Cord, and swung it around quickly before straddling down on it. Another of those intimidating-human moves she'd learned, mostly by watching Cord. "So...bar's good?"

"Bar's good. All good things come to the wicked."

"You used to be such a nice boy, too."

Cord grabbed a piece of scrap paper from the table, stuck it in the book, and closed it flat on the table. "That's up for debate. So what's up? Udo got you a drink?"

"Sure did. So...I have a favor to ask you."

Cord put the spooky smile away. The corners of his mouth curled down just slightly, and he was all business. "You're charming as hell, but getting less so by the second."

Quinn needed very much to be taken seriously, so she made sure not to register how much that hurt. She countered his bravado. "You used to listen to me, too."

"I used to do a lot of things." The business face tipped dangerously towards a snarl.

Quinn frowned, more deeply than her face displayed. "I know. So I'll try to be quick, and hope you have an open mind."

"Hm," he offered by way of response, and reclined in his comfortable chair. Quinn leaned further in.

"It's actually a pretty short story if you only want the highlights. It's mostly about the Queen in Waiting. Have you been keeping tabs on the Orphan?" She immediately regretted her choice of tone and phrasing, and wondered where all that practice had gone.

Cord smirked bitterly. "Dumb question. I'm the reason she's got that charming little nickname. If you believe all those tall tales, of course." He went inside himself for a second, but came back with, "But no, Quinn. I haven't been following our dear girl's exploits lately."

Quinn ignored the bait and continued. "The Orphan is due to assume the throne properly in less than a month. And the only thing she really wanted on that day was to have her lover by her side."

"Kid's too young to have a boyfriend," Cord groused.

It brought a moment of amusement to Quinn, but she kept that tucked inside. "Says you. That 'kid' is nearly a woman now, and she got herself a man."

"So *you've* been keeping tabs on her then?"

15

Quinn took the hit, answered honestly. "Of course I have. That's our little Allie. Like I wouldn't know when our girl got herself a sweet young guy to bring her flowers."

"And who is this nice young suitor?" he asked, faking casual, but the way his eyebrow jutted up, she knew she had tapped a nerve. The favorite uncle, wondering who was chasing after his niece.

"Who *was* that. He *had* been a young man name of Aiden, a sweet boy who wanted to make a good name for himself so that his princess might look on him favorably."

"So, a chump."

"A sweet chump. A sweet chump that went into battle down in the southlands – "

"Vic led the charge?"

"Of course."

"So...Aiden's dead, then."

Quinn sighed, frustrated with Cord's grudges and letting him know it. She took a scolding tone and clarified, "This'll go a lot quicker if you just let me tell it. Aiden died in battle, like a lot of sweet young men do, as you well know. And the Orphan might have just mourned and moved on, except she's got this advisor, name of Grolev. Grolev is a magician. A talented one at that – as I understand these things. I say he's a talented menace to anyone who ever came in contact with him."

Cord shrugged. "I remember some lanky, craggy fella in a black robe skulking around the halls and scowling when Keegan Morris was the head magic man."

"That's him all right."

"So how'd he get to be the Orphan's main guy?"

Quinn shrugged back. "How do they ever? Point is, Grolev tells the Orphan that death doesn't have to be the end of their True And Noble Love Affair. That he can bring Aiden back. And the poor girl went for it."

Cord thought this turn of events through, and could only offer, "Ah, crap."

"Yup. So Grolev does his thing. I don't know what exactly, maybe sacrificed lots of living things to lots of mean spirits...I don't...but I should go back a little bit. When I say 'died in battle,' I mean to say it was a massacre. The kingdom's got its eye on some of the deep southern territories."

"Huge mistake."

"Huuuuge mistake," Quinn agreed. "Those guys make the Fel wildmen in Eastern Sun look like teatotalers. Pretty much the entire battalion went down swinging."

"I remember the southlands. Just tell me Victor Mene was among the bodies."

"Sorry to inform you, but Victor is pretty much the only one who can tell the tale with any accuracy. Though...he's not the only one that could tell you how these soldiers died. See, Grolev cast this spell, and then Aiden was back up and walking."

She paused for effect before adding, "Sort of."

Cord leaned in, propping his elbows up on the table, making a steeple out of his fingers and pressing them against his face. "What's it look like down there?"

Thinking she had gotten Cord on her side, she leaned in and answered matter-of-factly, "Bloody Twilight has turned into a breeding ground for undead soldiers. It's chaos in there. And it needs to be fixed. Sooner, rather than later."

Cord nodded. "I'm getting what you want from me."

"Yeah?"

"Yeah." He shoved himself back into his chair. "And I'm going to ask you politely, this moment, to get out of this bar right now and think of a better favor to ask me some other time."

Quinn stood up from her chair, placed her hands flat on the table, and leaned into Cord's face. "This is important. This is a real danger, and I need help."

"Why do you care at all?"

Quinn's eyes stared down Cord's remaining one. Because she was angry with him, she ignored the question, no matter how many good answers she had, and went into her rehearsed pitch. "This is my proposition. We have a limited amount of time to take care of this situation before it spills out and we can't control it anymore. I'm asking you to meet me back at my camp in two days. I have a couple of guys I'd like you to talk to. I'll explain everything you want to know, but it has to be there, and it has to be then."

With that, Quinn turned around and marched to the door. Cord stood up. Raising his voice just above the irritable whisper he'd been using, he told her, "I won't be there. Anyway, I'm not what you need. I haven't picked up a sword since I moved out here."

Quinn peered over her shoulder just slightly, enough for the outside light to catch the reflection of her eyes and make them glow. "I've heard different. I'll see you soon."

Cord blinked.

She was gone.

4. Customer Relations

Cord grunted angrily and leaned back into his chair. After several minutes of sitting with his arms crossed, frowning as hard as humanly possible, he picked up his book, flipped it open, and stared at words he didn't absorb. Failing that, he shut the book and threw it at the far wall. It just missed a customer sitting at the head of a table in the opposite corner.

Startling him enough to spill his beer on his lap.

"What the hell?! Who does that ass-stain think he...son of a whore!" The customer stood up, ready for confrontation, but was quickly pulled back into his seat by Wallace Pitts, one of the regulars. One of the few that Cord ever saw and gave an approving nod to. Wallace quite liked this place, considered it a sort of haven, and was beginning to regret bringing his two nephews to his usual drinking spot. Good guys, but they got hot too easy.

"Wouldn't do that, Dale," Wallace advised wearily. He'd been in this kind of situation with his sister's boys before, and wasn't happy at the prospect of it happening in his local watering hole.

Dale shrugged Wallace's arm off. "You kiddin' me? Guy nearly took my head off."

"That guy's the owner."

"Hell of a way to run a place..."

Wallace leaned in, his face deadly serious. "Let me put it to you another way. If the things I hear are true? That guy would kill you without a second thought. He kills a king and gets away with it, what do you think your chances are?"

Dale sat back, his face suddenly blank as he processed this new information. "This is the guy killed Arius? Says who?"

Shrugging, Wallace said, "Word gets around. Can't say for certain what's true, but do you want to try him on for size?"

"That's the king-killer...well, he looks crazy enough. Damn...now I'm not sure whether to turn him in or buy him a drink."

Wallace smiled, and made a gesture to Udo. Udo registered the order with a nod and not much else.

But then Curtis, the younger of Wallace's two cousins, twenty-two and a 6'5" wall of muscular anger, stood up much the same way Dale had. "This is stupid, there's no way that's the king-killer. I heard the guy got captured trying to get on a boat, and his head's mounted in the Orphan's bedroom."

Wallace shook his head in embarrassment. "Damn, Curtis, that's the stupidest thing I ever heard. If the guy who killed the king had been caught, there would've been a public trial, a hanging...hell, they might have made a show of the Blue Knives kicking the crap out of him beforehand."

"Yeah, okay." Curtis gave serious thought on it, but instead of sitting down like Wallace had hoped, the kid came to an entirely different conclusion. "So that means that grumpy piece of crap over there ain't no king-killer. Means he gets beat just like any other asshole."

Having made up his mind through a use of logic that Wallace would under other circumstances have found admirable, Curtis shoved his way out past the table, and barked "Hey! Asshole!" in Nathan Cord's direction.
Cord looked up, expressionless, and, understanding the provocation, answered, "Didn't like that, huh?"

"Hell no I didn't like it. Made my brother spill his damn beer!" Curtis puffed his already massive chest out. "Stand your suicidal ass up!"

Cord, behind the table, did as asked. "And what are you going to do about it?"

Curtis crossed the barroom in several long, quick steps, until he stood facing Cord at the opposite end of Cord's corner table. "Get out from behind there, you hairy-ass coward."

Cord nodded, processing the request. Then he grabbed the edges of his table and flipped it, launching it violently toward Curtis. The edge of the table smacked him square on the jaw, bloodying his lip and sending him stumbling back. But it didn't knock him down.

With deliberate casualness, yet quicker than expected, Cord circumvented the table. He was standing a breath away from Curtis, his forehead just meeting the big man's chin. It was a good angle. Cord waited for Curtis to stop stumbling, and then plowed his forehead into Curtis's jaw.

The big boy dropped this time. When he hit the floor, Cord dropped the full weight of his knee onto Curtis's chest, knocking the wind out of him. Then he delivered three brutal punches. A right to the side of the face. Then a left to the other side. And then, as Curtis attempted to lift his head, a direct shot to the big man's nose. The back of his skull collided with the ground hard enough for everyone to hear.

Blood and spit stuck to Cord's fist as he pulled it back.

Cord looked up at his patrons, and as expected, found that a lot of perfectly good conversations had halted immediately in favor of watching the crazy man beat up a new customer. He stood up, nodded to no one in particular, and walked back to the table, propping it back up. Then he turned back to look at the far corner table, and noticed Wallace Pitts, hands hiding his face, sitting there with someone he didn't recognize.

"Wallace, this guy one of yours?"

Wallace noted that Cord wasn't even breathing heavy when he asked. Flustered and frankly annoyed that his usual quiet beer after a hard day's work had suddenly turned into a brutal spectacle he'd have to explain to his sister when he brought the boys home, he answered as calmly and apologetically as he could, "Sorry, Nate, they're my sister's boys. Thought they'd like the place, but...you know." He looked at Dale, then Curtis on the floor, and shrugged. "They're idiots."

Cord made a face that snarls come from, but nothing was heard. He glanced at Dale. Without any emphasis, he asked, "You the guy spilled his drink?"

Dale was frozen stiff, but hoped like hell that his head was nodding like he wanted it to.

"I'll have Udo get you another," Cord barked. "Wallace, this kid" – he jutted his index finger in the direction of Curtis's ragdoll form – "he doesn't come back here again, right?"

"Will do, Nate. I'll ship him off when he, uh...y'know, when he gets up."

"Good man." His customer service moment concluded, Cord walked back to his seat at the table. He sat, drumming his fingers tensely on the oak, partly because he was very keyed up, and partly because his book was still on the other side of the room and he'd be damned if he was going to walk all the way back over there to get it just so he could continue not reading it.

To his fortune, Udo came over with two mugs of beer, placed one in front of Cord and then sat down with the other one in his hand. He jerked a thumb in the direction of Wallace and Dale. "This was from them." Then he glanced at the limp body of Curtis Pitts. "Hope that got rid of some of the tension."

Cord muttered, "Not really," and made that snarling face again. After a while it relaxed a bit, and he took a long pull off his beer. "You know how I practice with the sword out back every day?"

Udo nodded.

"You mention that to anyone?"

Udo said nothing.

Cord pressed. "Maybe mentioned it to Quinn, last time you saw her at the market, something like that?"

Udo made a face like he was searching his memory. "Mighta said something about it, if she asked. Didn't know it was a secret."

Cord looked down at his beer like it said something rude to him. "Well, not that it does anyone any good now," then took another long swig. "...But it was."

5. Practice

One, two, three, four, dodge, kick, HOLD, lunge, one, two STAB, four, SWING, STOP, three, four, crouch, wait, three, four, one, be-HIND, four, PUNCH...

Udo occasionally watched Cord when the former brigade chief practiced out back. Sometimes it was because Udo needed to step past Cord's makeshift training course in order to get to his garden. Sometimes it was because Cord's performance verged on a dance routine, and Udo admired the rhythm.

He wasn't sure if Cord counted steps when he fought, but Udo had played drums when he was a child, and even though it had been years since he'd picked up any sticks, he could still hear the beats inherent in everyday movement. It was a personal quirk he decided not to share with others.

Every day, in the late afternoon – the routine varied along with the season, always when the sun began to set – Cord would set up his course and fight the dummies as they came at him, on a surprisingly complicated pulley-and-track system that Udo had deemed the sole example of Cord's building ingenuity. Cord had started and finished this project without announcing it or requesting any outside help.

When it was completed, and he showed it off to Udo, the barman understood why Cord had left the building specifications of the bar to him. This track was unwieldy, to say the least. An experienced craftsman could have made him something far more streamlined and effective.

But then Udo caught the sight of Cord practicing against the track, and realized that Cord had built it to be exactly what he required.

The dummies were set along a series of interweaving tracks. There were several air-packs strewn haphazardly along the ground that, when Cord stepped on them, would change the course, causing both continuous motion and randomized placement of the dummies.

Also of note: Cord practiced blindfolded.

All of this put together meant that Cord could never be absolutely certain when he would hit one of his "innocent" dummies. These were the ones sized like children.

The dummies were standard burlap sacks, raised up on sticks. Their torsos and heads were filled out with straw, raw potatoes, and eggs. Since Cord was blindfolded, he needed to hear when he'd struck a decisive blow, and had found that the noise made by the potatoes and eggs was close enough to the sound he needed.

Whenever Cord tagged a dummy, Udo found himself wanting breakfast. It was a strange, if instinctual, reaction. But then he attached the logic to Cord's routine, and found himself occasionally hating the taste of breakfast.

Today was the eve of Nathan Cord's personal holiday.

For lack of a better description.

Udo had known Nathan Cord for a long time now. And even ignoring his disappearance into the woods for two years, before his re-emergence as owner of Admiral Mudd's Lament, Udo considered himself Cord's closest – and frankly, only – friend.

He considered it a stewardship. Quinn Kind had once held that honor, but Cord had always seemed reticent to engage the Pic in casual conversation when they would occasionally run into each other at the marketplace.

Udo had initially held the theory that at some point during those two years, the Quinn and Cord had slept together. In his experience, that was how awkwardness between two friends usually started. But that didn't really account for the unspoken bitterness held between the two of them. In the end, though, it was none of his business, so he never asked.

He never asked much as a general rule. But he had just recently watched his boss – his friend – beat the living daylights out of a patron, in response to a minor provocation. This was a man who usually went out of his way to avoid talking to any of his customers, any more than he had to. And so Udo found himself a bit worried.

After Nathan Cord had returned from the Pic village two years ago, the former brigade chief seemed a master of calm, completely in control of the fires burning in his soul. At first, Udo had attributed it to whatever Quinn and her people had taught him.

But then the days went by, and some dark nights settled in, and Udo watched his friend sink into a deep depression. He saw it, but didn't know what to do. The man had been terminally afflicted. Udo was concerned that maybe Cord would kill himself. And again, he didn't know what to do.

And then one night Cord, drunk and chatty, as men get after too much whiskey, met a hack magician named Fehrer. It must have been Kayla's birthday, or maybe their wedding anniversary. It was a night where Cord's wife was on his mind, in any event. And Fehrer was there to listen.

Fehrer was, as far as Udo had heard, a dirtbag. But the man told Cord that he could use magic to bring his wife back, in a way, to let him talk to her. And Cord lit up like fireworks.

When Cord had come back from the Pic village, he still seemed a bit sad, but mostly contented. But when he made his deal with Fehrer...it was the first time in the many years Udo had known him that Nathan Cord appeared to be happy. This idiot had made his friend happy, for the first time since Udo had known him. Who would want to break that spell?

"Nate!" Udo hollered, to let the blindfolded Cord know he was in the vicinity.

Cord sheathed his swords and pulled off the blindfold. Huffing, trying to catch his breath, he glanced around as his good eye adjusted to the late afternoon sun, not really taking anything in. "How'd I do?"

Udo surveyed the scene. A tiny dummy hung backwards on the track, its head a pulpy mess of chopped potatoes and cracked eggs.

"Still hit a kid."

"Damn it." Cord looked around at his dummies. His face crunched up, and he grabbed one of the adult dummies by its stem, yanked it up from the track, and swung it into one of the others. "DAMN IT!" he spat out, his tone even more violent than his actions.

Udo took in the outburst. It was startling, but it wasn't exactly new. Cord took every error in practice as something to learn from, to work harder on. But whenever he hit a kid, Udo could always expect to see a bit of damage done to the course.

One of the dummies landed at his feet. He heard raw potato and egg splat inside. He looked down at the dummy's blank head as the yellow egg yolk seeped through the canvas. Then Udo looked back up at Cord. His boss – his friend – stood in the middle of his dummies, breathing heavily, angrily.

"She fricking...she uses the memory of that damn kid...thinks that'll push me into this nonsense...of all the manipulative horseshit..."

And at once, Cord remembered he wasn't cursing to himself. That he had an audience. "*What*," he pushed, glaring at Udo, though his tone wasn't a question. His voice was cold and harsh.

Udo blinked. His face betrayed no emotion.

Cord relaxed just a little at this. "Sorry. Sorry, Udo. What do you want to say." Again, a question, but without the proper tone. Cord stepped away from the dummies, back to his business partner, his barman. His friend.

"You stopping off at Wiggans' place tomorrow?"

"Yeah."

"I got some stuff for you to bring to Fehrer's. How are his kids?"

Cord chuckled, honestly amused by Udo's curiosity. "Fehrer's kids don't need any more toys, man."

"Kids always need toys. And they're already in the wagon."

Cord took the scabbard off his belt, traded it for his shirt, hanging off the birdfeeder. Pulling his shirt over his head, he muttered, "Why are you always so interested in giving Fehrer gifts? You don't even like the man, and you've never met the kids."

Udo shrugged. "He makes you feel human for a little while. Feel like I owe him something."

Very close to Udo's face, Cord looked into his tiny black eyes. Asked meanly, "You're looking out for my soul, is that it?"

Casually, he answered, "If not me, who?"

Cord had no response. He looked away, down to the ground, immediately sorry for his tone. There was no good reason for it, they both knew, but something about the way Quinn had dangled the Orphan's situation in front of him...

Udo moved on. "Anyway, I told Fehrer I'd send him some peppers when they came into season." He brushed past Cord, and then past the dummies, out to the garden, to pick some peppers for his friend's mystic.

Hoping silently that maybe this would be the last time.

6. The New Magic, And Its Masters

The Kingdom of Western Sun sits in the center of the Cabrea region. To the north are farming communities, and even further up, the annexed Northlands, the kingdom that had been retitled Northern Sun about eight years back or so. To the southeast, a coalmining community and Beasts Old Throne, annexed as Eastern Sun earlier than that. And in the deep south...well, there was no name for that area. It was just the south. And as the wholesale slaughter of Western Sun's finest soldiers over the last year had proven, anyone who thought they could annex the south like they had the Northlands and Beasts Old Throne were fools or madmen.

But to the west of the kingdom, out past a long flat field of nothing much, sat the forest. It had no name, and didn't really need one since humans, by and large, were not exactly welcome there, and so far at least, hadn't tried to take it for themselves.

It was the Pic Forest, and that was enough.

It took its name from the tribe of woodlanders known as the Pic Clan. There were plenty of questions revolving around what the Pics and other woodlanders really were, answered mostly via speculation from the humans in the neighboring kingdoms. Some of those answers were just the rumors and guesswork that always happens when people try to explain something they can't quite grasp. And some of that was the work of the Pics themselves, building up their own legend to maintain their privacy.

What was known to the humans for sure was that the average Pic was between four and a half to five and a half feet tall. They tended to live between one hundred and two hundred years. They possessed greater than average strength, speed, agility, and senses. They were a matriarchal society, in that the vast majority was female, and their ruling council was made up of seven of the oldest women in the clan, collectively known as the mothers. They had a communion with the earth around them that could be considered mystical.

26

And, perhaps most pointedly, they had very strict rules about letting humans live with them.

The rules had been broken twice over the last half-century, not that the people of any of the Suns knew it. The first occurred when Quinn Kind had persuaded the mothers to let Cord stay with them.

The second was not Quinn's doing. In fact, she had vehemently opposed the idea. But she was voted down when a magician calling himself Welles showed up six months ago, asking to learn from them. It had been a long time since a magician had shown interest in the Pic culture, and he made a very good case for himself, as far as the mothers were concerned.

The magician named Welles crouched in the middle of a clearing in the Pic Forest, and began to whisper out incantations.

The words, if you could call them that, were older and more obscure than history ever dealt with. But at the same time, they were so new that few modern ears had heard them.

He continued uttering strange sounds from the back of his throat, from the middle of his nose, and at one memorable point, from the cavities just behind his eyeballs. He was talking to the world, and these were the noises the world understood.

The trees around him bent casually to his will. Massive old oaks, crunching and rolling to the rhythm of his chant. Swirling and melting into each other.

If someone high above could see what was happening, as the trees danced around each other, finding their place in the formation Welles quietly called out, they could see the joining arcs that form a heart sign.

He pulled the hood down from his head, smiled, and coughed with purpose. From miles around, leaves charged through the trees, like a swarm of paper bees.

Someone high above would see an arrow of leaves plow through the heart of trees.

Satisfied, Welles casually sat his ass against the earth and began to laugh. He dropped his back to the ground and let the arrow-leaves fall all around him. Laughed louder, prouder.

The light exercise of a magician. Morning push-ups for the mystic soul.

Twenty years ago, the things he was doing were the stuff of fairy tales, a child's imagination. And then an eccentric academic called Keegan Morris and his likeminded colleagues in the field of esoteric knowledge, having spent decades in study, unlocked the greater meaning behind the old writings they had unearthed and poured over.

And like that, the magic of storybooks and folk tales become very real. The people marveled. And of course, they were just a little terrified to see the world in which they now found themselves suddenly so out of synch with the one to which they'd grown accustomed.

But for some, the eruption of magic in the real world was a sign that the world was as strange and wondrous as they'd always hoped. That there was more to it all than mundane family life and the certainty of working in coal mines once they were out of primary school.

Welles had been twelve when he ran away from such prospects to study with Keegan Morris. He wasn't alone. Young men, women and even some woodlanders came from all over to learn the secret codes that could give them the means to communicate, in a very real sense, with the world around them.

Nobody had even mentioned to them how much damn fun it would be.

One side benefit to studying magic, Welles remembered as he felt the footsteps of Quinn Kind tapping their way toward him from over a mile away, was that all the woodland dwellers, the Pics and the Fel and the Tree-bobs, everything mysterious to a human, were that much less baffling and secretive than they wanted to be in the eyes of an average human.

Welles was human, yes. But there was nothing average about him. He was a guy who liked knowing things. And over the past six months, he found he quite liked knowing the Pics. Some more than others.

A few more mumblings and non-words, and a tree branch lunged down, past his head, and grabbed Quinn by the waist, hoisting her up.

"Hey there, Quinn," he shouted up to her sweetly. "Nice morning, yeah?"

Quinn, stuck in a tree and wrapped in branches, just frowned and folded her arms, like this happened every day. "I hate you so very much, you know that?" She said it with a hint of a smile in her voice, if not her expression.

Welles sat up. "Well, that's debatable," he smiled. "But one thing's for sure: if you wanna sneak up on me, stop being so damn loud!" He chuckled to himself, and dropped his back down to the ground again, the easier to see his tree-captive.

Quinn put away her frown, and glared at him with her strange eyes. "Put me down nice, or I'll come down on you hard."

Welles grunted seriously, letting it echo through the dirt under his feet, and the tree branch bent and cracked its way back to the ground, easily releasing Quinn from its grip. She dropped to the ground weightlessly, a feather in a soft breeze.

Quinn smiled. "So very, very much, is my hate for you." Then, stepping closer to the magician, "Anyway…hi."

"Hi," Welles returned warmly.

"So you're in a good mood, it seems," Quinn chided.

Welles dug his heels into the ground, concentrated, and called up a wind to push him to his feet. "Yeah, I think I am. Lots of energy flowing around today. Anyway, how goes our dilemma?"

Brushing leaves off her shoulder, she replied, "Not great. We're going to have to go to Plan B."

"Oh, good. I take it this means I get learn what Plan B is?"

"Plan B," Quinn confessed, conspiracy riddling her words, "is where I do something totally reprehensible to one of my closest friends."

Welles frowned, then looked up to the trees, still in their heart formation. He let out something that sounded like a deliberate sneeze mixed with a bad foreign accent. The trees squirmed and cranked back to their proper shapes.

"Sounds interesting. When do we start?"

Quinn looked down at the ground, something in her hurt by the question put to her. She pulled something small out of her pocket, something round wrapped in a handkerchief, and showed it to Welles. "I already started. Why do you think it took me till morning to get back?"

Welles took a look inside the handkerchief, and nodded in sympathy. He had learned a lot from the Pics over the last six months. Training his senses to work like theirs. Getting a sense for their fighting style. He had even begun – he thought, at least – to figure out how it is they can sink into the ground.

But Quinn had managed to teach him, first-hand, the most startling trait her people possessed: the lengths to which a Pic will go in order to achieve a desired result.

7. Plan 'A' is Just the Start

Not too long after sunrise the next morning, Cord hitched up the wagon to his horse and left the Admiral's Lament, on a tight schedule by his reckoning. It was a half-day's ride to Fehrer's settlement up north, and he wasn't traveling light. Part of Fehrer's twice-annual payment was that Cord bring provisions for his family with each visit.

Not much was needed. Grains, whatever vegetables Udo grew out back that season. A couple bottles of wine – Beasts Old Throne vintage (during Coal Brigade's tour in the east, they'd all ended up with stockpiles of the red, and Fehrer knew it). And of course the toys for Fehrer's children (despite his outward bristling at Udo's soft side, Cord was willing to acquiesce, since they were good kids, as far as Cord knew from good kids at least). But it meant Cord needed to bring the cart to carry everything, considerably slowing an already long trek.

Many of Cord's friends (meaning: Udo and Quinn) had often pointed out that Fehrer's conditions were ludicrous and somewhat insulting add-ons considering there was no guarantee that he wasn't pulling off anything more than a hack magician's scam.   But it was the pact Cord had made, and while he didn't have much honor left to him, this was an agreement he felt obliged to keep, without any notions of renegotiation.

As he snapped the reins, he started thinking about Quinn, and the mission she'd hinted at. It only now occurred to him that she took his rejection far too easily, and that perhaps "asking nicely" was just plan A. Quinn had always been fond of contingency plans, and as Cord rode off, he wondered what her plan B was.

He wondered this as he headed to Fehrer's – a man who had in his possession the one thing that could bend Cord's will. And Quinn knew it.

It was a long ride. And no matter how hard Cord snapped the reins or how fast he could get his horse moving, the sense of unease in the pit of his stomach stayed with him for the entire trip.

8. Mene's Daydreams

Lashing the damn things together had been the hardest part. Not that hauling them roped behind him was that much easier.

The pixie girl hadn't requested it, but Victor Mene knew that all her plots and plans would be worthless if she didn't see firsthand what they were up against.

Mene looked back on the two dead things trudging behind him and wondered for just a moment: *if I had shown* these *things to the queen-in-waiting's council, would they have still advised the charge into the south?*

Just as quickly as the thought had come to him, he put it aside. It was a pointless notion, after all. What was done, was done.

The horse was dragging. The brainless, lurching things that had been soldiers weren't exactly hurrying along. Mene jerked the rope and they picked up their uneven steps.

Dolus and Tegan. Older soldiers. A decade ago, they'd been part of Coal Brigade, before Cord's disgrace made it necessary to dissolve the branch. They'd been living with an unspoken embarrassment on their records for years now, thanks to the man the citizens referred to only as the king-killer. The way they said it, equal parts spite and astonishment. "Nathan Cord, the king-killer." The yarns that they spread about him, like he was a storybook figure, a tall tale more than a man. They might have said it differently if they honestly believed he was still alive, and no one had done anything to bring him to justice. All because the queen-in-waiting of the Kingdom of Western Sun had quietly decreed it. The girl the citizens had snidely dubbed "the Orphan."

But Mene knew the man on which those ridiculous stories were based. The real thing, the truth: the sneering, cold, unstable nightmare of a soldier. In the end, nothing but a bitter veteran who went over the edge one night and committed regicide in a fit of petty jealousy.

The fantasies he had on bringing Cord to the kingdom's justice had grown more intense as Mene reached the outskirts of the Pic Forest. These were the thoughts he focused on as he drifted off to sleep at night. And that was when Mene realized that he was completely exhausted.

Unusual for him, as he was generally a master of pacing himself. As he'd told Cord many times, fighting is an endurance sport: the ones who make it out of a day's fight alive are the ones who prepared themselves to see nightfall.

But getting out of the kingdom had taken more out of Mene than he'd expected. Those dead soldiers might have been slow of reflex and pathetic in their fighting, but what they lacked in style, they more than made up for in sheer number. The dead that had piled up thanks to the casualties in the south had begun to number into the hundreds, and beyond that, some of the rotting beasts that had come at him must have been dead and buried for years. There was an army of dead men clawing at the walls of the kingdom. Stupid, and slow, yes. But also mean and vicious. It felt simple and easy as he was doing it, but looking back, Mene realized that it was blind, stinking luck that got him out of there.

Arriving at the Pic Forest, Mene glared at it irritably. He could not believe this was where he'd find his reinforcements. A bunch of weird little woodlanders who hadn't fought seriously in decades. Mene unmounted his horse to survey the land a little more thoroughly, but as soon as his feet touched the ground, Dolus and Tegan stumbled toward him, snarling.

Mene didn't mind. He took it as an excuse to punch the living hell out of them.

When it didn't look like they'd get back up again anytime soon, Victor Mene stepped toward the edge of the Pic Forest and spread out his arms. "This is Victor Mene, captain of the Royal Guard of Western Sun. And I want to see your little leader, the one called Quinn Kind!" A bit glibly, he added, "Tell her I've brought presents!"

He must have been tired, because in the blink of an eye, he was surprised to be surrounded by young pixie boys, armed with knives, crossbows, and stares they thought might be threatening.

Mene was not easily threatened.

One of them got close enough to him. They were fast, of course – the little Pics are always fast, Mene reminded himself – but the captain of the guard was pretty fast himself, and managed to grab the boy by his collar before he could try sprinting away, and yanked him up to eye level.

"You, my little friend," Mene glowered at him. "You will be my messenger."

A voice came from the trees. A tenor, and yet still somehow authoritative. "No, he won't. Put the boy down, Mene."

Mene set the boy's feet back on the ground, but maintained his grip. "I've been invited here by your friend Quinn. This boy here just tried to assault me. I'm within my rights." Mene explained this sternly, as he would to a very stupid child. It was probably a mistake. But Mene had gone to a lot of trouble to get to these woods, and would be damned if he had to explain himself to a bunch of kids.

"Have it your way," the voice in the trees sighed, and then Mene immediately felt a pinch in his neck. He let go of the pixie boy so he could grasp at his throat, and found a dart lodged in. Mene yanked it out, but realized it was too little, too late.

His legs grew numb, then bowed awkwardly, and then the captain of the guard fell flat on his face. "You little bastards have dosed me," he tried to yell out, but all that erupted from his throat was a series of angry coughs.

Though he tried to fight it, he nodded off. Exhausted as he had been, this was not the way he had expected to get any rest.

9. The Drugged-Up Détente

At camp, Quinn Kind found herself in a losing battle of cards with Welles, who had, to his credit, politely warned her that there was no way for her to win against him. As he put it, "I've got the universe on my side. You've got a few trees and shrubs."

She knew that beyond a fondness for hyperbole, Welles had enough of a decent streak to try to save her a few dollars when gambling with him. She didn't take the lifeline Welles had thrown, and so had been steadily losing to him. But it was a way to pass the time.

She was happy for the distraction when Victor Mene plowed his way into camp.

"Plowed" was the description one of her brothers used, and was not exactly true. "Stumbled violently" was more accurate. But Mene towered over the slightly-statured Pics, and ultimately it came down to a matter of wills. Mene, still in battle-mode and riled up from riding like hell out of Western Sun, was of a mind to hurt anything that came near him, and Quinn's thirty-odd brothers were under strict orders not to touch the man. No contest.

"Oh, please, William," she gently scolded her messenger. "If Welles' predictions are anything to go by, there's no way Victor Mene had the strength left to fight off thirty of you."

William, younger than Quinn by a good forty years, stared down at his feet as he delivered the news to his older sister. "He wouldn't stop and listen to us – just kept pushing us all to the side, and demanding to speak with you. The dart was Quentin's idea."

Quinn scowled, because she was allowed to within her big-sister rights, especially where Quentin was concerned. "So when I said, 'When Victor Mene gets here, no one is to lay a finger on him,' Quentin took that to mean that drugging him was still okay. Is that it?"

William thought on this for a moment before replying, "Yeah, that sounds about right."

"Ugh…" was the best Quinn could muster. "So where is he now?"

"Quentin put him in your room."

"Not on my bed…"

Laughing at the thought, William clarified, "Good lord, no, the guy's huge. We dropped him next to the bed."

Quinn glared harder than she even knew she could.

William checked out his shoes again. "We put a pillow under his head."

Shaking it off, Quinn put on her business face and called back to the card table, "Welles, come on. Victor Mene's in camp, and I am not having a conversation alone with him. Especially if he's doped up to the eyeballs with whatever horror my brother decided to dart into him."

Welles looked at the table – specifically, his giant stack of chips against Quinn's dwindling bank – and nodded happily. "Yeah, cool. You were done in four hands anyway."

"You're not as charming as you think you are, you know."

Welles grinned. "Now, we both know you're lying."

Before she could retort, her little brother tapped her shoulder. "Uhh, Quinn?"

"What's up, William?"

"Mene   brought   some…things   with   him."

"What do you mean, 'things'?"

"I mean…things from the kingdom. The monsters. He brought a couple of the monsters with him."

"I see. This just gets better and better."

They headed into Quinn's quarters, the most secluded of the family dwellings. It was slightly larger than the boys' rooms by a few square feet. She was the oldest of twenty-seven females, in a family of seventy, and preference was usually given to the sisters who would be next in line to take over a role in the motherhood.

Quinn was progressive, maybe the most forward-thinking of her entire clan, and as she was one of the oldest, it was pretty well implied that she would be the policy maker when her mother died. There were a lot of different clans around – the Pics, the Waters out by the sea, the Tree-bobs up north, the Fel clan to the east – and she wanted all of them to start working together with the humans. Being an enigma to humankind was all well and good in terms of protection of her people, but it wasn't doing anything positive in the long run, and in Quinn's view, it was becoming very important to create a larger community if they were to make any real progress as a civilization.

Her intentions were entirely noble. But that didn't mean she didn't love having a nice big room all to herself.

And now Victor Mene was working off a drug hangover on her floor. Just perfect.

Quentin was already standing guard outside her door. When Quinn showed up, he tried to hide his smile.

It did no good – Quinn could pick that shit-eating grin out of a line-up of hundreds. "I ask you to do one thing. One. Thing."

Quentin stood at a soldier's attention, even saluted like the humans do, but his triumphant glee snuck out just the same. "You said don't hurt him. And I would say the man's in a blissful, sub-coma state right now. You say 'jump,' I say 'Name the bridge,' ma'am."

"Don't get cute with me, brother. You just think he's sexy."

Quentin's eyes widened mockingly. "Don't you? I mean, the armor, the bald head with the two corn-rows, that big old scowl...c'mon. That's a fox of a man right there."

"I'll tell a fox you said so, just to confirm. You...you go away now. Big people business."

"What do you want us to do with those two thrashing corpses he was thoughtful enough to tie to the back of his horse?"

Quinn thought for a moment. "Lock them up somewhere. And keep your hands away from their mouths. I don't know if they're contagious or what, but best to take every precaution we can. Ugh. We're going to need those things, sadly enough. But keep everyone away from them, and use the heaviest chains we have. Last thing we need is those suckers getting loose. You understand me, Quentin? I'm serious, here."

Stomping off, Quentin threw back, "I serve at the pleasure of my sister, cranky though she be," and headed off to take care of their horrible prisoners. Quentin would get over her pulling rank on him, she told herself. He was her twin brother; he pretty much had to.

Quinn knelt down to check on Mene, but found that gently slapping his face did nothing constructive. Without her asking, Welles rummaged through his bag and found some smelling salts, which he tossed to Quinn. She wafted it under Victor Mene's nose, and he tossled around a bit before opening his eyes.

"Want some water?" Quinn asked, holding a canteen to his mouth. "My brother nailed you with a pretty severe sedative...plus, maybe some other stuff. So you might want some water."

Victor tried his best to curse Quentin Kind, but Quinn couldn't hear anything he said.

She tried again. "Seriously, some water – "

Victor coughed like it was some kind of challenge he was determined to overcome. Finally, he brought his voice to audible levels. "I'll settle accounts with your brother some other time. Whichever one he was. And you had better point him out to me when I ask. But for now, just tell me. Is your plan working so far?"

Quinn looked over at Welles, and focused deep on his coal-black eyes. For a reason she couldn't place, Welles didn't give his usual blasé smile, the one he thought was reassuring, but sometimes came off as patronizing. When he nodded, he almost looked noble. And a little concerned.

"So far, everything's gone as I'd figured."

Victor hacked a little more and then asked, "So what you say is true – you're bringing Nathan Cord here?"

"Yeah. But do I have to remind you about our agreement?"

Victor sat up, apparently attempting to will the drugs out of his system. "No, that's perfectly clear to me. I don't get to kill Cord until he's served his purpose."

Quinn frowned. "No. I said you need to listen to me when I explain Nate's situation. And I mean REALLY listen, not just – "

"Quinn?"

When she looked over, Welles looked like he had just passed a stone. He recovered enough to tell her, "Yeah. You wanted me to let you know, so this is me letting you know. Your boy Nate is headed over to Fehrer's. He hit that tripmine signal I gave you to install."

Quinn slapped her forehead and stroked it down her face. "Ahhh, damn it. We've got a little less time than I thought we'd have. Victor? Stay mellow. Things are about to get more interesting than I'm happy with."

10. The Broken Contract

By the time Cord had reached Fehrer's – far faster than usual – unease had given way to tension, and tension without release just created anger. Something was wrong. He just knew it. But he had to be sure.

He pounded his fist on the door with nearly enough force to break his hand. And waited. And paced. And pounded again. He could hear scurrying and muttered curses from behind the door. That was enough of an excuse for Cord to kick it in.

With adequate notice, Fehrer would have answered the door in ceremonial robes and burning incense, a welcoming environment waiting. But as Cord was two hours early for their appointment – an appointment Cord had stuck to like clockwork for nearly five years – Fehrer hurried toward the door in a bathrobe, and in a panic. He knew what this was about.

"FEHRER!" Cord bellowed from the doorway. The anxious bellow echoed through the house.

Rushing down the stairs from his bedroom, Fehrer tried not to look terrified as he greeted him. "Cord! Welcome. You're earlier than usual, but…welcome to my home, as always," the hack magician offered, hoping to quell the tension. He tied the rope on his bathrobe and then lifted his arms grandly, to signify his inviting nature.

Cord shoved Fehrer into a wall, pinning him there to keep his attention. A hanging family portrait shook and crashed to the floor.

"I already know something's wrong here. So think carefully about what you tell me next," Cord growled.

"Uhm," Fehrer gurgled, struggling against the force of Cord's forearm. "Obviously, we need to talk. Please, just…"

Regaining his composure slightly, Cord released his grip on Fehrer's neck. "Okay. Okay. I'm going to just ask you: do you have my eye?"

"Your…ah…" he stammered.

Tapping two fingers fiercely against his eyepatch, Cord bellowed, "My eye, Fehrer, my goddamn eye!"

Fehrer looked around the hallway, over into the kitchen, to his right into the living room. He was hoping to find at best an answer, or at least a means of stalling, but could only note how good his chosen profession had been to him. "...I...no. There's been a robbery."

Cord somehow saw humor in this, and began chuckling bitterly. "Of course," he waved his hands at the lovely, untouched furnishings. "Looks like they really ransacked the place. Clever thieves, too. Left the silver, left the vases...eyeball theft has really been on the rise, huh?"

"I only realized it was missing today, otherwise I would have sent word..."

Cord looked around the house too, and it reminded him to breathe. Inhaling deeply, he centered himself, and recalled being told on more than one occasion that he was never more frightening than when he appeared totally calm. "So you don't have my eye. Meaning I will not be able to see my wife tonight. This correct?"

Fehrer sighed sadly, and answered, "Yes. That's correct."

Again, calmly, Cord posed a question. "How did this happen?"

"I don't know. I woke up this morning, and I opened the cabinet where I keep it, just to prep everything, you know, and it wasn't there. I searched everywhere, thinking I might have misfiled it somewhere, but it's not here. I don't know. It's just...gone."

Having reached the end of his experiment in diplomacy, Cord reached to the back of his belt to unsheathe a six-inch dagger from its scabbard, then shoved Fehrer back into the wall and held the knife to the man's throat. That he was still able to do this with absolute calm on his face, and in his totally steady hands, surprised Fehrer. It surprised Cord more. Only Fehrer registered it on his face. "Please don't!" he sputtered.

Cord stared at the man for a moment, drank in the sweat and panic. It brought him back to his military days. He sniffed and remembered a distinct smell of fear that he hadn't experienced since he had commanded soldiers. "I cut that eye out myself. Because you told me that the pain was part of the ritual I would need, in order to see my wife. I gave that to you with complete trust. And instead of protecting it, you stuck it in a cupboard where anyone with half a mind and quiet feet could get to it."

"I'm sorry..." Fehrer told him. He had begun to weep. "It wasn't my fault...I'm sorry..."

Fehrer's fear brought Cord back to the present, forcing him to release his anger entirely. "You're right. It wasn't totally your fault. I know who's to blame here. I'm going to leave now. And you and me, we're not going to see each other again, you realize that, right? We're done. Contract terminated."

"Yeh…yes, I understand…"

Completely calm now, not just faking it for the sake of fear tactics, Cord released his hold on Fehrer and stepped back, his knife now at his side. "I'm gonna go now. You want those groceries, they're in the wagon. I'm leaving that behind, I don't have time to be weighed down. Udo packed a couple of toys for your kids, too, so you make sure to go get them." He stepped toward the door. Then he stopped, jumped back, kicked Fehrer's leg in and sliced the side of his face. The pain set Fehrer screaming.

Cord realized he had started to smile. Putting away both the knife and the smirk, he walked back out the door. The cut was just deep enough to cause a lot of blood, but no lasting damage. Close enough to mercy for a man with a reputation like Nathan Cord's.

As he mounted his horse, Cord looked behind him, and realized the sun was starting to set. He knew he could be in Quinn's camp in just a little time if he rode hard enough, snapped the reins, and rode off. The anger in him began to build again. This time he welcomed it, like the old partner he knew it was.

11. New Friends

Captain of the Guard Victor Mene sat by a bonfire, huddled inside a heavy blanket, still shaking off the effects of the drugs Quentin Kind had pumped into him. *Literally* shaking them off – he was still trembling and cold, hoping to hell the feeling would be gone before the traitor Nathan Cord showed his face in the camp. He would not see the so-called king-killer in less than completely imposing form.

He was surrounded by young Pics – he had to remind himself not to call them "pixies" in their own village – watching some of the clan putting on a show. Dancing, music...Mene was not stonehearted, and recognized that the performers were very talented. Which did not mean he was enjoying the performance. He was just there for the warmth of the fire. None of the Pics sat near him, so he at least had his space.

He shuddered involuntarily, then cursed under his breath.

And then with almost no noise, the magician sat down next to him. Mene cursed under his breath once more.

The firelight danced across the magician's face in odd patterns Mene found disconcerting for reasons he didn't attempt to understand. He never did like magicians, found them to be self-satisfied and cocky. He didn't expect to like this one any better.

"So you're Captain Mene, huh? I'm Welles," the man said, holding out his hand. "Quinn's said some really interesting things about you."

Mene grunted. When it became clear that Welles wouldn't put the hand away, Mene jutted his own out and grasped the magician's without saying anything.

"No, pleasure's all mine," Welles deadpanned, then eyed the performers. "Enjoying the show? These guys are pretty good. The Pics seem to like it. Good rhythm."

"I suppose."

"Hey, I was always curious, figured you'd know," Welles started with a snap of his fingers, "The Orphan's personal guards – "

"She is the Queen in Waiting, and you should address her as such, Mister Welles," Mene coldly corrected him.

Welles smiled genially and shrugged his shoulders. "Okay. Cool, no offense meant. But the Queen in Waiting's personal guard, the Blue Knives…"

"The Order of the Indigo Temple," Mene clarified. At this point, even he knew he was just doing it to be contrary; he himself referred to the Blue Knives as such.

"Yeah, those guys!" Welles exclaimed cheerfully, clapping his hands. "The Indigo Temple…is it true what I've heard?" He waved his hand down by his crotch warily as he asked, "Are they really eunuchs?"

For the first time, Mene turned to look at his tormentor. "The Order of the Indigo Temple is an elite unit independent of the Queen in Waiting's army. They are the most dedicated and skilled warriors I have ever known. They are not eunuchs. They are a celibate, silent order of monks whose primary languages are meditation and violence."

Still watching the concert, Welles kindly remarked, "So they're not as charming as you then, huh?"

Recognizing that slicing open the man's neck would not help in the long term, Mene merely sighed with annoyance, and stifled another shudder. "You have questions."

Welles gave Mene a *Who, Me?* kind of look, but then nodded, "Yeah, I do."

"About me, and my history with Quinn Kind and Nathan Cord."

Welles pointed at Mene, admitting, "You're good."

"Ask me what you want to know."

Welles frowned, thoughtfully. "Huh. Thought I'd have to weasel it out of you, but okay. What's the deal with Nathan Cord?"

Mene stifled a laugh he didn't know he had in him, then answered, "Nathan Cord killed King Arius the Bold seven years ago, then fled in self-exile. He hasn't been heard from since, other than rumor here or a whisper there. This is not a secret."

"Yeah, I know that. Everyone with an ear to the ground knows that," Welles said, nodding. With a hint of conspiracy to his voice, the magician pressed on. "But you've got a special mad-on for the guy, as Quinn tells it. I just wanted to hear it from you."

"We're going to be working together for the next few days, you and me?" Mene asked, attempting to look Welles in the eyes as he did so. The black pits that met Mene did him no favors.

"Yeah, pretty close," Welles answered sincerely. "So that means more knowledge will help me."

43

Mene nodded, accepting this uncomfortable truth. "I trained Cord. During the rule of Lucius, I nominated him for his post as chief of Coal Brigade. I introduced him to Lucius myself, and when Arius took the throne, I arranged for him to meet the new king and his daughter as well. He betrayed crown and country the day he murdered the king, and in so doing, he dishonored me."

Processing this, Welles said, "I see. I see, and I understand. So tell me, do you drink?"

Mene shook his head voluntarily, attempting to connect the question to the conversation. Warily, he responded, "When the mood strikes me."

"Well," Welles started, pulling an unlabeled bottle out from under his robe, "we've got a few hours before Cord shows up. And I think I kind of like you, captain, and I'd like to drink with you while we enjoy this fine concert. What do you say?"

Mene glared at the bottle, then at Welles, and then repeated that process twice more, before nodding, grabbing and uncorking the bottle, and then taking a strong man's swig.

"Well done, sir! Well done!" Welles exclaimed, taking the bottle back from Mene and swigging down a gulp himself.

Quentin Kind had been sitting in the audience as well, as quietly as possible, as a means of avoiding a confrontation with Mene, but once he saw a bottle come out, he decided to chance it. "Hey, Welles, mind if I grab a pull off that?"

"Come on, Q, you have to ask? Bottoms up. Here's to tomorrow!" he cheered, passing the bottle onto the young woodsman.

Mene didn't seem to recognize him. If indeed he had, it made no difference two drinks later.

Within no time, an entire row consisting of a soldier, a magician, and several young men of the Pic clan were cheering rowdily and laughing and passing around the bottle.

In a little more time than that, captain of the guard Victor Mene had passed out, because he had not received the lesson that you should never engage in a round of drinking with a magician like Welles.

Not with the bottle a magician supplies, at least. No telling what's in it.

A half-dozen of Quinn's brothers had to learn that lesson, too. Casualties of war.

Groggily standing, Welles put his hands to his chest, whispering forgotten old words. Once this little spell had eased the majority of his inebriation, he made his way back to Quinn, sitting far away at a table by herself and lost in her own thoughts. She looked terribly sad.

"Hey," Welles greeted her softly, putting the nearly-empty bottle in front of her on the table. "Saved you a couple mouthfuls. Don't worry, I took the mojo off it."

Shaken out of her thoughts, Quinn smiled sweetly and took a small drink. "Kind of you, thanks."

"So ol' Vic there should be out for a couple of hours. He's quiet, and he can sleep through the rest of your brother's concoction, so it's a win for everyone."

"Appreciate it. Last thing I need is to try calming Nate Cord while his former commander is looking to chop his head off."

Welles asked, "Do you think he'll help?" as he quietly put the bottle to his lips.

"Vic's a career soldier. He'll do it for the good of crown and country, he'll pull his weight."

"I meant your man Cord."

Quinn snatched the bottle back and finished it off. "Well he ain't gonna do it for me, that's for sure. But he'll do it for the Orphan."

She slammed the empty bottle down and headed off to her room to prepare her case.

12. Old Days

Being that Quentin was, in Quinn's eyes, the best fighter her brothers had to offer, Quinn decided to sober him up first. Her strategy consisted of a healthy glass of tea, some strong words, and finally, a solid kick to the crotch. Quentin was soon in fighting form, though he wasn't exactly enthused about it.

Together, the two of them went about the task of putting their younger brothers to bed. The performers had wrapped up, and a dozen Pic boys asleep on the amphitheatre benches helped nobody.

Welles would have helped, but claimed that he needed to meditate before Cord's arrival. To Quinn, Welles' "meditation" looked an awful lot like a power-nap.

After she had finished cleaning up after the boys, Quinn returned to her own room, in the mood for a bit of sleep herself.

Ever since Welles came to her with the information of what had been happening within the kingdom walls, it felt like she'd been going nonstop: prepping her brothers, sending a messenger to the Fel in hopes of enlisting their aid, working with Welles on the necessary spells to maintain the barrier and keep the dead soldiers from spilling out into the surrounding villages.

Trying to bargain with Victor Mene, and going into a meeting with Nathan Cord. Two events that would be exhausting in and of themselves. To schedule them both over the course of a day was just too much.

And then breaking into Fehrer's the night before Cord's appointment, and doing something that she recognized as underhanded – no, not "underhanded." That was a lie she had been telling herself. It was just a euphemism for "utterly reprehensible." Stealing a man's solitary link to the only thing that he ever really loved. That's not what a friend would do. It was, however, a strategy a leader would have to employ.

Quinn Kind found leadership to be exhausting. She headed back to her room, lit a lamp by the entrance, and lay down on her bed. She closed her eyes and breathed, slowly, rhythmically, and deeply.

She slowed herself down enough to remember why in the hell she was doing all of this.

The title she'd held when she had first stepped into the kingdom, nearly two decades ago by human timekeeping, was Pic Ambassador to the Human Realm. This was back when magic was really starting to explode in the popular consciousness of the humans. Everyone was watching Keegan Morris, as he extolled the virtues of the unseen world. And the woodland people, of whose existence the humans had always been unsure, were suddenly thrust into the spotlight, unable to hide from the eyes of this new generation of mystics, mages, and dimestore spiritualists.

Quinn had always been vocal about the necessity of making alliances with the other tribes of the world, woodlander and human alike. She had told her mothers time and again that the world was getting smaller, and those who wanted to be left alone would be cutting themselves off from the future.

So the mothers of the Pic clan nominated her to represent them, to live among the humans, both to learn from them and teach them Pic ways. To pave the road for broader integration down the line – and to tell her mothers if the wind changed direction, to warn them if the humans began to feel less "neighborly." The fact that she was the most conventionally attractive to human eyes – she was far less angular than most of the Pic women, with rounded features that humans seemed to like – didn't hurt. A little manipulation is sometimes justified.

It hadn't been her first time inside kingdom walls. In her youth, like most Pics, she and her friends dared each other to scale the walls or sink into the ground and swipe something from inside. Once, the young Quinn had snuck into some kingdom girl's bedroom and returned with a thin, curved knife that had sat on the girl's nightstand. She had kept it to this day.

But it had been her first visit in broad daylight, as an invited guest, welcomed by King Lucius himself, that she was thinking of. The citizens of Western Sun looked at her with everything from kindness ("How wonderful, they're real!"), to polite derision ("Bit on the short side, isn't she?"), to outright scorn ("Useless pixies"). That last batch didn't really bother her. She knew it was coming, and knew she wouldn't be changing their worldview. And really, she wasn't there for them, anyway. She started to work with people who were willing to be part of the larger world she envisioned.

To her surprise, this included a rising young star in the king's royal guard, 22-year-old Nathan Cord.

The quick rest Quinn had been hoping for didn't come. Her memory was dancing about. Quinn held a picture of Cord's younger self in her mind's eye.

With his short, regulation haircut and his smooth, clean-shaven face. He had two lovely gray eyes. And his smile didn't scare anyone back then. And thinking of this, Quinn suddenly found herself briefly but unbearably sad. She accepted the feeling, let it run its course, and then opened her eyes and roused herself from the bed.

Remembering Cord got Quinn to thinking, and she realized that if Welles' predictions were at all accurate, then Cord was now at least an hour late to his own party. And Welles' predictions had yet to fail.

So when Nathan Cord grabbed her from behind and put a thin, curved knife to her throat, Quinn realized that all the planning in the world wouldn't do any good if a girl didn't bother to close her damn door when she wanted to rest for a moment.

13. Old Days in a Haze

Sweet young Nathan Cord, Quinn remembered in a haze. No more than 22 years old, the youngest chief of Coal's Brigade ever seen in guard history. He had initially joined the guard for the same reason a lot of young men in the Cabrea region did back then when they came of age, under the law of Lucius the New. By accepting a five-year commitment in the guard, Cord was looking to gain full citizenship in the kingdom. Citizenship meant he could buy a plot of land, and marry his woman, Kayla.

Cord was the son of a cattle rancher, Cale Cord. Cale died of darkheart when Nathan was in his third year with the guard, but Nathan hadn't lacked for father-figures at that point. Everyone had their eye on the young soldier, though it was Commanding Sergeant Victor Mene who decided to "make a man" out of Nate, his most talented subordinate.

He offered Coal's Brigade to Cord. It wasn't as huge a deal as it sounded – in peacetime, command of a special strikeforce wasn't much more than a ceremonial title. But Coal's Brigade had always been an unconventional unit, not as bound by the restrictions of full-time military life, and so it afforded him the luxury of living like a citizen, since he wouldn't be called upon for any specialized military incursions.

But then Lucius died, and the brother, Arius, assumed the throne. And all the old rules were thrown out.

Arius was a devoted student of the region's history, longing for a day when the Kingdom of Western Sun would rise as the seat of power on the continent, the way it had been envisioned by the barbarians that founded the city-state.

Arius didn't waste any time in pushing his own agendas. He wanted total control over the neighboring kingdoms, and he needed soldiers more talented and fearsome than usual in place. With this mandate, Mene began making full use of the small band of specialists that had become known, under the calculating and clever command of Nathan Cord, simply as Coal Brigade. Coal Brigade represented the elite of Western Sun's soldiers. Warriors with unconventional strategies that could be put into play by virtue of their small size, strategies that might be hindered by the weight of a full army. These were the men who would head out before the royal guard on their most dangerous missions, to stop potential threats before full military force was deemed necessary.

During his first tour of duty, Cord had shown a special gift for animal cunning and creative strategy. That was what Victor Mene saw and rewarded. And it became obvious that Cord was also a natural born leader, even in spite of his tendency to contradict Mene's military style at almost every turn. The men and women of Coal Brigade would go to hell for the man. And because he valued their lives as highly as they respected his leadership, most of them stayed alive.

Sweet young Nathan Cord. At first, Coal Brigade had been dispatched to protect sympathetic leaders in the neighboring states. But eventually, the orders came down to them to dispatch violent dissidents in the early stages of insurrection. And not long after that, Cord's small band of brothers was quietly ending anyone who uttered threats against the Kingdom of Western Sun – the people who called it by its first name. Its real name, Bloody Twilight, because they knew the barbaric history from which this monstrous thing of a city-state had really been born.

Cord was asked, more and more, to do horrible things quietly. And he had learned how to do those things very, very well. His five-year tour was extended into seven when he took position as brigade chief, and then ten, based on the new laws Arius had put in place to keep his army strong and massive. The taxes on the land grew higher to accommodate that army. It didn't matter as much to Nathan Cord as the boy-become-man thought it might. Cord had discovered his true gift through the guard. The cattle rancher had learned that out of all his talents, the one that was valued most was his capacity for quiet and creative acts of violence.

Cord led the Coal Brigade through a number of undeclared battles, weakening resistance in both the Northlands and Beasts Old Throne in the east, and gained favor with the king for executing missions quickly, subtly, and successfully. Each mission left behind a minimum of brigade casualties and a maximum of terror.

Though she had never asked Cord about it, Quinn now pondered the horror of that realization. In retrospect, she knew she should have. What must it have been like for a rancher's boy like Nathan Cord, to realize that the one thing in the world he was best at was killing?

She wondered if, by the time he started leading Coal Brigade on those terrible shadow missions, it even concerned him anymore.

Questions she had put away a long time ago, coming back to her.

These were dreams Quinn had experienced often over the years. She hated the feeling every time.

The mix of dream and memory untangled a little as Quinn regained consciousness.

Cord must have put her in some kind of sleeper-hold, because she woke up tied to a chair, with a sizable headache and the feeling that a good bit of time had passed.

She studied her surroundings. She was still in her own room, tied to her own chair. Which meant that no one else knew what was going on.

Everyone in the Pic forest understood the first rule of a Pic female. Quinn had actually gone out of her way toward making this rule iron-clad, through a mix of kind request and general emotional terrorism: don't bother Quinn when she's in her quarters. Nathan Cord was very well aware of Quinn's rule, which had now proven to bite Quinn on the ass. Hard.

When Quinn was through shaking off her grogginess, Cord appeared before her. His expression was sanguine and betrayed no emotion. "Hey," he began gently. "I get what you're trying for here, but it's done. Just tell me where you stashed my eye, and I'll leave. And you can do whatever the hell you were going to do. No harm done. I promise."

Fully roused, Quinn smiled. "Or what, Nate? You'll torture me?"

Cord gave Quinn a look she took as sadness, as he displayed the thin, curved dagger in front of her. He brushed a flat side against her nose so cleanly that Quinn couldn't be certain she'd even felt it.

"Yes," he answered quietly.

Quinn nodded, "Okay," letting him know she understood the severity of the situation. Then she squeezed her lips together tightly and whistled in a decibel Cord's kind could not hear.

Sitting, bored to tears in his room and just praying for something to happen, Quentin Kind's ears perked up to an alert from his sister. It took him only a moment's sprint to get to Quinn's quarters. At which point he began savagely attacking Cord before either man could really process the situation.

14. The Violent Hello

Quentin Kind's foot collided into Cord's nose, letting him know that things were getting a bit serious.

Cord had intended to scare Quinn into giving up the location of his eye. He was confident in his ability to do so, though less sure of the odds that he would actually be able to use torture methods on an old friend.

This was neither here nor there, as he'd been stupid enough to leave Quinn's mouth ungagged, allowing her to signal Quentin. Quentin had been Cord's primary teacher when he'd sought refuge in the Pic village years ago. So he knew for a fact that the little guy was a bastard of a fighter, and Cord wasn't precisely sure that he could win without taking drastic - meaning, lethal - measures.

While Cord spied different parts of the body that would put Quentin down without killing him, Quentin, his reflexes several times faster than the average human, landed half a dozen short, sharp blows to Cord's frame. In addition to wounding Cord, there were the beneficial dual results of slowing him down and making him angrier, more likely to make stupid moves.

A Nathan Cord that had properly prepared himself to fight a Pic would have worn light armor and readied several backup weapons, along with no less than three pre-planted explosives. But in his rush to get in and out quietly, Cord hadn't given himself a lot of planning time, and for his error suffered three more quick punches to the ribs before he could even steady his breathing. He dropped to his knees long before he thought he would.

Quentin, well-rested and frankly a bit angry at an attack perpetrated in his village, let alone on his sister, picked up Quinn's souvenir knife and pointed it seriously at Cord's throat.

Cord, on his knees, calmly raised his hands. "Hey, Quentin. Good moves."

"Thanks, Nate. For a human, you're still pretty fast."

Cord nodded just slightly, as the blade was still pretty close to his neck. "Appreciate it. You know, if I'd come in here with my sword, you'd be in bits. Sliced up like a sandwich at the threshold over there."

Quentin thought on this. Then he knelt down, tilted the knife so the curve hugged Cord's throat, and nestled his mouth into Cord's ear. "Well aren't you a big scary man with a knife at your throat?" Quentin whispered with satisfaction.

Cord was stuck, and he knew it, so he said nothing.

By this point, several Pics had arrived just outside Quinn's door, wondering what they should be doing. Quentin motioned for a couple of his brothers into the room to untie Quinn and secure Cord.

Standing at full attention now, Quinn Kind stood behind Cord, wrapped her arm around his neck, squeezed, and looked at Quentin. Understanding, Quentin pulled the knife back and placed it on Quinn's dresser. He took two steps back and nodded.

"I have had enough of this," Quinn said simply, quietly. Authoritatively. She wrapped her palm around Cord's chin and jutted his face up toward hers. "Cord. I have had enough of this."

Cord shut his eyes and answered, "Okay."

As she stormed out of the room, Quinn tossed a serious look at her twin brother, and understanding, Quentin took control. He glared at Cord, then at the Pic boys, and ordered, "Tie him up, guys. Tightly."

15. The Prognosis

Quinn wandered the camp, looking for Welles. She checked the rooms of some of the younger Pic boys, thinking maybe Welles wanted to get to know them better, drink and make jokes. But she knew she wouldn't find him there.

She checked the fire, to see if maybe he wasn't throwing praise on the performers, even though she knew as well as he did they were done for the night.

It bothered Quinn that she was afraid to visit Welles where she knew he would be, because admitting that fear meant admitting that what they were facing was something she had no coping mechanism for. And like it or not, after gathering this group and planning the attack, Quinn Kind was in charge. And no one wants to see their leader practically wetting herself at the sight of the enemy.

But the enemy was something that people should never have to lay eyes on. She opened the door to a storage shed where her brothers had chained up the dead soldiers. "Almost human" was the phrase bouncing around her brain, and she hated it. They *were* human, after all. Just dead humans who shouldn't be moving anymore. They hadn't even begun to rot – these two must have come from the immediate casualties that Mene had brought home from the southlands.

And yet she could only think of them as monsters, these two, thrashing against their chains and howling to be let loose. With no idea of what was happening to them. She hoped, anyway.

She prayed that was the case, as she wondered if the Orphan's boyfriend, another casualty of that recent combat, was still lurching around somewhere inside the kingdom walls.

And she thanked her lucky stars that – her recent bout with Cord notwithstanding – there wasn't a being alive that could sneak up on her in the dark. Otherwise, the sight of Welles sitting cross-legged on the floor to the right of the doorway might have scared the living hell out of her.

But there he was. Welles' eyes were closed, and he was muttering to himself. She hated the whole scene, but didn't know how to explain it to him. She didn't think she'd have to.

The two undead soldiers roared at Quinn when she arrived. It was a terrible noise, one she had told herself to be prepared for, but it was no use. The noises weren't sounds that living humans were capable of. It sounded like muddy bones scraping against each other, choking, dry and wet all at once, and not at all like language. It chilled her.

"Hey, Quinn," Welles greeted her in a way he meant to sound calm, but they were well past that now.

"Hey," she returned. For a moment she thought about sitting down next to him. Thankfully, the idea passed, when the monsters rattled their chains again, keeping her on her feet, at full readiness. "So what do you think?"

Welles breathed deeply, closed his eyes harder, then opened them again as though he'd been asleep for ages. "Hmm?"

"What do you make of those two?"

Welles spun his torso in Quinn's direction, and looked up at her. There was no smile, no quirky comment. At this point, she would have appreciated it.

He looked up at Quinn and frowned. "Well, in my informed medical opinion, they're dead. Dead and gone in every meaningful way. There's nothing left to them but meat and rage." Welles shook his head. And for the first time since she'd met the mage, she recognized sadness in Welles' face. "I'm sorry," he finished his evaluation, sincerely.

"They have no souls," Quinn interpreted.

"Whatever you want to call it. Soul, spirit, internal spark of energy. Nothing. Whatever is making them move, it's not something internal, it's something that's pushing them from the outside. Like marionettes."

"There's little more than stimulus-response going on. All they seem to notice is physical violence, and that's all they react with. I tried so hard…" Welles stopped himself there, then tried again. "I really wanted to see something else. Something I could work with, either to bring them back to full life, or shut them down simply. But whatever makes them people is gone. They're just meat puppets."

Deciding that comforting the man was more important than her own guardedness, Quinn steadied herself against the monsters' thrashing noises, and sat down next to Welles. They stared at their captives for a moment, and she frowned along with him. She put her hand to his back and stroked it gently. "I'm so sorry, Welles. I know you hoped this would be different."

"The worst of it is, I can't really figure out how Grolev got them moving. But at the same time, the fact that I can't figure out the spells he used tells me a lot. We're talking about death magic here."

"Explain it to me," she urged sympathetically, then quickly clarified "As simply as you can, I'm not as well-versed in any of this as you."

"The magic I use, it's not terribly complicated, it's just an understanding of the living energies in the surrounding earth, the people and things living on and in it. Once something dies, well, that's more or less the end of my contact with it. But communicating with the energy in dead things, that takes a lot of devotion to the practice. Scary devotion."

"Well, isn't devotion just part of a magician's craft? You spend hours every day just practicing the fundamentals," she said, attempting to understand why there was an element of panic in Welles' voice as he spoke. "But wait, if it's so intricate, how is it a dimestore magician like Fehrer can bring Kayla's spirit to talk with Cord?"

"That..." Welles started, anticipating the question and deciding to tread lightly on the subject, "is a different type of trick. To be honest, I have a feeling Fehrer's conjuring a spirit out of Cord's emotional memories, rather than actually communicating with the spirit world. But even then, contact with the beyond is still another aspect of life – their souls are still living energy, just not housed in a body anymore. I don't have an exact theory worked out, but I would like a few minutes with this Fehrer to sort out just what he does. All I know is, it's not death magic."

"Because it's not complicated enough? I'm still a little confused."

Welles knew he wasn't getting his point across. After taking a moment to gather his thoughts, he tried again. "That's okay, it's not easy to understand. Let me see...okay, it's like, if I wanted to paint forest scenery using nothing but blood for paint, with enough dedication, years of spending time thinking of nothing but how to get green hues out of dark reds, it's possible I could do it. But you know what else I'd need?"

Answering the obvious, Quinn whispered, "Blood." She was beginning to get Welles' point, but wasn't quite there yet.

"Blood. I'd need to gut a lot of things to get all the different colors of blood I'd need to paint that picture. And when I'd finally done it, when my painting was completed, do you know what I'd have made? A forest scene colored in all the wrong ways. A perversion of something natural. And who in their right mind would spend all their time and energy to make something so fundamentally wrong?"

Quinn shook her head, absorbing the analogy. "So what you're saying is there aren't a lot of magicians who work with the 'medium' of death magic."

"Right. And those few that do, don't tend to mingle with the rest of us. They don't share their notes. But what I do know – and like I say, I don't understand the specifics, just the implications – is that Grolev has already spent years developing the kind of power it would take to raise hundreds of dead bodies from their graves just to start fighting and killing anything in their way.

Which begs the question: if Grolev's already got that kind of power, why would he use it just for this?"

"You think this is just a distraction?" Quinn asked incredulously. "That's sick."

"That's exactly the right word. It is demented. But beyond that, the really frustrating thing, is that it's totally outside my realm of understanding. This is stuff even Keegan Morris wouldn't be able to wrap his brain around." Welles hung his head. It looked like he was tired of thinking about all of this. He sighed heavily and asked, "So that's my assessment. Your call: what do we do now, Quinn?"

The simplicity of the question struck Quinn as almost amusing, and she actually found herself smiling as she got back up on her feet. The smile wasn't based on any sense of satisfaction or relief. She only knew that her answer was just as simple.

"You know, I've been thinking of these two as monsters. But they're not. Especially after what you just told me. They're just distractions, things that have to be put down in order to take out the real monster.

"But we've got monsters, too. We have two of the greatest beasts Bloody Twilight has ever birthed, and they're on our side. We have monsters that can destroy anything that comes at them. Victor Mene and Nathan Cord are here with us. And they really want to fight. So I say we let them in there and turn them loose."

Welles started to laugh, a bit nervously. "Heh. You used to be such a nice girl, too…"

Before she had a chance to retort, a very young Pic boy showed up behind her and tapped her shoulder. He whispered in her ear. She nodded like something good had happened, but didn't elaborate.

Then the Pic boy ran off, and Quinn, returning to Welles's comment, frowned. "I don't think there's any room left in this world for nice girls, Welles." She stuck out her hand, and he grasped it so she could hoist him up. They stared deeply at each other, and Quinn told him, "Maybe someday soon, but not now. We have to set our boys up now. We have to get ready them ready for one hell of a fight."

16. A Personal Thing

Bound to a small chair with nothing to do, Nathan Cord thought back to last time he'd been in the Pic forest.

It had been just after he'd killed Jonas Mudd, and buried him in a shallow grave he actually hoped somebody would stumble upon some day.

There hadn't been much of a need to kill Mudd. The man was pathetic from the start, and once Cord came back, and his reputation with him, Mudd had literally pissed himself in fear. Cord could have let him go, told him to never sail again. He could have told the "admiral" to do pretty much anything, and it would be done. Cord had complete power, but he was angry, angrier than he even realized he could be. Old feelings were fighting their way to the surface, and Cord decided to take them all out on Jonas Mudd.

He knew then that if he kept going on this way – the way he truly, desperately thought he should – then that rage would end up destroying him. He made a hard choice to save his own life, and sought solace from the one person he knew would grant it.

When Cord came to this village, he was disheveled, trembling, and damn near suicidal.

And Quinn saved him. Quinn and her people. They encouraged him to farm their crops, taught him meditative techniques, some basic magic. But mostly, they taught him to live as though life were something worthwhile. He had spent nearly a decade slaughtering people in the name of the crown, and it had cost him his wife, his professional honor, and he could argue, his soul. Teaching a man who had lost all of this that life is worth something was a lesson that took a long while to really sink in.

Cord had left the village hoping to carry those lessons in his heart. He went back to the haven that Udo had created. He became a bar owner, and it was satisfying, in its way. It became easier to forget about his past, at least for a few moments a day. He chatted up patrons a little, on the rare occasion that he felt he could manage a conversation. It felt like a new start.

But then there was the anniversary day. Whenever the anniversary of his wedding to Kayla came around, it became practically impossible for Cord to keep moving. On one particular anniversary evening, he had started talking with a so-called "commercial magician" named Fehrer, and any sense of rebirth in him stalled.

Cord had been quite blisteringly drunk that night, and as was typical in that case, he had started blathering on about Kayla. Usually Udo was around to pull him away when he got like that, but like an idiot Cord had given him the night off in order to let a young local train as a part-timer, so he had no friends in the bar who would recognize the situation for what it was. And Fehrer, sensing money, dug in his claws. The commercial magician told him that he could arrange a meeting from the spirit world where Cord could have the chance to speak with his wife. When the time, the place, and the price were right, of course.

And just like that, all the lessons the Pics had taught Nathan Cord went sailing out the window. Because when all was said and done, the only thing in the world Cord wanted was the opportunity to see Kayla again.

And Quinn just couldn't let this arrangement stand, could she? She used it as a means of extortion, stole the one thing that kept his heart beating just because she thought....

Cord didn't know what she thought, really, and he didn't care. Bound to this tiny chair in Quinn's room, Cord found himself wanting a little comfort, and as he usually did when in such a mood, started to picture Kayla's face in his mind, when Victor Mene showed up at the doorway, wrapped in a heavy blanket and appearing very much like he was trying not to shiver. Kayla's image in his mind evaporated immediately.

"Here lies Nathan Cord," Mene uttered in his deep bass, barely fighting a grin off of his face. This was Mene's version of humor.

Cord wouldn't give him the satisfaction, no matter how much the man deserved it. "Technically I'm sitting. How are you doing, Vic? Keeping your soldiers alive?"

Mene's non-grin disappeared.

Cord sneered, wearing his disgust proudly. "Yeah. Well done, Cap."

It startled Cord when that grin reappeared on Mene's mouth. "This might perk you up, Cord. I've got a couple of your Coal Brigadiers here in camp. Dolus and Tegan. They're not in the peak of health. Quite the opposite, in fact. But that probably wouldn't matter to you. They were disgraced the moment you fled the kingdom walls."

Cord closed his eyes and remembered the two boys Mene mentioned. They had been two of the few who actually managed to survive the last siege Cord had led, before the last of the bastards in Beasts Old Throne surrendered and accepted annexation as part of Western Sun. He had been particularly proud of them for that. The treaties had been signed that day, but nobody told either army. A dozen members of Coal Brigade took swords to the gut hours after peace had been declared. Those twelve men received hero's honors and were buried at Soldier's Memory, side by side with the rest of the boys that Mene and Cord failed to keep alive.

Coal Brigade had sustained heavy losses throughout the Beasts Old Throne battles, but that last day had been the worst. Cord might have rebuilt his team with some of Mene's up-and-comers, but things didn't work out that way. After Cord killed the king, there was a stain on the brigade and everyone who served in it. They were absorbed into the guard proper, but Cord knew it didn't matter; Dolus and Tegan were Cord's Men, and were likely pariahs in their own army for the rest of their tenure.

Cord tried his best, but couldn't even put together a deserving image of his wife's face in his mind after Mene shared this. All he could picture were the faces of the seventy-three soldiers that died under Cord's command over the course of seven years.

He reacted to those memories by spitting on the floor, then glaring at Victor Mene and uttering as fiercely as he could, "You useless, preening monster."

Mene stepped close to Cord, close enough to speak into his ear. "In the last two days, I've chopped the heads off more of my own men than yours, king-killer. Be miserable if you want, but if it's a competition you're looking for, I'll win it every time, and goddamn us both."

Cord found himself at a loss for words. It was troubling to have something in common with Victor Mene.

Finally, Cord asked, "So what happens now?"

Pacing around Cord, Mene answered, "We have a mission. We're going to retake the castle from those walking corpses we used to call comrades. And you're going to help."

"What if I don't want to?"

Mene nodded irritably. "Right. Your magic eyeball. Welles mentioned that detail to me. You'll get that back after we're done."

Cord opened his mouth to ask another question – "Who the hell is Welles?" – but Mene cut him off before any words came out. "You'll fight because you want to. I know you, Cord. You're angry enough to kill, and I know as truth that it's all you're good at. And that will come in handy very soon. Is this acceptable?"

He hated when Mene made sense, but even a broken clock is right twice a day. Cord nodded. "What happens after that, Vic?"

Mene appeared to reflect on this question, and replied, "The little pixie told me to keep my anger in check, so you're safe from me for now. But when this is over – assuming we both live through it, and I think we will – I am going to kill you. I am going to execute you for what you did, Nathan. This is my right, in my capacity as the law of Western Sun."

"Just so I know?"

Mene smiled. "Just so you know." The smile seemed to almost reflect pride.

Cord nodded. "Assuming I sincerely agree to do what you guys want...assuming my aim isn't to kill you once I'm let loose...when do I get out of this chair?"

Mene pulled a switchblade from his belt, walked behind Cord, and cut his bonds. "You're free, Nathan Cord. Come on. I think the pixie queen wants to address her troops before we head back into the kingdom."

Cord rubbed his wrists to get some feeling back, taking in Mene's taunting directions. "What do you mean 'queen'? Quinn's mothers are the heavies around here, don't they get a say?"

Mene grunted, "I don't pretend to understand the pixie ways. That's your interest, not mine."

When Cord looked up from his wrists, Mene was standing by the doorway. Still huddled in the blanket and trying to make it look natural.

Cord put that question aside in favor of another. "So how are you feeling, Vic?" he asked, standing up. "Gonna be a hundred percent when we get into some fighting?"

Mene fended off another shudder and started to pull the blanket in closer, then, spying Cord's amusement, threw the blanket into the corner of the room. "Yes."

They walked out toward the center of the village together.

"Man, what did Quentin dose you with?"

"Shut up, Cord."

17. The Situation, As It Stands, Part One: A Fine Example

Victor Mene and Nathan Cord walked toward the bonfire in the center of the village. Someone who didn't know them might say they looked almost like comrades.   They found they were the last ones to the party. Every bench in view was occupied by a Pic warrior, all ready for instructions. Quinn Kind stood before them in front of the fire, wearing a long brown coat and holding in her left hand a spear. Nothing about it looked special. It was a standard staff, five feet high, tipped with one foot-long blade. But though it was hardly extraordinary in design, Cord immediately recognized its significance.

"She's carrying the Stem," he told Mene, knowing the man would be ignorant of its significance. "That's the staff...the ceremonial weapon the warrior-mother carries into battle. Back when they did a lot of battling, anyway."

"Ah," Mene responded without any particular interest. A weapon was a weapon to him.

"What's Quinn doing with that? Would've figured one of her moms would keep it with her. Weird."

"Huh," Mene responded in the same bored tone, letting Cord know he was talking to himself.

Cord ended the chat, instead focusing on his memory of a beatific, life-affirming Quinn, but saw none of that in the warrior who commanded the attention of three dozen Pic fighters. The darkness and flame obscured their faces, but to Cord it looked like they were mostly boys. Granted, the Pics were a fairly androgynous people, but Cord had spent enough time with them to recognize boys from girls. And he couldn't make out any females in the crowd. It struck him as odd.

When Quinn had first come to the kingdom as ambassador, Cord had actually been concerned over how the seemingly peaceful nature of the Pics would mesh with Western Sun, a kingdom whose history was built on war. He had liked Quinn immediately, and was concerned that maybe her kind wasn't quite built for the harsh realities of a human political system, especially one founded by a warrior class. It was later that he realized their pacifism to be a bit of a ruse. They didn't show it outwardly, but they knew how to fight, and they knew how to wage war if necessary.

He had heard rumors that they had long ago engaged in battle with their woodland neighbors in the Northlands, and in Beasts Old Throne, but it had been so long ago as to be little more than fairy tales. But whatever their history, there was a good reason no one encroached on the Pic forest. They had their own homegrown fighting style, one based on striking quickly, hiding, and then striking again when their opponent wasn't looking.

When fighting humans, their natural visual camouflage, that weird talent they had of masking their presence from a human's field of vision without even trying, meant that they could hide in plain sight, just off to the left in the periphery, to toss in another hit.

While Cord knew for a fact that it was nearly impossible for a human to learn, he had also taken in demonstrations that were fascinating to watch. Fascinating, and frustrating. Like watching a primate swatting at a hornet. Funny at first, but eventually you just wished someone would fall down…

There wasn't a name for the discipline they employed. It was just the singular way that Pics fight, so why would they bother naming it? Eventually the humans got fed up with referring to it that way and started calling their sad attempts to mimic the form "Pixie-style."

The Pics were always cautiously aware that one day Cord's kingdom might find itself interested in annexing their village. In truth, it was in preparation for that possibility that they had sent Quinn in to make friends. When Arius took the throne and the Annexation Wars started in earnest, the Pic mothers pulled Quinn out, and instituted mandatory fighting instruction for everyone in the village. These Pic boys situated around the fire looked green, but Cord knew for sure that each and every one of them was dangerous.

But even with that knowledge, Cord looked around at the miniscule army Quinn Kind had assembled. Three dozen of Quinn's warrior siblings. A captain without an army. A magician nobody had ever heard of. And himself, a disgraced soldier.

What in the hell did Quinn think they would be able to accomplish?

"Everyone listening?" Quinn started. "Good. This won't take long. I want everyone to get some rest before we move in tomorrow, but I figured we should all be on the same page."

There was some commotion among Quinn's makeshift army. She pounded the Stem fiercely against the ground. Three sharp clacks against a rock rang out. Everyone shut up.

Quinn behaved like this was expected, and moved on. "Two days ago, the Orphan's mystical counselor, a disgusting excuse for a human we know as Grolev, raised an army of dead soldiers. The recently dead from the southern battles, and a lot of those boys that were buried in the kingdom, got raised. It's conjecture at this point just how many we're dealing with here – if Grolev's spell managed to raise every dead body in Soldier's Memory, or what. We're assuming that it's only the freshest dead still moving around – any bodies that had long been in the ground would fall apart the moment they tried to rise up. So we think the number may have been around fifty to a hundred initially, but they've been killing the citizenry for over two days now. Welles has the numbers around four or five hundred or so, and rising. We figure anyone who was there when the spell was cast is at risk of rising again once they are killed.

"Keep in mind, these aren't people anymore. No minds or souls to speak of. They've been brought back to life with no memory of themselves. All they know to do anymore, is to kill. Captain Mene was kind enough to bring a couple of them with him so we could see what we're dealing with...."

Welles came out of nowhere, into the light of the fire, with the thrashing corpses of Dolus and Tegan pulling against their chains. Welles smiled awkwardly by way of a greeting.

And then he let the chains go.

They charged straight for Mene and Cord. The two men reacted on instinct. Mene unsheathed his sword and sliced Dolus' head off swiftly, with barely a movement.

Since his weapons had yet to be returned to him, Cord found himself forced to improvise. When the thing that used to be Tegan lunged at him, Cord toppled over, struggling to keep his former charge from clawing and biting at him. It grabbed his arm, momentarily confusing Cord when he realized it was trying to yank it out of the socket. Not exactly standard attack strategy.

Cord crashed his free shoulder into the corpse's chest, rolled it onto its back and shoved his thumbs into its eyes. When the thing began to scream in ugly, squealing baritones Cord had never heard before, the former brigade chief went to work, violently pounding the thing's head into the ground. His thumbs remained locked in the thing's eye sockets.

When Tegan's corpse stopped attacking and started twitching, Cord pulled his thumbs out, reached for a nearby rock, and in one deliberate movement, thrust it down, crushing its head in. He held the rock firm. The twitching stopped.

Cord lifted the rock and proceded to pound it into the thing's skull twice more, then rested, breathed in and out deeply a few times until he regained his composure and no longer felt any need to throw up.

"So we're aiming for the head, then," he concluded, loud enough that everyone could hear and learn the lesson the easy way.

Not missing a beat, Quinn gestured at the two soldiers and said, "Now picture that, times hundreds. That's what we're up against. Thanks for the demonstration, guys."

As she said this, Cord and Mene lurched to their feet, both trying not to appear winded. They looked at each other, realizing that they'd just participated in a nightmarish bonding exercise.

18. The Situation As It Stands, Part Two: A Quick Question

"Hang on, hang on," Cord interrupted, waving his hands irritably. It had been a long time since he'd had to sit through a briefing, and found that age hadn't brought him all the patience he'd hoped for. "Maybe I'm asking an obvious question here, but indulge me: where the hell is the royal guard?"

Mene bored his eyes into Cord's skull, but since it didn't burst, Mene knew he was left with the recourse of answering the man's query. "Scattered," he stated officially, as though that would be enough.

It wasn't. "More words, please. Feel free to use ones with lots of syllables. I know it'll be tricky for your caveman brain, but – "

Mene squeezed a fist and started to raise it.

"VICTOR." Quinn halted him. "Just tell him."

Mene grunted. At some point he would get that punch in, but unlike Cord, age had granted Mene patience, so he unclenched. "We have regiments permanently stationed at Northern and Eastern Suns."

Cord processed this and responded, "Not a surprise, but that would only account for half the numbers, tops."

"And we've been pushing into the south for the last few years."

He remained silent, and Cord waited, realizing it wasn't for dramatic effect. The words were hard for Mene to speak. Finally, he continued, "It hasn't been going as well as the Queen in Waiting's cabinet would have liked."

"God. Didn't they learn anything from the first time we tried that? How many did we lose back then? Even Arius agreed that it wasn't worth it..."

"And Arius is dead," Mene countered pointedly. "And the Queen in Waiting has no real power to say otherwise. The decisions are made by Grolev and Arius's cabinet." He added, pointedly, "The cabinet that Arius had appointed *before you killed him*."

"And you," Cord pointed out, slipping a little accusation in his tone. "Captain of the guard. Surviving veteran of thirty years of service. You're telling me your opinion has no weight with those guys? Or did you not bother to speak up – I mean, one fight's as good as the next for you, I know, but goddamn. The southlands can't be taken, and you know that better than anyone."

"I spoke my mind," Mene said bitterly, practically choking on his own words as he added, "They chose not to follow my recommendations."

Quinn stepped between the two of them. This conversation would end in a fight or a complete shutdown, and neither would do her any good. "How they got there is a moot point right now. At the end of the day, the brunt of the royal guard is stationed outside the southlands. Most of them get to come home stacked on a cart. Since Bloody Twilight's not under attack, they must have figured that a skeleton crew left at home would be fine."

Starting to reel with disbelief, Cord clutched to the one thing keeping him grounded: his old friend anger. "And what, they couldn't stave off a few dead men that hadn't been buried yet?"

By way of explanation, Mene offered, "Most of them are draftees. Their training was not what I would have liked."

"But why wouldn't some reinforcements from the neighbor kingdoms have come back?"

Quinn fielded this one. She answered calmly, even though her inner rage on the subject was close that which Cord demonstrated openly. "One possibility is that they don't know. Communication between the kingdoms has been...spotty. Has been since Arius died. Say what you will about him, but as a king, he made sure there was interconnectivity between all the kingdoms."

Cord's eye flashed, letting Quinn know that there was a lot more than that one could say about Arius. "He was a rapist and a murderer. I don't give a goddamn if he was a good communicator."

Quinn was also a good communicator, so she was wise enough to step back from this line of inquisition, returning to the matter before them. "In any event, either they don't know what's happening. Or they do – they maybe have a basic idea that things have broken down over there. All the woodlanders felt something change, but we're patched into different wavelengths, and even then, we didn't know specifics. But I'd be surprised if some enterprising Tree-bob with a few guardsmen buddies in Northern Sun never let anything slip. In which case they've all decided it's not worth it to come down and check up on things."

This was too much for Cord. Stupified by what he'd just heard, he looked back at Mene, asking barely above a whisper, "What...what the hell happened to the guard, Vic?"

In what actually seemed like an act of compassion, Victor Mene shook his head with a trace of sadness that he would never consciously acknowledge. "Perhaps even you can grasp that seven years is a long time, Cord. Seven years of the central kingdom being run through manipulation and greed. Things became…unmanageable."

Cord felt Mene's despair, and softened his tone slightly. "Okay…yeah, okay. So Bloody Twilight's broken, and this sad lot is all that's around to fix it."

"Bloody Twilight can't be fixed," a voice came from out of nowhere. Cord looked up towards the fire. Quinn tilted her head back slightly. Welles had rejoined the conversation.

"Sometimes something gets broken, and no amount of glue or positive thinking will do the trick. And if you can't fix it, you can either ignore it, or destroy it before it starts hurting the parts that do work. And this isn't something we can ignore for very long."

Everyone took in Welles' words. There was a long moment of quiet. Cord decided to press on in a vain hope of making just a little more sense of the situation, even as he started sizing up this new player. This man who had shown up to sic Dolus and Tegan on him, disappeared into the shadows, and reappeared just to make some snarky comment.

"Okay, Spooky. So how did we even find out about this? Quinn, you haven't really been welcome there since the annexation days, and Vic," he continued, pointing a thumb still sticky with Tegan's ocular juices in Mene's direction, "he's not likely to send a distress call…"

Mene grunted – then nodded in grudging agreement.

"It was me," Welles offered, as though that brief admission explained things well enough.

Cord scratched his beard. "Yeah…who the hell are you again?"

Welles glanced over at Quinn. "You were right, he's a real charmer." Then, speaking to Cord, but with enough volume for everyone to hear, "My name is Welles, and I'm a magician. And about 90 percent of being a good magician is practice. Every day I spend hours 'working out,' so to speak. And the day Grolev cast his spell, I was practicing mind surfing."

Cord nodded, sadly, understanding none of what Welles had just said. "Okay, explain that one for the stupids."

Smiling in a way Cord found oddly unsettling, Welles answered, "If you can read the emotions of one person, it's called intuition. If you can read a whole group, that's just showmanship. If you can do that with a group of people you've never seen or met, from miles away? That's magic." He was channeling Keegan Morris's public speaking style, and quite enjoyed it.

"So that was my morning, sitting out in the fields north of the kingdom. Reaching my mind out to feel the mood of the people. It was normal, nothing too exciting. Then in a matter of minutes, I felt wave after wave of people's minds screaming, terrified. And then I felt something else. I still don't know quite how to explain it, it was a new one on me. But I felt those guys," he said, pointing to the remains of the soldiers Cord and Mene had just killed again. "Like nails against the chalkboard. If the chalkboard was in my gut.

"I had to figure out what was going on, so I reached out. Past the fear. Past the sickness of those in contact with the dead soldiers. And I found someone who was angry and righteous. I found Captain Mene, here." He gestured out to the captain.

Mene knew to continue the story. "There wasn't even time to think. One minute, I was in the stable, tending to my horse. And then I heard screaming. I looked out, and there were these men, some in bloody armor that we'd worn while fighting in the south, some wearing the ceremonial garb in which our fallen are buried, spreading everywhere, cancerous. Some had swords and were swinging at anyone who came close. Those without, just grabbed and beat on their victims. And then I saw those victims, clearly dead, pick themselves back up and start attacking alongside their own killers. My first thought was to go to the Queen in Waiting, but I couldn't get near the castle, not without wading into a hundred of the things. Then, in my head, I heard a voice. I later learned it was our magician here. He told me he was working on something to keep the monsters where they were, and that I needed to get out of the kingdom if I were to be of any help in saving it."

Cord, now sitting on the former Mister Tegan's body, snorted. "Bet you loved taking orders from a voice in your head."

Mene ignored his baser instincts, and answered the question. "It was not my finest hour. But it was easily my strangest. So I followed my instincts and trusted the man."

Quinn called attention. "By that point, Welles had made his way to our camp, explained the situation, and we started formulating a plan while we waited for the captain to make his way to us."

Cord's mood immediately darkened. "Right. Your plan. We're going to have to talk about that."

Quinn's eyes gave off a cold glare. "And we will. In private, if that's okay with you."

Cord waved it off, regaining his façade of wry bemusement. "Of course, Ambassador Kind. Can't help but notice that we're talking about an initial enemy count of a few hundred, minus however many Vic took out, plus an exponential increase if they're adding their own kills to their number. And I spy a fighting force here of less than forty, so while I appreciate the vote of confidence…"

The Pic fighters began to murmur among themselves. Quinn struck the Stem again, and regained their attention. "The fighting force isn't to beat the enemy, just to clear a path so Welles can get to the high tower. The goal is for Welles to break Grolev's spell, make those dead men dead again, but we need to make our way into the castle to get to him. We're just providing interference to make that happen."

Quentin Kind stood up from the ranks. "Still, sis, he's got a point. We're good, but are we as good as what the magician needs?"

"We'll be as good as we need the western front to be. And I trust the Fel clan to be as good as we've all heard they are."

Cord felt an odd tingle in his jaw and realized he was smiling. He'd forgotten just how clever Quinn could be. "You little sneak. You got in touch with the Fel?"

Quinn was clearly fighting off a satisfied smile of her own as she answered, "My messenger reached camp just before you did. They'll join our party when we get to the kingdom walls."

A silent pride hushed its way through the band of warriors. Quinn didn't bother hiding her satisfaction any longer, and beamed a hopeful smile. "Come on, guys. Did you think my plan amounted to nothing more than 'Let's see if we can mess some of them up before we die'?"

19. The Situation As It Stands, Part Three: A Slim Chance of a Bad Night's Rest

Welles cut through the murmuring invited by the mention of the Fel clan to explain, "Based on the strongest emotions I can pick up from inside the barrier, I believe the Orphan is holed up in the castle's high tower, protected by Grolev, and her personal guard – the Order of the Indigo Temple." At the mention of the Queen in Waiting's personal guard, he nodded respectfully toward Mene, letting him know that he was capable of learning. Mene made no gesture in return.

"Our primary goal is to make our way to the castle, get the Orphan out of there – that's assuming she's still alive – and get back outside the barrier. And then burn the whole mess to the ground."

Mene asked calmly, "Is that the only option?" but the trace of frustration was apparent. Asking the captain of the guard to burn down his own kingdom was very close to asking him to chop off his left foot.

Welles answered coolly, "The Kingdom of Western Sun is well beyond saving, captain. Its architecture is crumbling. Its government has been corrupted in every sense of the word. And its people are mostly dead, or worse. There is nothing to fight for. It is a poisonous growth, and we are a rusty butter-knife forced to do the work of a scalpel. Not ideal, but we'll have to do. We have to kill the magic that brought those soldiers out of the ground, otherwise the disease will spread to the Bastard Suns – " at the colloquialism, Mene raised an eyebrow, prompting Welles to correct himself, "Excuse me, the neighboring kingdoms. Western Sun is a lost cause, and it needs to go."

The group fell silent for several moments, taking in both the simplicity and the enormity of the task ahead of them, before Quinn returned to the front, telling her makeshift attack force, "Anyone who wants to get some rest, you've got about five hours. We ride out at first light. Figure we should be outside the barrier before twilight, at which point I'll meet with the head of the Fel and we'll make final preparations from there. Questions?"

No one spoke up. Quinn sighed. Whether it was out of disappointment at the lack of curiosity, or thankfulness that there were no further questions that she couldn't answer, it wasn't clear. "Okay. See you all in the morning."

The group slowly dispersed.

Quinn headed toward her room, leading her steps with the Stem, propping herself up against a feeling like she was lugging a boulder on her back. So she wasn't at all surprised when she got to her room and lit the lamp, only to find Cord already sitting on her bed. After all, Cord had been a heavy contribution to that weight all by himself.

His posture was hunched, his wrists resting on his knees and his fingertips pressing against themselves in arched formation. He stared placidly at them, and didn't blink when the light went on.

She frowned, sadness and exhaustion creeping into her face and voice. "Please, Cord. Not now. I know how you feel –"

"You couldn't possibly." He betrayed no emotion, and didn't bother looking at her.

She nodded. "No. Probably not. But there's so much more at stake right now than your anger toward me. Can you find it in you to just hold off until this is done?"

Cord stood up and calmly stepped toward her, until they were close enough for his frame to tower over hers by a foot. She could hear him breathing deeply, in a slow, steady rhythm. The benefit of a man who couldn't care less about dying. She realized that she was afraid of him. It didn't show.

"Just answer me this. Did you extort me into this mess because you needed a good fighter, or because you thought I'd have more of a stake in getting the Orphan to safety?"

Quinn looked up at him, frankly pissed that he felt he had the right to question her judgement at this point. This showed.

"For now, Nate? Just leave it alone."

Cord read her eyes, and decided it wasn't worth it to push further. "Yeah. Until this is done. Sleep tight, Quinn." He brushed past her, out the door, without looking into her eyes.

Feeling a tenseness in her back and shoulders that was new and completely unwelcome, which she attributed to the invisible rock she'd been hefting around, Quinn dropped the Stem to the floor, blew out the light, undressed, and crawled into bed. She didn't even bother trying to sleep. She just wrapped a thin blanket around her body, curled up and did her best not to think of everything that could go wrong.

Mene, knowing that sleep would only help his mental acuity, found an empty hut and rested his head on a pillow in a bed two sizes too small for him, falling asleep without issue. When there is nothing left to do, he had always told his soldiers, it is always best to rest for whatever is to come.

Welles began a meditative routine, part of a larger spell that he thought might keep him in a semi-comatose trance state until the time came to leave camp.

Cord paced the grounds for an hour, then found a tree far enough away from the camp that looked comfortable, sat down and propped himself against it. He scowled, took off his long coat and bundled it up for use as a pillow. And his anger eventually exhausted him enough to fall into an unsatisfying sleep.

20. Strange Acquaintances

That sleep lasted all of an hour. He woke from what amounted to a power-nap with a crick in his neck and restlessness everywhere else. Shaking the wrinkles loose from his coat before putting it back on, he wandered the campgrounds some more.   Eventually, he found himself back at the bonfire, where he came upon Welles, his legs crossed, his back on the ground, his hands on his belly, quietly spouting off a steady stream of...something. Cord could swear that there were harmonizing noises coming out of the guy's ears. He couldn't help but be impressed. He'd never seen Fehrer do anything like that, that was for sure.

Unsure exactly what to do now, Cord simply sat, cross-legged, opposite the magician. The chanting Welles mumbled was, in a way Cord couldn't quite place, strangely soothing. Then he noticed the neck of a half-full bottle of something sticking out of the mystic's satchel, so he reached past Welles and pulled it towards him noiselessly. But not quietly enough that it escaped Welles' notice.

"If you wanted a drink, you should have just spoken up," Welles said barely above a whisper. The solemn expression he showed during the briefing had worn off, and, his eyes fully open now, his onyx pupils reflecting against the firelight, he took Cord in, and half-smiled.

Cord half-smiled back. "I thought you might be busy."

"Sort of."

"Were you meditating, or putting some kind of spell together?"

Still sitting cross-legged, Welles raised himself up, then arched his spine backwards and was rewarded with sound of several vertebrae popping. He came back up, satisfied. "What do I call you? You prefer Cord, Nathan, Scary Bastard...?"

"So long as you don't address me by any rank, I'm fine. Cord, you can call me."

Welles nodded. "Cord, I've helped to develop a spell to keep those dead things inside kingdom walls, I've put together spells to lessen injuries for the entire Pic clan, and I even ingested a potion that, if I mixed it right, should make my skin completely unbreakable for the next forty-eight hours."

"And if you mixed it wrong?"

"I'll be covered in purple hives by morning. But I think I got it right. So, no, all I was doing there was focusing, and praying."

"To any particular deity?"

Welles cracked his knuckles, then his neck. "Does it really matter? When you climb high enough up the spiritual food chain, you realize they're all just parts of the same great unknown, and you hope like hell whatever's looking down on you, it sees your point of view."

"If it sees anyone at all," Cord mused. He started to pull the cork off the bottle, then, remembering his manners, tilted the neck toward Welles and made a grunting question for permission.

Welles waved his hand casually. "Go right ahead, but I get the second sip."

Cord spied the bottle, then, "Wait, this isn't that unbreakable-skin-potion thing, is it?"

Chuckling, Welles answered, "No, it's plain old rum. Thought you owned a bar?"

Cord laughed a little. "We don't get a lot of magicians in there. More of a farming clientele. Beer-and-a-shot type of folk." He took a swig. "That's pretty good."

He returned the bottle back to its owner. "Thanks. Got it off a pirate worked off the Cape of Cold Hope, about ten miles southwest of here. Used to work under Jonas Mudd, before the work dried up." He took a sip himself, then passed the bottle back.

Sensing trouble, Cord guardedly answered, "You don't say."

"Fella by the name of Gavin Barrows. Nice enough guy for a pirate, I felt. Anyway, you said you don't get a lot of magicians in your bar?"

Cord nodded, ready for the follow-up.

"You have contract with a guy, though. Fehrer?"

"You know him?"

"Nah. Heard the name, not much else. What's he do for you?"

At Welles' seemingly casual inquiry, Cord took a deep breath, exhaled slowly, and told the magician frankly, "Listen. I don't immediately hate you, and that's saying something. So I'll tell you straight: don't play me for dumb, I'll treat you the same." He took another sip.

Realizing the thin ice he was hopping across, Welles asked, "Sorry. I'm a curious guy, is all. Quinn gave me the general gyst of what he does for you, and

I'll admit, it's not something I immediately understand. Is it true it's a ritual? You get to talk with your wife?"

"If you're about to tell me Fehrer's rates aren't competitive, believe me, I've heard it before."

"No, I was just wondering how that works out."

"Twice a year, on the equinox, we sit out in a field, he chants out some nonsense, and my wife appears in the smoke from the fire I build. And we talk."

"Mind me asking what you talk about?"

Cord frowned. "Yup." The bottle exchanged hands once more without any further elaboration on Cord's part.

"Fair enough. I just remember...see, my mom passed away a few years ago. And I tried a spell, sounds a little like what your guy does. And I reached her."

"Yeah?" Then, mimicking, "Mind me asking what you talked about?"

Welles sipped from the bottle and shrugged. "Not a big conversation. She told me to quit bugging her."

Cord felt his mood darken, knowing that it had a baseline dark-gray tone in the first place. He offered nothing.

At this point, Welles felt the ice he was standing on begin to crack a little. "But, y'know, my mom wasn't the friendliest woman in the world. Probably why I ran off to join a bunch of egghead oddballs looking for magic, right?"

Cord said nothing. He just stared inscrutably at the magician.

When Welles became fully immersed in the science of magic, his eyes shifted from their original blue-gray color, into a shimmering black that completely hid his pupils and irises. Ever since, he'd never met a man that could successfully look him in the eye. But at that moment, Cord came very, very close.

Welles felt a chill dance through his skin, hoping very much that it was just that potion making him impervious. Especially if half of the things he'd heard about Cord were true. But to his surprise, Cord's demeanor softened.

"Are you afraid of me, Welles?"

"Only because I think I crossed a conversational line a little while back. And because you're a fairly large, scary man with access to weaponry." He held the bottle out towards Cord, hoping for the best.

Cord accepted it, and offered a small, unreadable smile. "Don't be. Your innate curiosity is what got you where you are today. Isn't that punishment enough?"

Welles' mood lightened. He found that he quite liked this man, despite a reputation that marked him with the beginnings of an empire's destruction. "Ask me again, assuming we survive tomorrow."

Cord's smile widened, just barely. Welles saw what Quinn meant when she spoke of it. It was eerie. Like he was mimicking human interaction – he recognized that a smile would be welcome in that situation, but the way he formed it was still somehow unsettling. "No promises," he said by way of agreement.

Welles stood up. "So, you don't sleep before a fight, do you?"

Pursing his lips as he took on the question, he answered honestly, "It's been a while since I've thought about it one way or the next, but no. Not usually. Here, take your bottle back."

Welles waved his hands in protest. "Hang on to it, stick it back in my bag when you're done with it. We'll talk more tomorrow?"

"Short of injury, I don't see any way of stopping you. And hey, you've got that impervious skin now."

"Just the same, that's not the way I'd like to test it out. Good night, Cord." He started to walk away from the bonfire, angling toward the center-right of the camp. "See you in the morning."

Without turning, Cord responded, " 'Night, Welles. Tell Quinn I said you're all right."

Welles froze. "…What was that?"

Cord maintained his position, took a sip from the bottle, and answered, "You're heading in the direction of Quinn's quarters. She's the only one set to the east, all the other dorms are to the west."

"Yeah, but how did you…"

"Only a hunch until just now. Hope you're better at spells and potions than you are at keeping secrets."

"Oldest trick in the stinking book," Welles muttered. He found himself completely unsure of what to do next.

Cord solved that riddle for him by waving. " 'Night, Welles."

"…Thanks, Cord." Welles left.

Cord sat staring into the fire, happy to be alone for a while.

21. Confessions in Bed

The normal, established guidelines put down by the Pic mothers say that if a Pic woman's door is closed, then no one is to open it. But there wasn't much about Quinn Kind that one would call normal, and even less where Welles was concerned. He turned the doorknob and walked into the darkened room. His black eyes could see clear as day.   It was a nice bit of common ground that he was happy to share with her.

Attempting to make no noise, he slid his robe off and undressed, then crawled into the bed from the foot of it, finally coming to rest his chest against Quinn's back, placing his arm gingerly around her waist.

"It's okay," Quinn whispered. "I'm not asleep."

"I didn't think so, but just in case…"

She reversed her position to face Welles. "Hi there." She smiled tenderly.

Welles returned it. "Hey."

They kissed, enjoying a rare private moment.

"You want to try to get some sleep?" Welles asked.

Quinn shrugged. "Hasn't worked so far. So who were you drinking with?"

"Heh," Welles said, remembering the taste of rum on his lips. "Sorry, but Nathan Cord sat down with me, we got to talking."

"Oh yeah?" Quinn half-asked. Not near sleep, but finding herself somewhat comfortable and moving away from full consciousness. "Anything interesting?"

Welles hedged. "Ehh, this and that. Nothing you need to worry about…"

Quinn giggled. "Oh good, because up until now I've been so totally carefree…"

She elbowed him playfully.

Venturing a little further, Welles admitted, "Yeah…so he knows about you and me. Figured I should mention that."

Turning to face him, she chastised, "Welles!"

"He suckered me into it!" Welles rolled onto his back, plopping his head down on the pillow. "We were talking, and I stood up, and then bam, he snuck up on me."

Propping herself up on her side, Quinn glared at him. "Serious magician, pain in the ass cardplayer, handle your liquor well, but Nathan Cord chats with you for a few minutes and you get duped into mentioning us?"

Welles thought about it, then offered, "Hmm. Well, I am an enigma. You mad?"

Quinn sighed, not unkindly, and rested herself against Welles' chest. "Any other night, maybe."

Welles settled his hand on Quinn's back. "But tonight?"

"Tonight I'm just glad you're here."

"Me too."

"Doofus."

"And I feel very welcome, with sweet talk like that."

Quinn picked up her head and kissed Welles again. "I mean it. Not the 'doofus' thing. The other thing." Then, "Are you afraid about tomorrow?"

"Terrified."

"Me too."

Welles wrapped his arms around Quinn and kissed her neck, then her shoulder. "So we won't think about tomorrow."

Together, they pulled the blanket up around them and didn't bother trying to sleep.

22. First Thing

The toe of a small, sharp boot jabbing Cord in the ribs woke him at first light. He first found himself surprised that he'd even managed to fall asleep, but chalked it up to getting old. Not too many soldiers live to see forty. Of course, not too many commit regicide and live to see sunset, so Cord knew to consider himself outside the bell curve on a couple of points.

He squinted to see the face of his tormentor, backlit and obscured by the morning sun. A pleasant tenor whisper urged, "C'mon, Cord, you'll want to see this," and Cord realized Quentin Kind was the scourge of his continued rest.

"Quentin. Come on, little man, what's in your head? You know I tend to react violently on reflex, right?"

Quinn's brother hunched down with a smile on his face, wordlessly reminding Cord that his scary reputation would get him nowhere. And he was right. For all his bluster, Cord knew, particularly from recent experience, that in straight-up unarmed combat, Quentin could take him down without any real trouble.

During the two years Cord spent living with in their village, Quentin had been charged with his physical rehabilitation – which meant teaching Cord to fight like a Pic.

Fighting like a Pic was about a lot more than just using their innate speed and heightened senses to their advantage. There was a philosophical component to it. Cord was an adept in most fighting styles, but Pic fighting didn't come naturally to him. Because like most human soldiers, Cord fought with an eye on an objective beyond the actual scrape: the mindset that told him that once he took out his opponent, he would be free to accomplish his previously scheduled task.

But Pics knew that when fighting started, there was only a single, crystal-clear objective: win the fight.

It was a subtle distinction, but it meant a world of difference. Humans fought on a timetable, while Pics paced themselves, prepared to engage an opponent for as long as it took. Pics were a faster species, yes, but a lot of that was illusory. Pics simply fought more casually, knowing that victory went to the patient.

Though Cord had started to wonder how patient they could be against an inexaustable army like the one they were about to face.

Still, he respected Quentin's lessons. At first glance, it would be hard to imagine Quentin as a strong teacher, with his blasé attitude. But Cord recognized that despite his manner, Quentin usually knew what he was doing.

It didn't make the early wake-up call any more inviting.

"Gripe, gripe, gripe," Quentin mocked the slowly-rousing Cord. "Come on, follow me." He started walking at a quick pace. Cord, with very little time to lose, followed.

Quentin led him to the edge of the woods. "Up the tree," he enthusiastically ordered. "You'll want a nice aerial view." The Pic bounced up the trunk effortlessly, pouncing on a branch fifteen feet up. Cord hauled himself up the tree branch by branch, feeling heavy and lumbering by comparison.

The view that greeted him was that of an army of Pic soldiers. Ten on horseback, twenty-five on foot. Generally speaking, Pics didn't require the use of horses, but they kept a few on hand for long-distance travels, particularly if they were traveling in large groups. Sinking into the ground presents a terrifying variety of hazards when multiple Pics are attempting it at the same time. Horses are slower, but on the upside, no Pic ever died from bumping into one another on a horse.

In front, Victor Mene, towering on his own steed, inspected them, spouting stern words Cord couldn't quite make out, but would probably recognize as pretty close to what he remembered from his early days in the service.

There they were. Small in number, small in stature, but each and every one a skilled and passionate fighter, willing to put his life on the line in service to a foreign civilization that, Cord knew, would not have been likely to extend the same courtesy.

If he hadn't been so sure most of them would be dead by morning tomorrow, Cord might have called the feeling in his gut "pride."

23. Pep Talk

Cord's instincts were on the money in regards to Victor Mene's rallying speech. The captain of the guard had decided to tell the Pics the same thing he had told his own soldiers time and time again.

"There is every chance in the world that many of you will be killed. Make your peace with this now. You're not going to have time once we've engaged the enemy. And if I see any of you attempt to run away from the fight, I'll kill you myself. It's important that you know this.

"Now, with a group of this size, it's going to be an eight-hour march to the barrier. We will stop for a brief rest only when we reach the barrier the magician has erected outside the kingdom. In this time we will establish contact with the Fel clan, and synchronize our attack.

"If you are frightened? Good. We're about to go into battle against monsters. Things that Should. Not. Be. Many of them used to be my comrades. A few of them I even called 'friend.' Believe me. I understand your fear.

"And for those of you who do not feel this fear, congratulations. You've successfully detached yourself from the reality of the situation. Your mental illness may come in handy. Try to put yourself in the initial wave of attack.

"The absolute voice of God in today's battle, as far as you are concerned, will sound like me, and it will sound like your tribal head, Quinn Kind. No one else's voice matters, since you will not be following their commands. If you obey the voice of God, you may live.

"For those of you out there who feel disheartened by my speech, here's your pep talk: We are alive. We have made a choice to save other lives, and fight for an ideal.

"We fight for a cause. That cause makes us strong. That cause makes us unstoppable.

"Now LET'S MOVE OUT!"

Mene waited for a reaction, keeping his feelings of uncertainty to himself. He had prepared human soldiers hundreds of times. But this army of pixies was a completely new experience for him. He wasn't sure exactly what would motivate them.

He gazed down at them. Their faces were serious, stony, and prepared. But they were restrained. No fierceness.

And then Quinn Kind rode to the front. Her horse was almost as stealthy as its rider. Her face was painted in gray and green. But her eyes shot through like bolts of lightning.

Every soldier's eyes held steady on Quinn. She raised her ceremonial staff, the Stem, high over her head in one quick, sharp motion.

"WE RIDE," she bellowed, loud and deep and soulful.

The army erupted, in howls of defiance to any death that may come their way. Mene was almost proud.

They began their journey to the castle. What noblemen called the Kingdom of Western Sun. What citizens called Bloody Twilight. And what stragglers like Nathan Cord, Quentin Kind, and Welles called a likely last stand.

PART TWO: THE ROAD TO BLOODY TWILIGHT

24. Elsewhere, the Queen's Awakening

Allison Kendra Quinn Dearborn should have been known among the three kingdoms and beyond as the Queen in Waiting. But then her life happened. And she knew full well that because of it, her people only ever called her the Orphan.

For seven years the title hung around her neck like an albatross, a mark of pity and resignation: Western Sun is so hopeless, even our princess is damaged goods, it said. But somehow, there was a part of her appreciated it. It marked her with great loss, but she believed it also imbued her with a strength not too many would ever know. Nor should they ever have to experience such a thing.

The Orphan looked out of the window of the high tower in which she found herself pinned down. "For protection," she noted bitterly to herself. She spied the lurching, shambling messes of men and women who were once someone's father or mother, someone's kin, and she knew that there were more of her kind than she had ever realized. Western Sun was a kingdom of orphans. And if it wasn't already, soon it would be a kingdom of the dead.

She felt like she should cry, but the Orphan hadn't been able to muster up a tear since she was eleven, and she walked into her father's chambers just in time to see Nathan Cord ram his sword through her father's chest.

At first, being only a child, she hadn't been able to find any sort of reaction in her, but she must have yelped, or gasped. A small enough noise to turn Cord's attention away from the two bodies lying at the foot of the bed and towards her. His face was drenched in blood. She knew some of it was her father's, but only in retrospect realized that some of it must have been his wife's.

She could never remember Cord's face in that moment as it really was. Only the whites of his eyes darting out from underneath a dark red veil had stayed with her, as it dawned on him who else was in the room.

But she could emember that shocked, anguished look on his face. She read it not as a reaction to the horror he had just committed, but rather at the realization that she had seen the result. That he had allowed her to see it.

As princess, Allison had always been surrounded by a surrogate family. They often compensated for her father's extended absences. But some meant more than others. That night, the princess's favorite uncle knew that he had just scarred his dear niece for life. That was the look she remembered. And that was the look that had made her cry that night.

She remembered him hesitantly stepping toward her. But she wasn't afraid of him. If she had been asked, at age eleven, if her wonderful uncle Nathan would lay a hand against the king, she would have laughed the idea away. But even having been proven grossly mistaken in that assumption, she still believed beyond a shadow of a doubt that he had not been stepping in her direction with intent to harm. She imagined that he wanted to comfort her – to tell her it would all be okay – but no longer had any idea how.

And despite what had clearly occurred, she found that she wanted to comfort him too, to take the horror away from his face. So she did the only thing she could conceive of that might help. She stepped away from the door, and knelt down next to the doorframe, her back turned to Nathan, so that she could cry by herself.

She only heard his footsteps as he ran out the door, and down the hall. Never to be heard from again.

Never to be heard from again, no matter how many times she prayed he might return to save her.

Those heavy boot steps now echoed in her mind, she thought, until she realized it to be the sound of Grolev pacing the creaking wooden floors of their sanctuary, the high tower where they'd been holed up, for two days now.

"Why are you nervous, Grolev?" the Orphan asked, sternly. "You've done nothing but assure me of our safety for nearly two days. Yet here you are, carving a ditch in the floor with your constant pacing."

The tall, usually languid man stared out at her through sunken black eyes. "And I maintain that assurance, my princess. But you can't fault me for growing tense."

Allison nodded. "So the screams outside are getting to you too."

Grolev sighed. The breezy tone of it disturbed the Orphan. Everything about Grolev the Wizard disturbed the Orphan. "The screams, yes. But not so much the sound of them…"

Turning her attention back to the violent view below, she finished his thought. "It's that they are growing fewer every hour. Those things. They're running out of people to kill, aren't they?"

She hoped she only imagined that she heard the wizard chuckle before he responded, "That's what it sounds like to me, yes."

Allison steeled her shoulders, arched her spine back. No fear. No tears. She had come to a decision.

They were doomed, she knew, unless they could reach help from outside that barrier past the kingdom walls that Grolev claimed he had erected for their protection. A part of her wished that her wonderful suitor, Aiden, would ride up on a horse, call out her name, and lead her to safety. But she knew the truth. She had been told many times what a smart girl she was. It was Nathan Cord's pet name for her, after all.

She knew that at best, Aiden was dead. And at worst, he was out there somewhere. A monster like the rest of his fellow soldiers.

A helpless princess locked up in a tower would cry for her lost beloved. But Allison Kendra Quinn Dearborn would be damned if that was her only role in this travesty. She would have none of it.

So that left only one option. Her teacher. Her warrior. Her nanny.

"Grolev, I want you to attempt to reach your mind out, past that barrier. You find Quinn Kind, and send a message for help."

"I'll try again, my princess, but -"

"'Your highness.'"

"Pardon?"

She had steeled her bones, and her will. "Address me as 'Your Highness,' Grolev. Right now, there are no more advisors, there are no more cabinets, there are no more generals. At this point, I am the only person who can command. And I'm telling you not to 'try' to call Quinn Kind. I'm telling you to do it. If you're as good as you claim to be, you will make contact. Your barriers can keep them out for a while. After that, it will be up to the Blue Knives. And I know they're very good at their job, but they're up against an army that doesn't recognize the fear of death anymore. I haven't heard you come up with any plan of escape, so this is mine. You call Quinn Kind and you let her know the Queen of Western Sun requests her assistance."

Grolev stood in cold silence for a moment before answering, "Of course. Your Highness."

No fear. Not tears.

Orphans may feel afraid. Princesses may weep. Allison Kendra Quinn Dearborn refused these roles. She was the Queen of Western Sun.

The queen placed her faith in a woman who had helped to raise her, though she hadn't seen her teacher in nearly a decade. And in doing this, she cast aside the prevailing feeling that she and her kingdom were deeply, deeply screwed.

25. An Enlightened Perspective

Snotty little bitch, Grolev grumbled in his head.

"Of course." He swallowed bile. "Your Highness." *Your silly little puppet.*

Years of work, years of subtle plans, pushing pieces around like a diplomat, suggesting, coercing, when he could have been shoving and controlling. And she thought putting on her big-girl voice would be all it would take to bring him around to her line of thought?

He was more than a magician, damn it, he was a wizard, he could have done anything he pleased, but he took this route, for this very moment. For a kingdom built on skeletons to sacrifice itself in bloody, unholy, hellish terms. All because he commanded it.

Grolev had to remind himself of his subservient role, and stifled another laugh. His role as the Queen in Waiting's mystic counsel. The thought of it made him choke. He coughed. When the little wench looked over, her eyes accusing, Grolev made vague waving hand gestures, like it was part of some meditative trance he was heading into, in attempting to contact the little pixie nanny the girl had grown so fond of.

Out in the courtyard, the undead hordes of soldiers were laying waste to their surroundings and anyone they came in contact with. In the tower, lining the stairs, were over twenty of the Queen in Waiting's personal protectorate. The Order of the Indigo Temple. Or as Grolev saw them, retarded inbred monks so trained and focused for fighting that they couldn't recognize easy action if it were sitting right on top of them.   And here he was, trapped with a little girl pretending to be nobility, oblivious to her only real use – the final sacrifice on executioner's time.

This is going so much slower than I wanted, Grolev thought to himself. But all good things come to those who wait.

He felt the little wench's eyes on his back, and so nodded deferentially to her, and walked to the far wall, where he plopped himself down and crossed his legs, making gestures like he was trying to find her savior, her warrior-nanny. He closed his eyes, and after a half-second of satisfied smiling, he put on a meditative face and slowed his breathing.

This ought to shut her up for a few minutes, at least.

26. We All Call It Bloody Twilight

The Pic army, such as it was, marched resolutely toward Western Sun, while Cord rode behind the rest, more comfortable bringing up the rear of the invading force. More comfortable there than around Mene, no matter how much he'd have liked to display otherwise. It was still difficult looking at Quinn with anything but bitterness. And her troops, if you could call them that – they were mostly Pic boys too young to know much about the annexing battles he'd spent his last few years in the guard fighting – they kept looking at him like he was someone who would lead them. Quinn had told them too many tall tales about the invincible Nathan Cord.

From a tactical standpoint, he needed them to be sure that everyone, himself included, would be taking orders from Quinn and Mene. It bugged him, yes, but he had enough soldier left in him to recognize the need for a chain of command. From a personal standpoint, he didn't want any of those boys or girls thinking that he was the one that could save them from the massacre that was likely approaching them all.

So he took the rear. Which made it harder for Welles to act like it was an accident when he slowed his own ride down enough to join Cord in the back. Soon enough, in any case, Cord had a traveling companion.

"Come on, Welles," he shook his head, not unkindly, "can't a guy be alone with his thoughts?"

"Heh. Around me, not so much, Cord."

Cord looked a question at him, to which Welles responded, tapping a finger to his temple, "Great and Mystical Powers of the Mind, remember? I get a vibe from people, it's pretty hard to ignore."

"Pretty sure I know the vibe I'm putting out. Admire your bravery trying to hang out with me anyway. Stupid of you, but still."

"The world takes care of fools and scoundrels, as I've heard it."

"I've heard thieves get paid and heroes get burned, and no one gets their prayers returned. But to each his own."

Welles nodded, like he was jotting that down in his mind. "So by my estimates, we've got another couple hours before we're at our stopping point, outside the edge of the kingdom."

Cord spied the distance. "Sounds about right."

"How do you refer to it?" Welles asked, going for a casual tone in his voice and mostly failing. "I mean, most people just call it 'the kingdom.' And legal documents, and guys like your buddy Victor, always give it its full title, 'The Kingdom of Western Sun.' All the Pics though? Ask them to refer to it by name…"

"They call it Bloody Twilight."

"Citizens too?"

"Most of 'em."

"Right. Now, I never lived there, but you moved there when you were eighteen, right? To gain military citizenship."

"Yeah."

"So, what's the name you use?"

"Like if I'm out abroad, and someone says, 'Which kingdom are you from,' what do I tell them?"

"Right."

"I tell them I'm not from around here. You know my history, right? Not a good idea for me to share my last known address."

"People seem to know who you are, though. That's what Quinn says."

"People have ideas on who they think I might be. I don't share. But the rumors are enough to keep people from asking me a lot of questions directly." He glared at Welles, who didn't seem to take the hint. "Usually, anyway."

Welles soldiered on. "So anyone did ask you, you'd say, 'Nope, never been to Western Sun myself,' something like that?"

The sun had positioned itself behind the pack as they continued their way east. Since they wouldn't slow anything down by lingering, Cord steadied his horse and turned it around to face the woods. The base of the sun had just started to drift along the top of the treeline. "You see that?"

Welles slowed and turned around as well. His horse started to trot backward until his deliberate pat stopped her. "Yeah. I mean, I know the kingdom faces west, toward the ocean. That's why they named it that, when they started building, however long ago."

Doing the math in his head, Cord clarified, "Must have been nearly eight hundred years ago at this point. Maybe more. The history's sketchy on the dates. Everything they wrote down was more about the men who started it all. A council of elders. Saw themselves as warrior-wise-men, claiming land they thought was their right.

"This was back before there were kings – that's another bit of messy history you can look up for yourself some other time. But those wise men, they took a ragged bunch of barbarian thugs they called an army, marched their way west to a bunch of loose-knit farming communities, and they took that land by hook or by crook. A lot of the people already living there fled. My ancestors headed up north, so…"

"You're of Northlander descent?"

Cord thought he caught a tone in Welles' question and responded, "Yeah, but don't believe the stereotypes, we pay our bills on time and don't back down from a fight, assuming we've had enough to drink."

He glared at Welles for a moment, then laughed a little to let the man know he was kidding. Welles didn't find a lot of comfort in it, but gave Cord a smile all the same.

"Anyway, those that stayed to fight got slaughtered, for the most part. The survivors surrendered. Those big cusses from the east went and built their castle on top of the graves of the people they killed. Understand, I'm not being colorful. You dig deep enough under the castle, you'll find skulls.

"Western Sun…this whole kingdom is a history of violence. Most are – it's not that surprising. But it's the lie the elders tried to sell afterward, that this was going to be a new kind of place, progressive beliefs, peace for all, all that warm nonsense. That's why they named it the Kingdom of Western Sun. Has kind of a bright, spiritual ring to it. When we annexed the offshoots to the north and east about a decade back, they were renamed Northern Sun and Eastern Sun. To make it sound like we were all one people, one region."

Welles nodded, letting Cord know he was listening, and that he could continue the story.

"I killed a lot of their soldiers so Western Sun could have a couple sibling states. I haven't been to either of them since the battles ended – I might do okay in the north, but I'm not sure I'd survive a trip out east, if anyone recognized me. But every now and then, I get a guy in my bar from Northern Sun. You know what they call themselves?"

Welles chuckled and answered, "Bastard Suns," before realizing that he maybe shouldn't find the humor in that.

"Yeah." Cord turned his horse around. "So I call it Bloody Twilight. Anyone who knows our history does. It's only got a pretty name on paper, and politicians' lips." Then, after a moment, he pointed languidly toward the front of the herd where Mene led the way, and added, "And true believers."

He dug his heels in, and his horse picked up the pace. "Come on, we're starting to lag." Cord's horse returned quickly toward the group.

Welles thought about it, and found more questions in his head that he wanted to hear Cord answer. He dug his heels into his horse to catch up.

27. Small Talk

"Hey, wait up!"

Cord groaned. "Can't you fly or something? Thought you magicians could fly."

"It's not that I can't. Just wanted to ride with the people I'd be fighting with."

"Thoughtful of you."

Welles grunted. "Thoughtful nothing, I need you guys to keep me from getting eaten by those freaks inside the bubble."

"What about that magic skin-hardening spell you were talking about?"

"Who wants to find out the hard way if it works?"

Cord grunted. Welles wasn't sure what that noise meant, but before he could ask, Cord put his own question out. "You put that bubble up yourself?" Something like disbelief in his tone.

Welles hesitated. "More or less."

"You had help."

"What makes you think that?"

"You're young. Haven't met that many magicians. But that guy who was advising for Lucius back in the day, Keegan whatever."

"Morris."

"Right, he was fifty if he was a day, wasn't he?"

"Yeah, but he wore it pretty well. I studied under him."

"Did he admire your zits and squeaky voice?"

"Actually," Welles corrected, hoping he didn't sound smarmy by doing so, "I started before puberty. Ran away from home when I was nine."

Cord squinted at him, scanning his features. If Welles were capable of blushing, he might have here. He wasn't, so he didn't.

"My parents never really 'got' me."

"Yeah, can't imagine why," Cord breezed, and turned his attention away from the magician.

Welles let that one hang, instead relocating the line of questioning Cord had broken up. "So I wanted to ask you..."

"Come on, man..."

"No, nothing serious, just a quick question: you were in charge of Coal Brigade?"

"Yup."

"So, why 'Coal Brigade'?"

Cord shrugged, not bothering with a deep answer. "Victor gave me the position, I accepted. Nothing sinister in there." He slapped his horse, and trotted ahead of Welles, hoping to send a message. Again. Wondering if next time he'd have to resort to physical harm. Wondering if that was part of Welles' master scheme to figure out if his stupid spell had taken hold.

Welles ignored the intended message and kept pace. "No, I mean, the name. 'Coal Brigade.'"

"Who gives a damn?"

"I do. Names matter. They give meaning. For instance, it's called Western Sun, but everyone who cares calls it Bloody Twilight. The Pics...the humans demean them, take away the mystery, by calling them Pixies. Names matter. So I figured, Coal Brigade..."

Cord laughed quietly to himself, then throwing a look to Welles, answered, "Sorry to ruin it for you, but Warren Coal was the first leader of the brigade, and after he died, it was called 'Coal's Brigade' in his memory. They dropped the 'S' at some point. Like I said, nothing exciting there."

"Huh. I'll admit – a little disappointed."

"Yeah, that'll happen. Truth's always pretty dull. Can we keep riding in silence, or is that against your code?"

Welles thought on that, then answered, "I'll be quiet as a church mouse, Cord."

"Good, good."

"Unless I think of something else to ask you, obviously."

"...Sounds like fun. Keep in mind I have a lot of edged weapons strapped to my person, okay?"

"Sure thing."

Cord trotted on ahead. Welles, unwilling to tempt the fates, of which he knew a good bit about, kept himself at the rear.

28. How Easily a Heart Turns to Coal

Cord's smile felt warm and funny at first, and then sank into the bitterness that he'd become accustomed to over the years. It wasn't a total lie that he'd fed Welles. Warren Coal had actually started the special team of advance men that would later bear his name. But that wasn't why the name stuck. At some point, after the possessive 'S' had been dropped, when people talked about them, it usually came out, "You know, Coal Brigade. As in, 'Hearts Black As'."

Almost twenty years ago now, after the peacekeeping mission out to Beasts Old Throne - what eventually was renamed Eastern Sun - Cord had been prepared to retire. He'd put in his five years of service and could be considered a member of Western Sun's society. But his captain, Victor Mene, not five years into his own post but wearing it like he'd been born into the position, took him aside one day.

"Son, you did good work out there," Mene had told him one day by way of a greeting. "I hear you're opting out of further service."

"Yessir, but it's been an honor," Cord answered unwarily. "Figure I'll marry my girl, cash out my service pay, buy a plot of land outside Western Sun. I'm a rancher's son, I think I'd be good at running a farm, herding some cattle."

He remembered Victor Mene scowling at this, apparently the stupidest idea he'd ever heard. "You'd be crap at running a farm, son. And that land out there's no good for grazing, what I've heard. Hasn't been for years. We both know what you're good at. You'd be shaming yourself not to use that gift for the good of the kingdom."

"Sir?" Cord remembered himself saying. He could remember the stupidity in his young voice. How could he have not seen what was coming?

"You're a great soldier, Nathan," Mene told him, putting his hand on Cord's shoulder. "You'd be a waste, if I were to let you just go farming."

"But I don't want to be a soldier anymore," the young Cord tried to explain. "I just want to be a citizen, marry my girlfriend…"

"What if I were to tell you that you can serve the kingdom as you have been, but be exempt from a soldier's lifestyle?"

"Sir?"

Remembering it now, Cord wanted so much to beat some sense into his younger self. Too little, too late.

"You are gifted at striking when it's quiet, Cord. I've seen you do it a dozen times over the past few years. It's an intrinsic part of you. I want you to lead Coal's Brigade."

"Captain Mene, that would be an honor. But I told Kayla my tour was coming to an end, and this...I don't know, it just seems like I'd be breaking my word."

Breaking my word, Cord remembered himself saying. What a special brand of stupid he'd been. He could have stopped it all right then if he hadn't let himself get suckered by flattery, by encouragement that the horrible things he'd done in battle were some kind of talent.

He flashed back in his mind, and pictured that big smile Mene had given him – a smile that even now Cord felt was sincere, since the old bastard really believed that military service was the only service worth a damn – when he'd said, "I'd like you to come with me to a special dinner. Don't worry, you can bring your girlfriend."

"Where are we going?"

"King Lucius is having a special feast, both to introduce a couple of new appointments, and to celebrate the soldiers, the heroes who policed Beasts Old Throne, when it couldn't help itself. And you *are* a hero, Nate. You'll be recognized as such."

And Cord had accepted that invitation, like any idiot would, who'd been called   a   hero.

29. A Good Memory in a Head Full of Bad

You just don't turn down a personal invitation to dine at the king's table. It's simply Not Done. So Cord accepted Mene's offer, and he and Kayla had one of the most wonderful nights of their lives together, tasting the life of royalty. It was their first time in the royal dining hall. They wore their best clothes. And everyone treated them like they belonged there.

So they dined, they danced, they even told the king funny stories about Cord's awkward courtship of Kayla. Lucius was as gracious a host as he was a sovergin. He looked the part, too: a big bear of a man, full-bearded with a flowing gray mane, and he carried his weight like it was nothing at all. But it was his personality that most obviously marked him as royalty. He was engaging, and good-natured, and funny. The king was *funny*.

Cord remembered how much that surprised him, that a king could be such a pleasant human being. And how far that went toward his decision to accept the position as chief of Coal's Brigade the next day.

That was also the night he first met Quinn Kind, the ambassador of the woodlands he'd heard stories about while he had been stationed in the east. She wasn't anything like the Fel crazies living in the forests out there. She was clean, polite, and…"elegant" wasn't the word. She didn't dress formally at this event, as might have been expected; rather wore what she usually did: boots and gloves, mud-colored clothing, with braids randomly woven in her hair. But still, she had an air of sophistication about her. Class. She knew why she was there: to introduce the world to the best her people had to offer.

If he hadn't met Kayla all those years earlier and given his heart to her so completely, Cord could easily have seen how a man could fall in love with Quinn. As it stood, Kayla and Quinn became fast friends that evening, and not much later, so did Quinn and Cord.

Thinking back to that night now, Cord remembered that Keegan Morris had been at that party too. But he'd been having too good of a time with Kayla, Quinn, and even King Lucius to get around to introducing himself. That's how wonderful the evening was: a bona fide magician stood in their midst, but with the company he had with him, things had been magical enough.

He never did meet Morris personally. Saw the guy around a few times at cabinet meetings and dinners, but never shook his hand or anything. It might have been his conversations with Welles sitting on his mind, but as he thought back over the years, Cord felt somewhat sad that he'd never gotten to know this man that so many, including his new "buddy," had idolized.

Riding alongside the marching Pics, Cord looked behind him to see if Welles was still riding behind. There was no sign of him. He peered up ahead, thinking maybe he'd sped up to ride with Quinn. The guy was nowhere. And Cord realized that Welles must be very good, to hide his presence more thoroughly and casually than even a Pic could. It didn't shock him that Welles and Quinn had gotten together.

He did have some questions about that, to be sure, but decided those were questions best answered by Quinn.

30. The Wizard's Lament

The barrier continued to irritate Grolev. And the fact that he couldn't outwardly display his irritation by killing something just made it worse.

He'd let the little girl believe that he had put it up himself, to contain the killing hordes. To protect the outlying regions. The thought baffled him. *Who would want to protect those hick mongrels?*

He posed the question to himself, but already knew the answer. Goddamned Keegan Morris. Everybody's favorite mystic.

That jackass.

He didn't know how the hell it could possibly be, but Grolev knew that somehow Morris was behind that ridiculous golden bubble that had raised itself up the moment the dead soldiers started wading out toward the kingdom limits. Someone was watching it all happening, and someone wanted to slow down the inevitable.

Goddamned Keegan Morris. Grolev had lobotomized the stupid old treehugger and locked his carcass away with his own hands, and yet the pompous geezer refused to lay there drooling like the waste of gray matter he should be.

He must have gotten out of his body, Grolev concluded, both bitter and admiring. *Took him nearly a decade, but he did it. Sneaky old longhair.*

The little wench was looking over at him, suspicion in her eyes. Grolev had ignored his façade of meditation too long.

"Taking a reprieve, your highness," he covered, remembering to throw in that 'your highness' crap to placate the bitch. "Despite what you may have heard, wizardry is not easy."

She stared at him, still in his sitting position on the floor. "I hadn't heard that, nor would I ever imagine that to be the case." Thoughtfully, she explored the notion further. "You know, I've met several mystic studies. And you're the only one who has ever referred to himself as a 'wizard.' Do you find that strange? I find that strange."

Grolev decided to play it spineless for a while, and bow to the Queen in Waiting's obvious intellectual skills. "I understand your highness's skepticism. Of course, most call themselves mages, or mystics, or simply magicians. A magus here or there. There is no true ranking procedure in our line of work. We tend to be a theatrical bunch, and choose our own titles. But I have devoted my life to my studies, to better serve your father and yourself. And I believe my skills warrant a more specific title, your highness. I apologize if it appears arrogance on my part."

There was a steel in the girl's gaze that he found a bit unsettling. "It 'appears' nothing, Grolev. You *are* arrogant. But I don't need your apologies. Don't let me distract you. Continue what you were doing." And then she turned her back to him, returning to the window.

He knew she didn't mean it as an insulting gesture, but Grolev decided to take it as one anyway. He returned to his false conjuring position, in his head trying to calculate his odds of killing Keegan Morris without the Queen in Waiting – and oh, did it make him cringe to think those words – realizing what he attempting. She was a silly little puppet, but she wasn't stupid.

He closed his eyes to make plans.

31. The State of the Girl

It was about a half-hour until sunset, and the marching troop was settling down for a short reprieve while their commanders made final preparations for the fight ahead.

Cord unmounted, and walked around camp as the Pic soldiers grouped together. They chatted, made jokes, played on small instruments. And Cord realized that despite Mene's rallying speech, they didn't have the fear of death in them yet. Maybe it was a Pic thing. Whatever it was, Cord found it deeply troubling. He felt the anger in him rising. That same anger he'd been fighting back since that initial relapse back at Fehrer's. He'd ridden it into the village, blanketed himself with it when he confronted Quinn, and let it charge him up enough to kill those dead soldiers Mene had captured, that Welles had put on display. But after that, sleep, along with those talks with Welles, had helped water it down enough that it wasn't so potent.

But it was creeping up on him again – in a moment of peace, of all things. Everything he saw around him spurred it on more. They were playing *cards* – nothing could be more benign! - and somehow *that* was ticking him off.

He felt a steadily overwhelming need to find an outlet for his anger, and caught a glimpse of Quinn, speaking with Quentin and a few of her other brothers, looking over a map of the kingdom grounds.

If he wanted to pick a fight, this would have to do.

When Quentin and the others walked away, Cord found his opening, and stormed up toward Quinn. "I admire your optimism," he told her, his voice nothing but hard and mean.

"What's that?" Quinn asked, caught off guard.

"That you think the Orphan's worth saving."

Quinn didn't give even a moment's thought before answering, somewhat insulted at the allegation, "Of course she's worth saving. It's Allison. It's little Allie."

"You're putting the safety of an entire region at stake based on your notion that she's still the sweet kid we knew back then. Be real, Quinn."

Quinn put her hard eyes into Cord's only good one. "Don't you dare tell me you think Allison's beyond saving."

"Physically? Yes. She's beyond saving. I believe you when you tell me she's still alive – not that we have much of a chance of keeping her that way once we get in there. But hell, let's say we do. What, you think she's going to...I don't even know what you think she's going to do for you. She's the only child of *Arius*, the monster, and she's had this jackass Grolev whispering in her ear as her chief counsel for the last seven years. Come on. You think she's still the same girl who drew you unicorns and fought off her bedtime?"

Quinn had only one answer, and she didn't care how weak it might sound out loud. "Yes. I do."

Cord took a step back, calmed his voice. "Quinn, that's not the way the world works. I loved the kid too, but she's long gone to us by now. If we go to the perimeter, set the place ablaze, and head out, we can stop this whole horrible plague before it creeps out to the Bastard Suns. But a rescue attempt is just going to get a lot of your people killed. I can't even fathom how that's an option to you."

A deep, frighteningly calm voice behind Cord answered the question. "Because the Queen in Waiting is all that is left of Western Sun. And keeping the kingdom alive is all that matters."

Without turning to face him, Cord responded, "Shut up, Vic. This isn't your call. At this point, you're just hired help, same as me."

Victor Mene rushed up against Cord, so fast that Cord actually found himself a bit startled. Mene's voice was rage on a leash. "The pixie and the magician managed to save me alone. My voice is all that is left to speak for the good of the kingdom, and I say the only way this mission is a success is if we get the Queen in Waiting to safety. If she lives, so does the kingdom."

Cord found his blood boiling again. He didn't mind it. "Do you realize how retarded that sounds? Nevermind, of course you don't. All about queen and country for you. Follow me here, Vic: The Girl. Is. Lost. She doesn't represent the damn kingdom. She's just a kid who's spent the last seven years getting her head filled up by a bunch of corrupt politicians and, from what I've heard, one toxic magician. If she represents the kingdom, then the kingdom is dead, and good riddance!"

Cord thought he might have heard Quinn whisper, "You can't really believe that," but he couldn't be sure, because this was the moment Victor Mene had chosen to rocket his fist into the side of Cord's head.

Finally, Cord thought with a smile, as his face went numb and he fell to the ground.

32. Throw Down

For just a moment – for the briefest second as he hit the grass – Cord thought of driving a dagger into Mene's gut and calling a decisive win, after all this time. But where was the satisfaction in that?

So he shoved himself up from the ground, clenched his fists together, and swung them into Mene's solar plexus, roaring as he made contact. It was the one of the few moments of joy he could count over the last several years.

Didn't last long.

Victor Mene is captain of the guard, and one doesn't get that title for dropping after one gut-punch. Using the stumble to drop down into a tackling position, Mene tilted his head up, eyed his target, and rammed into Cord, knocking him back into the dirt. His knees pinning down Cord's arms, Mene began punching the king-killer's face in with both fists. For queen and country. And because he'd wanted to feel his knuckles bouncing against Cord's jaw for seven years.

Somehow it never occurred to him that this dream-scenario would end with Cord jamming a knee into his nuts.

Wincing, Mene rolled off Cord. Cord, wheezing and bleeding, stumbled to his feet and kicked Mene in his side. And again. And again. Hoarse, violent cursing accented every new kick.

Nobody, least of all Cord, could have accurately answered how long he would have kept throwing his foot into Mene's torso, but they didn't have to. Because Quinn Kind had had enough of this. And there wasn't a force on earth that could dodge a roundhouse kick from a Pic woman.

Cord felt a dull, hard crack to the back of his skull and dropped to the ground, landing just beside Mene's feet. Just conscious enough, Mene took the opportunity to deliver his left boot heel into Cord's right temple, finally knocking Cord unconscious.

To make everything even, Quinn dropped her fist down against Mene's thick bald skull, knocking him out, too.

Quinn stood over the exhausted frames of her two prize soldiers. Her heroes of Western Sun. Her idiot friends who would jeopardize everything because they couldn't just play nice with each other for one stinking day.

Welles had been discussing the expected arrival time of the Fel with Quentin, which meant news of the two human guys beating the living hell out of each other reached them last, and they had missed nearly the entire fight. The rest of the Pic army, meanwhile, had gotten quite a show. Thankfully, being that the average height of a Pic male is 5'3", and being that Welles was a solid six feet tall and change, he got a pretty good view of how it ended – with his girlfriend delivering a well-timed, perfectly executed blow to each combatant. He had to admit that it was just a little sexy.

He cut through the audience, hurrying over to her, but the frustrated expression on her face warned Welles that she didn't need comforting just then. But she would probably need someone to curse at. This, he understood, is also the boyfriend's job, sometimes.

Standing at her side, Welles asked, "Think they'll be awake by the time we head in?" with a quiet calm meant to give the impression he thought they might just be napping.

Quinn's posture was rigid, her muscles still tensed and ready for more fighting. Her mood was pretty much the same. "Back off, Welles, just – " she started in, but immediately halted. It wasn't Welles' fault and she knew it. A few deep breaths and she regained focus enough to answer his question, "Yeah. They will. Assuming I won't have to beat them up again."

She stormed off, though they were in the middle of a fairly level, barren field, so it wasn't like she had a lot of places to get away to. But space is space, and Welles let her have it. He nodded to Quentin, who came over while trying to hide the enthusiastic grin on his face with his hand.

Welles smirked. "Just let it out, man."

Quentin dropped his hand, showing off a beaming, toothy grin. "Damn, my sister is cool."

Shaking his head with amiable incredulity, Welles just answered, "As long as she's on your side, man. Help me drag these guys away from each other so they don't start round two once they wake up, okay?"

Quentin grabbed the captain and hoisted him over his shoulder, jokingly clamping his hand firmly on Mene's ass. Since Victor was a fairly large man, each of his limbs practically touched the ground, but Quentin was strong enough to carry the weight. He pointed with his right hand toward the far right of their perimeter, closest to the castle, then with released his left from Mene's rear to gesture back in the direction of the forest. "I go this way, you go that way?"

Floating Cord up by waving his hands and making weird noises, Welles nodded in understanding. "Put the boxers in their corners? Good thinking, Quentin."

They marched in separate directions, hauling their unconscious comrades along with them. Both of them caustically noting to themselves that, of recent note, this was the first plan they'd concocted that didn't immediately appear to be life-threatening.

33. The Job Interview

When he felt sure the Orphan's eyes were focused on the carnage outside, Grolev, still feigning meditation in the corner, popped an eye open to make sure she wasn't watching him. Satisfied, he went back to his real task: sussing out where in the hell Keegan Morris's spirit had gotten off to. It was proving harder than he thought it would, confirming his suspicions that Morris had an ally outside the barrier.

That didn't exactly surprise him. Everyone loved Morris. But few of his students stuck around once Arius had given the mystical advisor title to Grolev, which was fine by him. He didn't play well with his classmates, historically. Most of them had dissipated when Arius assumed the throne, more when Grolev gained favor. Nomads by nature anyway, they spread out, formed little magic-enclaves out in the sister-states. He had heard that the seaside was big business for some of the weaker practitioners. There was even a rumor of a pirate ship entirely manned by magicians.

But there were Morris loyalists all over the Cabrea region, and while they had called Grolev angry, sadistic, psychotic, and even megalomaniacal, not a single one of them ever referred to him as stupid. And that was what kept them away. That, and the entirely true rumors of what he had done to their beloved, useless guru.

Way back in the old days, when Keegan Morris was appointed as King Lucius's royal advisor on the mystic arts, his first public act had been to host a symposium on magic. Grolev remembered that the royal hall was practically choking with attendees, all fascinated by this new art and awed by the charisma of its leading proponent. Grolev had stood in the back. His arms were folded the whole time, as he waited to hear something new and interesting from his former mentor, only to find himself satisfactorily disappointed.

A dull practitioner – and there were many – would have used the whole thing as an excuse to show off his book collection, to display diagrams and hand-positions. All while explaining how all these dusty old texts nobody ever bothered to look through were, when examined through a certain mindset, the keys to unlocking a power that had until recently been considered the stuff of cheap fiction and children's bedtime stories.

Grolev could toss a lot of words out describing the man – arrogant, self-satisfied, delusional as all hell – but the one word no one would use to describe Keegan Morris was "dull." The man was as much of a showman as he was a mystic. He loved crowds.

In Grolev's eyes, Morris was particularly fond of their love for him.

It made him a perfect salesman for the discipline. Nobody could sell magic like Keegan Morris.

In Grolev's eyes, that made him an overrated whore. Nevertheless, when Keegan Morris started to talk, he listened as closely as anyone.

"Magic," Keegan Morris began his lecture, to these new, civilian devotees, "is the most simple and yet mind-bogglingly complicated art that we as humans have ever stumbled into. I won't lie to you. It's strange and it's tricky, and I just want you to know that so that when I start doing strange and tricky things, you applaud approvingly." And then he grinned widely.

Laughs from the audience.

He explained that his discipline was at its most basic level about developing balance in a universe that primarily favors chaos. "Picture yourself as a tiny puzzle piece in the world." From a box sitting next to his stool on the stage, he took out a 2000-piece puzzle box, and tossed the contents out into the audience so that most of them had a piece in their hands. "You're all such small pieces, as you can see. You can't imagine anything you do making a difference," Morris started, smiling.

He was always smiling, that stupid, beatific grin that nobody ever found smug or condescending, as he produced a gangly puppet out from his box of visual aids, then tossed it onto the floor. "But you're connected by wires. We all are," he proclaimed. He held his hands up, fingers angled in the proper formation. Thin spindles of purple electricity sparked from his fingertips, shot up dramatically, then arced down, connecting with the limbs of his example-puppet. The puppet dangled to life, perking itself up by the electric wires and waving at the audience of sheep. They started to clap.

Morris manipulated the wires, dancing the puppet around on the stage. "This is what we are to the world. Not just the puppet, like we might assume, but the energy that makes it dance. That's us, too. These strands of energy are connected to all of us. All magic is, is recognizing how we connect to each other, and to the larger whole. If we know we're all connected by these wires, by *ourselves*, then maybe we can throw ourselves out further…" at this, Morris took one of the strands that held up the puppet's right hand, and zapped it back into his box of visual aids. A trumpet tumbled out, and a new magic wire bounced from the base of it into the mouthpiece. Then Morris blew out a long, comically exaggerated breath.

They started laughing again, while a series of purple sparks traced the breath from his mouth, to the puppet, to the trumpet. A pedestrian noise blew out from the horn.

The sheep clapped some more. Grolev's arms remained folded. He had always hated these people, and when they gleefully applauded such a rudimentary trick, he was happy for a new reason to confirm that feeling.

Waving off the claps (the puppet waved them off too), Morris continued. "I know, it sounds awful. But that's just the first step. Are there any trumpeters in the audience?"

One of the royal musicians raised her hand.

"And what's your name, my dear?"

"Katherine White."

"Ms. White, would you think of a song for me? Something upbeat, if that's possible."

Katherine White nodded, and Morris expanded his attention back to the whole audience as he continued, "We're all shooting out these lines of energy, even though we don't know it. What a magician does…is this."

He gestured one hand at the puppet, and the other out at Katherine White. The static energy moved the trumpet towards the puppet's mouth, and multiple electrical arcs started to push against the trumpet's keys, playing a rudimentary three-note song. And then he arced another bolt out to Katherine White. And suddenly, the rudimentary song became something far more complicated and welcoming. The puppet had learned Katherine's song.

More applause, as Keegan Morris gestured to Katherine White and started to put a cap on it all. "This is magic. We're small, and practically meaningless. But we have the power to play a song, if we just know how and where to put our energy. And just as simply as we can play a song – and a lovely song at that, thank you Katherine – "

More lines of energy shot out from the bell of the trumpet, out into the audience, gently snatching the puzzle pieces from their hands, and pulling them back up to the stage, where, in a swirl of cardboard, they began to join each other, finally creating a finished puzzle picture – a near mirror-image of the audience it looked out on. "We can create a picture of the future."

And everyone clapped again, louder and harder than before.

It had been one of the most excruciating nights of Grolev's life.

Back then, what had truly frustrated him about the people's admiration for Keegan Morris was that they never bothered to do any further research. Grolev had. After growing bored and disillusioned with Morris's teaching style, Grolev had ventured off on his own, dug a little deeper, reading the books and pages that had been deemed dangerous and worrisome. The ones that Morris and his cronies had decided weren't in keeping with the light, fluffy magic they wanted the discipline to be. He found magic that spoke of the energy in rot and putrification.

Keegan Morris preached that magic was about finding the hidden connections in life. But Grolev had learned that there was much more magic in death. So much beautifully hideous music to be played by manipulating the power of decay.

This understanding had made Grolev a non-entity among his peers. It wasn't that they dismissed him. They recognized that he had discovered something important and new to the school of magic, and it terrified them.

"You're missing the point," one magician had told him languidly. It seemed like every magician he talked to spoke with this easygoing, everything's-just-fine drawl. "Magic isn't about power, it's about connections..." The same old lines. Most people just dismissed it as an affect of drug use, but Grolev used drugs too, and if anything they made him more impatient than your average magician. So he decided that these magicians were just that – average. Average, and remarkably stupid.

This kind of live-and-let-live retort had been directed at Grolev years before he had first cut out a magician's brain. If he had known he could squelch the argument so easily, he probably would have started that particular practice much earlier.

No matter. Things had worked out well for him, in the end.

While Keegan Morris had commercialized the magical arts with public appearances, talk of starting a school for the more adept youngsters, and pats on the head like a good little lapdog from Lucius, Grolev had learned to use magic to its full potential. Out to the lands to the far east, even past Beasts Old Throne, out in the ancestral homelands of the savages that founded Western Sun, Grolev harnessed the power of earth that was green and abundant, thanks to the fertilizer of generations of slain barbarian ancestors.

This was when he truly understood the ugly truth that Keegan Morris had worked so hard to ignore. Magic wasn't about finding order in a chaotic world. To him, magic meant finding the order in the world, appreciating and loving it. And then shoving enough chaos into its veins that it would break, allowing a man of vision to make it do whatever he wanted, without the bother of negotiating.

Like a lot of young people back in the early reign of Lucius, Grolev had moved away from his people in order to study magic uninhibited. Like very few magicians, he had returned to his home and devoted time to slowly, methodically murder every member of his family.

The power he gained from this act was indescribably satisfying. Between his sojourns in the east and his act of familial slaughter, when Grolev returned to Western Sun, he carried with him a stunning cache of bleak magical energy.

As far as he was concerned, death magic beat out Keegan Morris's hippy love-powers any day of the week.

From his first protracted wheezing fit witnessed by his subjects, everyone with an ear to the ground knew that King Lucius had a terminal diagnosis of darklung. So it was no shock when he died, and Arius took the throne. Once that happened, the change in the wind was obvious.

Keegan Morris, the poster-child for everyday mysticism, found himself on the outs with the new political regime soon after that. Maybe it was his increasingly public rallies against Arius's annexation policies. Maybe it was that Arius couldn't stand anything connected with his dead brother's regime.

Either way, it didn't take much work for Grolev to take the man's place in the crown's favor. He didn't do much more than show up, a smile on his face, and a promise that he could take Morris out cleanly, and no one would ask any questions. After all, magicians were known as a notoriously flakey bunch. It would come as no real surprise if Morris just disappeared on one of his pilgrimages, and simply never came back. Frankly, it was astounding that Morris had stuck around as long as he had.

Keegan Morris claimed that magic was about finding order in a chaotic world. Grolev knew that the philosophy applied far more realistically to politics than it did to magic.

The very night that Morris turned in his resignation, after publicly proclaiming that he would as a form of protest, Grolev confronted his former teacher in his own chambers. He had planned all the things he would say, all the horrifying truths he would reveal to his old teacher before destroying him. But in the end, there were no words exchanged, because in that moment, knowing beyond certainty that Morris was a dead man, Grolev found them completely unnecessary. He was more powerful. He was Better Than Keegan Morris. He sent a powerful shock through his old teacher's brain and watched the man crumple like one of his teaching puppets, whose strings had just been cut.

And like that, the job interview was over, and Grolev was named the new advisor on mystic studies to King Arius the Bold. Phase one of his plan was complete.

The wizard – Grolev was so much more than a mere magician, and felt that a new, more imperious title would make that more obvious – had erroneously assumed that it would take a lot of subtle manipulation to guide the kingdom towards the kind of violent actions that would serve him, but Arius taking the throne proved to be a boon that not even Grolev could have foreseen. Arius wanted political power, and Grolev wanted mystical power. They got along famously. Only Grolev knew why.

While he had been developing long-ranging scenarios that would end in bloody upheavals, Arius was simply working out reasons why places like Beasts Old Throne needed to be brought under sterner rule. He decided that since the mining communities were a necessity to the entire region, they needed to be under Western Sun's control. For Arius, that was enough to bring the full force of Western Sun's army down on its neighboring city-state. The result was years of bloodshed and death. With the right incantations in place and a sacrifice here and there, every death gave more power to Grolev.

Then Arius noticed that the Northlands were mobilizing their forces awfully quickly. Another invasion, and some more dark incantations, and Grolev found himself ever so happy.

And all that time, Keegan Morris sat in his cell, a braindead, drooling lump of meat locked below the royal castle.

Or so Grolev thought, until the last day or so. There was clearly some part of Morris's mind still floating around, and try as he might, the wizard couldn't find it. Worse yet, he couldn't let his frustration show, lest the stupid little bitch-queen-to-be reverse all history and realize something obvious for a change.

Almost on cue, she requested, "Grolev, I want you to do something for me." He opened his eyes once again. She was still spying the kingdom grounds from the window. Her back was still turned towards him. It still pissed him off.

"Name it," the wizard said pleasantly.

"Find me survivors."

Grolev coughed politely, but with meaning. "Your highness, it's wildly unlikely that there are any survivors out there. It all happened so fast, I wouldn't want to get your hopes up…"

The Orphan turned toward him, her eyes cold with resolve. "The people aren't stupid. There are plenty of places to lock themselves up, where short of a battering ram, these monsters would be unable to enter. There are people still alive out there, Grolev. I know it. And if you've had no luck reaching Quinn Kind – on account of that barrier, I assume – then the least you can do for me is find my frightened countrymen inside the wall, so that when we *do* reach Quinn, we can tell her where she might be of assistance."

"I will do my best, your highness," Grolev said quietly. Inside himself, he grinned ear to ear, because he knew that at some point before the sun rose on Bloody Twilight, he would get to slit the stupid little bitch's throat with his own knife. He'd forged one himself, especially for the occasion.

34. Under a Tree

"I wish you'd talk to me," Welles said to Quinn. His volume was low, but in terms of intent, it was as bold a voice as he'd ever used outside a spell. The spells he used weren't just strange words and breaths. They worked because he had to believe they would, and part of that lay in charging his voice with meaning, faith, and confidence.

Right now, he needed all the magic he had in him to get his girlfriend to tell him what he could do to make things better.

In the six months that they'd been together, "needy" had never once been a word Welles would have used to describe Quinn. Her independent nature was one of the things that first drew him to her. But he had lately found that her closed nature – an aspect of herself that was necessary for any potential Pic mother – was starting to put a strain on things. If he wasn't sure that the steady increase in that nature over the last few days wasn't a reaction to certain dire circumstances, he might have become frustrated.

But as it stood, Welles was uniquely keen to the fact that, whether or not she said anything, he was about the only thing that could keep her from coming totally unglued at this point.

"What?" Quinn bellowed angrily, nearly catching the attention of her soldiers. Recognizing this, she pulled her volume down just a bit, if not her intensity. "What do you want me to say?"

Welles was a man who could manipulate plant-life as he saw fit. He could change the structure of the human body. He could speak, on a rudimentary level, with animals. He could read minds, when he knew what to look for. He could fly short distances. He could peer into the past, present, and future and communicate with the undiscovered country.

But coming up with the right thing to say to an angry girlfriend was something he still had trouble figuring out.

"I didn't have anything particular in mind," he started. He had an image in his mind's eye of stepping out onto an iced-over pond, hoping it wouldn't crack underneath him. "But I know you're mad, and I know you need to vent."

Quinn glared at him. But the ice felt thick enough, so he smiled gently, and held his hands out to his sides, like he was negotiating a truce. "And, y'know, I've got a little free time."

The frown Quinn had been wearing, pretty consistently since they left the woods, wore on her face harder than Welles had really seen up until now. It pushed her features down to the point that he could see tears beginning to form in her eyes. She walked quickly and resolutely toward him. For a brief moment, he wondered if she was going to kick the crap out of him too, as the only way she could successfully display the full extent of her feelings.

But instead, she hugged him fiercely, burying her face into his chest. He could feel tears melting into his shirt as she hid her face. She clutched the back of his robe. He could feel the fingers gripping close to the collar, like it was the only thing that could keep her in place.

"Rrrrrgggghhh…" she groaned out, her voice hoarse and exhausted.

Welles rested his hands on her head and back. "It's okay."

"It's not okay. Nothing's okay, I'm screwing everything up, I don't even know what I'm doing…."

Pulling her face away from his chest in order to establish eye contact, Welles put his black eyes to Quinn's gleaming green irises. "Look at me. I would never lie to you. You're doing great."

Quinn looked up, but her expression of fear and frustration didn't change. So Welles kept talking.

"I can catch a vibe off people pretty well. And those guys…they'll do what you need them to. Don't worry about that. You're doing great. You're leading."

The beginnings of a wary smile started to creep onto Quinn's mouth, so Welles ventured a little further out onto the ice. He enthusiastically elaborated, "Your plan might not get anybody killed!"

She cocked an eyebrow at him. It didn't matter that he said it with a tone of confidence and loyalty. That one put a few cracks in the ice, he knew. But he was a resolute type of guy.

"…Not what I meant, actually. My point, being, that…ahhh…bugger. Okay, let me back up."

But when he looked at Quinn, she was still smiling and warm – she'd understood his intention, thank his many gods.

"You're a sweet guy. Not a wordsmith by any stretch, but you're sweet. You know that?"

"I try," he stammered out. "Really, reeeally hard…."

She placed her hand on his cheek. "You succeed. I'm sorry, I just need to calm down. Just don't know how. This is all pretty new to me, you know?"

Welles nodded, thinking, then answered, "I actually think I do. Hang tight for a second." Then he crouched into a meditative state, and for a full minute, muttered out noises that were deeply meaningful to him, but had to have sounded like gibberish to Quinn.

And then a small oak tree no more than eight feet tall erupted from the ground. The thin, newborn branches creaked out, spreading leaves and creating a beautiful shade just for the two of them.

Welles explained, "You mentioned one time how you liked sitting under a good shady tree when you had to think about things. So...does this work for you?"

Quinn gazed into the branches, the leaves hovering overhead. And then she looked at Welles. "You're amazing," she told him.

Welles hugged her close to him. "About time you noticed."

Her face up against her lover's chest, Quinn opened up. "I need Cord up and running."

"Hm," Welles responded thoughtfully. "Doesn't seem like he's out of practice..."

"I mean, I need him to understand what he's fighting for. Because right now, I think he's just happy for a chance to go fight again."

"That's good, though, right?"

Quinn snorted a bitter laugh. "No such luck. He's had a deathwish ever since he killed Jonas Mudd. I thought we'd taken care of that when we took him into the village, but...I'm worried that he's just looking at this as a chance to die in battle."

"You should talk to him."

"I've tried..."

"No, you've tried bargaining with him, coercing him into doing things. You've told me how close you two used to be...just tell him what's happening. Tell him why you need him here. Why you need *him* in this fight."

Quinn looked up at Welles. She peered into his black eyes. She was the only one he knew who could see what was in there, and it filled him with a warmth a thousand spells couldn't conjure up.

For a moment, neither of them could find words.

Quinn rested her head back on Welles' chest and closed her eyes, enjoying the comfort while it lasted. And then Welles opened his mouth, hoping for some perfect words to come out.

But all he could manage was, "I...what I want to say, I shouldn't right now...you know?"

She looked up at him again, read his beautiful black eyes, and understood. "I know. Me too." With that, Quinn pressed herself up against

Welles one last time, then pulled away, standing up. "I need to talk to Cord for a second."

"Good idea. I'll catch up with Quentin, see if your Fel buddies are close by."

Welles watched Quinn walk away, mentally working through a thousand variations on "I love you." None of them were perfect enough to say out loud.

35. Saving Bloody Twilight

Aching and irritable, Cord woke with the feeling that he just wanted to sit under a tree. There was plenty of woodland up north by his bar, completely devoid of noisy elves or other mystery-people. Out back by Udo's garden, he'd set up a hammock. Laying in it, stretched out beneath two big shady trees, sounded just too perfect of an idea at that moment.

But even the Pic village was comfortable to him, after all the time he had spent there. He knew the land, and he loved the shade that cast itself about when evening came. Twilight in the Pic village was beautiful every day.

When the world starts to creep in too much and too fast, just get your ass out to the woods, sit under a tree – that was Cord's philosophy.

But out here, in the vast, flat expanse between the woods and the kingdom, there was no place to get away, to be alone for a moment. Even if Cord were a hundred feet from anyone else, they were all right there for him to see, and for them to see him.

Out at the edge of the perimeter, he could even spot Welles and Quinn, sitting by each other, comforting each other under a lone, tiny oak in the middle of nowhere. It took Cord way too long to realize that Welles had dreamed that tree up himself.

Cord was actually a little jealous.

He missed the woods. And then it dawned on him that he couldn't possibly be the only one. After all, he was surrounded by Pics who called the woods their home. More than that. It was their entire existence, ingrained into them from birth – housing, mode of travel, food source, protection, religion, and more things than any human could ever really understand.

Cord checked out his comrades, like he'd been doing before his altercation with Mene. It was old soldier's instincts, inspecting the men, and now that his fight with Mene had helped ease his unaimed frustration, watching the soliders was oddly comforting.

116

There they were – a petite army of woodland kids with no real battle experience. In the middle of a field, only a few miles from their intended fighting ground.

The sun was beginning to set. It would be dark soon. And yet none of them displayed any real recognition of danger. Just the boredom that comes from waiting. He'd been so pissed at that, just a few moments ago. Scrapping with Mene had drained a lot of that tension. Wouldn't be long before it filled up again. He knew he'd have to start fighting again soon, take on some of those dead soldiers, otherwise he might try to pick another brawl with someone who didn't quite deserve it.

He didn't like being so sure about that.

Cord understood the slow, lumbering nature of the enemy – it's not like they were planning some grand counter-strike. Still. Felt weird, just sitting at the edge of a field. Nursing a fat lip, a bloody nose, and – Cord gingerly felt around his torso – yes, a cracked rib, too.

He saw Quinn walking toward him. Sadness and annoyance blending in her expression. And he realized where the phrase "to add insult to injury" might have originated.

"How you feeling, Nathan?" Her tone didn't exactly reek of concern.

Cord hung his head, trying to convey embarrassment. "Sorry, Quinn. Tempers flared. You made me and Victor ride together for the better part of the day, you had to know this might happen."

He tried to laugh at his joke and was rewarded with a tiny shock of pain on his right side. He made a mental note to favor his left side when the fighting started. The fighting with the dead men, anyway. He could probably throw another right hook at Mene if he had to.

Quinn didn't humor him. "That was dumb, Nathan. Real frickin' dumb."

"Now, I know you're mad, since you're using my first name, but I get the feeling it isn't because, wonder of wonders, me and Vic hate each other."

Quinn sat down next to him. She pointed to the not-quite-army. "You see anything weird about the soldiers we're heading into battle with?"

Cord came up with a couple of pithy retorts, but decided they wouldn't get him very far. Instead, he surveyed the troops. "Well, you've got me, Vic, and your magic boyfriend. And…what's the count, thirty?"

"Yeah, around thirty," Quinn confirmed, her tone trying to lead Cord toward a specific conclusion. "Look at them. What do you notice about them?"

Cord felt obliged to make a serious inspection. Mostly male. Mostly young. They were filling up their downtime with cardgames, telling stories, tossing jokes around. A few of them were tossing a ball around. Like young Pic boys will do. Young being a relative term with the Pics…

Young Pic boys.

It hit Cord, finally. That ton of bricks had finally been delivered. "Oh."

Must have shown on his face, too, because Quinn answered, "Yeah. My fighting elite is made up of people I would never think of bringing to a fight."

"They're all young Pic men. No more than 50 years old, most of them," Cord continued along Quinn's line of thought. "Where are the women?"

Quinn laughed bitterly at a private joke. "Figured you might not have noticed, as focused as you were with the wanting to kill me and Victor."

Cord felt how blank and confused his face must have appeared. He needed to get rid of that dumb look, so asked, "I noticed it back at camp, but I didn't really think about it. Quinn, where are your mothers and sisters? You're a matriarchal people. Why aren't any of the girls fighting?" The word "girls" spilled out too fast for Cord to catch and fix it, but he attempted damage control. "Quinn, you have a dozen warrior-queens ready to fight, so why is it just you?"

Quinn's severe expression broke, recognizing something in Cord that he didn't understand. "When Welles came to the village, told my mothers what was happening in Bloody Twilight, do you know what they said? 'Good riddance.' That sound familiar, Nate?"

"Sorry," Cord muttered, not entirely sure why he was apologizing.

Quinn kept on as though he hadn't spoken. "They'd been waiting for the kingdom to try annexing the forest for years. So seeing the kingdom just eat itself? As far as they could see, this was a blessing.

"But when Welles told them he didn't think his shield would hold for more than a few days..."

"...They packed up and left," Cord finished for her. "But...they're Pics, where...?"

Quinn smirked angrily. "Your little bar and its pig-farming neighborhood have some new neighbors. Udo's probably pouring them a round as we speak. They headed for the woods up by Northern Sun. The Tree-bobs will take them in. They're friendly that way. I went with them, then snuck out to see you before heading back to my village to prepare the guys."

Cord looked at Quinn. The anger he'd felt toward her had disappeared, he realized, and all he saw now was an old friend trying desperately to hold her homeland together with both hands.

"Why in the hell would you stay?" There was no frustration in his voice. No sneering superiority. Cord was suddenly quite frightened for her. For this decision she'd made. It hadn't occurred to him until this moment how hard her choice had been.

Quinn's expression softened. She felt like she was finally talking to the Nathan Cord that she had called her best friend. "Allie," she answered simply. Saying her name, she laughed a little.

"Quinn, she's not our little girl anymore..." Cord started, his tone suddenly sad.

She cut him off. "No, I don't want to hear your cynicism, Nate. You don't even believe it yourself. You remember all the same things I do. You remember her first steps, and the way she'd say 'baf' when she wanted a bath, and how, when the carnival set up shop, she wasn't afraid of the performers because of the time you and Kayla took her to see the Blue Knives and you told her they were like clowns…and how she always made me and Kayla read her that nursery rhyme about the arguing ducks together before she went to bed, because she liked how our voices sounded together."

"How you taught her those tumbling exercises, like gymnastics," Cord added, automatically. "You were training her to fight like it was a game…"

Quinn kept up the momentum. "You remember the pillows Kayla helped her make? They were supposed to spell out her name, but it looked more like 'Alpie'?"

"Yeah…what about that hideous dog you got for her, one of Big Jack's litter."

Quinn broke out laughing. "Oh god, that thing…think it chewed up half the boots in the kingdom before it ran away…"

"Man, did she cry that night. That sweet little girl…" Cord trailed off, as a thousand more memories flooded his heart. He was suddenly speechless.

Quinn was not. "That's right, Nate. That sweet little girl is trapped in there with monsters swarming everywhere she turns. And we need to save her. She can change things for the better, if she's allowed the chance. Because we raised her. You, and me, and Kayla. *We* raised her. Arius might be her father, but we are her parents. And we both did her wrong, leaving her there. That was unforgivable. We both got wrapped up in our own shit, and we left her in the care of horrible people. But I don't believe for a second that they tainted her.

"I know her, Nate. I've kept an eye on her, I know the woman she's become, and I know she can make Western Sun more than Bloody Twilight, make it mean what it should. What Lucius tried for, she can do that if she gets the chance. We screwed up a long while back, not protecting her like we should have. But we can do that now. When it counts the most.

"I didn't bring you into this because you're a good fighter, Cord. I've got good fighters. I need you because she needs you."

Cord heard and absorbed every word his friend had to say, but fought off their intent. He shook his head. "I killed her father. She saw me do that. And then she saw me run, without explanation. I can't help her." Saying those words out loud for the first time hurt. He concluded sorrowfully, "She wouldn't want my help."

Quinn stood up angrily. "Why do you think you're not dead, you stupid son of a bitch?"

Startled, Cord had no answer ready.

119

"She protected you! When you disappeared, she called off any search. Called you dead to the kingdom. Think about it, if she wanted revenge…she's the commander of the most powerful army in the hemisphere! Your head would have been a decoration on her mantle by the end of the week! But she said 'No. Let him go.' She kept you safe for seven stinking years."

"Mudd…" Cord weakly argued, remembering the bastard's greed and bloodlust when he'd realized who Cord was.

"Jonas Mudd was a corrupt, money-grubbing thug of a man. You've got a bounty on your head in the sister kingdoms, but not because of Allie. You pulled off some horrors before you killed Arius, if you'll recall."

Cord coughed out a brief chuckle. "Guess I figured those horrors are what kept people away."

Quinn smiled. She sat down again, gave him a friendly elbow to his left side. "You know what they say about believing your own hype, king-killer." Then, her tone once again serious, "Cord, I hate – I *hate* – how I got you into this. I'm never going to let myself off the hook for that. But I needed someone who would risk his life without question to save a wonderful girl who might be destined to do great things. Ugh…I nearly gag at the thought of saying this, but Victor Mene is right, in a way. If we save the Orphan, we save Western Sun. Not Bloody Twilight. We save *Western Sun*, Nate."

And then the time of day forced its way into Quinn's argument. They both noticed it at once. The sun had begun its descent in earnest. Shimmering against the ocean. Casting its brilliance through the thin leaves covering the Pic forest. Letting the light and shadow reflect itself toward Bloody Twilight. Granting Western Sun its title once again. A dying city, covered in orange, red, purple and gray.

"Sunset," Cord remarked, as nonchalantly as he could muster. "About time your Fel buddies should be making contact. Better get ready."

Quinn stood once more. In the twilight, she looked majestic. Cord was almost in awe.

"Yeah. I'd better get the boys prepped." She turned to leave Cord.

"Quinn?"

"Yeah?"

Cord got to his feet, stood firmly. He tried to think of a way to convey his feelings, to speak with meaning and conviction the way Quinn had. But all he could get out was, "I'm your man."

Quinn looked at him, a question on her face, even though she knew and understood the answer.

"On this one, I'm your man."

Quinn said nothing as she began walking toward her troops. Then she looked over her shoulder and smiled, honestly, gratefully. "I never had a doubt. Thank you."

Quinn left Nathan Cord with a smile on his face that he found confusing and uncomfortable. And the first mission in nearly two decades in which he had absolute faith.

36. A Soldier's Prayer

Victor Mene sat in what he recognized to be his corner of the campground. A tiny spot of exile in which he was implicitly ordered to stay, so as not to frighten the little pixie boys. It didn't make much difference to him. It wasn't like he planned on socializing. Frankly, he was content with the opportunity of a few minutes of quiet. A few minutes to strategize in his own head. And recent experience had taught him that his new cohorts were a chatty bunch.

He peered out at his soldiers. None of them had ever seen combat – real combat – before now. But they had been in battle.

Pics age at a quarter of the rate of humans, and he had heard rumors that decades before the dead king Lucius had invited them to the kingdom, they had been involved in shadow skirmishes with the other woodland peoples. There had never been any confirmation of these battles, but he had heard Quinn Kind allude to such fights when speaking publicly with Lucius. When he broached the subject with Cord, he received a vague confirmation that the Pics had had to fight to keep their land free of the Fel and nameless southlanders. No one would tell him much more than that.

Mene understood well enough, in any case, that their fighting expertise wasn't just a matter of keeping fit. They had learned to use their natural abilities aggressively for a reason. And whatever those reasons were, they contributed to the unspoken rule that humans were not allowed in their forests.

For this reason, Mene had always been frustrated with the relations between the kingdom and the Pic clan. His reputation classified him as stubborn, clinging to old ways, but that wasn't true where fighting was concerned. Before Quinn Kind's mothers – her superiors – had decided to withdraw her from activity with the kingdom, he had hoped to develop training regimens that could teach their fighting style, that strange mix of casual, languid movement and quick, deliberate strikes, to his troops.

Unfortunately, his limited social skills proved to be a detriment to that plan. He could never find the right words to begin a meaningful dialogue with the pixie ambassador. On the rare occasion that they would encounter each other in a social environment, Mene had always been terribly aware of his own frame towering over Quinn, perhaps too imposing a figure for the girl to feel comfortable around. And while he sat back and worked on new means of communicating with her, to more casually approach her in order to learn her techniques, Quinn had allied herself with Cord, and to his endless annoyance, they had become friends. Social acquaintances, without any thought to sharing fighting secrets. It had made both of them useless to him in terms of advancing the guard's abilities.

Worse yet, Mene had always felt deep down that their friendship had planted the seeds of Nathan Cord's self-destruction, taken his allegiance away from the kingdom just slightly. Just enough that regicide would eventually become a possibility to Cord. In a way that Mene knew to be irrational but nevertheless stood by, he believed that Quinn Kind was indirectly responsible for the death of Arius the Bold, and ultimately, for the current collapsing state of the Kingdom of Western Sun.

Victor Mene found himself daydreaming of his own troops, alive and well and fighting, a cunning fleet of human soldiers with the magical Pic fighting prowess added to their own formidable guard training. In his mind, they would have been unstoppable.

The captain of the royal guard was not prone to daydreaming. It struck him as odd, to wonder what could have been, when every electric impulse in his brain usually devoted itself purely to what is, and nothing more. Perhaps this was Mene's way of grieving.

The image in his mind of this perfect fighting force nearly made him smile. As much as anything ever did.

It was possible, Mene accepted, that he had become aware of his own slim chances for survival, and that was leading his mind into unexplored areas of imagination. When they served together, Cord had always chided him for his lack of lateral thinking. He wasn't wrong. It was, after all, why he had installed Cord as chief of Coal Brigade – to have someone under his command that could make plans that were more fluid and adaptable than he himself was capable of concocting.

No matter the plans he took into a fight, Victor Mene had never once felt the fear of death in battle. It simply wasn't in him. But he had long suspected that Cord was always prepared for his own death while fighting, and that was somehow the source of his creativity.

Nor did Mene fear death now. But this was the first time he recognized it as a possibility. The thought intrigued him, if nothing more. But he would not allow himself the luxury of such a frivolous thought. He focused on what he knew for a fact.

But the fact was he had escaped Western Sun through a mix of instinctual self-preservation and blind luck. And he was not sure that those odds would ever be in his favor again.

Frivolous thoughts, once again. He shook them off, reminding himself that luck doesn't enter into battle. Just calm, focus, and a steady hand with a blade. As he had often told his troops, embracing these three truths can keep a man alive.

Victor Mene breathed in deeply as the sun began to set on his kingdom. His beautiful kingdom, the only home he had ever known. Bathed in orange, red, and shadow. Warm and dark.

"I would be honored to die for you," he said as softly and tenderly as he had ever spoken. "But I hope that honor will not be mine tonight, that I might continue to serve you."

Someone who had never met Mene might mistake this for a prayer.

Nathan Cord only saw Victor Mene whisper and smile at nothing, as he marched across the field toward him.

37. The Ballad of Cord and Mene

Nathan Cord walked towards Victor Mene, completely clueless as to what he intended to say to his former captain. An apology? If it was for fighting with him earlier, he didn't want to – frankly, he wanted to fight him again, under less heated circumstances. He'd long suspected that the captain could use a good beating, and Cord figured he was exactly the man for the job.

An explanation for killing Arius wasn't on the table either. He could call Mene stubborn, myopic, and bull-headed. But these were all synonyms for a True Believer. Victor Mene believed in king and country, and there was no explanation that would give him cause to accept regicide as an acceptable offense.

Cord had not come up with anything terribly profound by the time he came to a stop in front of his former commander. He stood in front of the man with clenched fists – clenched everything, all his muscles were tensed – as Mene glared up at him, eerily calm.

"How you doing?" Cord asked, and was absolutely stunned that of all the stupid things he could have started with, that was the one he'd picked.

And a horrifying thing occurred. Victor Mene smiled a little, and let out, "Heh." That was as close to a belly-laugh as Cord had ever heard from the man. It amused him. That he found himself amused by Mene was incredibly annoying.

"Yeah, all right. Listen, we're gonna have to work together for a while, and after talking with Quinn, I realize what happened back there was probably a bad idea for morale and all. So…"

Mene's face tightened. Cord didn't know how to read it. "So you're sorry?"

"What's that?" Cord asked in order to buy himself some time.

"Is this an apology for attacking me earlier?"

Cord swallowed hard. A little pride went down, and it tasted terrible. "Yeah, let's call it that."

And then Mene started laughing. Loudly. It was the scariest thing Cord had ever heard. "My word, Cord. One little chat with the pixie and you become a complete pussy."

"Bite me, Vic." But despite himself, Cord could understand the humor Mene saw.

"I know what's happened. Your sentimentality for the Orphan's finally overtaken your rage. It was an eventuality."

Cord sniffed. "You know me so well, is that it?"

"I believe so, yes. Well enough to know you want a rematch as much as I do. Don't worry. When this is over, you and I will beat the living hell out of each other, because I think you know as well as I do that it would do us both some good. I'm fairly certain that I'll kill you. And when I do, I'll take your head off and parade it in front of the locals, so they know, finally, after all these years, what happens to a man who kills a king."

Mene smiled genuinely as he explained this to Cord, without malice or threat. It was almost friendly. Mene believed that Cord should be honored, that he was worthy of a personal beating and beheading at the hands of the captain of the guard.

Cord nodded, understanding. "And hey, maybe I'll kill you, and parade your head around, so people can see what happens to a guy so rigid in his ideals that his brain is no longer capable of new thoughts." Then, though he was surprised to do so, he sat down next to Mene, to get a better view of the kingdom as sundown kissed it. Something about the camaraderie of the whole thing, maybe. Cord decided not to think too deeply about it.

Mene didn't look at Cord, but answered, "You people. You, and the magician and the pixie girl. You all judge me, because I believe in Western Sun. But I know the truth, Nathan."

"Yeah? What's that?"

Mene stared off at the kingdom walls and something like a smile crafted itself on his face. "You admire my resolve. All of you are so conflicted. You, the king-killer drafted back into service. The pixie and her army of peace-minded tree-people. And the magician...I won't even pretend to understand where his mind is. You're all torn between your hearts and your brains."

Cord finished the thought. "And your heart and brain want the same thing." He rolled that around in his mind for a moment, before continuing, "You know, Victor...I hate you. I mean, I truly despise you. You trained me, you promoted me, and yet you will never give a moment's consideration for why I did what I did.

"So yeah. I hate you. But you might be right. Out of everyone in this camp right now? You're the only one whose mission is completely clear to him. And I envy you that. I think that might be what I came over to tell you."

"Good work, then."

They sat staring at the kingdom, before Mene said, "That roar you use, when you attack. It's not startling for anyone who recognizes it."

Cord nodded, taking that in, and responded, "And the fact that you're like nine feet tall isn't all that scary for anyone who knows you don't guard your midsection. One good shot to the stomach and you're a ragdoll."

Mene grinned, honestly, happily. "When our final battle comes, Nathan Cord, I imagine it will be something people write songs about."

Cord thought on that for a moment. He entertained the idea of a song written about himself that didn't involve lyrics about 'killing the king-killer dead,' as went one particularly jaunty tune he'd heard. It wasn't an unpleasant notion.

"And you call me sentimental. What do you think they'll call this song of yours? 'The Ballad of Cord and Mene'?"

Mene nodded, "I suppose."

"You suppose. I thought you hated ballads."

Without hesitation, Mene confirmed, "With all my heart." And yet he said this with a hint of a smile.

Cord smiled too.

38. Family Reunion

Quinn Kind was with Welles, analyzing a map of the kingdom she had spread out across a folding table in their makeshift command center. Welles had been talking about a feeling he'd gotten now that they were closer to the kingdom walls.

"I need to be close to the city to get a real read on what's in there, you understand," Welles said, trying his best not to sound embarrassed for any earlier oversight. "I haven't been this close since I came to your village, and at that point, all I could hear was screaming."

"And now?"

Welles stared intently at the kingdom. "I still hear screaming. And I hear violence, and madness, and death. But I'm picking up something else now, too. I hear prayers. Prayers sound different. They sound like sad sighs. 'Please someone, save us.'"

He grabbed Quinn swiftly by her arms and calmly pulled her closer to him. For a moment, she thought he was going to kiss her, but before she could chastise him for it, he told her in a quiet, solemn whisper, "I think there's a group of survivors in there." And then Welles' solemn expression broke, revealing a tiny bit of hope.

It was infectious. Quinn felt a warm tingle in her chest, and asked, more eagerly than she had intended, "Do you know where? This might change the whole gameplan, Welles. If we can save these people…" And as soon as she had said it out loud, she was crestfallen.

Welles read her expression. "If we want to save the Orphan, and save these people, it makes things a hell of a lot trickier, I know." Welles turned his eyes back on the maps. "But see," he started, putting the pieces together in his mind carefully before he offered anything, "we've been looking for an angle of the city we could attack first, so if I can just figure out where the hell they are, we can start there, put your guys in, put the Fel in, and…"

Welles stopped himself there. He didn't have anything further because anything else depended on the Fel actually being a part of the initial attacking force. And so far, they were exceedingly late to the party.

Quinn had grown impatient as well. "I don't know where they are, Welles." She squinted, and put her thumb and forefinger to the bridge of her nose to massage her growing headache. "They're a half an hour later than they should have been. Maybe they were just messing with me, I wouldn't put it past them. But damn it, I was hoping they'd be here by now."

Welles looked around with his magician's eyes, hoping to see some warm bodies entering the camp. He picked up...something. Something strange and foreign to his eyes, that he couldn't quite make out. It could have been anything, a wild animal, an unusually charismatic shrub. Whatever it was, he decided against pointing it out, against getting Quinn's hopes up. "Doesn't matter. We can do this. We don't need those psychos."

Quinn appreciated Welles' dedication. "Check the maps one more time, find us an entry point, and we'll work from there." Welles turned back to his map, while Quinn surveyed her camp. Her brothers.

A naked eye might see them goofing around and think that they weren't ready for a fight, but Quinn knew better. She trusted her boys to be glorious when the time came.

And then she looked to the far right of the camp, and came upon the strangest sight she could count over the last few days. Stranger than undead soldiers, stranger than a giant golden bubble covering a kingdom, stranger than anything Welles could do.   Nathan Cord and Victor Mene were sitting together. Talking. Talking, while not trying to kill each other. She was practically hypnotized by the sight of it.

Wild noises swarming the camp from all sides snapped her out of her trance. Hoots and howls and cackles of vicious glee. Some jumping out of nowhere, some erupting from the ground below.

She heard Welles mumble, "Those sneaky sons of bitches..." The exact same thoughts had just crossed her mind.

The Fel had finally arrived.

Late, as usual.

The Fel were of the same kind as the Pic and the Tree-bob clans. They all came from the same offshoot of humankind, and all had the same peculiar abilities not possessed by the people of the Suns. The superior senses, the environmental invisibility, and the ability to travel under ground, among other talents. But their individual cultures tended to reflect their neighboring kingdoms.

The Tree-bobs were, much like their Northern Sun neighbors, a peaceful, placid people, without any strong warrior instincts. What they lacked in tenacity, they made up for with warmth and welcome. The Tree-bobs had the best relationship with their neighboring kingdom of any woodlander clan. Because of this, Quinn had to agree with the general concensus: their woods were a lovely place to visit.

The Pics, though they kept mostly to themselves, had a reputation that was not to be taken lightly, and as such had what Quinn could only refer to – though she recognized the inherent arrogance – as a somewhat more regal temperament. She had long ago decided that it had been a possible byproduct of living so close to Bloody Sunset, the cradle of the kingdoms.

Of course, to the far south were lands no one spoke much of. The loose conglomeration of human villages there was made up of angry, violently tempered humans. If their attack on the kingdom nearly a century earlier hadn't been enough of a lesson, then the slaughter of Victor Mene's army was a grim reminder to everyone, human and woodlander alike. Simple and deadly, and three words long: Do Not Enter.   Quinn knew there was another tribe down there, further south, past those psychotic human villages. She didn't know what those woodlanders called themselves, nor did she want to meet any of them if she lived to be 300.

So that left the Fel. Unlike their sibling clans, the Fel found great pleasure in dealing, both socially and fiscally, with the people of Beasts Old Throne, and its later incarnation as the Kingdom of Eastern Sun.

Eastern Sun was a mining community. And the Fel liked making bombs. Their woods housed the elements of explosive powders and fluids, and over a hundred years ago, they struck up a deal with the Throne's ruling class, creating a commercial agreement of explosives-for-favors that worked mutually well for both communities, until twenty years back, when the Throne elders got greedy, increasing taxation and twisting labor laws to their own ends. The Fel, sensing a threat to their livelihood, sided with the workers, putting them at odds with the royal guard of Western Sun. The resulting police action lasted years, and ended with a treaty presided over by Lucius. The Fel had to work more candidly if they wanted to sell their wares to the miners without Western Sun demanding money off the top.

But within two years of Lucius's death and Arius's rise to power, Beasts Old Throne had been annexed, "for its own safety," as the king had put it. Beasts Old Throne was renamed Eastern Sun, and taxes were renegotiated to nobody's benefit but Western Sun. They practically shut the Fel out of business altogether.

So there had been little love lost between the Fel and Bloody Twilight.

Quinn had been put through her paces these last few days, getting what she needed for a strong attack force. Extracting Mene. Manipulating Cord. Sneaking away from her mothers. Convincing her brothers to fight.

But those howls of excitement and raucous defiance of battle preparations that signaled the Fel entrance actually put a smile on her face, because it had been the easiest bargain she had ever struck. She offered them the one thing they wanted. The chance to break things.

Quinn had sent a messenger into Fel territory to pass along a simple note that she had hand-written. It read:

"Bloody Twilight is falling to pieces. Want to help burn it down for good? Of course you do. Tell my brother that you'll meet us in the fields to the west of the kingdom before sundown tomorrow. Bring your craziest sons of bitches. XO, Quinn Kind, Acting Queen of the Pic Clan."

She looked around and estimated about a hundred Fel boys and girls. All long-haired, wildly unkempt, bare-armed. A few of them buck-naked, save for a bandolier of bombs strapped to their chests. In stark contrast to the clean-faced Pics, all of the Fel were proudly bearded. Even, upon close inspection, a few of the women.

The Fel encroached further into the camp, closer to Quinn's brothers. On the Fel's entrance, every Pic boy stopped what they were doing and stood on guard, in an attempt to show these crazy men that they were warriors, too. She was bonded closely enough to all of the boys to know they were wary of their cousins from the east.

Not that they were wrong to worry. They'd heard plenty of stories about their maniac cousins. But their apprehension didn't exactly bathe her in faith for her army.

And then Quinn witnessed the second strangest thing her eyes had taken in over the last few days. Each of the Fel started laughing joyously, and embraced the nearest Pic.

Quinn remembered a night, early in her ambassadorial role, where Cord and Kayla had attempted to explain, amusement clear on their faces, the notion of a "family reunion" to her, and how alien it sounded. How could you call them family if you didn't live with them, weren't bound to them by blood and obligation?

"Okay, so people just show up in a camping area somewhere every few years to…what, to say hello and remember they have the same ancestors?"

Kayla nodded, encouraging Quinn's credulousness. "That's about the size of it, yeah," she said, chuckling. "There's usually some drinking involved."

Cord, hugging Kayla in amusement, tossed out, "When my family did it, one of my uncles would hold an auction of old family junk."

Quinn's mind had been thoroughly boggled. "That sounds like something crazy people do."

"Well," Kayla concluded, "that's family for you."

Quinn hadn't been able to wrap her mind around it.

And yet here she was. Witnessing what could be dubbed the first official family reunion of the woodlander clans. Immediately, she understood that jokingly ambivalent tone in their voices when the Cords had spoken of such an occasion.

And then out of nowhere she was lifted up in a bearhug from a massive Fel. "Hahahah! Quinn Kind, yes?"

Oh god, Quinn thought. *These idiots are going to kill me before I even make their acquaintance.* "I am," she answered quickly. "And you are?"

"I'm Saymon Q'iln. Ruling Brother of the Fel." He set her down. "Don't tell me you haven't heard of me." He stared at her intently. Quinn wondered if he was gauging her response to a joke he'd just told.

She smiled, weakly. Samyon Q'iln glared at her, then his eyes flashed and he grinned.

Somehow that must have done the trick.

"EXCELLENT!" he bellowed. "Quinn Kind, I've received your note and brought my greatest warriors to help you tear this place apart. What do you want us to do?"

Quinn regained her composure. "For a start, maybe tell your guys to stop hugging my guys?"

"OY!" Saymon hollered. "Knock it off, you bastards!" Each of the Fel released their hold on the Pic boys. The Fel looked amused. The Pics looked about ready to wet themselves.

Quinn nodded approvingly, trying her hardest not to fall down at the sight of it all, as peculiar as this meeting was. "Thank you, Saymon. We've got a bit of planning to do, you and me."

"Sounds like fun," Saymon grunted happily. Everything he said sounded like he was ordering a round for his men. Quinn couldn't tell if that was good or bad.

So she simply looked him up and down, and answered, "Then I haven't explained it properly."

"Ha-haaaa!" Saymon answered.

Quinn remembered Kayla's words. "That's family for you." Quinn repeated them under her breath, and added to herself, "Huh. I think I finally get it."

39. Warm Memories of Beasts Old Throne

Mene and Cord sat together, as the sun finished its descent on the Kingdom of Western Sun. The deep blues that come at the end of twilight cast themselves against the region, signaling that the time for fighting was close behind. And Victor Mene found himself in a rarely nostalgic state of mind.

He tried to remember his first kill and found that he couldn't. Other soldiers do. Most do, actually. But nothing sprang from his memory. His whole life, he'd been in battle. It felt like that, at least. He wouldn't have it any other way.

He looked at Cord, then turned his head back to his kingdom. His home.

Mene couldn't remember his first kill, but he could remember Nathan Cord's. For a brief moment he considered saying this out loud, but thought better of it. He acknowledged that it wouldn't fill Cord up with fond memories. Cord had always been conflicted regarding his experiences in battle. Bitter, when he should have been proud.   Maybe bitter *because* he had been proud. Whatever it was, it all seemed idiotic to Mene.

Cord hadn't been in training for all that long before they received orders to police Eastern Sun. Technically, after two years in the service, a cadet is considered an accredited soldier, but to Mene, his soldiers were considered trainees up to the moment they saw actual combat. Eastern Sun – Beasts Old Throne, back then – shouldn't have been the struggle that it ended up becoming. And for that, they had the Fel to thank.

Sitting and staring at the kingdom, Cord finally broke the silence. "You know, if we're gonna sit and stare for a while longer, I should grab that bottle of rum from Welles…"

"I don't drink before battle."

"This isn't any kind of battle you've seen before, Vic. Any old rules you had flew out the window the minute your casualties woke up and started waving weapons around."

Mene thought on this for a moment. "I see your point. But my rules still stand. I just want to look on my home for a little longer."

Cord had teased Mene earlier about sentimentality. But observing the look on the captain's face, Cord couldn't find it in him just then to crack any jokes at Mene's expense. He simply nodded, and said nothing more.

Had Mene realized back then that there were Fel fighting undercover in the armies of Beasts Old Throne, he might have prepared his soldiers differently. He liked to think that, anyway, but couldn't know for certain, and so put it out of his mind.

The militia of coal miners that made up Beasts Old Throne's army fought just as he had figured – like desperate, untrained men who hadn't gotten paid and thought staging a revolt was the only course of action left to them.

Mene had been ready to take them out, restore order, and be done with the mission in a week, two at the most. But with the Fel interspersed in their number, their fighting force became a confusingly random blend of sloppy rabble-rousers and fearless lunatics. The mix had proved unpredictably dangerous.

Nearly twenty years ago, but Mene could still remember his embarrassment after their first charge had proven so completely unsuccessful. They'd been driven back into the hills outside the valley where Beasts Old Throne rested. In the dark of night, they made camp as Mene and his sergeants debated strategies. All very typical plans of attack. Mene pointed out that they were not a typical army, and so had grown frustrated listening to the uselessly conventional strategies his men suggested. He excused himself from his tent and took a walk into camp, through his men.

They had been quieter than these pixie boys were tonight, Mene remembered. More reserved, readying themselves for the next day's siege just as they had been taught. This night, Mene found that he missed that feeling of calm before a storm, and it dawned on him that he may never have that pleasure again.

It was plenty calm that night before they attacked Beasts Old Throne. During what his troops must have assumed to be an impromptu inspection of their ranks, Mene came across a young man sitting alone by a fire, writing in a notebook.

"What are you doing, cadet?"

The young Nathan Cord looked up at his commander, and answered obediently that he was writing a letter home to his girlfriend.

"That's thoughtful, but if all goes as planned you may well beat that letter home, Cord."

"With all due respect, sir, I have a feeling we might be here for a while." Mene remembered the boy's tone as quiet, but completely unafraid to speak his mind. It was an interesting change of pace, if not entirely welcome from a subordinate.

"What gives you that impression, Cord?"

"Well…" he put his notebook back in his satchel and stood up, pointed a finger down into the valley. "For one thing, I think we both know by now that they've got some of those woodland people, the Fel? If their reputation is at all true, then they're in the fight just for the fun of it. Beyond that, they're the Throne workers' chief source of mining explosives."

"Your point?"

"We haven't even been hit with any explosives yet. Which means right now, the Fel are just playing around with us."

Mene silently chided himself for not being as well-informed about the woodland people as he probably should have been. But the popular belief was that most of the legends surrounding the Fel were simply that.

Cord continued. "And they know where we are. I mean, everything I've heard about these woodland folk says they don't light torches or anything at night. So they can see in the dark. Even if we put out our fires, they'd know we were camped out up here. So they know where we'll be coming from tomorrow." Then he stopped. He seemed self-conscious, telling his commander something he was sure must have been obvious.

But Mene found himself enjoying a new voice, and told the young soldier, "Go on. What do you think our options are?"

Cord looked down at his boots. "Sir…"

"Look me in the eyes, soldier," Mene said coldly. "If we attack tomorrow as we did today, we'll meet with the same resistance. If we move our troops, they'll see us and change position accordingly."

"So send us in tomorrow like they expect, but put Coal's Brigade into position tonight, quietly, to attack at a different point. Or split them up further, get them to infiltrate the Throne without initiating the enemy, get them inside to protect the elders and then…" Cord's idea had run out of steam. He smiled half-heartedly. "I don't know what then."

Mene very nearly smiled back at him, but found the proper reserve to avoid it. "I think I do. Tell me, Cord, did you have any kills today?"

"Not sure any of us did, sir. But no, I was in the back, mostly just pulling the wounded out. Mostly just used my shield." He gestured over to a dented piece of metal underneath his satchel. "It's seen better days. Those Fel guys use hammers and maces, came as a bit of a shock."

Mene registered the complaint, and replied, "Shake it off. Hammer out the dents. Tomorrow, you're with me." He turned to head back to his tent, his mind suddenly fresh with ideas.

"Sir?" Cord asked. Not meekly, but not exactly brimming with confidence.

"You're with my attack team tomorrow. I'm putting Coal's Brigade on duty, as well. We leave before first light tomorrow."

Once he was out of view of his soldiers, Victor Mene began to smile. Tomorrow would be a very different story.

"Vic."

"Hm?" Mene tried to pretend that he hadn't been completely lost in thought. Nathan Cord stood above him, extending a bottle of rum and doing something he thought of as smiling. It was really closer to baring his teeth in order to scare off weaker prey.

"I told you I don't drink before a fight."

Cord plopped down next to him, popped the cork out of the top with his thumb, took a swig and gestured it to Mene. "And I have told you, time and time again, that your rigidity would get you killed someday. Besides, this isn't drinking before a fight. This is a requiem for Bloody - for the Kingdom of Western Sun. Win or lose, that sucker's going down tonight. Figured you might want to pay your last respects."

"You think you know me..." Mene snarled.

Cord started laughing. "I think you've been staring at the castle walls long enough for me to walk over to Welles and ask for the bottle, listen to Quinn talk to her Fel buddies about lines of attack, and come back to find you in the exact same position I left you in. I think you're gonna miss your home, Vic. Tell me I'm wrong."

Mene hesitated, then took the bottle from Cord and swallowed down a drink. "You've always been an annoyance to me." He passed the bottle back to Cord.

Cord raised it in a salute, smiled, and kept himself quiet.

40. Nathan Cord's First Kill

To Victor Mene's chagrin, Cord might have been onto something. He had been feeling an emotion in his gut that could only be called Sadness. He had been born and raised with the singular, wonderful purpose of serving the Kingdom of Western Sun. He had protected, attacked, fought and killed for his homeland. But now he was following his final order: destroy the place that had created him.

Victor Mene was a man of such strength of will that he would chop off his own arm if it would suit the needs of the kingdom. And yet he found himself struggling with the notion of bringing the place down on itself.

Things used to be so much simpler. His mind drifted once again to that first week at the perimeter of Eastern Sun, to Cord's strategic gamble. At first light, Mene, Cord, and a dozen men handpicked by Mene from the regular regiment and from Coal's Brigade made their way to the easternmost part of the city, and while the primary force of the royal guard engaged the enemy at the western walls, Mene's tiny crew quietly took out the few soldiers who had, somewhat ironically, counted themselves as unfortunate that they would have to guard the eastern walls, thus missing the action on the main battlefield to the west.

Mene and his men scaled the walls easily, climbed them before those coalminers even knew what hit them. Mene took out three within the first minute of engagement. It gave him a moment to breathe. It gave him a moment to look to his left and see Cadet Nathan Cord shove his sword into the belly of the sentry that met him at the top.

Mene found himself the sole audience as the body slipped off the young man's blade and slumped to the ground, and saw something like horror creep up on Cord's face, apparently disgusted by what had just happened. Cord's reaction irritated the captain. He had hoped for more of a killer instinct from such a clever young tactician. Instead he saw a young man frozen by his own actions. And as he stood still, another guard approached Cord, ready to gut him with a short blade.

Mene didn't bother with a moment of thought. He pulled a throwing knife from his belt and let it fly. The blade breezed by Cord's head before sinking into the attacking soldier's forehead.

His hand still poised in the direction of the dropping corpse behind Cord, Mene still managed to notice another enemy sneaking up on him, and shoved his sword behind him, up into the man's belly.

Just another day's work for Victor Mene.

After that last kill, everything seemed calm. It was a welcome respite, but not one that would last for long. Yet Cord was still making like a statue.

"Cadet, at attention!" Mene barked at his subordinate, his voice low and guttural but easily heard.

Cord snapped out of his trance, shaking the fright off of his face. "...Sir. Apologies, sir. I didn't mean to..." And then, looking Mene dead in the eye with something Mene would later understand as remorse, he continued, "Sir, I killed that man."

Mene looked down at Cord's first kill. Nothing special. A small man, a bit on the pudgy side. One of the rebel miners. Not exactly a threat. He glared back at Cord, stepped up close to him, close enough that his spit could hit him easily. The boy needed a pep-talk.

"And you will kill many more, Nathan Cord. Get your head out of your ass. We're fighting for our lives here. You'll take off any head that doesn't look friendly at you, and you'll do it for king and country, do you understand me?"

"Yes sir," Cord had answered. Mene recognized a resolute tone in the boy's voice that he decided was for real.

"Good boy. Let's get in there."

And this small fighting force chosen by Mene worked their way to the throne room. On the way, they took the heads off soldiers, ran their blades through grunts, pointed their shortblades threateningly at young draftees. It took less than a day for Victor Mene to watch Cord turn into a real soldier. His first kill was a momentary shock. After that, he showed his real talents. He took out men twice his size and three times his savagery, and the further along they got, the quicker Cord used lethal force. And by the time they reached their destination, Nathan Cord had developed a fearsome growl. Mene figured that it helped make his kills feel more animalistic. It helped remove that juvenile sense of morality from the equation. Cord created and set loose a caged animal, a predator, born out of necessity, to absolutely destroy all oncoming threats.

On that day, Nathan Cord became a real killer. On that day, he made his captain proud. But if he were to ask Nathan Cord now about that day, Cord would mark that as the first time he had cast off a bit of his own humanity. With many more to follow.

"Yo! Vic!"

Mene realized that he had been reminiscing again. He shook the thoughts loose, returning himself to the here and now.

"C'mon, man. Two sips of rum and you're daydreaming?" A much older Nathan Cord glared at him. Mene still had the picture in his head of a shell-shocked, blood-spattered young cadet, and tried to reconcile that with the long-haired, one-eyed, bearded lunatic tapping him on the shoulder and still wearing that pitiful thing he thought of as a smile. "Guys at my bar would have a field day with you."

"I still remember your first kill, did you know that?" Mene told him, as close to pleasantly as he could muster. It still sounded like a scolding.

"No kidding?" Cord scratched his beard and pondered the idea. "Man, I don't even remember...that's a bit weird, Vic."

Mene accepted his lie and sternly returned, "Try not to be such a pussy this time around, Cord."

Before Cord could respond, Mene stood up and headed toward Quinn's command center. Cord looked at Mene, then at the kingdom, and chuckled to himself.

41. The Plan

Quinn Kind looked around. Her soldiers were getting antsy. That was good. It meant they wanted to fight. Maybe "wanted" was the wrong word, but they recognized the inevitability of fighting in the air, knew there wasn't any more waiting left, and were ready to accept what would come next. For better or worse, now was the time. She stepped out from the tent where she, Welles, and Saymon Q'iln had been finalizing their attack plans.

"EVERYONE!" she shouted, and raised the Stem. Each member of the Pic clan looked up. The Fel took no notice. So Quinn took a few steps forward, found a rock on the ground, and slammed the base of the Stem into it in two short sharp thrusts. It clacked loudly enough for everyone to hear.

All eyes were on her.

"Everyone. We're ready to go. Pic clan, Fel clan, listen up. Right now, those dead soldiers are trying to force their way out at the northern end of the kingdom walls. They know there's a whole new kingdom for them to head off to. The Northlands are closer than Kings Old Throne. So that's where they want to be. They smell live meat up there, so that's where they need to go. Acting Fel and Pic troop leaders, stand up."

Quentin Kind stood to attention. Quinn looked at her brother and saw no trace of the sarcastic lounger he only pretended to be. His face was deadly serious and absolutely ready to follow the orders of his acting queen. She quite loved her brother in that moment.

A young woman sitting among the Fel stood up. Quinn was actually surprised, but didn't let it show. She was covered in...at first Quinn thought it was some kind of war paint, but quickly realized her body was tattooed all over. The girl looked exactly like Quinn would have imagined the fiercest female Fel warrior would look. Terrifying, and yet oddly beautiful. She was happy the reality lined up with her imagination.

"What's your name, soldier?"

"Elaina Q'iln," she answered easily, pride in her voice.

Quinn looked behind her, and saw that same pride reflected in Saymon's face. "Your daughter?"

"You bet."

Turning back to the troops, Quinn continued. "Okay, listen up. Elaina, you and your troops are going to stay here, wait for the dead boys to head on over to this wall. When you hear enough of them to know they've caught your scent, go underground, erupt inside the wall, and flank them on each side. When you come up from the ground, keep your wits, don't get disoriented. You hit them with everything you've got. No room for error here. You take them out, or they'll eat you alive. I mean that literally."

"Yes Ma'am!" Elaina barked.

"Quentin, I want you to split your people up into two teams. Team one goes with Cord, Mene and Welles. You are their support crew. When the dead boys on that side start to thin out to a reasonable number, head down then come up, outflank them just like the Fel. You're going to make a path so our poor human friends here can come through the field without having to wade into a whole pack of hostiles."

Quentin responded respectfully, "Yes Ma'am."

"Cord and Mene."

Respecting Quinn's position, both men stood tall. Two leaders at her command. "Whatever you need, Quinn," Cord answered to her call. Mene stood silent. It was good enough.

"At the northern wall. The scouts tell me the hole those things have made is big enough for you to get through. Welles will brief you on your objectives when you're in position, then he'll get you through the barrier. You've got a special mission. It is essential that you succeed. Do you understand?"

Cord tossed a look at Welles. Welles gave a dead look back at him. Cord wouldn't have even recognized him as the man who had been drinking and joking with him by the fire the night before. He had to admit to being just a little impressed.

He didn't show it.

Then he glanced over at Mene. They silently shared the realization that their operation had become much more complicated than the initial "Re-Kill the Dead Guys" idea that they'd been both been working on in their heads during the ride toward the kingdom.

The fact that he was relieved to have Mene fighting with him disturbed him to no end.

Mene's was thinking mirrored Cord's.

He didn't show it.

"This is it, guys," Quinn continued, her tone low, sober, and serious. She gazed out at her troops, pride in her eyes. "I know we're not much. A small collection of Pics and Fel, and we're staring at a bunch of monsters numbering in the hundreds. But they are stupid and slow. And we are smart and fast.

"This is how we'll win.

"They can only react to what's in front of them. And all they can think to do is lunge at us or swing weapons haphazardly in our direction. They have no plan. They just want to kill. We know how to outmaneuver them. We know to take off their heads and aim for their hearts.

"This is how we'll win.

"All of you need to focus. You're going to sink into the ground and come up into the kingdom. From the moment you erupt, these things are going to start attacking you. And they are not going to stop. Focus. Make your movements swift, deliberate, and immediate.

"This is how we'll win.

"Take out anything that moves. Do not hesitate. I say again: Do. Not. Hesitate. We are here to be direct. We are here to be violent. We are here to be final.

"This is how we'll win. This is the only way we will win."

Quinn looked at her soldiers. Her Pic brothers. Her Fel cousins. Their attention, each and every one of them, was trained on her. She saw their faces. They heard her, and they believed everything she told them. It made her proud. And at the same time, their faith in her was terrifying.

She needed comfort, so she focused her eyes on finding friends. She peered out at Victor Mene and Nathan Cord. They were working so hard at keeping their faces expressionless, but she knew what they felt and gave them both a quiet nod of gratitude.

She looked over her shoulder at Welles. He tilted his head just slightly in her direction. She returned it. It would have to be enough.

These three men, who could not be more different. All with their own place in Quinn's heart. A man she respected. A man she trusted. And a man she loved.

For just a brief moment, Quinn lost track of her warrior-queen demeanor and wished she could break it all off, walk over to Welles and tell him just how much she loved him, and kiss him so long he'd never forget it. And though she hated it, she shook off that feeling, frustratingly aware that now was not the time or place.

She knew what Welles was going to have to go through very shortly. It was enough to break her heart.

But this was not the place for people with hearts. This was the place for warriors with armies.

Quinn Kind returned her eyes to her army. She pounded her staff against the rock once more, and shouted, "Tonight, we do the impossible. Tonight, Bloody Twilight falls. Who's with me?"

Cheers erupted. Not enough.

Quinn pounded her staff again. She shouted as loudly as her voice could carry. "TONIGHT, BLOODY TWILIGHT FALLS! WHO IS WITH ME?"

Every man and woman in this field, Pic, Fel, and human, roared in response.

They mobilized, and moved out to their positions.

Ready to kill Bloody Twilight for good.

Or die trying.

Part 3:
Burning Down
Bloody Twilight

42. The Hardest Part

Sword at the ready in his left hand, short blade handy in his right, Nathan Cord stared at the gaping hole in the wall that usually protected Bloody Twilight. That low, ugly wall had been there for hundreds of years, a symbol of strength and protection for the citizens of the Kingdom of Western Sun.

And it had been porous as all hell, if the gaping hole in it was any indication.

When he and Quinn had first become friends, the Pic girl shared with Cord a dozen stories of her people using their weird abilities to slip underneath that wall, into the kingdom, where they committed petty acts of thievery and vandalism in the name of youthful rebellion.

Once, Quinn had apparently stolen a curved short-blade from the bedroom of Cynthia Batale. Cynthia was just a kid at the time, but eventually became one of Kayla's friends. It made Cord laugh when Quinn told him about it. He told it to Kayla, who also laughed, but only after swearing to him on her life that she would never mention it to Cynthia. She was a big girl, quick with her fists, and so Cord couldn't see any benefit to her knowing. Her father had given that knife to her on her sixteenth birthday to fend off unwanted suitors. Lord knows what her mind was like with that kind of upbringing.

Looking at that hole in the wall, Cord was struck by the relative elegance of Pic thieving. He knew so many people who could slip under, or bounce over that wall. And those things inside were just pounding away at it, with their weapons, their fists, even their heads. It seemed violent and pathetic at the same time. And for a moment, Cord wondered how entwined those two traits actually were. He might have thought more about that, gotten downright philosophical in his mind, if he didn't have Victor Mene so close at hand.

"You're pacing," Cord heard behind him. He darted his good eye as far back into his skull as it would go, without turning his head around fully.

Mene was sitting on the hillside, flanked on each side with their personal array of Pic and Fel soldiers. He looked strangely comfortable, as though a patrol of woodland creatures watching his back was a regular occurance.

"So what if I am?" Cord asked, calmly. "I'd be stupid not to be nervous."

"Nervous." Mene rolled the word around in his mouth, then snarled when he looked back on Cord. "That's just the thing I like to hear from the former Coal Brigade chief. You continue to inspire, Cord."

Cord thought about arguing some more, but glanced again at the giant hole in the wall and decided it wasn't worth it. This massive barrier, set to keep enemies out and scare off anyone else who gave even a little thought to attacking...and these undead bastards were taking it apart brick by brick. Because they smelled live flesh to the north.

Quinn was banking on the fact that their senses of smell were keen enough to sniff out a tiny army of woodlanders at the western side of the wall. That they'd be more interested in a close target, and move away from the progress they'd made at their northern destruction site.

This was their great plan, Cord grudgingly accepted. And despite his incredulity, it was beginning to work. He could just make out the lack of bodies working the hole in front of him. Most of the dead soldiers had left this project, opting instead to pound their way through the wall to the west. They smelled the bigger sect of Pic and the Fel troops, and wanted to take them on. It was an obvious baiting strategy that no living soldier would fall for – "Come at us, we're so ripe and juicy and slow!" – but Quinn was also banking on the dimwittedness of their enemy, the fact that they would go for the close meal over the big one.

But some of the dead soldiers remained at the northern wall. Cord theorized that they were the fresher dead, the ones from the wagon Mene brought home after their most recent failure in the south. Maybe their senses were sharper than the ones who were just barely whole enough to dig themselves out of their graves, under Grolev's spell. All conjecture at this point.

Those remaining dead must have smelled the live fleshy things sitting on the hillside waiting for change, and crept through the hole. Free of the kingdom wall, a few of them ran the twenty feet it took to get them to Welles' big yellow energy-field. It zapped them. Hard. They stepped back into the hole, angry and confused. It wasn't a major shift from their previous demeanor. But they got close enough that Cord could make out one of their faces.

"Holy hell, that's Silas Platt." He checked back with Mene, surprise and curiosity on his face. "Vic, you remember Silas Platt?"

"Platt?" Mene asked, similarly curious, but not alarmed. "I thought I'd taken him down on my way out."

Cord thought for a moment, then remembered out loud, "No, Platt was a dead ringer for Artie Boggs. We used to tease them about it. Platt was like a tall version of Artie, you remember that?"

Mene made a face like he was thinking on what Cord had just said, but then responded, "You're talking a lot."

Cord knew what Mene was implying. He dodged, "Somebody's got to carry this conversation."

Mene ignored the attempt at levity. "Pacing. Chattering. You'd better still be useful in a fight, Cord."

"Just hang back, Vic. It's what you're good at. Hanging around with your big old army while the little guys like Coal Brigade do all the hard work." Cheap shot, Cord knew, and not exactly accurate. But he found himself aching for a fight, and this would have to do, before the real thing kicked in.

Mene answered quickly and calmly, "And now you're revising history. Honestly, Cord, the pixie girl's crush on you must be coloring her judgment if she thinks you're still the fighter she remembers." It actually took Cord off guard, the quickness of Mene's rejoinder. It bugged him more than he thought it should. He thought for a few moments, and remembered some of the more bizarre moments he'd had with the royal guard. Particularly his time as chief of Coal Brigade.

It wasn't a fight he wanted, he realized, so much as interesting conversation. The urge to kill Mene had quelled, leaving the reminder that the captain was one of the few men Cord knew who remembered the same things he did. And since being drafted back into service by Quinn, he had developed a tendency to dredge up old memories. For the first in a long time, he felt the urge to share them. Because Cord had always been a clever tactician, he searched and finally found some middle ground to share with Mene.

He offered, "You remember that time in Beasts Old Throne where me and my guys hid ourselves in Plague Creek? Not sure if there was more mud than waste in there, and we laid in that crap for the better part of three days breathing out of reeds, picking off the advance scouts one by one, just so when your guys were ready to go, the enemy didn't have any kind of intelligence on your numbers when you finally – FINALLY – bothered attacking."

"That was your idea, if I recall. Sounds strange and improbable enough that it would be one of your ideas, anyway."

Cord folded his arms. "Well. It worked."

"That it did."

If Cord could have picked one thing about Victor Mene that pissed him off more than anything else, it was that the man never raised his voice in an argument. He used that same cool, level, mildly condescending tone, every time. The popular opinion was that Victor Mene was a great leader and a crap conversationalist. But Cord knew that wasn't quite the reality. Mene strategized arguments the same as a battle. Keep the high ground.

Cord hated so much about Mene, but he really did admire that aspect of the man. Sometimes.

Noting with some irritation that the dead soldiers weren't leaving their hole as quickly as Quinn and Welles had figured, Cord sheathed his weapons. He found pacing much more comfortable with his fists empty and clenched.

There was no sound for a while. Just the air lazily breezing past them. Springtime. Cord only now noticed that winter had passed them all by without any heavy weather. He felt like it had been deathly cold only a few days ago, but realized this warmth must have been around for a couple of weeks, at least. Now that he recognized it, the new air felt good. It occurred to Cord that under normal circumstances, this would be considered a beautiful evening.

Mene's low bass voice broke the serenity, startling Cord in the process. "Do you remember the monk gambit?"

Cord glared at Mene, but sifted through his memories just the same. Both of them were still reminiscing over Beasts Old Throne days. Probably the last time things felt right. Felt normal, like they were doing something that needed to be done. He remembered the monk gambit. The memory made him laugh.

"Okay, that was one of my worse ideas."

Mene stood up from his perch on the hill, walked down to Cord. "Yes, it was," he confirmed, then checked over his shoulder. That's when Cord noticed that their miniscule regiment of Pic and Fel soldiers was listening intently to their conversation. They probably had been the entire time.

It was the war stories. Everyone likes listening to war stories. Especially when they're being told from two points of view that lived to tell the tale. They like comedies this way, too, Cord knew, and indeed it did feel like the two of them were performing some well-rehearsed routine. Cord wondered which of them was the joker, and which was the straight man.

He glanced at Mene for the briefest of moments, and caught it in his eye. Mene was actually enjoying the attention. Despite all his instincts, it made Cord crack a smile. He didn't mind the attention himself. Before he knew it, he was storytelling.

"Even during the war years," Cord started, offering the tale just as he had to his own soldiers, back when he had soldiers to call his own, "Beasts Old Throne – it's Kingdom of Eastern Sun now, but back in the day we called it Beasts Old Throne, like you Fel boys know it – they would take in the monks from that abbey out in the northeast. It seemed pretty obvious to me at the time, that a quick way into their kingdom would be for Coal Brigade to masquerade as monks, bringing in their usual batch of wine, like they didn't know there was a battle going on..."

Mene added with some small amusement, "Hearing you tell it now, I can't imagine what I was thinking, that I signed on to this plan."

Cord looked Mene and pointed, mock-accusingly, "You wanted unconventional thinking! So blame falls on you. As far as you were concerned, I was still a rookie, so I don't know what you thought I was doing. But yeah, we dressed up like monks and tried to gain entry through the front gate."

Both Pic and Fel were captivated by the story. Cord continued.

"What we didn't know, even after a full week of recon, was that they had a codeword. We never picked up on it. When the actual monks showed up at the door – and by the way, we never hurt those guys, we just stripped them down, tied them up, and stuck 'em in the woods – we heard the same words, over and over. 'You've brought our wine?' 'Yes we have, good sir.' Every time, that's what they said."

Mene added, "If Coal Brigade had simply staked out the front gate for one more day, they would have realized that the code word *changed weekly*…"
Cord reacted as though he had been offended, but in reality he still felt the embarrassment from his first major folly as a strategist. "Well, that's neither here nor there. Point is, if we had just said 'Yes we have, *fine* sir,' Coal Brigade would have been in the main courtyard cutting those guards up like there was no tomorrow."

The Pic and Fel both started laughing. Cord loved telling the story, and realized that during his exile, in those seven years of sitting in a boat, sitting in the woods, sitting in a bar and pretending not to be the former leader of Coal Brigade, the man who killed the king…he sort of missed it.

"Well, long story short, those guys pulled their swords real quick, and my guys – you have to realize, they were in disguise, and monks don't carry swords…"

Mene finished the thought. "If you've never seen men in monk's robes beat the living hell out of trained soldiers, you've missed out. It was an awful plan, but it may have been worth it simply for that image."

"We won that fight, by the way," Cord finished, hoping to keep the honor of Coal Brigade intact.

For another hour, Cord and Mene took turns watching the number of dead soldiers by the hole decrease, as they passed the time telling war stories to their men. But Cord periodically scoped out Welles, who stood a hundred feet away, high up on that hill, far from their small group. Staring intently at something Cord knew he didn't have the proper eyes to see.

Eventually, Cord checked in with Mene, in order to feel out his assessment of the magician. "That Welles is a clever son of a bitch," he offered, hoping to get some reaction.

"I don't disagree."

"If he keeps us all alive, you remind me to thank him for that later."

Mene made no movement either way, just responded, "I'm sure he'll appreciate it."

The cliché stands that the waiting is always the hardest part, Cord thought to himself. He never really understood that. The waiting is hard. But

149

then, of course, there's the battle. The battle makes the waiting look like a stroll in the park.

He glanced back up at Welles, wondering what the magician thought the hardest part might be.

43. Protected

Welles pretended not to listen to Mene and Cord as they shared war stories. It was fascinating stuff, to be sure, and a part of him was happy to see the two falling back into a comfort zone with each other. Anything that kept them from killing each other was good news, as far as Welles was concerned.

During their planning sessions over the last two days, whenever Welles had broached the subject of how two men who apparently hated each other would be able to partner up, Quinn had only ever smiled and answered, "I have faith in them."

It was the only point in the planning stages when Quinn would smile. So he let it go.

Of course she was right. That said, he was still as worried as ever.

More so, since they'd reached the barrier. Now that he could feel the citizens still trapped inside. He was worried about them, and about his team's ability to save them. But he was also concerned for himself. He'd experienced quite a bit in his time, but this was new. For the first time, he felt unsure of his abilities.

He was a very good magician. Why be modest – he was a great magician. Ego aside, there was simply no question. Studying with Keegan Morris, he was the star pupil. And when he lost contact with his teacher, he used the absence of a mentor as an opportunity to spread his wings. For years, he traveled, met other mystics, and learned from them.

A peacefulTree-bob who had managed first-person direct communication with the earth. A group of Fel brothers who could start fires with their laughter. A hermit south of Beasts Old Throne who used sex to alter probability. And there was that strange, off-putting little man to the north, Wiggans, who could see through time. He learned lessons from all of them.

By the time he headed to the seaside out west, Welles had made a dozen foreign techniques his own. Out there, he met a healer who sold him a case of rum and an invulnerability spell for the knowledge of a dying day. Not his own, but rather a pirate by the name of Mudd who had wronged the healer in some way.

Welles had used Wiggans' techniques, and in doing so heard the name Nathan Cord for the second time in his life. The first...well, everyone knew Cord's name after they found Arius's body.

Welles was almost curious enough to ask Cord why he had needed to kill that man just as he had predicted. He hadn't found an opportune time, and highly doubted that he ever would.

Especially since he would likely need the former chief of Coal Brigade to keep his ass alive. Though Welles had lately been wondering if he really would need Cord. Or Mene. Or any of them.

He felt something else inside the bubble, something he only sort of recognized. But it was powerful, familiar. And without really understanding why, Welles knew he could use it.

"Hey, Welles!" Cord hollered up from the bottom of the hill. "Quick question!" Cord was smiling. Welles had many times been assured that this was a bad sign. His entire body tensed up.

Cord must have noticed, because as he got closer, he slowed down and put his hands out to his sides, to display non-aggressive behavior. When he reached the top of the hill, close enough to look Welles in the eye, Cord chuckled good-naturedly. "Man...what'd you think, I was coming up here to beat you up?"

Welles unclenched, just a little. He felt dangerously self-conscious. "Well, y'know. I'm a career magician. People like to pick on guys like me."

Cord frowned like it was new information he hadn't taken into account. "Really?" His pace quickened. "Why would..."

"Ahh, just, guys like me don't blend in with soldiers and the like. Or farmers, or ranchers. Not even scholars, really. Magicians tend to spook people out. They usually respond by picking fights. And I'm not really a fighter, if you couldn't tell..." He raised his hands, palm-up, to show off his thin, lanky frame. "Y'know?"

Cord made a thinking face, then looked Welles in the eyes, and answered seriously, "I'm not most people, Welles. Never have been. Not great odds that I ever will be." He actually looked a bit hurt at Welles' insinuation.

"Just a reflex, Cord."

"Nathan. Told you, call me Nathan."

"Sorry. Nathan. Just years of paranoia – "

Then Welles saw Cord's left fist shoot up, aiming to collide with his jaw. The punch connected fiercely.

And he felt it like a ten-year-old was hurling a pillow at him. It sent him staggering a good two inches back.

It was still an unwelcome feeling. After shaking off the initial shock, Welles glared accusingly at his attacker. But Cord – who had been knocked to the ground as a result of the blow – was mostly enamored with his own fist, and the lack of damage it had done.

Welles felt no sympathy. "What the hell, man?!"

Cord gave a look to his fist, then Welles, then his fist again. And then he grinned, and Welles reminded himself never to question Quinn's "Cord smiling is a bad thing" theory, ever again.

Still on the ground, Cord propped himself up to a sitting position, and hollered down the hill, in Victor Mene's direction, "HA! Told you! You owe me twenty bucks!"

Dumbfounded, Welles put the pieces together. "You wanted to see…"

Cord hopped up to his feet and brushed the dirt off his butt before finishing Welles' sentiment, "Yeah, wanted to see if that invulnerability spell of yours worked out for you. Mene bet me it wouldn't take. I was in your corner, man." He patted Welles on the shoulder proudly. "Good job!" Cord seemed genuinely pleased.

Then his grin dropped. "So now that we know it's up and running, any way we can put it on our guys? Not me, necessarily, but Vic's such a fragile flower – "

Welles lobbed a punch into Cord's jaw, sending him tumbling down the hill.

After stopping his fall, Cord looked up at Welles. Startled, but mostly amused.

"Didn't see that coming, I'll admit. I'll take that as a no?"

Welles scowled. "I spent hours putting up that spell. I can't just throw it around like confetti."

He paced for a few moments, before concluding, "DAMN IT!" louder than he had planned.

Properly chastened, Cord stood up and started his walk back to his troops. "Fair enough. And I'm sorry to have snuck up on you like that. But Welles? It's gonna be a long night. I know you're scared. We all are. But if you don't get a grip on it…you're no use to us." Then he turned and finished his walk down the hill.

Welles looked at his fist, and saw that it was trembling horribly. He closed his eyes and concentrated, until he felt the trembling stop.

Cord couldn't possibly understand. Welles wasn't afraid of the coming horrors. He understood the severity of the task.

But he had barely felt that punch land. And now his hand had started glowing. A color very close to that of the dome that covered Western Sun.

Welles was fighting off the terror of realizing that since they'd reached the kingdom, it seemed that he had grown more powerful than anyone, himself included, could imagine.

And if that wasn't concern enough, he'd also never been in a fight before.

44. The Signal

Quinn had decided that her grand plan – act as bait to get the majority of the dead soldiers over to her wall, giving Cord and his boys the opening to get into the kingdom – was perhaps stupider than she'd originally considered. These are the opinions you form when you have nothing to do but dwell on your own ideas, and no one around you to tell you otherwise.

She was the lone advisor to a bunch of rowdy Fel and quietly panicking Pic. She could have used Cord to calm them with a quiet "There's a good chance we won't all die" pep talk, though she knew it had been years since he'd had to deliver one of those, and figured he'd be rusty anyway. She would have even settled for another one of Victor Mene's "You'll die for Queen and Country and love every bit of it" rousers.

What she had was Saymon Q'iln periodically hollering "GET PSYCHED!" to his troops, which elicited raucous "YEAAAAAAHHHH!!"s from his people, and sideways glances from hers.

No. When she thought about it, what she really needed was Welles subtly reaching for her hand when he sensed that she was getting stressed. But Cord and Mene needed him more. This is the kind of decision a leader makes.

If that's what a leader does, Quinn frowned to herself, it ain't worth it.

But of course holding hands with her boyfriend wasn't any kind of strategy, and she knew it. She was too smart, too well-versed in the roles of Pic motherhood, to think that just running away with your lover was anything other than a nice, calming fantasy.

It still hurt.

At that moment, she truly understood how deeply Welles had gotten into her system, and wondered when that had happened. She'd only met him a little under a year ago. And had distinctly disliked him that first time. He was so...*haughty* about the whole magic thing. He liked who he was *so much*. But that arrogance brought with it this genuine, wondrous fascination toward the things he didn't know. He very much wanted to understand the Pic culture, and it wasn't just because it was a source of knowledge he could exploit. Quinn had been wary of magicians since Grolev dug his claws into Bloody Twilight. But when this lanky, boyish magic user, this enthusiastic student of Keegan Morris showed up, she couldn't help but be infected by his enthusiasm. She wanted to teach him things. And he was such an adept student.

She introduced him to her mothers, and they reacted much as Quinn had, but everyone knew that it was beneficial to them, to have a magician immersed in Pic philosophies and moreso, Pic ideals. He made himself at home in the village, but never became a burden. He had even offered to help with daily chores. He was terrible at them, but it really was the thought that counted.

Looking back, Quinn figured that that was the first time she'd seen Welles as more than a voracious student, started to see him as a truly interested, good-hearted man.

And he'd become friends with Quentin. She had never been the most popular member of her community. That role fell to Quentin, and she was perfectly happy for that to be the case.

Though Quentin would never say it, Quinn knew that her brother had gotten the shortest of short straws by being born only minutes after her. He was a boy in a girl's world, and would never get the family benefits bestowed upon Quinn. She had made pains to compensate over the years, especially after the mothers had appointed her ambassador to Western Sun. In an unofficial but, in her mind, much-needed capacity, she had appointed Quentin to be her own personal advisor.

If Quinn had genetically received leadership capabilities, Quentin had gotten the people skills. Everyone liked him, he was probably the most adept student of the battle arts, and he could get people around to his way of thinking just by being him. It was a talent some could learn, but not in the intrinsic way he displayed. She admired that, and so she made sure he knew that she looked to him to tell her how to make people like her.

Not that she was always the best student. But just as she learned how to be a better leader from Quentin, she had begun to learn how to be a better learner from Welles. Her schooling from these two teachers eventually intersected.

A little over six months ago, when she and Quentin had been talking idly, the subject of Welles came up. "I think he's working out pretty well here, right?" she fished, waiting for Quentin's more thorough opinion to come out.

"Very well. He's learned a lot here, and better yet, he likes being here. We were playing handball the other day, and he told me – "

"You guys play handball?"

Like she'd asked whether they both breathe air, he answered slowly, "We play ball. We joke around and drink together. We play cards and one of these days I swear I'll win a hand or two...why is that surprising?"

Quinn didn't really know for sure, but quickly realized that she still viewed Welles as an outsider to their community, when that was apparently no longer the case. If Quentin and Welles had become friends, then that meant everyone else had accepted him, too. She felt behind the curve. "I guess I figured people were still a little wary of him."

Giving that Quentin smile, charming and mocking at the same time, he answered, "No, *you're* still a little wary of him. You've stood back this whole time, letting him into the village, letting him learn from us, but have you ever, say, talked to him?"

"What, like a conversation?"

Quentin's eyes popped out a little. "Wow. Yes, like when two people talk to each other, that's a lot like a conversation. Do you even know his first name?"

It felt like an anvil had dropped on Quinn's head. "'Welles' isn't his full name?"

Quentin reiterated, "Wow."

She shoved him on the shoulder. "Shut up, I have a lot of stuff on my mind."

"Sure, sure. Want some advice?"

Quinn smiled and sighed, the conversation finally ending up where she had hoped. "Always."

Quentin advised his sister to take a walk with the magician. She still wasn't sure why she had worked hard to avoid him up to that point. There was just something in her that felt like making friends with Welles would be a betrayal of the Pic code in reference to non-clan – namely, "Don't get too close with those outside your clan" – especially since they had been trying to recede from the looming threat that Western Sun had slowly become. There had been enough concern from her mothers when they learned how close she had gotten to Nathan and Kayla Cord.

That simple little walk, with this gawky wizard...thinking back to that day, Quinn smiled with her eyes closed. Which is always a bad sign. Happy people do that. And now was not the time for Quinn to be happy. Undead monsters clawing at the walls waiting to take a bite out of everyone she knew...not a place for the contented to be.

That first walk. Quinn had put on her business face, telling Welles all about the Pic social structure, and how their distrust of humans was trumped only by their fears of humans mastering mystic arts. She had been trying to scare Welles, but to what purpose, she couldn't really remember anymore. Maybe if he had been afraid of the Pics, and her in particular, he wouldn't get himself further involved with them. And he'd stop trying to make her like him.

But he hadn't been scared off at all. Quite the opposite; it looked like everything she told him about Pic culture and their concerns regarding magic-users...he was so curious about everything. Completely fascinated, amazed, and absolutely without guile. And as they walked, Quinn couldn't help but notice that roses sprouted up from the ground wherever the walk led them. She pretended not to see them. Didn't want to give him any ideas. But occasionally, she glanced over at him, and found that he was unable to hide his smile. He beamed with admiration and contentment. But he never once let on how much he was showing off, just to impress this girl he met and found that he quite liked.

Quinn fell in love with Welles right there and then. But she held off on telling him that for months.

She managed to avoid telling him for so long, that it took Bloody Twilight being overrun by reanimated dead men to make her even broach the subject.

It was after he came into her room. After he had, in embarrassment, confessed that Cord had deduced their relationship. And after she had welcomed him into her bed, disregarded his silly transgression. And they made love, even if they didn't call it that.

After the passion was over, he wrapped his arms around her. When she felt his warm body on hers, she finally broke her silence. "Welles?"

"Hmm?" He exhaled casually. Not a care in the world. Typical guy behavior, though Quinn actually enjoyed it when the veneer of magician dropped and he showed himself to be just a regular human male.

She tried for the same breezy tone, but looking back, she wasn't sure how casually hers came off. "I think, you know...you being you, and me being...uhm. Welles?"

"Still here," he acknowledged.

"I think I love you." She didn't like how it sounded, and tried again. "Yeah. So. I'm in love with you. And, uh...that's what's going on, there."

There was silence for several excruciating seconds, before he responded, "Well, yeah. Obviously."

She elbowed him in his ribs.

"Aaoww!"

"I'm serious."

Welles ran one hand through her hair, as he caressed her body with his free hand. "I'm serious, too."

He placed his hand on her cheek, turned her so that they were facing each other. And he looked at her, his face nothing but honesty and pride. "Quinn Kind. I am absolutely, hopelessly in love with you."

She clung to those words. Just a matter of hours earlier, but suddenly she felt like they'd been spoken a lifetime ago.

It just wasn't fair. Two people confessing love for each other should feel immediate, always. Not like this. Not wondering if it was just something to say because death seems imminent.

Staring at the wall, Quinn wanted to shout out violent curses to the sky. She could have told the man at any point that she felt that way, but decided to wait until the central kingdom of the region started eating itself alive just to tell him what he had been waiting to hear for months?

"What the hell," Quinn found herself muttering. "That poor son of a…"

"QUINN KIND!"

Quinn rubbed her temples wearily. "Oh god, protect me from this crazy man."

Saymon Q'iln wanted an audience. He was beaming with glee.

"Yes, Saymon, what's up?" She had her diplomatic face on. This was a face she had learned from her mothers. One of the few things she knew that Quentin didn't.

He grabbed her shoulders excitedly. "We've counted a couple hundred at the wall, m'dear. Now's the time. Let's wreck these things up. My boys have been waiting all day!"

Quinn scanned the barrier. Her own heightened senses could hear their movements, could smell their rotting flesh. And Welles had taught her rudimentary means of reading through the barrier, seeing their shadows. She knew there were masses of bodies clawing at wall. They smelled her makeshift army. Quinn's plan had fallen into place after all.

Only one thing to do. When she looked back to her men, she saw that they were already in position. The waiting was over. She felt no hesitation, and gave the order.

"LIGHT 'EM UP!"

The Fel and Pic worked together to shoot fireworks up into the sky, giving Cord and Mene's secondary team the signal, that the plan had worked so far. That they could attack the dead men's remainder, while Quinn's Fel and Pic attack force took on the brunt of the monster population.

Saymon Q'iln gave Quinn a curious look. It frustrated her. This guy was supposed to be the big chief of the Fel clan. And he was looking to her for confirmation of attack plans. For a moment, she wondered how far up the Pic chain of command he thought she was.

She wondered herself, for a moment, and then decided that it didn't matter. She was the only Pic Mother here. She may not have been branded in ceremony, might not have spoken any official oaths in front of her entire clan. But the boys with her right then knew that she would go to hell for them, and that was enough of an oath for them to devote themselves to her, as they would any Mother.

She wondered briefly if Quentin had told them to. And if he had, then bless him and keep him safe. The fireworks went up. She raised the Stem, and shouted, "LET'S GO! YEEEAAAAAHHH!"

Both Pic and Fel erupted in kind, and charged toward the kingdom.

Quinn was proud of her fighting force. Stem raised high, she charged in with her people into certain oblivion. But in the back of her mind, she held on to Welles. She hoped he would see that the fireworks her people shot up were more than a signal.

She hoped he would see that they were a love letter from her, to him.

45. Go

And there it was. Finally. Fireworks, lighting up the night sky. Victor Mene was first to notice the signal. And to him, it looked…beautiful.

Immediately, he shrugged the feeling off. Mene was not one to use words like "beautiful." He liked words like "work," and "fight," and "cunning." He had never had much use for words like "beautiful." But those lights popping in the dark. He couldn't help but admit that they were perhaps the prettiest things he'd seen in a long time.

"Cord! Welles! Stop your tea party and get ready!"

Another word Mene liked was "orders."

He stared down the hole in the wall. Still a great many of his dead men milling about, working to get free. He instinctively catalogued in his mind which ones had weapons and which were simply clawing at the bricks barehanded.

"You sad bastards," he growled, a smile curling on his face. None of them had ever seen Victor Mene smile when they were alive. That was by design. Mene never wanted any of them to like him. He wanted them to obey. In his tenure as captain, he had been mostly successful. With very few exceptions.

One such case came running down the hill, swords brandished and battle-ready. "We're on?" Cord asked calmly.

"We're on." Mene started toward their small band of soldiers, but stopped. Under normal circumstances, he would shout an order and his men would follow, but as Cord had made painful strides to explain, normal circumstances had gone and vanished on him. He looked at Cord, and then at Welles, who followed the king-killer down the hill. He didn't walk down it, he hovered. Mene decided then and there that he would not mind hurting the magician, just to introduce a little humility into his life. But Cord had just made it clear to him that Welles was beyond injury. And though it wounded his heart, he was honor-bound to give Cord twenty dollars because of that.

There was almost nothing happening at this point that Victor Mene was happy about. Except for those lovely fireworks. Those bright spots that told him he could commit to violence for a little while against deserving foes. Probably the only language he could consider himself fluent.

"So. Who wants to lead the charge?" Mene asked his two compatriots. It made him feel unwell, to ask such a question. Maybe he was growing as a person. That thought made him feel worse.

Cord looked at Welles, then back at him. "The Pic boys already heard you giving your 'Let's all go and die, it'll be fun' speech. Probably you should do it."

Mene nodded, then checked Welles' expression. The magician seemed frightened enough to mess himself, but nevertheless asked, "I don't suppose you want to say anything...?"

It surprised him when Welles did speak up. But not to him. He turned to the hill, and shouted, "Quentin!"

The first among Pics was down the hill and in front of them faster than the blink of an eye. "So we're ready?"

Welles nodded. "They know you. They trust you. Call them out."

Quentin made no accepting motion, simply glanced at Welles, then at Cord. Cord looked at him with a rare expression. It wasn't the devil's grin Mene had grown to know over the years. It was something like respect.

The Pic boy turned to his brethren – brothers and cousins.

"Rise up!" he shouted.

Each man rose. "Present arms!"

Each man drew his weapon.

"We go in now. You men will fight off the enemy. Go for the head and the chest. Anything else will be a failure. You are to clear a path for the magician, the captain, and the king-killer. That is your sole mission. Wherever they go, you are their shadows. Anything comes within twenty feet of them, you kill it. Is that understood?"

The troops answered yes. But not quite forcibly enough.

Quentin bellowed out the order again, "IS. THAT. UNDERSTOOD." Not a question.

"YES SIR!" their soldiers shouted out in unison.

Quentin looked a question at Mene, silently conveying, *These are* my *men. Will you respect the chain of command?*

Mene stared out into the pack, then looked back to their leader. "Quentin, you seem to know these idiots' names. Direct them where they need to go, should they get confused."

Though Mene expected some annoying, quippy rejoinder, Quentin only nodded proudly and responded, "Sounds like a plan, captain."

Satisfied, Mene checked out Cord and Welles. "I think they're ready. What about you two?"

Welles shrugged his shoulders, and then seemed to realize that was the exact wrong move. So he focused on Mene and answered, "We're ready."

Cord just grinned. Back to that shark's grin Mene remembered. "Wow. You almost, kind of let Quentin take the lead. That was nice, Vic."

He glared into Cord's eye, and after a moment finally said, "Let's go." Then, to the Pic leader, simply, "Quentin." The Pic stood front and center, though Mene recognized it to be little more than offering a courtesy to the captain. He gave one back. "Give the command."

To every man that took his word as an order, Quentin bellowed, "LET'S GO!"

Victor Mene liked the word "go," too. He liked shouting it, and he liked hearing people shout it back. But it had become clear to him over the last day or so that this battle was about more than him. The Pics had their stake in it too. The Pics, and the Fel, and Welles, and even Nathan Cord. In spite of himself, Mene understood.

They charged together, into the hell that had become the Kingdom of Western Sun.

46. Saviors

The Orphan heard bombs exploding, rubble crumbling, and then shouting. Lots of shouting. Remembering the Pic teachings of Quinn Kind, she focused, and found that within that cacophony, she could pick out different tones. Some of it was excited, some even gleeful. Most of it sounded like people trying to scare off their own fears. But to her ears, it all sounded glorious. It sounded like hope.

She checked on Grolev. Still sitting there in his corner. She suspected that he wasn't doing anything magical. She felt like he was waiting for something. And it wasn't rescue.

Allison hated being in the same room as this man. She was too young to really remember Keegan Morris as a person, but she knew that she had met him as a child, and he had informed her idea of what a magician was supposed to look like. Bearded, long-haired, a friendly smile and kind eyes that looked at you like they really knew you.

The first time she had met Grolev, she might have mistaken him for a scarecrow, garbed in dark colors, greasy black hair, that pale, sunken expression. His eyes looked at you like they knew you, too. Knew you, and everything in you you didn't like, and he hated you for it. She remembered the first time he'd held those bony fingers out at her to shake hands, saying something in a voice made of toxic smoke and spent charcoal, about being sure they'd become great friends. Not even pretending to believe it in his own wheezing voice.

She found him completely reprehensible from the moment she'd met him, and the years had done nothing to change that opinion. For her entire life, she had felt her skin crawl with every minute spent in a room with this nightmare masquerading as a man.

Peering out through the window, she saw something that could be called a miracle. But she had read a lot of Keegan Morris's writings, and embraced his philosophy by simply deeming it "exquisitely good timing."

A small army was plowing through the barrier and past the western walls.

Quinn Kind had come to save her and her people.

"Grolev, have you made contact with Quinn?" She asked it as a test, but knew that a hint of excitement had come through just the same.

"Quinn Kind…" Grolev started, uncertainly. He wore a scowl. He always wore a scowl, but this was different. Nobody ever gave Allison enough credit for her ability to read the nuances of expression. She knew that Grolev had done nothing, and was thinking quickly to cover that up.

He gave an approving look like this was entirely possible. "Quinn Kind has made her way through the barrier," he non-answered.

"She knew we were here!" This time the Orphan made no pains to hide her enthusiasm. Another explosion erupted outside. She ran to the northern window. More soldiers. Hairy, crazy, chopping at everything. One man seemed to be floating. But she focused her eyes like Quinn had taught her, and saw two men she recognized.

"That's Captain Mene." Then her voice hushed. "And…no, it couldn't be."

Grolev must have read her tone, the mix of wariness and pride that she herself was trying to make sense of. The wizard's response marked the first time the Orphan had ever seen him stumble to his feet and run. It was awkward and unflattering, and unintentionally funny. Not at all the pompous way that he carried himself usually, and it made him oddly human to her just for a moment. He regained his footing when he got to her side, and asked breathlessly, "What? Who is it?"

With just a slight hint of smugness, she answered, "That, sir, is Nathan Cord."

"The man who killed your father." He said this with a frown. And then it twisted up into a smile. And the Orphan was more frightened than ever, that she was locked in the same room as this man.

"So then Quinn received my summons," Grolev lied to her. "She has come for you, my queen."

She put her fear away, stuffed it in a box and decided to let her anger loose. "Stop it, Grolev," Allison scolded. "I know you think I'm stupid, just a silly little girl, but you're not half as clever as you think you are. I don't know what you've been doing, but my Quinn did not come here because you summoned her."

She had expected him to lie some more, with increasing eloquence as he concocted a story out of thin air, like a magician might.

She hadn't expected Grolev to backhand her across her jaw, dropping her to the floor.

Towering over her, trying too hard to appear threatening, Grolev peered down, and cracked his knuckles. Without bending any of his fingers.

"I've been waiting years to do that," he sneered, hate and pleasure rolled up in one declaration. "For the record, dear girl, I never considered you stupid. Just…" he stopped hiding his smile, and it was grotesque and horrid in full view. "No, I think I *have* considered you stupid. You want to play the big girl? Fine. I'm going to kill you, little Allison. Little Allison Kendra Quinn…named after all your mothers. One a dead whore, the other a silly little wench fancies herself a leader. You've got a pathetic pedigree, little Orphan. I'm going to kill you when I'm good and ready, so just shut up and sit down like a good girl."

He raised his hand. Allison attempted to stand, fully expecting him to strike her again, and preparing herself for the impact. But he just twisted his palm and she fell flat to the floor, suddenly unable to move, like a long flat slab of granite sat on her entire body.

She wanted to curse him defiantly, but "Gghhh!" was all she could manage.

Grolev towered above her. "Just shut up, dear. This will all be over soon." Then, after examining his remark, he clarified, "Though hopefully not too soon."

47. The Blue Knives

Crushed against the floor, completely unable to move, the Orphan had never felt so vulnerable. But from the day she was born, it had been ingrained in her, that when things looked as bleak as they could be, there was one phrase that could save her. And so she reached deep inside herself, inside lungs that felt like they were being pushed through her chest. She found just enough air to shout, "Blue Knives! Come to me!"

Her warrior monks. Her Blue Knives. Like many things in the region, their name was a product of the location of their home and training grounds, in the Temple of the Indigo Sunrise. The Kingdom of Western Sun has the privilege of watching twilight, as it reflects off the water of the ocean, through the trees of the Pic forest, casting the kingdom in a wild pattern of orange and shadow. The temple of the Order of the Indigo Sunrise is located at the easternmost boundary, in the shadow of the kingdom. The light they see is the muted blue that comes just before dawn.

In the kingdom's shade hundreds of years ago, they had founded their order, devoting themselves only to the preservation of the royal bloodline. They successfully protected their charges, each member of the royal family, for centuries. But the last decade had not seen their finest moments. King Lucius the New died of a disease they had no means of combating. When he died, they pledged themselves to Allison's father. And somehow, they failed to save him. No one knew how this could have happened. And none of the Knives would explain. They did not speak.

So it was only conjecture that their failure to protect Arius caused them to redouble their efforts in keeping the Queen in Waiting safe. For seven years, she had no family of her own and few friends. And she knew that her death would allow any number of would-be sovereigns to take the throne. But there was never a single instance where she learned of a threat to her life. All because of the Order of the Indigo Sunrise. Her Blue Knives. Silent, lithe, and for all practical purposes, invisible, unless they wished to be seen. Ready to kill, ready to die, for the orphaned princess alone.

A dozen of them burst through the door, weapons ready. Rough canvas masks, matte black, covering their stolid expressions. They held no love or hate in their hearts. Only devotion to an ideal. Protect the sovereign of the Kingdom of Western Sun.

Their devotion was a strangely warming presence to her, much as an imaginary friend is to a small child. She took comfort in them. There was some irony in this, because as a child, the mere idea of them had terrified her. Her father had tried to introduce them as friends once, but it hadn't helped. That introduction to their nameless, mute commander when she was five years old gave her nightmares for months afterward.

They were completely unlike anything she'd ever come in contact with. She'd known soldiers all her life. But these men weren't soldiers. They didn't even seem to be human. In her child's mind, they were ghosts. Terrifyingly alien in every way.

When she had confessed her nightmares to her father, he tasked Nathan Cord as her chaperone to their temple, where they would present a performance, a demonstration of their prowess. Cord treated the excursion as a holiday for the young princess. She remembered him knocking on her door the evening before, telling her that he and his wife, Kayla, were going to see "some acrobats. They're really neat. They're kind of like jugglers, but they do this stuff with swords even I can't do." He admitted in a conspiratorial whisper, "Aunt Kayla thinks they're better with a blade than me," then rolled his eyes, "but I'm not so sure. You want to see them with us, maybe tell Kay that I'm still the number one swordsman in the land?" He gave her a quick grin, and that was all it took to get her excited.

She hardly slept that night.

After a half a day's ride on a wagon, they reached the monks' monastery. Cord took her by one hand, and Kayla took the other, and they lifted and swung her around as they headed into the temple. Allison remembered Kayla breezing out, "Whooosh!" every time she swung between them. And she giggled, and Cord laughed this big, baritone chuckle. Because they made it feel like they were going to a carnival, she felt only anticipation as the massive, ancient architecture of the temple entrance loomed over them. The whole time, Cord enthusiastically rattled on about their discipline, their talents. But all Allison remembered was "Whooosh!"

Whooosh. She hadn't thought about that for years, but remembering it now she was suddenly reminded of how often they would play that game with her. It brought a tear to her eye, and all at once she found herself missing Kayla Cord so much.

That day at the temple, the monks performed for them, showing off their almost superhuman capabilities in the most entertaining fashion they could muster. The swordfights were intense, but they tumbled around on the mats like clowns and bonked against each other, even though Allison half-expected them to (and prayed they wouldn't) lunge at one another with their oddly- shaped swords. They danced about like entertainers, in hopes of amusing her, and that day, Allison's fears regarding these strange, masked, tattooed men began to disappear.

Kayla held her hand and cheered enthusiastically when they pulled off death-defying stunts and masterful swordplay. "See, they're not so scary. They're just fighters, like Nathan," she told Allison sweetly. But there was a bit of apprehension still clinging to the little girl.

Cord took a different tack. "Hey, Allie," he said softly, tapping his index finger on her forehead. When he had her attention, he drew the finger up to the bridge of his nose and tapped it. "Up here. You listening?"

"Yessir," she responded obediently.

"You know you're the princess, right?"

"Yes."

"So you know there will be times where you're in danger."

"Yes." Allison always liked it when Cord would talk to her like she was an adult, like she could handle harsh truths.

"Good. You've always been smart like that. So let me ask you, if you're in danger, who's gonna help you?"

Little Allison gave the briefest moment's thought before answering, "You and Quinn."

Cord smiled broadly and tugged the girl close to him, jostled her hair proudly. "Damn right, little girl." She remembered that Cord gave a look to Kayla, who returned it somewhat coldly, but she didn't really understand what it might have meant at the time. Then she looked at Kayla, and whatever expression Kayla showed her husband disappeared, as she looked at the little princess and cocked her head warmly. "You're a smart little girl, you know that?"

Cord picked up the thread. "Yeah you are. Because you know me and Quinn, we're gonna look out for you. Forever and ever." He put his hands on her shoulders and lowered his voice a little. "But sometimes, we won't be around as much. See, your pop, he's gonna send me on a mission soon, so I'll be away for a while. But what did I say? I said I'd always look out for you, right?"

"Right!"

"So tell me what I said."

Excitedly, she parroted back, "You and Quinn will always look out for me."

Cord grinned. "Good girl. So how am I looking out for you? Who are these guys?"

"Blue Knives..." she knew what he wanted to hear, but didn't understand what he was getting at. When Cord put his arm around Kayla, she curled up onto their adjoining laps. Where it was safe. "But I want *you* to save me if I'm in trouble."

Cord stroked her hair gently. "I know. So listen up, because this might be important some day. If I'm...if me and Kayla aren't around, and Quinn's not around, the only people we'd trust to look out for you are these guys."

She frowned, staring at the empty expressions of the monks as they bounced around mimicking violence on their demonstration floor. But Cord kept on. "I know they're weird. They don't look like you or me, they don't act like it, but then, think about Quinn's people. They can be weird sometimes too. Doesn't mean they're not looking out for you, right?"

Allison heard what Cord was trying to get across. It was still a lot to take in.

"So what am I telling you?" Cord prompted. She liked when he tried to teach her things. He never made her recite anything like her regular teachers. He just put the information out in front of her and trusted her to come to the proper conclusion.

She looked up at her aunt and uncle. "If you and Quinn aren't around, and I'm in trouble..."

Kayla nodded encouragingly, "Yeah, sweetie?"

"I should call for these guys."

Cord grinned proudly. "You got it, Allie."

Kayla finished the lesson. "So what do you say, when you need help?"

Fully understanding, she screeched out in her tiny girl's voice, "Blue knives, come here!"

Her face was still buried in Cord's chest, so he tapped her shoulder, and gestured out to the demonstration floor. "Look."

The little girl uncurled herself and did as instructed. She saw a dozen masked monks kneeling in front of her. In that moment, Allison understood what the Blue Knives stood for.

Crumpled on the floor, that imaginary slab of stone pushing down on her even harder, Allison coughed out again – the last bit of breath she had in her – "Blue Knives! COME HERE, damn it!"

And the warrior monks erupted through the door, graceful as cats, bombastic as a drumline. Her face was firmly pressed into the floor, so Allison could only see their feet. She counted ten pairs. But as Cord had assured her, ten Blue Knives were worth a hundred of Coal Brigade.

One of them knelt before her. They were all interchangeable, without names, as far as she or anyone knew. The one who knelt down must have been their leader. For want of a better savior, he would have to do.

"Take..." it was so hard for her to speak. With the pressure on her chest, she could barely get any words out. "...Grolev..." she gasped.

They had taken it upon themselves for generations to cut the humanity out of their souls, the better to serve the throne. It was a righteous sense of duty that should perhaps be admired. Cord had told her that himself.

But their skin, heavily tattooed in blue tribal designs. Their vacant yellow eyes. Their mouths, hidden behind black shrouds. Not that it mattered – she doubted that they understood the emotional process that might lead to a simple smile of reassurance. These were not men built to tell her things would be okay. Physically and mentally, they had crafted themselves into organisms meant only for combat. She had periodically wondered how they could serve Western Sun, when they had no connection to its humanity. But Nathan Cord had assured her that human or not, these were the men who would save her in her darkest hour.

They were there to obey orders. And so Allison struggled, against the mystical weight Grolev had forced onto her, to give an order. "Take…gheh…take this man…into custody." Coughing and gasping for a decent breath, she forced out, "Arrest Grolev!"

And they did nothing.

"Heh," she heard Grolev utter. "You really are stupid. Did you know that? All this time. They weren't protecting you, you silly little wench. They were protecting me. Come on. They're just zoned-out monks! Too rot-brained to resist even a fraction of my suggestion. They listen to me now." He looked up to what Allison assumed must be the leader of her personal guard. "You. Blue Knife Retard. Stab yourself."

His yellow eyes gave no reaction to the command. He calmly, smoothly pulled his strange blade from its scabbard and shoved it effortlessly into his chest. Then he dropped to his knees and fell to the floor next to Allison without a word or a scream. His yellow eyes remained opened, as probing in death as they had been in life.

The sight of this crushed the Orphan even more thoroughly than Grolev's spell.

His demonstration over with, the wizard got down to practical business. He commanded the remaining Blue Knives, "Hold your blades on the Queen in Waiting, would you? If she moves, cut off her fingers. If she moves again, even out of pain? Run your blades through her knees."

Another member of the Blue Knives, apparently their new leader, stepped to Allison and pulled a five-inch blade from his belt, knelt down, and placed it a breath away from her fingers.

Grolev knelt down and lowered his head between Allison and the dead monk, so she could see into his pitch-black eyes. "If your big heroes come for you, these inbred monks will gut them for dinner with one word from me. So just lay there and wait, would you, princess? Adults are talking."

Allison did as she was told. To Grolev, it appeared that she had acquiesced to his demands.

But she was just waiting.

She knew that Quinn Kind and Nathan Cord were out there, fighting to get through the hoards of undead.

Her favorite aunt and uncle would come to save her.

48. Come Back

You're getting slow, you stupid old bastard, Cord thought to himself after taking his sword to three men that he almost recognized. He'd felt no effort in dispatching them, but when they fell at his feet, he suddenly felt exhausted. Looking down and scanning their faces, he attempted to reason with himself.

They're not your men anymore. Haven't been for years, and certainly not now. They're just bodies that the Orphan's magician is parading around. Just rotting meat with weapons in their hands and no idea how to use them.

Finding the discussion one-sided and fruitless, Cord managed to shut his brain down long enough to see more attackers coming at him. With great concentration, he managed to tap into that violent side of himself that had grown atrophied from disuse, and killed another half-dozen of them. The weariness set in again, creaking into his bones.

Not even that old, man. What's your problem? Vic's got fifteen years on you, and he's barreling through them without a second thought.

Then he blinked, and realized he'd blanked out. Again. The only reason he remained standing could be credited to five Fel who seemed to constantly hover around him. He realized that they had taken surrounding positions at his sides. Nobody would claim that the Fel were wild about battle plans or strategy, but they were plenty happy to attack enemies who didn't remember how to defend themselves. That they had stationed themselves meant they had received orders. Someone had lost confidence in Cord.

He couldn't remember any of their names. These Fel boys. Pretty sure he ever bothered to ask. It troubled him.

Everything troubled him.

He'd nursed plenty of reservations before the fighting started, though he was hardly alone there. But he'd assumed that once swords were drawn and things got going, he'd fall back into his old rhythm. But it was all too much, too much shouting and things coming at him and he kept hearing a voice in his brain asking *Why am I even in this craziness?*

This wasn't how he remembered fighting. He thought back to those dummies he practiced on in the backyard, and it all suddenly felt stupid and self-indulgent. And useless.

What, have I been misremembering things? Did I actually get nostalgic about this stuff?

The idea stopped him dead in his tracks. While Cord stood like a scarecrow, easy prey for a few of the dead soldiers, the Fel fighters, apparently acting as his personal guard, took those pathetic things out before they got within ten feet of him. He watched it all like he was at the top of the hill, not in the mix. He hoped the Fel boys didn't notice that he had become completely locked in. Rooted by...what? Fear?

Fear...since when do I get scared?

"They just keep coming at us," he quietly muttered, stupidly, to no one in particular. Like the severity of the situation hadn't occurred to him before now.

No. Not fear. What the hell is this? Shake it off, damn it!

He turned to his right and saw Victor Mene, a long-blade in each hand, sawing through the enemy like he was clearing brush. Mene's face betrayed no emotion. That was his strong suit, of course. If Cord recognized some of them, Mene had a crystal clear recollection of each man he had ever led. And if Western Sun's war with the southlands was anything like Cord had imagined, then Mene had very recently led many of these men into a slaughter. Yet the captain showed no hesitation when it came to killing them all over again. This time by his own hand.

And here stood Cord, completely at a loss for action.

He had been in fights every bit as vicious. Especially after Lucius died and Arius took hold, and the battles became less about keeping peace and more about enforcing the will of the king.

When they took the Northlands and renamed it Northern Sun, there was no sense of righteousness, no feeling of victory. It had been the first time Cord had felt like a bully. A thug. He'd killed so many before, all in service to the crown. But those battles were the first time he'd felt like a monster.

And then during their first brief foray into the southlands, in order to stay alive, Cord tapped into that part of himself that he knew had been festering throughout his entire career. That monster in the box. He let it out more and more, and hated himself more and more after every battle.

He tried to bully himself into action. *Stop thinking about back then, you stupid old bastard, you're in it now!*

But nothing happened. Some pep talk. He was still stuck. And every time he tried to put a coherent thought together, map out the situation and plan an attack like he'd been trained, like he'd accepted as instinct, something along the lines of *Vic just took the head off Donald Coggins...he was our only decent cook,* would creep into him. And Donald's head would tumble down to the ground and land at his feet, and Cord would lose himself again. *He has kids in the guard, too, doesn't he? I wonder if they...*

Other men might give a name to Cord's hesitance. Not knowing him, they would call it "fear." But Cord had an understanding of fear few men could reach. Coal Brigade's specialty was essentially in cultivating fear. The terrifying reputation of violence and startling destruction Coal Brigade had earned during the years Cord had been its chief had been the best weapon he could have imagined. They were talented at holding precarious points. Situating themselves in high-risk positions, while praying to gods they didn't believe in that they didn't get caught. Waiting for days, sometimes weeks, and then, just when it felt like it would never end, they would attack. This was Coal Brigade's purpose. The point of their existence. To live with the fear of what might be, until the time for violence finally came and there was only what was. And when they moved, it was to spread terror among their enemies.

After a while, the mere suggestion that Coal Brigade might be operating in the enemy's theatre of attack was enough to send their opponents running scared.

More than any member of Coal Brigade, Cord was adept at utilizing the mechanics, the nature of fear. He had been its most devoted student, because it kept him and his men alive. But it had never held him back before. If anything, he had always used it to propel him into hopeless situations. He welcomed fear and turned it into cold cunning and savagery.

Every. Single. Time.

It occurred to Cord then that perhaps his worship of fear was, if he understood Welles' discipline correctly, itself a type of magic. He wondered if that made him anything like Grolev. Magic or not, whatever this talent was, he had come to believe that it was a disease in his soul that made him a good soldier. That was at his worst.

But at his best – though it was something he hated to admit to anyone, himself most of all – it made him an unstoppable force.

He was the monster in a box that Western Sun opened when it needed one.

But in the here and now, these things kept coming at him, and he didn't know what to do, and the only thing keeping him alive were soldiers who didn't give a damn who these men used to be.

One of those non-men, rotten and without any semblance of humanity, charged at Cord. In response, he pushed himself past his Fel protectors and shoved a blade through its chest, removed it, then swung the sword back around and removed the head. When it all dropped, he looked down, and recognized the emaciated remains of Percy Windham. Percy Windham had been a recruit Cord had personally selected from Mene's rookies a couple of years before his exile. Smart and resourceful, Windham had shown great potential for Coal Brigade.

Nostalgic or not, Cord had never romanticized war. But he imagined Percy Windham as a future leader. Not as a lump of rotten skin and bones lying there at his feet. Still twitching.

Something finally erupted in Cord's gut, and started choking him as it made its way up his throat. He coughed it out angrily from his system. It came out as a howling, uncontrollable curse. His monster, trying to escape.

"Damn it…goddamn – SON OF A BITCH!"

He had felt several different, specialized brands of anger over the last few days. Quinn and Menc had personified the bulk of them. He understood that anger. They were based on a trust that had been broken. That made sense to him.

The shuddering remains of Percy Windham didn't make any sense at all. Somewhere behind Cord, a voice shouted, reedy but authoritative, "Good work, move on!"

The Fel that had been guarding him disappeared. Cord was still stuck.

"HAAAAIIII-YAAAAAHHH!" The battle-howl behind him only barely perked Cord up.

He turned around, and saw Quentin Kind standing atop a dead soldier's carcass, one that had targeted Cord. Cord glanced down at the body Quentin had sunk his blade into. He didn't recognize the man. The lack of recognition made him feel good, and then it made him feel awful. But it woke him up.

"Quentin. Thanks."

Quentin shrugged. Then he stepped in close to Cord. The Pic was a good six inches shorter than Cord, but his eyes beamed bright and brilliant, and to Cord, at this moment, he might have been a giant. He pushed his hand into Cord's shoulder, shoving him backwards. Unrooting him. "Get your head in the game, man. I don't know what you're doing."

Cord looked out at the battlefield. So many bodies. Dismembered. Pathetic. Uncared for. Forgotten, moments after their deaths.

Cord couldn't deal with it anymore. He couldn't figure out what the hell he was doing there. If Quinn could see him. She'd had such high hopes, and he was killing every one of them. He wasn't a soldier. Not a leader of men. He was a just a burnt-out barman who picked fights with drunks and shoved swords into potato sacks to relieve stress….

I'm gonna die here. What a stupid way to die….

He tried to verbalize these feelings to Quentin, but they only came out as a funny, stupid look on his face, gawking at his Pic friend. Quentin looked out at the battlefield, avoiding Cord's gaze. Then finally, he stared the former brigade chief in his one good eye.

"They're going to keep coming at us until they kill us." There was a casual nature to Quentin's declaration that Cord found unsettling. Quentin finished, "You want to let that happen?"

Five dead soldiers came at them, and Cord let the rage inside him boil over. He let the monster out, and he slaughtered them as easily as he had ever killed in his life. He was barely aware of what was happening. They kept coming, and Cord started working on the instincts he'd been praying would take over. He sliced with his long-sword, chopped, slashed and pierced with his short blade. He moved like a man possessed by his past self.

Then, realizing that the monster was making his moves, he stopped suddenly. When he woke up, he and Quentin stood among five dead bodies.

"There you go," he heard Quentin say quietly – and a bit condescendingly.

"I can't get to it, Quentin," he replied, shaking his head, trying to jar something loose. "I thought I could. Felt the rage build up with Fehrer, I swear I was ready to kill your sister, and Mene, c'mon, that should be easy. But I can't access that hate I used to have. It's in there, I know, but...I don't want to let it out. I got too good at keeping it where it was."

Quentin stifled a sad laugh. "What the hell, Nate? I thought I shook that notion out of you when you came to us, when I trained you. You think there's some beast inside you that does all the fighting, but that's crap. It's just you. No monster, no freak spirit that powers you up. It ain't magic. It's. Just. You."

The idea shook Cord. He flashed back to the time he spent in Quentin's village, studying with him. Learning from him, how to merge the savagery inside him with the enlightened perspective on violence that the Pic had cultivated. Fighting as a form of meditation.

Quentin kept at it. "You're not a monster. You protect things. You fight for what you think is worth guarding. What's worth saving. Quinn knows that, I know that."

Cord looked around, tried to remember what exactly he had done that had resulted in the chopped up bodies that surrounded his feet. And the root of his personal horror revealed itself. He wasn't afraid. He was deeply, truly sad. "Crap. That's what it...Quentin, I don't want to kill my own people. I know they're not...but, y'know. They still are."

Quentin shrugged. Not callously, just acknowledging Cord's position and countering it with his own. "They're already dead, Nate. Everything that made them your people, that's all gone. But their bodies have been pressed into service by a man with no respect for them. You're here to help send them to their final rest. Don't think any further than that. It's unnecessary. And it goes against your nature."

"My nature," Cord repeated, rolling the idea off of his tongue.

Another dead soldier came at them, and Quentin swept his blade through the air, dispatching it without taking his eyes off Cord.

He didn't even bother taking a breath before continuing his thought. "And I can't keep telling those Fel guys to watch your back. I mean, they're Fel. A lot of them don't even think you're really Nathan Cord. So they'll only listen to me for so long before they decide you're just some punk who's not worth the effort." Quentin concluded what passed for his motivational speech by giving Cord a gentle slap on his cheek.

Cord absorbed Quentin's words, and tried to get a bearing on his surroundings. Sight alone never really did it for him. It was always the smell of it all. He breathed in deeply, through his nose, taking in the aroma of a battlefield unlike any other he'd encountered. Old meat, and debris, and blood that smelled like rust. Finally he looked around, checked his surroundings again. He nodded.

Nothing was like he remembered. The fighting, the allies, the enemy, the battleground. Everything was different and disconcerting and strange, like new things usually are.

No anger. That wouldn't do the job of motivating him anymore. Just sadness at what had befallen his men, and his kingdom. But he'd never used sadness to fight before. So he searched for the one thing that was still clear and true. And finally he could brush the dust off his soul. The mission became completely clear to him.

"Protect the Orphan. Avenge my people."

Quentin smiled, like someone had reminded him of a promise he had forgotten. "Yeah."

He said it again. "I'm here to save Allison." It sounded right this time.

"And Quinn made sure that me and my guys would be around to see you do it. So what do you say?"

Peering up to the central high tower, Cord answered, "I say point me in the right direction, and I'll get the princess out of here. Or die trying."

Quentin's smile faded. "Well, let's hope we figure something else out in the meantime."

Cord grinned. That scary grin that everyone took for bloodlust. Cord knew what it looked like. He always knew. And he also understood what it really meant, to him at least: the pride that comes with righteous clarity in a fight. "Nevermind. I think I know where we need to go."

He raised up his sword, and bellowed his commands. "Fel, listen up! Clear a path, we're heading to the high tower! We're going for the Orphan!"

The Fel all stopped, took a moment from their killing to look up at this guy, this human who suddenly looked like one of the leaders of the Beasts Old Throne battles. One of those men they'd heard insane tall tales about. The chief of Coal Brigade. The king-killer. The Orphan's exiled favorite.

"Who's with me?" he barked. It wasn't a question, or a command. It almost sounded like a threat.

Some of the Fel finished the killing they'd started before the crazy man started shouting orders. When everyone was finished, they raised their weapons high in solidarity.

"WHO'S WITH ME?" Cord repeated.

More arms went up.

His blade still held high, Cord reached down and grabbed a hatchet from one of the corpses at his feet, spun it around casually on his palm, feeling out the weight of it before gripping it firmly. This would do nicely.

He pointed it toward the high tower. "Whoever's with me, let's move, and screw any one of you who isn't!"

The Fel started cheering and shouting enthusiastically. Cord started running, and like a nest of hornets, they funneled behind him toward the tower.

Quentin smirked. "Well *there* he is," he pointed out to no one in particular, yanked an axe from Percy Windham's rigor-mortis-stricken fist, and ran in with them, imagining how wonderful it might all be, if the reinvigorated Nathan Cord didn't get them all killed.

49. An Endurance Sport

Well, Quinn mused to herself, as a naked screaming Fel charged past her and into a pack of the monsters. *This could actually be going worse.*

She put the cautious optimism aside to engage a pack of six attackers coming at her. Twisting the Stem fluidly, viciously through each of them, lopping off heads and boring into chests. It was the fifth such attack in as many minutes and she hadn't yet broken a sweat.

Two remained, so she took a standing leap, flipped around and pounced lightly on one's shoulders. Drove the Stem down hard through its clavicle. Then she somersaulted and used to momentum to heave the Stem and flip the dead man over her. The thing slipped easily from her staff and careened into its partner. They both writhed on the ground, giving Quinn enough time to walk over and jam the base of the Stem into both of their necks, severing their spines and killing them for good.

Wasting no time congratulating herself, she looked up and saw her primary concern come to pass: a dozen of her boys had gotten bunched together, backed up against a wall, and the monsters had taken the opportunity to swarm them from all sides.

Raising the Stem and running into the fray, she commanded, "Anyone without an opponent, over here, now!"

Within moments, she had the backup she requested and together they picked apart the onslaught. When there was a moment's peace (save for the customary Fel victory whooping), she surveyed the scene.

Two of hers dead. One Pic, one Fel. The Pic was Kennedy Forsythe. She didn't know the Fel's name.

First casualties on her side. That she knew of, at least.

There was a savage frustration clawing its way out of her, but she invoked the stubborn cold streak of Victor Mene and tamped it down.

The surviving crew was all Pic. They appeared completely bewildered by what had just happened to them.

"What did I tell you?" Quinn scolded them. "Keep moving, don't bunch up. They're slower than you but their numbers can still pin you down. The price you pay for this lesson is Ken Forsythe." She gestured the Stem toward their kinsman's body. Their eyes followed.

Quinn would indulge no self-pity. "What are you gawking at? We're not done! Get out there, keep moving, keep killing! GO!" They dispersed. Fleeing her disappointment. She had no problem with that, as long as it kept them mobile and put their minds back on alert.

Before heading out again, she took another moment to look at her two fallen. And she told herself again that they could be doing worse. She could have lost them all.

Cold comfort.

It continued on this way, charging through near-empty streets, locating patches of undead men and putting them down. As they moved further into the kingdom, she saw that fewer of the things wore guard uniforms, and more of them were clothed in civilian dress. Townsfolk. Likely the first to be killed after Grolev's spell took hold and brought them back, same as the soldiers. Welles had assured her that the spell would only reanimate those who were in the kingdom when it was cast. But she kept a wary eye on Forsythe, half-expecting him to start twitching. But its body remained inert, and she reminded herself to trust that Welles knows his business. She moved on.

An hour went by without any break in the fighting. Her simple plan – stab and run, don't stop for anything – continued to achieve the desired effect of keeping her men alive. For the most part. She periodically heard screams that she knew the enemy was no longer capable of making.

Running around like this, her people had begun to spread all over the smaller villages situated by the base of the high tower. And the monsters were lumbering in all directions, tracking them by smell. Quinn had begun to sweat, and it dawned on her that she was leaving a heavier scent trail for the enemy to follow. And there was another problem: as more time went on, she found that the major drawback of her plan was an inability to gauge the results.

There was no real way to tell how they were doing. With only vague estimates of the initial enemy numbers, she couldn't figure out how many more there could be. Finding herself in an alley down in the King's Bend neighborhood, she came across a pile of bodies. A quick headcount told her the Pic and Fel had already come through and taken out twenty former citizens of Bloody Twilight. And it looked like the woodlanders had lost five of their own in the struggle.

Before she could add them to the total woodlander bodycount she'd come across since Kennedy Forsythe, her ears perked up to the shuffling of clumsy running boots, and her nose caught that stink of salt, copper and ash that warned her to get ready for another oncoming skirmish. They were close. Surprisingly close. She couldn't believe it had taken her this long to notice.

Time for that later. She followed her own strategy, charged at them, took them apart just like before. No flips this time, nothing fancy, no showing off. She just systematically broke them down.

When they were all dismembered and heaped into a grotesque pile, Quinn checked her surroundings and came to a number of conclusions, all of them bad:

The battle had gone into its second hour.

She was now well into the city, nearly two miles from the barrier.

Though there were only three more monsters than her first fight, it had taken her almost twice as long to dispatch them.

Three of them had been children.

And when it was over, Quinn found herself a bit winded.

Conclusion: she was starting to wear out. Not good.

When it was finally calm enough for her to take in her surroundings, she noticed she had heaped a bunch of bodies in front of the Farr Bar.

Back in the old days, the early days of her role as ambassador twenty-odd years ago, Quinn found herself needing Cord, in his role as her first real human friend, to give her an insider's perspective on the ways of his people. She was there to learn, after all.

Cord would return home from a mission, go to his wife, and catch up on things however married people do. A heartfelt embrace, then marathon lovemaking, and then maybe arguing about money – she assumed was how those things went. After all that was wrapped up, Cord would come out with Quinn to the Farr Bar and they would drink beer and share stories into the wee small hours. It grew to be a favorite tradition of hers through the years she spent in the kingdom.

At first, the conversations touched on notions of community, relationships, family, that kind of thing. Cord would share what he knew, but unfortunately he didn't know too much. He was a rancher's only son, his parents had both died within a couple years of his moving to Bloody Twilight. His only family, really, was Kayla, but she had never been close with her own kin. And while Quinn's friendship with Cord, and later Kayla, became deep and rewarding, Cord never opened up too widely regarding the state of his marriage. Quinn wasn't a complete alien, and one of the first things she picked up on was that no matter where you go, or what kind of folks you're dealing with, people are basically the same all over when it came to dealing with loved ones. The customs might be different, but the end result was always pretty much the same. And it was never easy.

So with Cord and Kayla, she knew when things were good, and she knew when things were strained. In those last couple of years before Kayla's death, she knew when things were really bad.

But these were just impressions she got, and she knew Cord well enough to understand that was something he wished to keep to himself. As a member of the guard and a prominent citizen of the kingdom, perhaps the only private thing he had was his relationship with his wife. So while the student of human nature in Quinn remained curious, the part of her that loved her friend let it go.

And as far as friends went, she couldn't have done better than Nathan Cord. He was kind, and loyal, and honest. But as far as mentors of the human condition went, Quinn realized that she could have chosen a little better.

It was the understanding of what she could learn from Cord that led her to pick his brain over something she knew he understood instinctively. So one night when he got home, they met at the Farr Bar and she got him to tell her what it's like to fight in a battle.

Cord sat quietly on the question, sipping his whiskey while he phrased a response in his head, and finally leaned in and offered, "It's an endurance sport." Then he leaned back in his chair, satisfied.

Quinn shook her head. "Okay, you're gonna need to give me a little more than that," she nudged him.

Laughing at himself, he assured her, "I know, I know, just give me a second, I'm trying to think how to put this…"

After scratching the back of his neck for a few moments and staring at a bunch of rowdies at the next table, he seemed to have formulated a response, and continued, "Yeah. Marathon. You figure that out in your first battle, and usually it's a hard lesson. At first you think, 'If I can just take 'em all out quickly, we'll be done.' Because you can't comprehend the sheer numbers involved – how many of your guys, how many of theirs, the size of the battlefield, just how far you have to go to take the position. It's too much to theorize about, when you're just a grunt.

"So you just try to get it done as fast as you can, so you don't have to worry about it anymore. But if you're lucky enough to make it back to camp, you realize the only reason you're still alive is other guys were moving even quicker than you did. But when the call rang out, they didn't have enough left in them to get out of there when there was an opening." He shrugged. "No soldier makes that mistake twice. From there on out, it's about pacing yourself for a lot of long days."

In the here and now, Quinn glared at the darkened windows of the Farr Bar, and thought about what Cord had said. She inhaled deeply, to catch her breath and to sniff out any more dead folks coming toward her. The coast clear, she exhaled fully, and dropped to her knees. She let the Stem fall clumsily in front of her. And the state of things grew awfully clear in her mind.

"Oh, you stupid bitch…" she cursed herself. "You utterly idiotic bitch." She put her hands on her face, half-expecting to hide tears, but to her relief, nothing came out.

When all the Pic women – the Mothers, and the older women like herself, the Mothers in training – left for the north, and Quinn had taken it upon herself to rally her younger brothers into an army, Quinn's chief concern was that they might not be up to the task at hand. But after drilling them relentlessly, she thought they might have a solid fighting chance.

And they had been doing so well. Initially. But it occurred to her that she'd never passed along that bit of wisdom from Cord. Because she didn't really think it would matter. Quinn knew Pics don't tire half as quickly as humans. It's just a difference of biology.

But it's also because Pic fights don't last very long.

All Pics know how to fight. Those teachings are used as a form of meditation and discipline. A means of self-defense against humans and other woodlanders was a benefit of training, not the reason for it. This is why, as humans had observed, it didn't seem like Pics fought with a secondary agenda in mind – because that wasn't how they were trained to wage war. There were never any objectives beyond the fight itself.

So waging war – fighting on a timetable to achieve an objective – was, in fact, a less familiar concept.

Historically in Pic culture, the women were the best fighters. And here was Quinn, alone at the mouth of a King's Bend alleyway, needing an extra moment to catch her breath and regroup. How well could her boys be faring? And the Fel – for all their bluster and enthusiasm, their specialty was in guerilla combat, letting enemies step on hidden explosives, and lying in wait to pounce out of trees and onto invaders. This run-and-hunt strategy wasn't in their nature either.

How much more of this can we take? she wondered, both genuinely curious and deeply concerned about what the answer might be. No one was around to offer it to her.

She took a few more deep breaths, then retook the Stem and leaned against it to hoist herself to her feet. Quinn steeled herself for more, found the direction from where she'd come, focused the energies in her body, and bolted in a dead sprint back toward the barrier. She was within a mile of the wall when she smelled another cadre of walking dead.

She had faith that she could kill them on her own, just like she had the others. But as an experiment, she struck the Stem into a nearby stone wall, held it high and let it ring.

In addition to being a suitably dramatic gesture for a Mother to make, the vibration of the metals in the core of the staff resonated a frequency woodland ears can hear for miles.

Her voice wasn't too shabby either. "PIC! FEL! I NEED YOU HERE!" She shouted. The echo of her voice ricocheted off the walls of the empty city.

Watching her would-be attackers trudging toward her, arms reaching out, their throats making that awful gurgling, sucking noise she had actually grown used to, she waited for reinforcements.

No one came.

Accepting the reality, she nodded in understanding. "It's an endurance sport," she reminded herself. Readying herself for this fight and the next one, and the next after that, Quinn wondered just how much worse this could get.

And then, when they were close enough for her to inspect each of their cold expressions, Quinn recognized one of them. And she got an answer to her question. Things *could* get a lot worse.

It was Aiden Fletcher. The Orphan's dead lover had come out to play.

50. All in a Day's Work

"You almost look like you're having fun, Vic!" Cord shouted as he hacked his way through ten of the enemy dead on his way to aid Victor Mene. Mene was doing well enough, but it had become clear enough that as they made their way closer to the high tower, the monsters had started to follow him, rather than engage the woodlander troops down at the base of the hill, closer to the barrier. It was strange to see Mene acting as an unwitting marching leader to a bunch of shuffling corpses. And it led Cord to an unnerving conclusion. He decided to wait for a quiet moment before he shared his thoughts.

"Fun?" Mene echoed, shoving himself into one of his attackers. He bounced himself backwards when he saw another attempting to sneak up from behind, swung his sword around, and jammed the blade into the second attacker's neck. He tried to pull it away, but found it was stuck in there, so he simply let go of the hilt and tackled his initial target to the ground before it could get back up, getting a good grip on its head to twist it around. And around again. And then yank it right off.

There were a lot of disturbing sights to choose from this night, but Cord decided that Victor Mene ripping a dead man's head off with his bare hands was, so far at least, a top contender.

While Mene had busied himself with this, Cord had gone over and tugged the sword out of the second attacker's neck. "Hey!" he called to Mene, getting his attention. When Mene looked over, Cord tossed the captain's sword back to him. Without batting an eye, Mene threw the severed head over to Cord in exchange.

Catching it instinctively, Cord gave it a good long look, and was happy enough not to recognize this one. "Okay, 'fun' might not be the right word."

"Talk later," Mene advised, and Cord realized that they were surrounded. Again. It felt like over the last...how long had it been now, two hours? Three? Since Quentin had shaken him out of his stupor and he pulled himself together to lead the men up the hill toward the tower, things had been going smoothly, if not quietly. But still, even though Cord had gotten back to his old instincts, he couldn't relax for more than a minute before the dead men attempted to box him in, and it was starting to wear him down. Sheer stubbornness kept him returning their attacks. He tensed his muscles, gripped his sword tightly, let out a roar and swung forcefully in a clockwise motion, vivisecting every last one that came at him.

Mene observed the strategy and mimicked it against his own opponents.

Then they both went around and mechanically dropped their blades into each dead man's chest. Drop, pull out, repeat with the next one.

Clockwork violence.

51. The Discovery

Quentin was happy enough to have Cord back in a lead position. Cord's new push to their objective split the groups, so Quentin was left with a smaller, more manageable team to direct. Looking after his own brothers was a task by itself. Throw in cousins who were as averse to commands as they seemed to be towards clothing, and Quentin enjoyed Cord taking a little bit of the pressure off.

Cord's charge had had the unintended consequence of leading the dead men after him and Mene. Even though Quentin's Pic and Fel squad were comparatively stationary, the dead men were going after a moving target.

Seeing an opportunity, he called over one of the Fel, an older warrior by the name of Cade Coogan. "New plan, Coogan. Take a few of your guys, start hacking away at whatever's hounding behind Cord's team. We can thin them out from the rear. By the time they're close enough to Cord, there aren't going to be enough of them to put up a decent fight."

Coogan pounded his fist onto his bare chest enthusiastically. The Fel must have all heard the thump, since they looked to Coogan for further instruction. "OY! Meedy, Raines, Goodall, come on, you bastards! We're chopping off some tails. YOOOWWW!!"

As Coogan and his boys darted off, Quentin decided that the Fel just weren't his type of folks. But this was his type of leadership. He'd never been terribly comfortable out in the front of the pack, but Quinn had always counted on him to be front and center. It was her way of compensating for his lack of official power within the clan. He appreciated the thought, but he was a behind-the-scenes kind of guy, quietly moving pieces where they needed to be, nudging opinions without forcing them. He didn't need glory or credit. The results spoke for themselves, and earned him a cache of trust and respect among his people that didn't need to be shouted from the hills.

Let Quinn and Cord and Mene be the leaders. Quentin was the backbone, and it worked for him.

With the Fel tackling the dead soldiers from the tail end, Quentin was left with nine of his own soldiers, against a few pockets of resistance that he was sure would pose no threat. Especially since they didn't appear to notice the Pics at all.

Instead, the dead men seemed more interested in a nearby stable generally reserved for the royal guard. Their sudden focus on a landmark rather than a moving target boggled Quentin's mind. It bore further investigation.

"What, do they want horses? Why would they want..." he mused for a moment before stopping that train of thought. It didn't matter. They were distracted, and that was all Quentin needed.

"Pics, listen up," he calmly requested, without raising his voice above his usual calm tone.

Cord needed to shout to get the blood going. Quinn raised her voice to boost morale. And Mene's deep base tones never needed increase. He just liked it. But Quentin's brothers were attuned to his voice. They could hear him easily from hundreds of feet away. So he gave an order. "Get on 'em."

And nine Pic warriors swiftly surrounded the dead men who had honed in so intently on the livery. Quentin's men were as sleek as a school of fish.

The fight didn't last a minute.

Arturo Fagin, one of Quentin's more familiar brothers, came back to him with a report. "Taken care of. I ran through the local shops, it's all clear, save for a few light pockets of resistance. We're doing great."

"Don't ever say that out loud, Arturo, it only invites trouble. While you're here, let me pick your brain for a minute. Do you have any idea why they keep heading toward the stables? Why not the armory? It's so close, if they wanted weapons they could shove their way in without much hassle."

Arturo thought for a second, then offered, "Transportation to ride up to Northern Sun?"

"But nothing we've seen tells me they're smart enough for that," Quentin countered. "What else could they be interested in?"

Arturo perked up his head. As he focused deeply on their surroundings, his ears twitched, and finally, he turned pale. "Quentin, listen. Smell."

Obliging Arturo, he focused his senses on the area. "I smell dung. We're by a stable, that's not...oh."

Arturo smiled broadly, but warily all the same. "Yeah. Do we - ?"

"We don't do anything just yet. Give me a moment, I'm going to ask Cord what he thinks."

The notion threw Arturo off. "Why? You're in charge, Q, we all know it. You don't have to take orders from a human."

"No, but I want that particular human's input." He started off toward Cord's battlefield, before finishing, "They're his people, after all."

Leaders like his sister, like Cord and Mene, have to keep focused on the big picture, the main objective. An army can't survive without a strong, assured command. But leaders would always need someone like Quentin around, to catch the smaller details when they presented themselves.

Quentin thought of them as one body. If Quinn was the mind, and Cord was the heart, and Mene was the muscle, then he was the nerve center, taking in the bits of information the battlefield gave him, processing it and figuring out what it all meant to the big picture.

With the discovery Arturo had just made, Quentin recognized that the picture had just gotten a little bit bigger.

52. Survivors

There were nine Pics standing a few yards from the livery, awaiting the order to save lives. But this was not known to Big Jack Barry.

All Big Jack knew was this: he was hungry as hell. And he knew he wasn't the only one.

He'd locked himself and twenty-three of his fellow citizens behind the doors of the stable nearly three days ago. He figured it was nearly three days, anyway. Boarding up the windows meant he only had the barest idea of sunrise and sunset. Gordy Nesmith swore it had been closer to a week. But Gordy was an idiot, so his math was spotty at best.

Big Jack stood by his three-day estimate, and his stomach growled in agreement. The only source of food and drink available to them was usually reserved for the horses. Nobody touched it for the first day. Everyone willfully went hungry. But it didn't take much longer for hopelessness and fear to catch up with them, and soon the horses had competition for their dinner. It sustained his people. But Big Jack was the type of guy to scarf down a plate of steak, eggs, chicken, ham, and five potatoes for breakfast. And then two hours later was lunch. Grains and water wasn't exactly a full and balanced diet as far as he was concerned.

Another day of this crap and he was going to put down one of the horses, and everyone would have a nice dinner.

As soon as the thought entered his mind, he tossed it out. He'd do a lot of things to survive, but he'd never seriously entertain the notion of killing one of his horses. He'd sooner put down Gordy Nesmith.

As if on cue, Gordy took that moment to chirp up. "I think I hear people!" he gasped, louder than he should have. And he knew that, because Gordy had been subjected to three days of his fellow refugees hissing "SHHHHH!" at him, terrified every time he opened his big dumb yap.

"Gordy, goddamn it!" Big Jack snarled, irritably, but not without sympathy. It wasn't Gordy's fault. He was just a bit slow, was all. The young man's dimness had actually worked to his advantage. If he'd been any smarter, he would've been drafted into the guard years ago. And then Big Jack would have to worry about Gordy's reanimated corpse banging its head against the stable doors.

Without really thinking about it, Big Jack tapped his knuckles against his own wooden leg. He hadn't spent a lot of time praising his own crippling, but it had kept him out of active service. His clumsy old prosthetic had kept him alive, in a way. And since he was a guardsman who couldn't fight anymore, he had been placed on support staff. He was aware of the irony, that his inability to fight had put him in a position to save his people. A few of them, anyway.

Not that he had any plan bigger than "Ride it out and hope for the best."

Though he never counted himself as much of a strategist, it was a plan that had gotten him through years of battles, so he didn't knock it.

"Jack, don't yell at him," he heard a dusky female voice from behind him.

Milla Coggins had been doting on Gordy since they'd reinforced the stable doors. Milla was a soldier's wife and a mother of four young guardsmen. Which was a nice way of saying that she was a widow with four dead kids. It only made sense that her motherly instincts would latch onto Gordy.

"Sorry Milla," Jack answered automatically.

"No, that's not...I hear it too."

Big Jack looked back at her. Milla met him with a stern look. "Something's going on out there."

He stepped close to the doors. He heard shouting. The dead soldiers out there didn't shout. Not anymore. Who the hell could be out there?

Kim Pettit piped up. "It's rescue. We're being rescued!"

And of course, everyone heard her say it. Jack was having a hard enough time keeping order among their little enclave of survivors. He didn't need Kim getting them all riled up. But he couldn't exactly yell at her. For one thing, he didn't want anyone to raise their voice. For another, he and Kim had had a thing a few weeks back, and he wasn't sure trying to order her around would be to his advantage in the long run.

That he had given consideration to the long run startled him. It was a bit of hope he didn't realize he still had in him. After all, he held little hope that they'd be rescued. Certainly not by the guard. After all, he'd seen the captain ride out of town at the first sight of trouble.

When it got bad, it all got so bad so quickly that nobody knew how to react. One minute, Big Jack was tending to the horses like usual. Captain Mene had just brought his steed into the livery for tending. Mene had made some vague comment about how he needed to see the Orphan, and how it wasn't going to be pleasant. It was as chatty as Captain Mene ever got.

Jack had never been a huge fan of Mene's leadership, but he didn't blame the loss of a leg on his commanding officer. Not exactly, anyway.

But you always remember the fight that cost you a limb, and you always remember who ordered the charge.

Still, whatever could be said of Victor Mene, Big Jack Barry knew as truth that the man held every loss close to him, be it a battle or a soldier.

So it was that much more of a shock to him, that when everything went to hell, and a nice spring day turned into the goddamned apocalypse, and dead soldiers picked themselves up off the murder wagon, and out from soldier's field, and started killing the townsfolk indiscriminately, only to have those dead folks pick themselves up and start doing the same…

It happened so fast it was insane. Big Jack remembered hobbling out of the stable, finding whatever living souls he could and dragging them back in for protection, confused and angry and terrified, him and them both. And then there was that one point, when he found Milla Coggins, hollering and disoriented, trying to find her husband. As Jack had started hustling her toward their makeshift stronghold, he saw Victor Mene, looking like was in a trance or something. Like he was moving under orders, the captain took a horse from the stable, whistling it to follow behind him as he stoically started cutting his own men to bits. The horse trailed behind, contentedly.

Big Jack Barry called out to his commander, "Oy, captain! Captain Mene! VIC!" But no answer was returned. And that was the moment he realized that Bloody Twilight had been completely abandoned by its so-called protectors. Some were dead. Some fought feebly – those drafted bastards with no training – and their leader just up and left, as if there was nothing of importance to stick around for.

The idea that any kind of rescue might be at hand made him understandably wary. But just the same, he put his ear to the door. He heard it, too.

"Son of a bitch," he mumbled. He heard talking. Casual, at first, nothing he could make out. He thought they might be behind that glowing…whatever the hell it was, he couldn't make out a damn thing from inside the stable. But an hour passed, and he heard the clanging of swords, and whooping and cheers that reminded him of the bygone Beasts Old Throne days. And then the moaning and grunting. That pathetic wheezing noise that the dead soldiers made whenever they started to exert themselves.

Another hour of this went by. Everyone inside that Jack had managed to save, all of his folks went deadly quiet, without any request from him. Then suddenly it was all quiet, inside and out. And after a few moments that went on forever, some whispers could be heard just outside the door. The voices actually sounded familiar to Big Jack. Nothing specific, just their tones. They sounded like those woodlanders the Coal Brigade had gotten so close with, all those years back.

They sounded, of all things, like Pic voices.

Big Jack Barry decided that his massive growling stomach had finally driven him mad. If he had ever entertained a rescue in his mind, it hadn't been at the hands of some hippie pixies. Saved by pixies. Big Jack tried to process it, but it just wasn't working in his brain.

"Jack, answer them!" someone urged from the huddled masses.

"Eh?" Jack gulped by way of recognition.

Kim stepped forward. Close to him. Held his arm. "Jack, they're trying to see if we're in here."

Jack listened again, and finally heard it all clearly. Those faint voices had gotten louder.

"Iello? Anyone in there?"

He felt Kim's grip on his arm, tight and scared. He thought back a few weeks, and wanted a little more time with Kim all of a sudden. Before he consciously understood what was happening, he answered, "Yes! Yeah! Hey! This is Jack Barry! I have people with me!"

He heard cheers outside the door, and then a voice replied, "Hello! This is Arturo Fagin of the Pic clan! Don't worry, we're going to get you guys to safety, just hold tight!"

Hold tight. Music to Big Jack's ears.

"We're just waiting on Nathan Cord to get over here!"

"Nathan Cord?" he repeated to himself.

At the mention of this name, Big Jack Barry decided that he must have surely gone mad, and all hope was indeed lost.

53. Stage Two

Drop the sword into the heart, pull out, move on to the next body. Repeat. Sometimes, just to break things up, Cord would aim to sever the spinal cord. The depth perception issues Cord faced made it a little tricky, but the sound the axe made alone was worth it.

Since it was relatively easy work, this cleanup procedure, Cord decided now was as good a time as any to offer Mene his theory. "I think maybe these things have some kind of post-hypnotic suggestion. Or whatever, I don't know what you'd call it, but have you noticed they start chasing us whenever we get closer to the towers, rather than go after the bigger groups of Quentin's men? I think Grolev put something in them, some instinct to protect the...you're not listening, are you?"

Mene stood high, his spine completely straight. Whenever he did this, he looked eight feet tall to Cord. "No."

"Fair enough. So what's up?" he asked, so casually it surprised him. He had gotten entirely too used to this fight. That realization actually made him feel good. Meant he was finally back in the game.

Mene squinted as he spied the terrain. "I think we've thinned them out. Some of the woodlanders are still engaged, but I think we've actually taken care of most of them."

"On our end of it," Cord corrected. "I can't even guess how many of them Quinn's people have been taking on. Hope they're doing okay."

"What about the magician?" Mene asked without any particular concern.

Cord raised his hand over his good eye, looking for Welles. He could barely make out a robed figure in the distance, a few hundred feet away. Before he could decide for sure that it was Welles, the figure shot out savage bolts of energy from his entire frame, dispatching a mass of dead soldiers in one fell swoop.

"Oh," Cord answered blithely, "he's fine." He was about to say, "What next?" but before the words came out, he heard in the distance, "Cord! Mene! Get over here! It's important!" It was Quentin.

The two guardsmen ran over to the Pic. Quentin stood cautiously at the edge of a series of stables and cabins that were primarily used by the guard's support staff – their weaponeers and horse trainers. When they reached Quentin, Cord patted him on the shoulder proudly. "Good to see you're still up and about, man." Then, more quietly, "Thanks again. For earlier. You know."

Quentin just nodded slightly, then asked, "You smell that?"

Mene and Cord gave each other a look. Cord answered, "Only things we can smell are dirt, horse crap and old blood. What are you picking up?"

"Sweaty fear."

Cord looked at Mene again and cocked an eyebrow. "Must be you."

Mene folded his arms. "Not likely," he groused.

"No, not him," Quentin clarified seriously. "Them. Now that we're through most of the dead men, we've all had better use of our senses. I think we've found Welles' survivors. They've boarded themselves up in the stables."

Without a moment's hesitation, Cord shouted, "Welles, get over here!"

The magician made the distance to them in the blink of Cord's eye. He hovered above them momentarily before drifting his feet down to touch solid ground again. He looked to the cabins Quentin had been spying, and immediately read the situation. "The survivors."

"Yeah, we think so. What about you?"

Welles stared off, apparently contemplating the question. Cord noted that he seemed a little...distracted. Distracted even for Welles, as though he had disconnected himself from the severity of it all. This, coupled with the raw power he had recently displayed in taking down his attackers, concerned Cord.

But then magician snapped back to life and started outlining the next steps of the plan. "This area's secure. Quentin, we're moving on to stage two. Gather as many of your men as you can. Move these people back out through the barrier, leave a few Pics to guard them, then send the rest over to help Quinn." Then, to Cord and Mene, "You two. We're close to the high tower. Get in there. I'll be behind you soon."

Mene spoke up first, asking a question to which he already knew the answer. "What's guarding the Orphan?"

Without any particular emphasis, Welles answered, "Blue Knives. About twenty of them, I estimate, but figure on more. All at Grolev's command, if I've judged the man's power levels right."

Cord started to ask, "Understood. How is Grolev..." but saw he was talking to no one. Welles had started walking off. Like he heard something important.

All Cord noticed was a familiar and yet no less eerie stillness, of a field after the end of a battle. "Welles!"

Cord ran after the magician and grabbed his arm to spin him around. "Welles," he tried again, more gently this time.

"Cord. Sorry," he offered apologetically, but he was still miles away. "What do you need?"

"For starters, I need to know why you've gotten all zoned out. I thought this was the point of the secondary target, to get these people out. But you're acting like you couldn't give a damn." Cord wasn't sure if he was concerned or just irritated. He got the sense that Welles instilled that feeling in a lot of people.

He also picked up on the notion that back at the village, and on the trek to the kingdom, he'd been dealing with Welles, the man. Casual in a sort of awkward way, trying in his own way to make friends by showing off simple tricks. This was his first experience in dealing with Welles, the magician. More powerful and confident than Cord would have guessed. A different beast entirely. "What am I missing?"

Quietly, confiding, Welles explained, "You guys can take care of the people. I have absolute faith in that. But there's...I can feel someone close by. I can't quite pinpoint him, but I know he's there."

"Who...?" Then it dawned on him. "Keegan Morris." Then, upon hearing his own words out loud, "Wait, Keegan Morris? No way. I thought..."

"Yeah," Welles admitted. "Cord, this close to the high tower, do you know of any...did Arius use dungeons? Torture chambers?" Disgust tinged his voice. Maybe on the subject, or maybe that he had to ask.

Cord frowned. "I've heard rumors. Whispers of rumors. But it wouldn't surprise me, knowing Arius. I don't know exactly where, but I'd say look for cellar doors. Anyone Arius wanted to keep locked up, he probably didn't give them much in the way of a view."

Welles processed the new information. "Okay." Pointing toward the sparse dwellings that made up the soldiers' and support staff's quarters, he proclaimed, "I'm going this way." Then he raised a finger and pointed to the top of the high tower. "You're going up there."

"Riiiight," Cord nodded, hoping in vain that Welles might pick up on the sarcasm. "And all we need to do is fight through twenty Blue Knives."

"Or more," Welles corrected sincerely, ignoring Cord's tone. He then sized Cord up, smiled, and slyly added, "Like you've never wanted to try."

The accusation earned a brief laugh from Cord. "Me? Fighting was never about competition for me. I never really wondered if I was better than a Blue Knife. But I'll bet you Vic's chomping at the bit."

Welles put his palm out. Cord grasped it, and they shook hands. Almost like friends. "Good luck, Nathan Cord."

"Yeah. You too."

Cord walked away, toward his next mission. Wells lifted his feet off the ground and floated toward his.

54. The Stories Victor Mene Will Tell

Nathan Cord stared up at the high tower. Where all the important business of the three kingdoms was decided. Where all the horrible choices of Arius and his successors were born screaming. Small, nondescript rooms, where Bloody Twilight was damned for all time.

At some point in history, the high tower must have stood for something good. When Lucius lived there. When the king of Western Sun looked out on his people and hoped to build, if not something as grandiose and ephemeral as "a better tomorrow," then at least something as simple a way of living where people could wake up and fall asleep without feeling they'd done something wrong.

Now, it only stood as the final stronghold of a dead empire, tenuously protecting a queen it didn't even want.

When Cord realized he was starting to picture the damn thing like an evil old crone, he rattled his head around to get his mind straight, and summed up for himself, "The high tower. Holy hell."

He'd been all bravado speaking with Welles and Quentin, but for the first time, Cord stared up at the central feature of Bloody Twilight's long and storied history, visible for miles on all sides. Practically impregnable, if cleverly guarded. There was only one entrance, leading up to a narrow spiral stairwell that stretched up ten floors. An invading army could send their best soldiers, but the stairwell was too tight for a full-on assault to be any good, and even then, the royal guard would hold the high ground. And if the guard was indisposed, there were always the Blue Knives.

Cord knew getting up there to Allie would be perhaps the most trying fight of his life. Excitement and terror mixed in his blood while he plotted out the task.

It was an unusual sensation – warm and shivery at once. He welcomed the freshness of the feeling.

Objectively speaking, the tower was a beautiful piece of architecture, really. Tall and imposing as it stretched up to infinity, and yet still it was inviting in its earthy simplicity. That might not have been the truth, but it was how Cord always chose to see the damn thing. Even when it all turned bad, the high tower remained the one piece of geography in Bloody Twilight that Cord couldn't find it in him to hate.

And then Victor Mene stepped up behind him and ruined the whole thing by pointing out the obvious.

"Blue Knives in there," Mene told him, as though he were stupid. It was Victor Mene, and that tended to be his default tone, so Cord didn't take any offense. Not as much as he could have, at least. The captain was just doing his best to quell any sense of hope Cord might have developed. It was his way.

"Yup. You never got to fight any of them, right? Not even a sparring match?"

Mene frowned. But a Victor Mene frown could mean a lot of things, and in this case, Cord knew it translated to a smile on the faces of normal folks. "No. But I always wanted to. I won't lie. That's been a dream of mine for some time. Never saw a day where I'd get the chance."

"Well, who could've seen days like these coming?"

A silhouette stepped into the open frame of the tower's only narrow entryway.

Torches from inside the corridor backlit the figure, draping him in shadow. Cord had to focus his eye, in that special way Quentin had taught him, just to make out some detail. It stood motionless. Masked, though even if any of them had been able to see its face, there would have been no difference. Those yellowed eyes beamed out at them.

One of the many legends surrounding the Blue Knives was that they'd trained themselves not to blink. Cord was sure that was about as true as most of the stories told about him, but seeing this warrior monk rooted in the doorway, glaring without hate or malice, he could see why tall tales spread around.

He hadn't mentioned it to anyone, but knowing the possibility of fighting a Blue Knife might come up, Cord had been preparing himself mentally the entire day. But then he looked over his shoulder at Mene, who stood, sword at the ready and eyes steely. And he saw a man of limitless pride who had been preparing himself for years – maybe decades.

There was only one thing he could do. Cord stepped aside, and raised his arm to present Mene to his opponent. "Here's your chance, Vic. Y'know, if you wanted to go first or anything."

Mene puffed himself up, checked the angle on his sword, adjusted his hands along the hilt. Charging straight ahead into a fight with a Blue Knife was certain suicide, even Mene knew that, despite his enthusiasm. So the captain calmly approached the threshold, held his sword out by way of invitation, and stood there, waiting.

And waiting.

And waiting.

Cord waited along with them. Waited so long he gave up his own fighting stance and folded his arms. And while his head told him all of this standing around and posturing was necessary, the action junkie in his gut told him this was taking entirely too long. Not on Mene's end – he was making the only play available to him. It was that lone Blue Knife. What the hell was his holdup?

Then Mene gave him his answer. The captain's patience must have been at an end. He stomped up to the entryway, within spitting distance of the Blue knife, and jabbed his sword toward the monk.

Moving on instinct, the monk swatted it away with his own blade. And then he went back to his still position.

"Are you kidding me?" Cord blurted. This wasn't at all how he expected this fight to go. A little more...movement, at least. Was the monk toying with Mene? Giving him a few moments to think he had a chance in this fight, before laying the hammer down?

Mene had gotten even more irritable. He took three steps back, raised his arms out to his sides. With his free hand, he slapped the plate of armor covering his chest. "Come on! I heard Blue Knives were tough! What are you, huh? I've fought things that have been rotting in the ground with more fight in them than you!" He pounded his chest again.

This got the Blue Knife's attention. He released his position guarding the threshold and came at Mene. A cat's quickness. A pitbull's ferocity.

"Now we've got ourselves a fight," Cord thought out loud, nervously. A sense of concern for Mene's wellbeing crept up into him. It disturbed him.

Mene stumbled back a few paces, off guard from the quickness of the Knife's attack after all those moments of nothing. But he nearly regained his footing just in time to raise his sword up and block a downward swipe from the Knife's blade. With the momentum from his crouched position, he shoved his full weight up, used his gloved hand to grip the blade of his sword, and pushed into the monk, preventing him from moving his own sword as Mene pressed it closer to his chest.

Blue Knives might not blink, but Mene did, and it was all the time the monk needed to display the weird cleverness his people were so revered for. He dropped the sword and somersaulting to the right, then again, so that he was behind Mene.

It gave the monk a good enough angle to sweep a leg around and knock Mene flat on his back. Adding to Mene's humiliation, he flipped over the captain, dropped an elbow into Mene's stomach, and tumbled backwards to retrieve his sword.

Cord, watching through his fingers now, thought back to the time he likened to them to clowns for Allison's benefit, and felt incredibly embarrassed.

Standing no more than fifteen feet away, but too far to be of any assistance if he properly understood the monk's response time, Cord reached to the back of his belt and felt the handles of three small throwing knives. He unsheathed one, flipped it around so the blade was perched between his thumb and forefinger, and held it ready.

In the years since losing his eye, Cord had worked hard to adjust for the loss of depth perception, and had for the most part succeeded. But he still preferred close-in combat, as there was less room for error when he could integrate his other senses into the fight. Long-distance assaults like, for instance, accurately tagging a quickly-moving target, was not his forte. But Mene was losing – badly – and Cord knew he would have to step in to keep the old bastard from getting killed.

With his free hand, he reached back and grabbed the other two knives. Just in case.

Mene had gotten back to his feet, though, enough time to grab his own sword and dodge another attack from the Blue Knife. He seized the moment, pressing the advantage with his size and weight, pushing himself and his blade close to the monk, not giving him time or space to recover as he made short slashing motions once, twice, three times, while the Knife could only back up.

And then Mene freed a hand and quickly punched his opponent right in the face. "Ha. Come on, asshole." He punched the monk again, not a jab this time, harder, meant to put him down. The monk only stumbled back a few feet, but Mene considered it a small victory. "Impress me."

Still at the ready, Cord heard Mene's verbal barbs. "What are you doing, Vic? You always give me grief for talking during a fight. Stop enjoying this and get to business."

And as predicted, Mene lost the upper hand just as quickly as he'd gained it. The Blue Knife had only been using Mene's punches to get the distance needed to double-backflip, giving him some space to move. With that room, he started darting around Mene, jabbing at him with hands and feet, hitting pressure points, until Mene's nerves couldn't keep him standing anymore, sending him crumpling to the ground.

The Blue Knife raised his sword.

"Now or never," Cord told himself, and threw the blade.

It missed, whizzing past the Blue Knife's head. But it got the monk's attention, and he turned to face his new attacker. Cord threw the second knife, hoping for a headshot. It lodged in his chest. If the Blue Knife was hurt, he didn't show it, and took a killing swing at Mene.

The ringing of metal against metal echoed all around as the Blue Knife's sword dug into the armor situated on Mene's shoulderblade.

"It's armor, you moron," Mene grunted, and found the strength to pick his sword up and run the monk through. It was thoroughly embedded.

That one, he felt. Mene pushed the sword and the monk away from him, letting both go.

The Blue Knife stumbled backward, wobbling like a drunk, stabbing his hands out in front of him and trying to grip the sword's handle. When he got a hold of it, he tried to remove it with three good, excruciating yanks. The last one did the trick.

Cord didn't hesitate, and threw his last blade. It lodged into the monk's throat, giving Mene enough time to stand up, tear his sword out of the Blue Knife's hands, and lop off his head, sending it tumbling downhill. A few seconds later, the body fell.

Cord rushed up. "Vic, you okay?"

Mene coughed hard, spat, and then inspected the dent in his shoulder armor. "Hh. Thought you said these guys were tough."

Cord rolled his eye. "Yeah, you're the baddest of the bad, we get it. I'll just ignore all that labored breathing." He bent down to inspect the Blue Knife's body, then found the head and removed the mask. It was completely hairless. Indecipherable blue and black tattoos – tribal markings, Cord assumed, not unlike what the Fel wear, though far more drastic and involved – covering practically every inch of skin. Eyes still opened. Cord opened his mouth. Several teeth were filed down into fangs, and all of them were nearly as yellowed as the eyes.

But there was something else. Things suddenly made a lot more sense to Cord.

"Vic, check this out." He tossed the head to Mene. "Sniff its breath."

Like it was far more of a chore than it actually was, Mene did as he was asked. "It smells terrible. Not unexpected."

"There's something on his breath, can't put my finger on it, exactly. If Welles was here, I bet he could confirm it, but…it's faint, but there's just a tinge of some kind of a mushroom or something."

"So?"

"So I shouldn't smell that. The Blue Knives have a strict diet, only what they grow. Roots and greens. That's it. There's no variation. They don't add spices to their food or anything. I shouldn't be able to smell anything other than roots and greens on his breath, but I'm catching something else."

"Again: so?"

Cord looked back up at the tower. "Grolev dosed them. He probably couldn't hypnotize them outright, their brains are too disciplined – and, for that matter, limited – for him to crawl in that way. If he was going to sway their allegiance, get them looking out for him instead of Allie…" He clapped his hands together with satisfaction. "Ohh, this is fantastic!"

Mene looked an annoyed question at him.

"Not to take the wind out of your sails, but if this guy had been operating at full capacity, you wouldn't have lasted a minute. You're good, but this is all they're built for. Killing is all they know how to do. But Grolev's sacrificed efficiency for loyalty."

When he saw Mene's face go from annoyed to nearly-murderous, Cord knew to clarify. "They're stoned, Vic."

Mene caught on. "Grolev doped them so they'd be suggestible, do his bidding. But the drugs are slowing them down, interfering with their instincts."

"Yeah. Which means we've caught a break. I hope killing one of them isn't going to be enough for you. Stoned or not, there's a good twenty more of them in that tower between us and the Orphan."

Mene peered over at the tower's entranceway. "Some closer than others, it would appear."

Cord turned to look. Three more Blue Knives had come out to fight.

Mene picked up his sword. Cord unsheathed his. They stood side by side.

Mene grinned. "Telling the story of how I killed a Blue Knife was attractive to me. Telling the story of how I killed twenty of them…"

Cord laughed. "You'll be a popular guy."

Mene nodded in agreement. "Then let's go to work."

55. Goodbye Teacher

Outside the fighting continued. Blood was spilling. People were dead or dying. Some of them still fighting even after. The sounds of violence carrying through the air, loud and serious as thunder.

Welles walked through the empty ghost town that had until recently been a community of laborers, blacksmiths, cooks, and all the other support staff that had been the first to go in the dead soldiers' initial attack. Hunting for that feeling that told him he was close. But he still kept an ear on his comrades. It was strangely comforting. He needed to know they were okay.

The deranged howl that Nathan Cord carried with him into battle could be heard echoing off the kingdom walls. Irritable grunts of derision from Victor Mene sounded off as he collided his shield into one attacker, the crisp metallic swipe of his sword ringing out in the air as he took the head off of another. He was cursing and laughing at his opponents, whereas before he had been calling them all by name and offering them heartfelt, if brief, apologies. Welles knew then that Cord and Mene must have engaged the Blue Knives.

They were making their way into the tower. It sounded like they were doing well. As well as could be expected, anyway.

Further out by the barrier, Quinn Kind was shouting commands to her troops, telling them to stay loose and mobile, but watch each other's backs. Her voice clear and confident. During one of their hushed lovers' conversations, she had confided in Welles that she felt like she was just posing at leadership, but Welles told her then, with absolute confidence and admiration, that she was a true warrior-queen, born and bread. A force to be reckoned with. Listening to her out there, he was happy to have even more proof.

When he focused, he could hear her heart beat a rhythmic staccato. But just a little bit faster than usual.

Welles listened to it, and tapped his chest in time. His own heart sped up briefly, matching hers, and he made a quick, silent prayer for her safety. Then he prayed for the safety of everyone else out there.

He could hear all of those sounds of violence. But then he found the rear outer door to a wine cellar, adorned with locks and attached to a long-disused hovel. He zapped the locks off it, and hoisted the heavy door open. Once he took the first step leading down into that cellar, nothing else registered in him. The view absorbed all of his attention.

In the far corner of this hovel that nobody ever referred to out loud as a dungeon and certainly not as a torture chamber – because Arius would never imprison dissidents, now would he? – underneath a single pathetically tiny barred window, a crumpled, naked figure sat motionless. His legs carelessly crossed, his long, thin arms limp at his side. His eyes staring out at nothing. Beard and hair grown wild and unkempt for years without concern. Figure withered to a husk.

All that violence outside, friends and lovers fighting for their lives, and maybe for something greater. But for that one endless moment, none of that mattered to Welles.

Not more than this shell in front of him that used to be called Keegan Morris.

"Oh, Kee…" Welles whispered, sad and horrified and angry and all those terrible emotions that Morris had taught him to dispel in order to unlock his potential.

He shut the door behind him and approached the body. Welles could hear Morris's heart, too. He had to wait a few moments to be sure it was still beating. "Keegan, I'm so sorry."

"You and me both," the voice just outside Welles' mind agreed.

That voice was the only thing that kept Welles from crying. It wasn't completely unexpected. But this was the first time in the past few days that Welles had heard it so distinctly that he could make out actual words. Up until now, it hadn't been more than a nagging thought at the back of his mind – a sense of something Keegan Morris might tell him, if he were there. Different enough from his own thoughts to assure him that he wasn't going a little bit mad.

It wouldn't have surprised him if that had been the case – better magicians than him had lost their minds over the years. Occupational hazard.

But when that non-voice got him to turn his attention to Bloody Twilight, Welles went out, just in time to see the dead men rising. And then that voice turned into something else, a reserve of power that he knew wasn't coming from him. It gave him ideas, and helped him put up that dome, to lock the monsters in. That big yellow burst of energy had been Keegan's trademark for the last few years before his disappearance. It was the signal to let Welles know he was still out there.

The longer his mind stayed in touch with the non-voice of his teacher, the stronger his intuition became that something awful had happened. And once inside the barrier, it led him here, to what he could only describe as a tomb for a living man.

Welles walked closer to Morris's body and knelt down in front of it. "Keegan, tell me what happened." He looked at the pathetic, lifeless face, expecting an answer to come out of its chapped lips at first. He was relieved that Morris's voice, ever clearer, came from somewhere else.

"Grolev happened. The skinny little prick always had it out for me. Clothes, not the face...Crap...He weaseled his way in with Arius, got the king...not Lucius, the king, the other one, what did I say?...got him to agree to take me out. I didn't see him coming. His magic is all about death, that's not something I'm usually attuned to. He always said my 'hippy-dippy nonsense' would be the end of me, didn't realize he'd be...bebe...damn it...."

"What's wrong?" Welles asked, and, looking at Morris's body again, felt incredibly stupid for asking.

"Where to start?" Morris answered, sanguine. "I don't really have a lot of time here, though...lot of time...time in lots, big empty lots..."

Welles nodded gravely. "You're slipping out. I don't get it, you managed to stay alive for all these years, why is it now...?"

Morris's voice, lazy and racing all at once, did its best to explain. "I spent all these years locked inside my own brain. That's what he did, took every bit of me that was connected to the world, shoved it into a tiny box inside my mind...spent years trying to pull enough bits of energy out of my body to get out...that spell, wh-wha-whaaatever Grolev did to start this horror, I think that wave of magic everywhere gave me just a little boost, enough to pry myself free, but it's keeping every bit of concentration just to hold together and I...dammit dammit DAMN IT, come on..."

"It's okay, Kee," Welles told him, stroking his body's head to comfort him, even though he knew there was nobody in there. "You did it, it worked."

That initial clarity of tone that brought Welles to the dungeon was beginning to break down, he realized. Morris's voice was growing tinny and confused. "Listen," Morris started, uncertainly, "I'm really happy to see you, really happy it was you who picked up on what I was really happy it was you...crap...you picked up what I was putting down," the teacher told him.

Welles felt tears fight their way out, down his cheeks. "Yeah, me too. Just tell me, what can I do? Can I get you back in there? Together, we could probably get something going, counteract the spell..."

"No, I was thinking something else." Welles thought Morris was just pausing for effect like the showman he remembered, but then Morris continued, "...I had a dog before I got here...can't remember his name now. Ray, Roy, Roger...an R name...wonder if he's okay..."

"Keegan, keep it together, man. Just tell me what I can do." He was doing his best to keep it together too, as he cradled his mentor's useless body.

"Kill me."

"...What?"

Sounding far away inside a tin can, Morris repeated, "Kill me. Welles, just snap my neck or smother me, or something, just put my body to rest. Not hard, I barely breathe and I think, 20 heartbeats a day babum...ba...bum...I can feel myself slipping back into that box and it's too much abersuch, such a crutch to doubledutch...come on, come on..."

Welles made no more attempts to stop the tears and they began to pour freely. "Keegan, I'll do it, but I need some help, man, I don't know what else I can do here! The monsters aren't stopping, your barrier won't hold too much longer, and Grolev's more than any of us can handle. And that's even assuming Mene and Cord can get past the Blue Knives. You're the smartest man I've ever known. You're my teacher. You've got to have some idea."

"If you kill me you'll figure it out."

Welles nodded. He didn't understand the instruction, but knew there was more to it than just euthanasia. Morris simply couldn't find it in him to get it out any better.

So Welles kissed Keegan Morris's forehead, and whispered, "Goodbye, teacher."

Then he clamped one hand over Morris's nose and mouth, and the other on his bony chest. Welles felt the already shallow breathing stutter, and after long, agonizing minutes, eventually stop. His chest fell for the last time.

It was the most awful moment of Welles' life.

And then suddenly it was astonishing.

56. Sing Songs for the Crazy Man

It was a miracle that Mene and Cord had gotten into the spiral corridors of the high tower in the first place. Even with the blessed handicap of the Blue Knives being a little too out of it to fight properly, killing five of them just to get through the door had proved to be more life-threatening than a hundred of the undead soldiers. A mucked-up Blue Knife was still ten times tougher than the best of the royal guard.

But they made it through. By sheer force of will, it seemed. Saving the Orphan had given Cord a newfound stamina; Mene had deemed it necessary to survive in order to tell his soldiers that he had personally slaughtered an entire cadre of the queen in waiting's personal warriors. It didn't matter to him that at that moment, he had no soldiers. He would rebuild. And then they would learn what a real guardsman could do.

Mene always found it best to lead by example. When the two old soldiers had finally killed the last of the Blue Knives that had engaged them, Mene knew that there was no better example he could make.

Now, in the narrow spiral staircase leading up to the top of the high tower, Mene and Cord found that their greatest advantage – that the structure of the high tower precluded a massive assault – worked both ways. Only a few attacks could come from above, but the corridor was only wide enough for two at a time - Mene and Cord – to charge up.

Their Fel backup stayed near the base of the stairwell, swarming and picking off whatever Blue Knives the two guardsmen could shove past them on their way to the top. But the Blue Knives had the high ground and would continue to hold it, sending only a few of their number at a time, careful not to crowd themselves but still engulfing the men who came to kill Grolev. Victor Mene and Nathan Cord both noticed they were fighting the actual definition of an uphill battle.

"Vic, sweep the leg!" Cord barked as Mene took first position into a fresh wave of the Knives.

It must have been a serious situation, because Mene didn't waste time telling Cord that he knew what he was doing and didn't need any advice. He swung his sword up at the incoming monk's knees. The monk leapt past the attack, bounced against the corridor and hurled himself over Mene and into Cord.

"Nicely done," Cord whispered, grabbing the Knife and using the momentum to hurl him over his shoulder. Cord turned around to watch the monk land on his back at the bottom of the stairwell, where the Fel, as instructed, gleefully hacked away at him.

"One more down!" Cord called up to Mene, only to find Mene out of view – he'd already turned the corner of the spiral stairway. Cord increased speed up the stairs, then heard a clanging noise of metal against brick, and felt his own foot nearly trip over Mene's longsword.

"Son of a bitch," Cord spat out and ran faster, half-expecting to find the captain's body. But when he turned the corner, the sight he took in told him he would never need to worry over Victor Mene's safety: Mene plunging a short blade deep into the chests of two Knives.

With a moment to spare, Mene faced Cord. "The long sword's no use in a narrow space like this. Thought I'd change tactics."

"Wasn't worried for a second," Cord covered. "How many have we taken down?"

Mene yanked the two swords out, put his back against the wall, and knelt down while he did the math. "The six outside, and we've managed…hold on." He returned the short swords to their sheaths on his back, gripped the shirts of his two fresh kills, and hurled their bodies down the steps. Then, cupping his hands around his mouth, he bellowed, "Hey, Fel! How many bodies are down there?"

A moment's quiet was followed up with the echo of, "Eight!" from the base of the stairs.

Cord looked at Mene, then nodded. "Let's keep moving. Hang back, I'll take point for a while."

Mene, for once, didn't argue.

As he ran up the steps, Cord scooped up two of the Blue Knives' short curved blades without pausing. Mene had the right idea. And just in time, too – the next turn brought three more Knives into play.

Cord crossed the blade in his left hand over his chest, slicing into one of them while jutting the sword in his right upward, hoping to jab the second monk in the gut when he lunged for Mene.

But the second monk didn't jump. Instead he curled himself up and barreled down the stairs in a ball, plowing over Cord as he made way for Mene. The Knives had adapted to their fighting style.

"You utter bastards..." Cord started, rubbing his ribs. From the way he had hit the edge of the stair, he was sure one of them was broken.

It was the first serious wound he'd sustained through the entire battle so far. A few cuts and scrapes here, a couple bloody noses, but this was the first injury that he couldn't ignore or patch up on the fly. It pissed him off.

"Never fight angry," he reminded himself, then remembered that it was Victor Mene who had first given him that advice. But his entire career had proved it wrong – when Nathan Cord fought with rage in his belly, anyone in his way was just a body that hadn't yet been counted.

He hoisted himself up, let all those mean feelings seep into his muscles, and just to make himself feel a little better, he stabbed the Blue Knife corpse laying next to him, dipped a hand into the wound, and smeared the blood over his face.

He knew it was just theatrics, but he didn't care. Nathan Cord was ready for some more violence.

There had been three Blue Knives in this last wave. One was busy fighting Mene behind him. Cord was wearing the second one's blood. Where was the third...?

Just when it dawned on him, he crossed his two blades in front of him to block the third's assault. Cord dodged a few more swordthrusts, but the moment he leaned to his left, the searing pain of his broken rib ran through him.

It distracted him just long enough for the monk to casually, elegantly run him through.

Those yellow eyes gazed at him. Intent and yet completely uninterested. Cord tried to return the stare as best he could, but his vision blurred slightly, and he looked down. He saw the hilt, and then a bit of the blade, and then...

He craned his neck around as far as he could to check out his back. The point was sticking out behind him.

"Oh," was all Cord could muster. He felt terribly stupid. And then the Blue Knife gripped the handle and shoved deeper, and then Cord felt terrible agony.

"GGGGhhhhhhh!" he groaned savagely. It caught Mene's attention.

Mene had been going back and forth with his own opponent in the narrow corridor, neither of them able to press an advantage, when he heard a sadly familiar noise – the impending death of one of his soldiers. Without a thought, he pushed himself harder, shoved his body into the monk, knocking him viciously into the stone wall, again and again and again, until the Knife's muscles relaxed just enough for Mene to grab his head and twist it all the way around. He didn't even wait to watch it drop, just turned and sprinted up the stairs, around the bend.

He saw Nathan Cord with a Blue Knife's sword all the way through him. Cord had a hand locked on the monk's throat. And then he saw Cord look down at the wound, touch his own blood, and smear it on the Blue Knife's face.

Then Cord gripped the monk's head, gurgled, "...your stupid ugly fricking eyes..." and jammed his thumbs into the monk's eye sockets.

That the monk did not scream fascinated Mene, just briefly, but he tossed his curiosity aside when Nathan Cord slumped down onto the steps.

Mene knelt down beside him. "Cord, this is a mortal wound."

Cord coughed out a laugh. Then he coughed out blood. "Really? That's a shock, Vic, it really is."

Ignoring the sad attempt at bravado, Mene turned to the base of the stairwell and bellowed, "Fel! Three of you, up here NOW!" Then, turning back to Cord, he stated calmly, "I'm going to pull the sword out. Then the Fel will take you out of here. If they can find Welles, he may be able to help you."

"Don't be stupid, you'll need them to – "

"On three," Mene continued.

"Ah, hell," Cord coughed. More blood sputtered out.

"One. Two."

"Three!" Cord hurriedly finished for him. Mene pulled the blade out swiftly.

Cord's scream echoed through the entire corridor. "Hhhhh...hhhhh..." he eventually heaved out.

"It's a good death, Cord."

"It's a crap death, Vic," Cord snarled. He looked down at the gut wound that Mene pressed his hand against. Fighting through the pain, he continued his lecture. "A good death is after Allie is safe. You do that, damn it. Keep the Fel close by, use them. Don't worry about me."

Mene had no words of comfort in him. All he could say was, "I will." Then, remembering Cord's sense of tradition and sentiment, he asked, "Do you have any last requests?"

Cord rolled his eye. Enduring Mene's attempt at humanity was almost as painful as his injuries. "Yeah, sure. If she's still alive...tell Quinn I'm sorry. And if everything works out...make sure they sing songs for the crazy man. Good songs. Mug-swinging, foot-stomping songs, all about me. That'd be..."

"Cord?" Mene asked.

"That'd be fun..." Cord thought he said, but Mene called his name out again, from far away, and Cord realized that this was it.

57. Aiden Fletcher's Last Stand

"...And you used to be such a sweet young boy, too," Quinn said to the snarling, dead-eyed thing that had once been Aiden Fletcher. She had said that recently to Nathan Cord, chiding him, but though she was now going for bravado, she meant every word of it. Aiden had been a sweet young boy only days ago. And now she was going to have to take his head off.

When Allison had first been born, Quinn never would have imagined herself taking an active hand in raising the daughter of a king. Particularly a king like Arius, who had, in the few short years that he had been in power, turned away from everything his brother had set in motion, seeming ready, even eager, to revert Western Sun to its barbarian roots. What Arius, ever the historian, had deemed its "glory days."

Allison's mother, Emma, had died only weeks before the child's third birthday, and though the idea was rarely given voice, everyone – citizen and Pic alike – assumed that Arius had had something to do with the death. He was exactly that kind of man. With her mother gone, with only her father's influence to guide her from now on, everyone looked at Allison as a monster just waiting in the wings.

But Quinn would have none of that. She had always been a firm believer in nurture over nature, and would be damned if the girl turned out to be her father's daughter. After Emma took her fatal fall down the stairs of the high tower, Quinn cemented her position that this child would not take after her father. She enlisted Nathan and Kendra Cord to her cause. They had no immediate plans to start a family, but they took to Allison all the same. She was such a lovely little girl, how could they not?

"Aiden, can you hear me?" she attempted, knowing full well that it was a useless attempt. He coughed and spat out his thoughts, such as they were. She kept on. "My name is Quinn Kind. I'm a friend of Allison's. Can you hear me?"

He tensed up his frame, and Quinn recognized that Aiden was about to charge at her. She firmed up her grip on the Stem.

"Ngyaaaaarrrr...." Aiden's corpse bellowed as it ran towards Quinn. She was tired from her previous encounters with his dead brethren, to be sure. She figured that made it closer to a fair fight. After all, she had fought ten-to-one odds. One-on-one was no challenge at all.

Aiden's corpse ran towards her, and she danced to the left, stabbing him in the side as she dodged. He stumbled further on, confused and angry.

Quinn couldn't bring herself to put him down. His presence brought with him a terrible sense of loss.

"Aiden, listen to me," she said, in her most commanding voice. For Allison's sake, she had to try, just one more time. "Allison loves you. Do you remember Allison?"

Clutching his side, Aiden made another move against her. She sprang up over him, bashing his head with the blunt end of the Stem as she made her landing.

"Fine," she concluded. "The girl's going to hate me for this forever, but okay. Let's do it."

With the help of Nathan and Kendra, it had been easy to raise Allison. She was such a smart little girl, and why shouldn't she be? In place of actual quality time with his daughter, Arius had made sure she had the finest teachers Western Sun could produce. But it was Nathan who taught her about honor and justice, and the kingdom that was her birthright to lead. Kayla who had taught her courtesy, dignity, and how to be a lady in the most amazing sense of the word. And for her part, Quinn had used her years with Allison to pass on all the lessons of leadership that she herself had been taught. If Quinn had been allowed to stay, hadn't been pulled out of the kingdom by her panicked Mothers, she may have helped raise the first human warrior-queen of Bloody Twilight.

If she had been allowed to stay, she might have been able to counsel Allison through her grief. And Grolev wouldn't have been able to put the ugly lie into her head, that Aiden could be revived.

"I suppose if she gets to be mad at me, I get to be mad at you, Aiden," she grumbled, preparing the Stem for its inevitable killing blow. "Let's face it, if you hadn't gone and died, we wouldn't be here now, would we? So this is as much your fault as mine."

Aiden made his final, flailing, clumsy attack. Quinn assured her balance, and jammed the tip of the Stem firmly, decisively into Aiden's chest. Then she shoved forward, knocking him onto his back.

No more words, she decided. She stood over him. Before he could make any further movement, she pulled the Stem from his chest and made the killing blow. And Aiden Fletcher, the Queen in Waiting's one and only love, was dead once more.

Sitting down next to his body, giving herself a moment to recharge, she addressed him again. "I kept tabs on her, you know. I can come and go through this kingdom without being seen, and enough people were around that I could watch her progress. When I heard about you…I truly regret never having gotten to know you, Aiden. I heard you made my girl very happy."

She stood up and walked away from the body. "Won't get to meet you now," she admitted mournfully as she looked to the high tower. "But I suppose I can try to avenge you."

58. The Wisdom of Dying Men

Nathan Cord hunched there, limp against the steps, weak and tired and mostly feeling very stupid that this was how he was going to die.

It didn't help matters that he couldn't stop thinking about Jonas Mudd. Specifically, Jonas Mudd begging and crying just before Cord cut him open and dumped his body in a shallow grave.

Plenty of soldiers think about how they might die – no big shock there – but Cord had never been one of them. When he was active with the guard, he was completely aware that death might come to him, but never had much interest in trying to predict when or how it would come about. He only went so far as being certain that he would die violently. Men like him don't croak in bed at a ripe old age, he knew. Though over the last few years, he had worried that his death would come at the hands of an angry bar patron wielding a broken bottleneck. To be killed by a Blue Knife...that was something, at least. "A good death," by Mene's standards.

Mene...Cord wondered where he had gone off to. A shout from up the corridor gave him his answer.

"I bring death, you sorry shadows of soldiers!"

So Mene was taking his death in stride. Cord smiled at the thought, then frowned at how mundane it was.

He always assumed that before he died, he would think Significant Thoughts. He would look over his life, see his friends and loved ones, put into context his triumphs and his failures. But no, it was just the image of Jonas Mudd on his knees, pleading with Cord to spare him. He couldn't get it out of his head.

Cord had long ago lost track of how many men he had killed in his time, but figured it had to number in the high hundreds. But very few of them had meant anything to him. In fact, he could only think of two: Arius, and Jonas Mudd. He had killed so many. Today alone, he had even managed to re-kill a lot of men. But Arius and Mudd were the only men that Cord had ever murdered.

That said, it still surprised him that Jonas Mudd, rather than Arius, would haunt his thoughts as he bled out on the cold stone steps of the high tower.

Killing Arius had happened in a fit of rage, and try as he might, Cord would never be able to clearly remember exactly what had happened that night. He knew why he had gone up to Arius's chambers – Cord had just finished a mission that involved assassinating a group of potential dissenters, just punk kids with some silly armbands and half-baked plans, and it had been the last straw for him. He was going up there to tender his resignation, and tell Arius just how bad everything had gotten. But once he made his way into Arius's room, it was just a jumble of recollections. Kayla in Arius's bed. A lot of shouting and threats. Arius snapping Kayla's neck in a fit of pique. A mean grin while he did it. People always commented on Cord's smile, but they'd never seen anything like the satisfied hate spreading across Arius's lips that night.

Then he could remember nothing but red. The blankness was followed by the image of Allison looking at him for the first time with terror and tears in her eyes.

When it came to Jonas Mudd, however, Cord could remember everything clear as day.

It had been one of Cord's dumber ideas, after killing Arius, to commandeer – no, not "commandeer," he stole it, that cruddy little scooner from the harbor, to make his way to the next continent. He had no idea what he would do there, he only knew that nobody would recognize him. He also had practically no idea of how to sail a boat by himself, and that lack of knowledge had nearly killed him. A storm came his way, wrecked his tiny craft, and left him adrift on a piece of driftwood for days. For one time only, the appearance of the Royal Hell was a cause for celebration. Though Cord had been too dehydrated and delirious to cheer.

The Royal Hell had been a notorious vessel along the coast. It was one of the first ships that Arius had authorized to be part of the royal navy, but the fact of the matter was Western Sun had no true cause to develop a naval fleet – they had no enemies out past the coast, and commissioning a ship for that reason was all at once stupid, arrogant, and terrifying in its implications. It sent the message that annexing the north and the east were not enough for Arius's agenda; he wanted to expand to the seaside, and possibly beyond it, to parts unknown.

In commissioning that ship, he'd given Jonas Mudd, a thug and a pirate, the mandate to do whatever he liked with the approval of the crown. And Mudd had enjoyed that privilege for years. He made sure he looked the part of the admiral, with a military-styled jacket, epulets and all. But it didn't change his pockmarked skin, the curly, greasy hair hanging down past his shoulders, the sharpened gold tooth. He could dress however he liked. No one ever mistook him for anything but a thug and a pirate.

The seas were terrified of him. He would keep small ships in dock, board larger freighters that might have been carrying curious shipments across continents, and sometimes simply pick fights with other boats just for the hell of it. To give his men something to do and put off the possibility of mutiny.

Cord spent a few days on the Royal Hell, nearly out of his mind from hunger and exposure. Once he had regained his senses, got a grip on his surroundings, he decided that it would be his pleasure to bring Jonas Mudd down so hard he never got up.

He bided his time, worked on the ship quietly, made only a couple of actual friends while observing the other men closely, being careful not to piss anyone off in the process. It hadn't been easy for Cord. He wasn't a social person in normal circumstances. And hiding his own identity on a boat of pirates was nothing like "normal circumstances." But over the course of the next year, while working as a deck hand on the Royal Hell, he developed his plans. On shore leave, he would hang out with the other crewmen, subtly feel out where their loyalties lay. Figuring out which were the men who simply loved sailing and got in over their heads with the Royal Hell assignment. Men like Udo.

Eventually, he felt he was ready to take Mudd out. His plans afterward were more vague – he had no real interest in stealing the boat, or anything so elaborate. He simply couldn't stand to see this bastard Mudd waging a guerilla naval war that didn't exist anywhere outside of his own swelled ego. It gave Cord a purpose when he was desperately in need of one.

It hadn't occurred to him that he wasn't the only one with extracurricular activities when on leave. Jonas Mudd had been checking out his new charge's background every time they got back to shore, slowly pulling apart every bit of Cord's vague and hasty cover story. He'd told them he was rancher from the Northlands who'd just lost his wife, and thought he'd get away from it all, try something new for a change. It seemed a convincing enough tale to Cord, but in retrospect, he wasn't surprised that it didn't hold up to close inspection.

When Cord sprung his trap, calling on the men he thought were in his camp to take the boat for themselves, he had been surprised when so few of them followed his orders. Udo. A couple others. Not nearly enough to win an argument like this.

The rest of them had been told that that one-eyed man they'd all come to know and trust as a brother was the killer of the king. There would be rewards for his death. It was the sale of the century for a bunch of pirates who were of late in the kingdom's employ. And Mudd played it up, made a big show of arresting Cord, "by the right bestowed upon the Ocean's Hand of the King." He actually used those words, the pompous bastard.

And then, because Jonas Mudd was a traditionalist, he took the Royal Hell out into deep waters and made Cord and the other mutineers walk the plank. Those few men who followed Cord died. Blind, stupid luck left Cord and Udo alive. Driftwood, waves, and the sacks of coin they'd stolen from the war chests and hidden on their persons that gave them weight. They managed to get to shore despite all odds.

The only thing Cord could focus on at that point was the complete stinking idiocy of his actions. Actions he took out of misplaced rage, actions that cost decent men their lives, at the hands of a preening egotistical lizard of a ship commander.

Udo and Cord sat on a beach that day and discussed their next move, pointless as that was. Cord caustically suggested tossing it all aside and building a bar somewhere, gave Udo the money he had on him, and walked away.

Angry and frustrated, Cord knew he had few options left to him. He knew that suicide was slowly but surely becoming one of them. But he also knew that there was one bridge he hadn't yet burned, and made his way back to the Pic forest.

His time there rescued him from madness. Quinn looked after his soul, and Quentin took the task of rebuilding his body and mind. Two years with them, and he began to make himself a new man. But he never shook off that anger. He had so much hate stockpiled in his heart, and nowhere to direct it. So when he took his leave of the village, he went back out to the seaside. He asked the right questions, followed the trail, and one night ambushed Jonas Mudd in a brothel. What was it called? "The Peg-Leg's Delight"? Something like that, anyway.

Bound and gagged him, and dragged him off in the dead of night.

Cord could still feel the exhilaration that came when Mudd started begging to be let go. Not the actual words – Cord only remembered a lot of "Please!" and "Don't do this!" gargled out through Mudd's gag, but his mind was made up. Killing Jonas Mudd wouldn't do much. But there was a chance that it would quiet down the anger in Cord's gut. There was even the possibility that it might feel very, very good.

Cord walked Jonas Mudd up to the hills just north of the Pic forest. Up to a hole Cord had dug especially for the occasion.

"You awful, murderous son of a bitch," Cord accused, when Mudd was on his knees at the mouth of his own grave. "You are a blight on this world. And you're going to die."

Mudd screamed some more pleas, but they were incomprehensible with the gag. So Cord yanked it out of his mouth. Along with a couple of teeth.

"Please, Cord. You don't know what you're doing! I can help you! I'm the royal fricking navy, they'll listen to me, whatever you want, I can get that to happen!"

The begging made Cord hate him more. "I don't want anything," he answered. Sad honesty coating his words. He kicked his heel into Mudd's face and the admiral fell back into the ditch. Then Cord pulled out his sword and plunged it into Jonas Mudd's chest. And then twisted and dragged the blade. Mudd's screaming was musical to him.

After that, he made his way back to the Northlands, just south of Northern Sun, found the bar that Udo had built, and irritably named it. When Quinn came around, wondering about "Admiral Mudd's Lament," Cord simply told her to spread the word that the kingkiller was back in town, and he would suffer no fools. And she spread a lot of stories, some more plausible than others, to scare people away from him.

Looking back, Cord remembered Quinn telling him how much fun it was to spread tall tales of big bad Nathan Cord. But as he lay dying on those steps, he came to realize how awful it must have really made her feel, that she had to tell stories that cast her friend as a monster, just to keep him out of trouble.

Between killing Mudd and making deals with Fehrer, Cord had systematically dismantled all the work the Pic clan had put into trying to put his broken soul back together. But Quinn told those stories anyway, built up the frightening legend of Nathan Cord. Because that was all she could do anymore, for a friend at the end of his rope.

Bleeding and coughing, Cord amused himself with the knowledge that what he had once thought to be the end of his rope wasn't even close. The real end was sitting and bleeding to death on the steps of the high tower, knowing that he hadn't accomplished any noble goal. In his life, he had quelled insurrections, assassinated rebels, killed a king, and murdered an admiral. Not exactly a righteous pattern.

He wished he could tell Quinn how sorry he was for disappointing her. And he knew then the curse of all dying men: the knowledge that they'd never get the chance to apologize for the wrongs they had done.

Cord coughed. The feeling of warm blood running up his throat and out of his mouth was disturbing to him. But he knew he deserved it.

This was why he couldn't stop thinking about Jonas Mudd, he decided. Like it or not, that was the defining point in his life. Killing a stupid bastard out of hate and anger. No glory of war, no protecting the people he cared about. This was the death Cord had earned, through viciousness and petty revenge. And he'd never get the chance to rise to anything better. He wanted to so badly. He didn't want to die having accomplished nothing but savagery. He wanted to do something good.

But looking down at the blood pouring out of him, Nathan Cord realized he just didn't have the time left to do it.

He was mistaken.

59. Goddamn the Mothers

Quinn was exhausted. Since meeting back up with her soldiers at the perimeter, they had managed to take down wave after wave of dead men. And women. And children. Along with her people, she had managed to kill Bloody Twilight all over again. But they kept on coming. She soon found herself looking back with something almost like fondness for her one-on-one fight with Aiden. In retrospect, it was the only restful period she'd had in hours.

Reports from her people told her that the residential villages, Crowsback, Hanging Tree, Dead Courtyard and the like, were clean. One go-around of the Dovebone Alleys and cross-streets that connected those inner neighborhoods was enough to convince her that the bulk of the threat remained in the outskirts, close to the border walls. But the dead men had begun to swarm again, and her ranks were thinning.

Her mothers were right, she thought. All seven of them.

They had chastised her throughout her tenure as ambassador to Western Sun, for growing too close to the humans. She never quite understood their frustrations. She had been sent to learn human ways and in turn teach Pic ways to those she felt would be most accommodating to them. Nathan and Kayla Cord were prime examples.

Granted, their whole marriage was strange to Quinn at the outset. They claimed to love each other, but spent so much time arguing, about...well, no topic was off-limits. At first, it was about when Cord's tour of duty would end, when they were going to leave Western Sun. But eventually the arguments focused on where they would live, and if they would have children. When Allison was a child, they argued about what they would teach her about her own people. She remembered a mild debate over when she should first hear the name "Bloody Twilight."

It was as fascinating as it was strange, and Quinn had gotten front-row seats for this prime example of human behavior at its most concerned and strenuous.

How could they ask her to leave all of that?

Arius had been a deciding factor. During Lucius's reign, the Pics held some hope of spreading their way of life, but with Arius in power, there was nothing left to offer. He didn't care about expanding ideas. He just wanted land – places that were Western Sun, and places owned by Western Sun. The Pic mothers understood that, even if Quinn thought there might be a chance. A ray of possibility.

She believed that people like Nathan and Kayla Cord might spread that ideal among their people. She told the Pic mothers that this would be the case.

How wrong that all turned out.

It wasn't that Cord had let her down. It wasn't his fault, really. He was a soldier, one of their best, and went where they sent him. And they sent him to Northern Sun, and Eastern Sun, and before she even realized it, Cord had been away for two years without even getting a chance to speak to Quinn.

Or Kayla.

Only now did Quinn realize just how big a folly that had been, keeping Cord away from his wife. How much that might have cost her people in the long run. A Nathan Cord with a strong marriage could have become a leader in his community, helped open minds and pave new roads. But the endless campaigns instead created a Cord that was isolated from his wife, and by extension, his people.

Quinn put the idea aside. More monsters were attacking her section. She called, and her warriors attacked as instructed, destroying the monsters as they came. Quinn wondered how many more onslaughts they could endure. She cursed her mothers.

"There's nothing left to care about," Mother Dalla told her frankly, one autumn afternoon. "Those humans are going to murder each other, and if we're not careful, they're going to kill us, too. We had a chance with Lucius, but this Arius fellow…"

"Yes, he's warlike, yes, he is focused on his own agenda," Quinn began her argument. "But I believe they can evolve. I have become friends with some of the humans, mother. Like Nathan and Kayla Cord. These are good people. If given the chance, they can steer Western Sun toward something better, if we only give them some support."

Mother Dalla laughed at her. *Actually* laughed at her. "Oh, sweet child. You want us to put our faith in the leader of a team of assassins, and his neglected wife?" And then Mother Dalla added insult to injury by patting Quinn on the head. "Dear, you've been with them too long. You've lost your objectivity."

"Lost my objectivity," Quinn growled as she fended off another group of monsters. "Screw those old bitches."

The Pic mothers had sent her into Bloody Twilight to learn what the humans were like. She told them about their greatest qualities: their curiosity, their compassion, their sympathy. But when Arius came to power and instituted his aggressive policies, those same qualities were nowhere to be found in the Pic clan.

"Arius will bring his war to our people. He will look west and wonder if he can claim it for himself. This is not an opinion. This is fact," Mother Caulder told Quinn during one briefing session. "Look at them. They've even turned away from Keegan Morris, and you know what hopes we had for him."

"Arius doesn't speak for all of them, damn it!" Quinn pushed, though she knew she spoke upon deaf ears. "If you give Nathan Cord a chance, I believe he can turn Arius's opinion towards something better."

"Cord?" Mother Caulder scoffed. "I know you have affection for this human, dear, but he's as corrupted as any of them. Why, your own brother has told us of some monstrous deeds he's performed just recently. He killed some youthful dissenters to the throne. On Arius's orders. This is what the humans do, dear Quinn. They kill their own children to preserve the will of the kingdom."

Quinn had been blindsided by the accusation. Cord had never spoken much of his Coal Brigade missions. She had assumed it was simply military code. Only then did it occur to her that it might have been shame.

It crushed her.

What she heard next crushed her even more.

"Your mothers and I have discussed this at length. We're pulling out of Western Sun. You are to have no further contact with this horror of a place. They are beyond our help, Quinn."

Quinn remembered the moment, just a day before the Pic clan gave up on Western Sun, when she asked Cord to explain what her mothers had told her, about his assassination missions.

"I can't talk about it," Cord told her coldly. But she had known him a long time by then, and understood his tone. She knew that Cord had done something he was having trouble living with. That he had likely done a great many things he was having trouble living with. Those deeds were beginning to poison him, and he didn't want to bring Quinn into it.

He turned away from her that day, and Quinn knew that she couldn't turn him back around. The Pic clan gave up on Western Sun. And believing that someday Bloody Twilight would turn its attention on the Pic forest, they instituted mandatory combat training for all of their people.

Without actual provocation, the Kingdom of Western Sun had put the Pic clan on a war footing. She had gone to change Bloody Twilight, and instead it changed her people. The horrid irony of it all broke her heart.

Quinn found herself thankful for all that combat training, however, when more monsters came at her and more of her brothers came to her rescue.

"I think we've killed them all!" David Archolm exclaimed proudly. Quinn slapped him in the back of the head.

"There's always more of them, damn it! Always! Keep on alert!"

But then, bursting up from the ground and then running up from the horizon, she saw Gavin Beglari. If it had been anyone else, she wouldn't have cared, but Quentin always had a crush on Gavin, so Quinn recognized him.

"Quinn! Quinn!!" he shouted.

"What's up?" she asked urgently.

"Man, what isn't?" he huffed. He had made his way through miles of dirt to deliver the message. "Quentin's found the survivors. And Cord and Mene took some of the Fel into the high tower."

Quinn took it in. This meant a lot. It meant everything. It meant that all this fighting might not be a suicide run after all. But she could only think to ask one question.

"Have you heard anything about Welles?"

Gavin answered, "From what I heard, Welles went on his own to track down someone. Or something. I don't know, it's all pretty speculative at this point." Quinn glared at him. He knew more details were expected, and after searching his memory, continued, "Quentin said Welles just started barking orders, then flew off into the support staff's quarters. Cord just said he 'had his own mission,' nothing more."

Quinn accepted the answer. "And Cord and Mene are in the high tower."

"With some of the Fel, yes ma'am."

Quinn gripped the Stem fiercely. "I'm going to join them. Help with clean-up here. I have faith in all of you. But if events take a turn for the worse, you get back to the high tower and alert me. I want updates the moment things go wrong."

"Yes, ma'am," Gavin answered.

"You got me?" Quinn pressured.

"Yes, ma'am," Gavin answered again, resolutely.

"Good boy," Quinn gave him, and ran off toward the high tower.

She could run quickly to the tower, but quick wasn't fast enough. She needed to be like lightning. So she sank into the ground.

Humans couldn't possibly understand what happens to a Pic when they go underground. Some of the stupider ones think the Pics are a burrowing people. Like gofers. And some think it's like magic, a disappearing act. The truth was somewhere inbetween. Pics literally become one with the ground, their bodies becoming a liquid version of their own forms, traveling through the earth on the waves of water held in the dirt. There are no human words to describe the act.

When Quinn erupted next to the entrance of the high tower, she gave some consideration to writing out just what sinking in entails, how it's done and why the Pics are so good at it. Maybe Welles could teach it to humans. It wasn't likely, but it was a possibility.

Then she realized she was thinking ahead. Thinking past this terrible night. She still had hope. If nothing else, she had that. But if Cord and Mene had managed to get through the gauntlet that was the tower, she might have more than that.

Quinn entered the high tower, saw a few Fel happily lopping off Blue Knife limbs left and right. The hope inside of her actually grew upon viewing the gruesome display.

She ran up the empty staircase, renewed in believing that maybe they might win this fight.

The groaning sound of a dying man stopped her in her tracks, and killed that hope dead.

"Quinn..." Cord strained, his voice hoarse and nearly inaudible.

He had managed to prop himself up against a wall. A sword was jammed into his gut.

"Cord!" she shouted, and ran toward him. She cradled him in her arms, careful not to disturb the wound. "No, no no...are you...how do you feel?"

"About ready to die..." he answered slowly, honestly. "But I'm glad you're here. Thought I wouldn't get the chance to tell you..."

"I'm here, I'm here sweetie..."

"...so sorry...for everything" he started, then soldiered through the pain in an attempt to complete the thought. "...messed it all up, so sorry..."

"No, don't worry, we're going to..." but Quinn had no words of comfort in her. She didn't know what lie she could feed him that he might believe. Cord represented hope that some part of Western Sun was worth saving. She believed that if he could survive, and save Allison, then her faith in these people would be worth something.

But he was dying on these steps, and Quinn knew of no way to save him. And her faith in these people wasn't doing a damn thing.

She perked her ears up, and heard Victor Mene spewing obscenities at the Blue Knives who were surely overwhelming him. It didn't sound like it was going well.

"I'm sorry too, Cord," Quinn told her friend. "For a moment I thought we could win. I'm so sorry."

As Cord lay there dying on the steps, his head cradled in Quinn's lap, she recognized the loss and accepted that Western Sun was done for. And Bloody Twilight would march on in kind.

She would soon learn just how wrong she was.

60. Magic is Nothing but Love

Keegan Morris was dead and gone. In a sense. But any magician knows that being dead is just another state of being. The spirit is no longer conscious. But that doesn't mean it's not still working.

And at the moment of Morris's death, it started working for Welles.
His eyes had been trained to see more than what was, strictly-speaking, visible. Magicians can see up and down the invisible spectrum, see the tendons of energy, the connective tissue of life, death, and everything in between, everything that makes up the world. But Welles had never been able to see that without putting in the effort. Before now. Now he saw Morris's spirit, his soul, his body's reservoirs of energy, whatever a man wanted to call it. And naturally, it was lovely.

He watched as Morris's soul sank into the earth below, spread out, and then rose back up, into Welles's own body. Welles's skin began to hum. Every cell began to vibrate and dance inside him. It felt good. It felt amazing. For a brief moment, Welles thought the feeling was indescribable, but then he realized that he'd felt something very similar, the first time he realized that he was in love with Quinn Kind.

"Magic is nothing but love," Morris had once told him, only a few months before Welles' apprenticeship came to an end, and he went abroad to further his studies by actually interacting with the world for a while, instead of reading books and chanting. "You can go ahead and roll your eyes now, Welles."

Welles had realized he wasn't doing a good job of hiding a slight smirk. "I'm sorry, Kee, it's not that I don't get what you're saying, it's just a little…"

"Corny," Morris finished for him. "It absolutely is. But that doesn't make it any less true. That's what I've been trying to drive home to all you guys. If you want to be masters of this art, you've got to keep that in your hearts. Love, love of the earth, love of the people, love of things you can't see. Compassion, trust, hope, faith…these traits will guide you through."

Welles had nodded in understanding, then asked, "…you been drinking, Kee?"

Morris laughed and answered slowly, "...little bit."

"Fair enough. Okay, so love. I understand. Where does hate enter into it?"

"That's easy. Hate, everything that goes with it; that's the past, man. That's what people are at their worst. Magic is about looking forward to the best people can be. Using all those good traits to work past the bad. Hate, pettiness, jealousy. No one can dispel those feelings. But if you're a good enough magician, you'll be able to recognize those feelings and go beyond them. If you can find some kind of love within those feelings, see the care and concern living even in negative ideas, and transform them into something better, something new...that's the mark of a great magician."

"Easy to say, harder to do," Welles countered honestly, but not unkindly.

"Actually, it wasn't that easy to say, either. There's no guidebook to learn this stuff. This is the kind of magic you can't conjure up."

The words rang in the back of Welles's mind as he felt Keegan Morris's soul enter into his, entwining the two into one. But more than his soul. His power. All those reserves of energy stored for years in his crippled body. Years of drawing in the living essence of the world, without anywhere to release it. Welles realized how awful it must have been for Morris all that time. A sponge for power, and unable to use any of it.

Welles could access all of it. And it enveloped him completely. Love. Compassion. Trust. Faith. Hope.

"I hope to hell I can pull this off," he muttered to no one in particular, other than perhaps the embers of Keegan Morris burning inside him. And then he sat down and began to chant out the beginnings of the invincibility spell that had so far protected him. If he could just get it out fast enough, direct it to Cord and Mene and Quinn and all the others, maybe there'd be a chance...

He mumbled out the ancient words he'd memorized, but it wasn't quite right. It wasn't that the words were wrong, it was that they were so needlessly complicated. He was listening to them from a new perspective. Just as he could now see the invisible, he could hear the building blocks of his own language. Every little bit, he heard with a fresh awareness. Like reading a children's primer when you're already fluent in a dozen languages. The words weren't necessary anymore for him to access the end result. He could bring forth what he wanted because he knew what to say, he had the power, and most importantly, he needed it done.

Understanding this, he whispered joyously, "Thank you, Keegan." Then he held his hands up high, looked up at the ceiling, and roared, "NOW SAVE MY FRIENDS, DAMN IT!!!"

Purple and yellow light beamed out in all directions.

61. Brotherhood

These stupid blue bastards might just kill me yet, Mene thought to himself. He kept hacking away at them all the same. Guardsmen don't take certain defeat as a reason to lay down arms.

He stabbed a Blue Knife in the heart, but the stupid thing didn't take that as a reason to give up either, and yanked himself away, blade still lodged in him, tumbling down the stairs and leaving Mene with only one short sword to fight with.

"Clever little hump," Mene grunted. He couldn't deny that was a smart play. He wondered how long he would have lasted with these men if they had been in full possession of their faculties. He brushed the idea aside. *If wishes were horses…*

With just a bit of sadness, it occurred to him that he had probably lasted a little longer than Nathan Cord. If Cord was going to rise up, power past his wound and come to his aid, he would have done so by now. Which meant that he was down there, dead on the steps behind Mene.

The two men had never been what anyone would call friends. At first it had been due to Cord's position as a subordinate, but even after he had been promoted to command of Coal Brigade, there was still a distance between them that could never be breached. Mene had always chalked it up to differing desires. All Mene ever wanted to be was a soldier. He was living his dream. Cord wanted to be so many things – soldier, husband, leader, teacher, farmer – that he would never achieve any of those goals to his satisfaction.

Mene wondered if there had ever been a time when a man who had all he ever wanted, and a man who wanted more than he could ever have, had ever really enjoyed one another's company.

Then he remembered that brothers don't necessarily have to like each other. And he knew in his gut that like it or not, through shared experiences, trials, and bloodshed, Nathan Cord was very much his brother.

His brother was surely dead down there.

"A toast to Nathan Cord," he barked at the Blue Knife he currently found himself fighting. He'd lost track of how many he'd dispatched, so he only knew that there were more coming for him. Mene didn't care. He had developed a simple strategy over the last few minutes of fighting alone: take them as they come. He stabbed the Blue Knife in the forehead.

Then the damn thing headbutted him in the chest. It drove the sword further into his skull and drove Mene staggering back. With room to move, the Knife pulled the short sword out of his head, threw it down the stairwell, and crumpled to the stairs. Silent the entire time. Once again, Mene had to admire their dedication and focus. By way of compliment, he spat on the corpse and sneered. "Clever little hump," Mene repeated. It was becoming his mantra.

So this was it. Victor Mene, last of Western Sun's royal guard. Left with just his fists against a bunch of brainwashed, intoxicated warrior monks. Not the end he had imagined – and really, who could have? – but it would do.

Mene raised his fists, ready to box his way into oblivion, mustered every ounce of bravado he could find in him, looked another Blue Knife right in his dead yellow eyes, and offered, "Come on, then."

But before the monk could respond physically, the entire corridor went golden. The walls, the air, Mene's vision. It was all engulfed by an overwhelming wave of misty beautiful light. Golden, with edges of purple.

Despite himself, Mene dropped his fists as he attempted to understand what the hell was happening. The Blue Knife didn't care, and wasted no time driving his blade towards Mene's belly.

The blade bounced off him.

If a Blue Knife ever looked confused, it was then. Mene looked down at the blade, and blurted, "Huh," before regaining his composure, snatching the blade from the Blue Knife's hands, and hacking away with wreckless glee. He had an idea of what might have just occurred. Rather than attempt to pave his way further up the corridor, he instead charged back down the steps, and found Nathan Cord and Quinn Kind. Cord had a sword jammed in his gut, and Quinn had her small hands wrapped around the handle.

"Pull it out, pull it out!" Cord was shouting in a mix of panic and annoyance.

"I'm doing it, I'm doing it!" Quinn was shouting back, mimicking Cord's tone as she slid the blade out. It was a long sword, so it took more time than one might hope. Particularly for the recipient of the stabbing.

Mene made his way down to the two in time to watch as Cord's wound, finally free of the sword, instantly mended itself. The three of them looked down at the gaping hole in Cord's shirt. Clean, warm, untouched flesh.

"Holy hell," Cord remarked. He looked up at Quinn. Quinn's smile beamed almost as brightly as that golden something had moments before.

"That's my man!" Quinn clapped her hands. "Hahahahahaa!"

Mene looked down at Cord. Cord glanced up. "Looks like Welles gave us a reprieve. Nobody's dying just yet, I guess."

Mene said nothing, just put out his hand. When Cord gripped it, Mene hoisted him up. The two of them very nearly smiled at each other.

Mene looked quickly at Quinn, who still held the sword that had nearly killed Cord. "He's going to need that."

Without thinking, Quinn passed the sword off to Cord. "Yeah. Guess so..."

Cord wrapped his fingers around the handle, held it steadily. He looked at Mene. "How many did you manage to take down while I was out?"

"Stopped keeping count."

"Early senility setting in, I guess. You wanna bring on some pain?"

"Always."

Nothing more was said. Three invincible warriors charged wordlessly back up the corridor and slaughtered every enemy that came their way.

Finally, they reached the narrow doorway that led to the round room at the top. The Orphan was in there. And the bastard that had started this whole mess.

The three stood in single file – Mene, Cord, and finally Quinn, bringing up the rear.

"You ready?" Mene asked Cord, already knowing the answer.

Cord nodded simply, and walked to the entrance.

But during those few seconds of conversation, Quinn had, with her freakish speed, stepped past the two men so that she could viciously kick the door down herself.

"You boys coming?" she asked without turning around, as she stepped through the threshold.

They followed, brothers in arms, like it or not, ready to finish a hell of a fight together.

62. Reunion

They each surveyed the scene. Quinn and Cord located Allison, pinned down to the floor near the window. Mene began a headcount of the Blue Knives stationed, seemingly inert, by the throne. And then in unison, they saw Grolev.

At that moment, three leaders stood in front of the orchestrator of unspeakable horrors and nightmares. The man who had managed to destroy an entire kingdom for reasons they still didn't understand. This man, this gruesome, hateful pestilence of a man. And they recognized real, flesh and blood evil. And in that moment, they found themselves at a loss for just what to do next.

But there was no time for that to be their undoing. Because Grolev's eyes weren't taking them in like they were him. Grolev was more curious about the soft, steady golden-purple glow shining its way up the corridor toward the throne room. And a sound like static electricity bouncing off of stone walls. And then finally, a tall young man, clad in black with a red robe, appearing in the doorway.

The room felt a little warmer. That sense of a heat source made Quinn, Cord, and Mene turn around to the doorway, to see what had transfixed Grolev.

Welles looked at them and smiled gratefully. "It's good to see you guys."

Quinn stared in amazement at her love, and could only sputter, "Holy crap, Welles, you're glowing."

Welles looked down at his hands and nodded that yes, it certainly looked like he had a bit of a shimmering quality to him. "Looks like. I've had an interesting couple of hours. You guys look pretty good yourselves."

Cord nodded, containing his amazement behind his well-honed stoicism. He poked a finger through the shirt in his hole from where he'd been run through. "Feeling pretty good, too, though this shirt is done for. Guessing you had something to do with that fatal wound being a little less than?"

Welles pointed his eyes up to the ceiling, making a coy face. "You can thank me later."

"Wyatt Welles," the magician heard his name called out, and realized that it was time to get back to work. Glowing might be an interesting topic of conversation for most people, but for a magician, it's just a productive day.

Grolev wasn't interested in discussing Welles's day. "Wyatt goddamn Welles. All pretty and glowing. You look like a queer."

Mene had also found the novelty of Welles's new condition dissipating. He grunted, "Enough of this," and took several strides up to Grolev, raising his sword to the wizard's throat. "Grolev, as captain of the queen's royal guard and sworn protector of this kingdom, you are hereby under arrest in the name of Western Sun. You'll forgive me if we forego the trial and get on with the execution." And with decisive force, he dropped a killing blow at Grolev.

The wizard grabbed the blade angrily, and it melted in his hand. "Shut up, you ignorant meathead. No, I don't recognize your goddamn authority, and frankly, I've always hated you and your self-satisfied bullshit. So it's time to grow up, big man. There are some problems you can't just hack away at."

Mene was still looking at the bladeless hilt in his grip when Grolev slapped his palms against Mene's ears, gave a look of utter hatred at him, and then smiled. His eyes began to glow red. His hands did the same. Mene began to quiver, and then seize. And then smoke began to pour out of his eyes, and his nose and his mouth and his ears.

Victor Mene, the captain of the Kingdom of Western Sun's royal guard, fell to the ground, dead.

Once more, three leaders stood staring at the monster called Grolev, completely at a loss for what to do next.

63. The Magic Hour

"Victor!" Cord called desperately across the room to his comrade, but he had seen enough dead bodies in his time to know that Mene wasn't going to get back up. Time for mourning later, he told himself. There's always all the time in the world to mourn, but a soldier knows he has to survive to make use of any of that time. Cord took a single instant, refocused, and looked an accusing question at Welles. "What happened to that invulnerability spell, magic man?"

Grolev answered for him. "Invulnerability. Heh, not quite. Try 'impenetrability,' Mister Cord. Nothing cuts through that skin of yours. But I'm pretty good at this. I can boil a man's insides without any trouble. Wanna see what it feels like? Mene's eyeballs just burst in his head. I know you've cut one out, but you wanna see what it'd feel like for the other one to pop and ooze down your cheek?" His hands crackled red electricity just to impress the point.

Welles felt for Quinn's hand. She saw this, and placed hers in his without a word. She looked up at him. He looked back. It was all the time they had.

Welles released her hand and walked to Grolev. "This is over. We're taking the queen, we're burning this whole thing down behind us, and then I'm going to do my best to forget that a thing like you could ever exist." The golden aura covering Welles radiated as he spoke.

"Piss off, Wyatt," Grolev sneered, and shoved his left hand into Welles's chest, launching him across the room, His back crashed against the far wall behind Quinn. Then Grolev snapped his fingers, getting the attention of his entourage. "Blue Knives, deal with Mister Cord and that pixie bitch, I want to focus on the little magician."

The six Blue Knives, who had up to this point stood motionlessly at either side of the empty throne, sprung to life, presented arms, and charged at Quinn and Cord. Quinn swept behind Cord toward the door and slammed it shut. "Come on you blue bastards," she growled. "Let's see what you've got."

Cord grinned at the bravado. "Brace yourself, dear – they've got a lot." He brandished his two short swords and the two warriors charged into the fray.

Grolev stomped over to Welles, still on the floor, grabbed a fistful of his cowl, and punched him savagely. "That's the thing about us magicians, we never get to just hit someone. It feels great, Wyatt, it really does." He punched him again, harder. Welles's nose and lip began to bleed. "Doesn't this feel just great, you little pissant?!"

A third punch. One of Grolev's rings caught flesh, cutting Welles's cheek. "And this is what I think of your chickenshit protection spell. I've got a thousand years worth of dead souls powering me! I'm taking energy from a place built on slaughter! You think a little spell's gonna keep me from mutilating you?"

Grolev stretched back up and delivered a roundhouse kick to the side of Welles's head. "And when I'm done, and the Knives have killed Cord, I'm gonna take that little pixie whore and I'm gonna screw her while she's bleeding to death. That'll be fun, right? Never done that before, I'll bet it'll be pretty damn satisfying." He delivered another kick.

"This is pathetic, little Wyatt. You took all this time, you raised a miserable little army, you even went to rescue poor old Keegan Morris, just so you could get your face stomped in. Well, points for effort." He lifted up his foot, then   dropped   it   down.

Welles reached up and caught it effortlessly in his hands. Calmly, he whispered, "Fire," and a shock of flames shot up, through his hands and up Grolev's body. The wizard stumbled back, made some squealing noises before extinguishing the flames. He looked at Welles, who picked himself up from the ground without his hands, and then dusted himself off. Again, without his hands. "Just seeing what you've got, Grolev."

Welles placed a palm over his face, pushed it down from forehead to chin. When he removed it, all the cuts and bleeding had vanished. He snarled, his glow intensifying.

"I am not impressed."

64. Fire and Rain

"Fire," Welles requested a second time, no strain or effort in his voice, only absolute conviction. He said it, and Grolev began to burn again.

"RAIN," Grolev roared in frustration, and the deluge of a summer storm burst out of nowhere, put out the fire, and died out in a puff of steam. Grolev stood soaking and seething. Welles remained bone dry. "See, I can do it too. I was just trying to make it last a little – "

"Let's try bats," Welles interrupted. He lifted his arms. His robe turned a muddy black, disintegrated around him, and flapped hundreds of leathery wings. He pointed at Grolev, and they swarmed him.

Grolev screamed, raging blindly. Black lightning shot out from every part of him and the bats dropped to the floor, dead. "I ruined your pretty coat, Wyatt!" He stepped on the bats as he marched at his opponent, still crackling fiercely. "Okay, so you've got a contact high from sitting in Keegan's pile of piss, how exciting. Don't need to deal with the long incantations, right?"

Welles shook his head with something like pity, and then tossed off, "Sink." And the next step Grolev took plunged him into a deep liquid that had once been floor.

Welles took two steps toward Grolev, and leaned down to his level. "I can't believe you don't get this. All your posturing about death magic, and this horrible place and how it powers you, and you just. Don't. Get it. No, it's not a contact high. Keegan's a part of me now. Years of soaking up the power of this world and unable to use it…it's with me now. His parting gift."

While Grolev struggled against the soupy mix that trapped him, Welles stood up, stepped closer, and kicked him in the throat. "I won't lie, that does feel good." Then he knelt back down to look Grolev in the eyes. "But that's not how we play, is it?"

He grabbed Grolev's head in both hands without unlocking his gaze. His hands began to vibrate. His fingers penetrated Grolev's skull. "Confusion."

Grolev found that he couldn't hold onto Welles's eyes. It was all getting fuzzy around him. He tried to pull himself out of the soup, out of the spell –

*Spell…soup? No… I'm stuck, stuck in something, there's…what is that noise, clank clang. A couple a few, knives all blue…*Blunt notions that should have been coherent thoughts failed to coalesce in Grolev's mind.

"Bssssttttrrrrddd…" he hissed out, trying in vain to pull his senses back together.

Welles stood and surveyed Grolev coldly. "I hope that feels really terrible. That one is for Keegan Morris. That's what he felt every day since you killed him. That cruelty of yours…it sickens me."

He listened to what he'd just said and sighed sadly, then added, "And it amazes me. It actually proves you right about one thing – Keegan didn't know it all. He didn't think intellectual obsession alone would be enough to drive a man to become a truly powerful mystic. He thought mastering this kind of power takes love and devotion, not some bitter quest to be the smartest guy in the room. So I suppose you are just a bit right. Keegan was a little naïve."

Welles stepped away from Grolev and finished his thought. "But honestly…who would want to imagine something as awful as you?"

He took a second of quiet to think about that. Just long enough to hear Cord shout in the midst of his fight with the Blue Knives, "If you're not too busy, Welles…!"

Without a word, Welles closed his eyes, and the glowing field around him expanded through the room. The Blue Knives stopped fighting. Quinn and Cord felt warm and protected. And then the Blue Knives all fell to the ground at once. Deep in sleep.

Cord raised a hand up at Welles. "Thanks," and then yanked an axe from the grip of one of the Knives and walked around to each of them, hacking off their heads.

Quinn ran over to Welles and they kissed. "I love you," they told each other simultaneously. Then she pulled back, and looked at him curiously. "…Wyatt?"

Sheepishly half-smiling, Welles murmured, "I was going to tell you my first name eventually, I swear."

She gave him an odd stare, like that didn't make sense to her. Before Welles could question it, Quinn's eyes rolled back into her head and her frame went limp as a ragdoll in his arms.

Grolev rose up, grabbed the back of Quinn's shirt, and ripped her out of Welles's arms, hurling her into the heavy wooden door.

"NAILS!" Grolev shrieked, and the nails in the floorboards ripped themselves out and shot at Welles. Most of them bounced off his skin, but Welles felt a few of them drive their way into his shoulderblades. He looked at Grolev and saw that the wizard was strenuously forcing them through his protection spell. They broke the skin and sank into his nerves. Welles screamed as he dropped to his knees.

Grolev towered over him. "Don't you ever turn your back on me, you piece of shit. Now *you* burn."

In the instant he spent trying to retreat his thoughts from the intense pain in his joints, Welles was bathed in fire.

His screams echoed through the room.

Cord looked up to find Welles lit up like a torch and Grolev scowling in Cord's direction. "And you, Mister Cord. It's a shame. I really should be thanking you for all this, but mostly I want you to scream like your pathetic friend here."

Coughing violently, Wells hoarsely managed, "...Ooouuuttt...," and the flames died down slowly, in patches. He was left useless and burnt, lying in agony on the floor. The room smelled of cooked meat.

Still trying to process this rapid turn of events, Cord didn't notice Grolev start muttering out incantations. But then he saw the bastard pull out a knife and cut into his own palms. His blood dripped to the floor. And then it spread, making a beeline for the dead Blue Knives. All at once they began staggering back to their feet, finding and reattaching their own heads. Grolev shouted, "I'll keep putting those idiots back together if I have to use horse glue and twine, Mister Cord! You just keep trying to kill them!"

Suddenly surrounded by six very dead and yet still very ambitious Blue Knives, Cord reaffirmed his grip on the axe.

"Sounds like a plan," he muttered stubbornly.

Something about his tone gave Grolev pause. He looked at the crumpled, smoking corpse of Victor Mene. And an idea struck. He grabbed Welles and yanked the nails from his shoulders, then plunged his thumbs into the wounds. Then, licking the blood off his thumbs, he walked over to Mene's body and spat on it.

And Victor Mene rose again.

Grolev looked back to Welles, who gasped in pain as he struggled up to his knees.

"There's your fucking 'life magic' at work, Wyatt. I can raise the dead. What the hell can you do?" He grabbed one of the Blue Knives' swords off the ground, raised it. "Other than make for a decent sacrifice?"

The sword sank through Welles's heart and pinned his body to the floor.

65. Cord's Curse and Mene's Rebirth

"Vic, can you hear me? Are you in there?" Cord shouted at the trudging monster he so recently called Victor Mene. But it was just a hollow shell, burnt up from the inside and cursed to keep attacking him.

The Blue Knives swarmed at him too, but they could barely see straight, any more than Mene's corpse could. They didn't pose much of a threat. Cord was able to hack at them with the axe in his left hand while keeping Mene's corpse at bay with the sword in his right.

"Vic!" Cord tried again. Of course Mene couldn't hear him. Victor Mene was dead, no question. Mene's body was nothing but a puppet, another fine example of Grolev's hatred of humanity in general, and the royal guard in particular.

Cord kicked Mene back hard, sending him staggering a few feet away, enough time to slaughter the reanimated Blue Knives. When they fell this second time, Cord didn't waste a moment, just started lopping off their limbs before they could get up.

But Mene moved faster than the Knives. Came back at Cord before he'd had a chance to chop off the legs of the last monk. Cord blocked Mene's strike with only a moment to spare. The corpse of Victor Mene grabbed a sword from the ground, brought it up, and gripped its blade with his free hand, shoving it into Cord's defense, very much like he had done in life. This time, the blade cutting into his palm wouldn't distract him.

So Cord let him push, let him think his strength was winning the fight, before tossing himself back toward the floor. The reverse momentum threw Mene's corpse off-balance, and when he stumbled to the ground himself, Cord snatched away the long sword Mene had wielded. With strength borne of desperation, he jammed it through Mene's chest plate, pinning the corpse to the ground.

But Mene still had a short blade in his hand, and stabbed upward, managing to slice into Cord's side.

He ignored the wound long enough to offer, "Vic, I'm sorry." Then he stood up, with a gash along his ribs, wheezing and trying to catch his breath. He walked away from Mene's corpse, retrieved the axe he'd become so fond of, and returned to the former captain.

"I'm so sorry," he said as he hacked Victor Mene's body apart, bit by bit. And when he was done, he groggily threw down the axe, yanked the sword from Mene's hand, and pointed it in Grolev's direction. Cord's own blood dripped off the tip.

Exhausted and bleeding, "You..." was all he could manage. The hate he used to fuel his fighting had reached critical mass. Cord could barely see straight. He wanted only one thing in this world – to kill Grolev by any means possible. But only after he'd made him suffer like no man had ever suffered before.

Grolev held his hands out to his sides in mock-surrender and muttered, "Damn, but you're an impressive son of a bitch, Mister Cord." Then he sent a quick bolt of black lightning through the brigade chief, dropping him effortlessly.

Cord fought his way back to his feet, growling, "Stop calling me 'mister.'" It was all he could think to say. It felt very stupid and quite important to him all the same.

"But I respect you too much," Grolev admitted casually. "I couldn't have gotten where I am without you, really."

Realizing he'd dropped the sword, Cord looked around the room blearily for something he could stab Grolev with. "Shut the hell up...hhh...you asshole. I'm gonna rip your goddamn guts out..." he muttered, but slowed with every step he took toward Grolev.

The wizard took the moment to gloat. "No, you're not. But since you've been working so hard, I think I should let you know: if you hadn't killed Arius, I never would have been able to pull this off.

"I had my eye on a lot of you guardsmen, y'know. But you were the unstable one, you were the one that looked about ready to pop. Arius could have banged any guard's wife in the kingdom, but he put his eye toward your dear sweet Kayla. She was so lonely, Nathan. She really missed her husband..."

Cord found another sword, grabbed it and swatted, but he was too far away from Grolev. The weight was too much, and he dropped to the ground trying to hold it. He hung onto it for dear life though, while feeling around on the floor for the axe he'd had such good luck with, while Grolev continued his gloating.

"So yeah...you killed the ruler of Bloody Twilight. Such a major blood sacrifice, and I didn't even need to raise a hand! Arius was a simple beast, really. All I had to do was mention to him how damn hot your trollop of a wife was, slow up the Blue Knives so they wouldn't interrupt, and just let it all play out. So I really need to offer you my praise, Mister Cord. All this is thanks to you."

The rage took hold, and Nathan Cord couldn't see anything but red, and he ran at Grolev, both weapons held high. And then the headless bodies of some Blue Knives fell on top of him, holding him down, making him useless.

Cord was pinned against the floor. He saw Quinn Kind, unconscious. Allison, crushed against invisible weight. Welles, burnt to a crisp. And he saw the remains of Victor Mene – his own handiwork.

And he got the distinct feeling that they couldn't win this one.

66. Just One Moment to Think

Welles looked around himself. It wasn't the round room anymore. It was something vague, warm, and without an exact shape. He understood that he was in some kind of dreamspace he'd never visited before. And he wasn't alone.

"I'm dying, aren't I?" Welles asked Keegan Morris.

"Well, you have a sword crammed through your heart and spine, so I'd say yes, you sir, are dying," Morris answered caustically.

"So we lost. Grolev's going to kill the Orphan, and then…what?"

"That's the worst part," Morris responded. "It'll just power him up some more. All his power comes from the killing that started Bloody Twilight. He already got the king killed. Sacrificing the Orphan ends the whole bloodline, and that will just open a little more power up to him. That's it. That's all he wants. Isn't that pathetic? All he wants is a little more juice. And he killed a whole kingdom to get it."

"My friends are dying, Kee. Cord's done for, and you heard Grolev say what he'll do to Quinn." Welles heard his own voice and realized to his dismay that even dying doesn't prevent a panic attack.

"So go save them," Morris offered.

It was the second time Welles could remember ever rolling his eyes at his mentor. "There's a sword jammed between my heart and my spine. I have a bit of a handicap," he understated.

"Me being awake in your consciousness isn't going to last for too much longer, so you'd better learn some lessons, Welles."

Welles thought for a moment. "What am I missing?"

Morris rolled his eyes right back at his student. "What is everything I've taught you? What is magic?"

Welles turned his thoughts inward, and recited, "Magic is love."

Morris nodded theatrically, silently telling his student that he'd answered well, but not correctly. "That's what I said you had to *have* in you to *use* it. What is it that we *use*?"

Welles thought again, slapped his head as the proper answer came to him. "Magic is just the energy we have inside ourselves, meeting up with the energy the earth offers."

"Good boy," Morris offered.

"So the energy's up for grabs, if we just know how to get to it." Welles continued.

Morris nodded, prodding his student. "Yeah..."

"So I'm dying, and Cord's dying, and Quinn's dying, and Mene's just been brought back with my own blood."

"Keep going."

"So my people, they aren't in a position to use their energy. But it's still available. And I can..."

"And what kind of energy do they have in them?"

It dawned on Welles. "Oh."

"Good boy," Morris repeated.

Welles rose inside himself. "It's all so simple," he noted.

"It always is. Go save your people, Wyatt Welles."

Welles absorbed all of Morris's teachings and spirit, and packed them with his own survival instincts.

"I can save them all, Keegan. Thanks."

"No thanks needed. You were a good student, kid. Not a student anymore, you do realize that, right? You're the man now."

"I'm gonna miss these talks of ours, just the same."

"So become a brilliant magician and figure out a way to keep having them." He smiled cleverly. "But you gotta survive to do that. First things first, right?"

Welles had a clever smile all his own. "First things first."

And he disappeared from this short respite in the back of his mind, returning to the land of the living, to save them all.

67. The Magic of Life and Love

Grolev watched Welles die for a second or two. He seemed to be talking to himself. That was bound to happen. "Just croak already," he suggested. Then he looked over at Quinn's unconscious body and smiled horribly.

Before he could posture any further with future plans of rape or torture, a voice from behind told him calmly and without any particular emphasis, "You won't get the chance, Grolev."

A part of the bad wizard knew what was coming next, but he stubbornly tossed the possibility out of his mind. He refused to turn back to look. He just skulked toward Quinn. He took one step. And then another. And then he couldn't move anymore.

Quinn's body began to glow, and then gave off lovely sparks of gold. Grolev cocked his head to look at Cord. His body was doing the same thing. Their bodies radiated gold, while purple strands of energy stretched back into Welles.

"Give me a break," Grolev muttered. He attempted to reach a hand out at Quinn, but nothing happened. He tried with the other arm. Nothing.

Every muscle in his body told him he had only one option, so despite himself, he followed those commands and turned back to look at Welles. The magician stood tall and completely still, his wound fully healed. Welles held the sword that nearly killed him at his side, the point meeting the floor.

"Magic is love. Keegan Morris told me that, once upon a time," Welles casually remarked. "Does that make any sense to you, Grolev? Does that sound at all familiar?"

"It sounds like the useless crap he generally blathered on about, yeah," Grolev answered. He found that he once again had control of his left hand, however limited, so he balled it up into a fist and worked on conjuring up something really painful while the silly boy kept talking.

Welles frowned sadly and asked, "Do you love anyone, Grolev? Do you care about anything?"

Feeling the energy pulsing in that left hand, Grolev decided to use the time given to him while little Wyatt Welles tried on his big-boy pants. "I care very deeply about hurting you, boy. Does that count?"

"I'm afraid it doesn't. See, I get that you're powerful. Scarily powerful. I mean, you are a force to be reckoned with. No one would ever say different. But you've invested so much of yourself in murder, and hate. You gained so much power from the death in the ground that birthed Bloody Twilight."

"Goddamn right, boy," Grolev confirmed, and feeling the power stored in his left hand, he unleashed it all towards the young magician.

Black electricity surrounded Welles, and dissipated limply.

Welles stepped closer to the wizard and put out his hand, placing it gently on his cheek. Grolev dropped to the floor like a ragdoll.

"I'm. Not. Finished."

Lying there on the floor, he had enough time to realize that things might not be going his way, and might never go his way again. It had been so long since Grolev had felt fear that he didn't immediately recognize it when it crept up in him.

"You've killed so much in your time. Look around the room, and you'll see your handiwork. Victor Mene. Nathan Cord. Quinn Kind. You did your best to kill them, but you can't. Do you know why?"

Grolev attempted to give a cold retort, but found that his mouth had been locked shut.

Welles stepped closer, until he stood in front of Grolev's prostrate body. "There's so much love in their hearts, Grolev. Love, and hope, and…look at them. You might not guess it at first glance. Quinn's not human. Mene is – was – a hard-bitten soldier. And Cord killed their king. Their king! You wouldn't see it at first glance. But they all came here together, to stop you. Not because of the kingdom. They know this kingdom is done for."

He looked over at the Orphan, exhausted from struggling against the weight Grolev had put on her. He waved his hand to release her.

"They did it because they love that girl. And the love they have for her…my gods, man. Did you never realize it? I guess not. You being you, after all. These are three people who could have given up and gone home. But they needed her to be safe. That girl there, her safety…that singular goal is what has driven them through utter horrors over the last few days. That makes them righteous – which makes them powerful. And I've got their power with me now, Grolev. And it is immense."

Grolev managed to find his voice. He used it to spit out a curse. "Eat me, you little turd. I'll kill you all…"

"No, Grolev. You won't. I have the energy of men and women who would sacrifice their lives for a wonderful ideal. Screw your death-magic. It is hollow and weak. These people have the magic of life and love in them, and that's more powerful than a man like you could ever imagine. There's an amazing world just waiting to be made, and that girl is the heart of it. And these friends of mine are its soul. I can't wait to be a part of all that. But you..."

Welles placed his hand upon Grolev's face.

"I'm sorry. But there's no place in that new world for your kind of magic."

A burst of light burst out of Welles in all directions, embracing the whole of Bloody Twilight before receding back into him. When it was gone, so was Grolev. Not even a speck of dust was left.

Quinn and Cord got to their feet, groggy and more than a little confused at what had just happened.

Welles wasted no time running to Quinn and wrapping his arms around her. She gripped him tightly in return. In that moment, they both held everything they ever really needed.

Cord looked around the room, still a bit disoriented, and saw Allison lying on the floor. He ran to her and picked her up in his arms. "Allie, can you hear me? It's Nate, dear. It's Nate, can you – "

Welles and Quinn looked over when they heard Cord's pleas end so abruptly.

They saw the Orphan holding a knife to Cord's throat.

68. Failures

"Allison, sweetie, we came to get you out of here…" Quinn started stepping cautiously over to the Orphan. "Allie, you can put down the knife, it's all over."

"It's not over," the Orphan corrected coolly. The regal confidence in the girl's voice startled Quinn. "This man has to answer for his crimes."

Welles decided it was his turn to try talking her down. He spoke calmly, but his words came out faster than he would have preferred. "Your highness, my name is Wyatt Welles. I'm a student of Keegan Morris, I believe you know his name. I'm here to inform you that Western Sun is no longer safe or sustainable. We have to get you out of here."

But it was clear that the girl wasn't listening to him. She was focused only on the man she held at knifepoint on his knees.

So was Quinn, and after all she'd been through, she'd be damned if it ended like this. "Allison, you put that knife down right now. That's Nathan Cord, girl. He's risked his neck, nearly died to save you!"

Allison turned back to Quinn, tears held in check behind her eyes. "It's his fault I needed saving at all!" Her shout was tense, but measured. Despite what it may have looked like, she was keeping herself collected. She looked back at Cord. "Did you even stop to think of what would happen, when you killed my father?"

Cord looked up at the girl, but said nothing.

"Answer me, damn it!"

"No," Cord answered honestly. He could never lie to Allison. "No, I didn't think at all."

"You said you would always be here to protect me, but you left me here! You killed my father, and then you left me here to watch this place be poisoned and corrupted by the men who took over for him!"

This was a man who had just been impaled not too long ago. Her words cut deeper.

They affected her, too. Finally saying these things, after so many years of keeping those awful feelings at arm's length. "You could have kept me safe and I could have done something! I could have saved this whole place if you'd just been there to help me, but you LEFT! How could you do that to me?!" She demanded an answer. The tears found their own way out.

The knife remained steady at Cord's throat.

Cord swallowed, feeling the knife's point against his throat as he did. "I don't have an answer for you, Allison. I'm more sorry than I could ever explain, but I don't have an answer to that question. Not one that would make it right."

Quinn had stepped closer while the two spoke, until she was nearly close enough to reach the knife. "Allison Kendra Dearborn," she sternly addressed her former charge just as she had when the girl was little, "You put that knife down right now."

Allison cocked her head to address her former caretaker. "You too, Quinn! How could you leave me here? You knew what was happening! You knew my father wasn't right, and you did nothing. You knew the kingdom was dying and you never came to save me. I was counting on you two for years. And. You. Never. Came!"

The part of Quinn that had helped raise and teach the girl wanted to pick her up and hold her close and tell her everything would be okay. The part of Quinn that had led an army into hell to save her needed this to be done with, and wondered if slapping her down now and apologizing for the rest of her life would be worth it. Before she could decide which part to favor, she saw Cord make a small gesture with his hand, a signal to wave her off.

"We failed you," he started. Every word soaked in sorrow. "Good god, how we failed you. It's the worst part of being an adult. You break promises, and you make bad compromises, and you walk away when you should stay. And your heart hurts every time.

"You're right. This whole thing is our fault. We made the wrong decisions and it cost us all everything. Coming in here to get you, it was an attempt to make up for those failures. So if you need to…if you need to punish me for failing you, then I accept that judgment. I've earned it. But…hell. It took too long for us to do it, but for now, you're safe. So I can die knowing we managed to do that one more time. It might not mean much to you, but it means everything to me, if that's the last thing I did on this earth."

He looked up at the Orphan. His little girl, all grown up. His queen. "I serve at the pleasure of the Queen of Western Sun. So I trust you to do what you think is right."

Allison Kendra Dearborn stared down at Nathan Cord, on his knees and accepting his fate. Her hand trembled. She threw the knife across the room and knelt down, and began sobbing uncontrollably. She tried to say something, explain or scold or apologize, but she couldn't form the words between the tears and exhaustion.

Cord pulled her close to him and held her as she cried.

Quinn ran over to them and dropped to her knees. She stroked the girl's hair and kissed her forehead. "It's okay, baby," she told the girl softly. "It's gonna be okay."

And she truly believed it.

69. Sing Songs for Victor Mene

"Everything's set to blow, Miss Quinn," Saymon Q'iln confirmed proudly when she passed through the barrier, battered and weary, but warmed in spite of herself by the feeling of Welles at her side. Cord and Allison rode on horseback close behind them.

"Thanks for waiting," she deadpanned, but was too exhausted to know if she was even joking.

Allison looked out at the men and women who had fought so hard to save her. Battleworn Pics and Fel, sitting wearily along the hillside. And between them, her own people. Those few survivors of an apocalypse. The last vestiges of the Kingdom of Western Sun. They stood at attention when they saw her. Very few of them had seen the Queen in Waiting up close. But they knew without a moment's pause who she was.

Allison half-expected them to pull her down from the horse and tear her limb from limb for failing to save her people. But they knelt down respectfully.

She turned and looked a question at Cord. He half-smiled. "I got nothing, I'm just a beat-up old barman. I think they want you to tell them something good."

The royalty had drained out of her voice. All that was left was a traumatized, teenaged girl worriedly asking her uncle, "What could I possibly say?"

Cord shrugged. Then, remembering his role, he smiled proudly at her, and answered, "Just tell 'em what they need to know. Be the queen they deserve."

Allison thought about that. She cleared her throat, and said in her most regal tone, "Stop the horse."

Cord gently pulled on the reins, and the horse trotted to a halt.

Allison dismounted and walked to her people. "Get up. Please. I appreciate it, but after all that's happened…"

There were no words. Slowly, the citizens of Western Sun stood up. And Allison knelt before them. "My name is Allison Kendra Dearborn. I am the last queen of Western Sun. And if you will have me, I swear to you all, I will do everything in my power to keep you safe, to protect you, from now until my dying day."

No one said a word. Hesitantly, Allison repeated, "...if you'll let me." She was afraid to look up. Then she heard the mismatched footsteps of a giant man with an artificial leg. She looked up and saw Big Jack Barry towering over her.

He patted her on the shoulder gently, took her hand and helped her back to her feet. "Wouldn't doubt you for a moment, my queen." He turned to his people. "Come on then, let's hear some noise!"

The people of Western Sun erupted with cheers and claps in unison.

Jack Barry gestured out at them and suggested, "Maybe go say hello to your people, my queen. I think they'd like to meet you." She looked at him uncertainly, then looked over to Cord, who had dismounted and began to walk over to them. He nodded approvingly. She returned the nod, and then walked into the crowd.

Big Jack Barry and Nathan Cord were left alone to eye each other up.

"Nathan Cord," Big Jack started. "Heard talk you were dead."

Cord waved his hands over his body to show he was intact, then returned, "Big Jack. Glad to see you're not."

Jack stepped closer and stroked his beard pensively as he inspected Cord. "Say...didn't you use to have two eyes?"
Cord smirked. "That's funny, because I seem to recall you having two legs." He heard himself laugh as he added, "Maybe we're just getting old."

He put a hand out, but Big Jack slapped it aside and bearhugged Cord. "Good to see you, my friend."

Cord patted his hand appreciatively on Jack's back, both to let him know he returned the sentiment, and to let him know that the big man was crushing him.

Setting Cord down, Big Jack offered, "So I heard Vic Mene didn't make it out, huh?"

Cord nodded, feeling the sadness creep up into his throat. "Yeah." He fought it off. "Yeah, we lost him."

Sensing Cord's tone, Jack pondered casually, "Wonder how he'd like to be remembered."

"He'd like to be remembered as a patriot, I know that. A man who went down swinging, for the sake of his kingdom."

"Sounds good," Jack agreed.

"Yeah." Cord thought on it for a moment, then added, "But the craziness I saw him pull today? I'm gonna get some of the Pics to write a song about him. 'The Ballad of Victor Mene.' It'll make for an amazing tune, I'll tell you."

Big Jack shrugged and said, "That sounds like something he'd really hate, Cord."

"Maybe," Cord nodded, "but I'd like to hear people sing about him. Whether he thinks so or not, he's earned it."

70. A Delayed Mourning

The Orphan found herself surrounded by her people. None of them seemed to hate her. It was confusing.

Quinn's approach gave her something she could understand. When Quinn offered quietly, "Allison, I have something I need to tell you," she was more than happy to go with her.

They stepped away from all the crowds, to an empty spot on the hill. Allison felt like she should say something, but before she could find the words, Quinn came out with, "I need to tell you, I came upon Aiden, after the spell took hold. He was past the point of saving. I killed him. I'm sorry."

Allison began processing the information, as Quinn put a hand on her shoulder and repeated, "I am so sorry. I wanted so badly to help him, but there was nothing I could do."

Quinn looked at Allison, eyes pleading for forgiveness.

All Allison could offer was, "I'm glad it was you that found him, Quinn. Thank you for telling me."

"Oy, Quinn!" they heard from behind. Saymon Q'iln was, in his own way, requesting the attention of the Pic leader.

Quinn looked pained eyes towards Allison, but the girl smiled weakly. "Thank you, Quinn. Go. See to your people."

Quinn reluctantly left Allison's side, to her relief. The truth of the matter was that Allison would need ages to come to terms with the death of her love. A death that had resulted in untold levels of destruction.

Allison missed Aiden so much the feeling threatened to eat her alive. And she knew she was so numb that this was the least she'd feel about it in the days and months to come. She very much wanted to cry. But she knew that this was not something queens do in front of their people.

And she understood that all she had left were her people.

71. Burn Down Bloody Twilight

Big Jack and Nathan Cord had been enjoying their reunion, as they came up with the first verses to 'The Ballad of Victor Mene.' Cord couldn't think of a better starting lyric than "Well Victor Mene was a son of a bitch, the best the kingdom knew," while Jack tried to ween him away from it and into something less obviously insulting.

"I mean son of a bitch in the good way," Cord protested.

"All the same, I think we can come up with something better," Jack insisted.

But before any further brainstorming could take place, Quinn walked up to them. "Cord, you got a minute? Jack, you should come over, too."

They followed her back to Saymon Q'iln and a few of the other Fel. All of them held torches. "Saymon wanted to see if we'd like to be the ones to lay down the fire."

Big Jack cocked his head, a question to the Pic girl.

She answered, "We've got to burn it down to the ground. There're still a lot of dead folks running around in there, and Grolev's spell will keep holding on as long as those walls stand. The Fel have laced the whole city with explosives. They thought we'd like the 'honor' of burning Bloody Twilight down to ashes."

To drive the point home, Saymon Q'iln gleefully jutted his torch out to Cord.

Quinn clarified, "They're funny that way."

With no obvious recourse left to him, Cord accepted the fire graciously. "Do me a favor, Saymon, and ask for the queen's presence. I think she should be involved in this, too."

Slade cupped his hands to his mouth and bellowed, " 'Ey, Queenie! Getcher tiny butt over here!"

It was good enough, as far as Cord was concerned.

More torches were passed around. Finally, Nathan Cord, Quinn and Quentin Kind, Wyatt Welles, Big Jack Barry, Saymon Q'iln, and Allison Dearborn stepped up to the fuses that started just outside the golden barrier and led deep into the city. They looked at each other, and then without a word, each set the torches down to light the fuses.

They saw seven sparkling snakes of fire charge into the city. Within moments, it began erupting into flame. A bigger fire had never been seen. When every wall of the city started burning brightly, and bomb-bursts could be heard beyond them, radiant blue lights shot up into the sky, popping, crackling, and beautiful.

"Fireworks...?" Quinn asked Saymon.

He smiled broadly. "Well. It's not every day you set fire to a whole kingdom, is it?"

Quinn admired the display. "I suppose not." She looked over at Welles. The light of the fire reflected against his face, and she saw that he had some cuts and bruises on him. The healing magic he had performed on himself took care of the major wounds, but some of the smaller scratches and burns had still scarred him. But he was smiling, and totally distracted by the display. She leaned into him, and he instinctively wrapped an arm around her. Together they watched the fire, like it was roaring there just for the two of them.

Pics, Fel, and humans sat contentedly on the hill, watching fireworks shoot through the night sky as an old, dead city burned to the ground.

It was indescribably beautiful, and more than a little bit sad.

Cord and Big Jack stared up quietly, until finally Jack broke the silence. "Hell of a homecoming, eh, Cord?"

Cord nodded. "Hell of a sendoff, too."

They returned to their silent admiration. Cord knew there was still a lot to do. A great deal of preparation if they wanted to make it to Northern Sun. And after that, he didn't know exactly what the plan was.

But he wasn't worried. All of that could wait until the morning.

EPILOGUE:
Six Months Later

72. Goodbye, Love

It was about an hour from sundown when Cord stepped off his horse and tied the reins up at the post in front of Fehrer's homestead. Cord looked around, breathed in deeply. It was early into winter, and the air was becoming thin and clean. But the temperature was still pleasing to him. Cord had noticed that even though Welles' invincibility spell had worn off months ago, his skin remained toughened against extremes of heat and cold. So the weather might not have been as nice as he thought.

Whatever the case, he felt good. After all, he was going to see his wife one more time.

He knocked on the door. There were shuffling sounds behind it, noises of double-clicking locks and chains, so Cord knew that Fehrer had come to answer, but had seen his face through the peephole and given second thought to opening it.

Cord waved pleasantly into the peephole. "It's okay, Fehrer. I'm just here to honor our agreement."

A few more locks clacked. The door opened just a crack. Fehrer poked an eye out. "Cord...I, uh...I didn't expect you to come."

Cord shrugged. "I realize I didn't leave things all that well last time I was here. I'm sorry about that. Come on, let me in. I'll be good."

Cautiously, Fehrer removed the last chain and opened the door the rest of the way. He was in that bathrobe again. And using a cane. *What a drama queen,* Cord stopped himself from saying out loud. "See, but...I still don't have the, ah..."

"My eyeball? That's okay, I got it back myself. Matter of fact, I brought a friend who wanted to talk about that with you, if that's okay."

"Where...?" Fehrer started, but then saw a tall young man in black, draped in a red robe, standing next to Cord, like he'd been there the whole time.

"Hi, I'm Welles. You're Fehrer, that's great. I've heard a lot about you. We've got some things to talk about. May we come in?"

His politeness did nothing to set Fehrer at ease. Though the young man's voice was quite soothing. For reasons that were beyond him, he waved them in with his hand.

"Boy, it is nice in here," Welles marveled at the décor. "Business is good, I take it?"

Fehrer stammered, "Yes, it's...business...good business."

Cord growled a little. "Fehrer, seriously, you won't be hurt as long as we're in this house...Welles, do you have like a mystical sedative you could slap into him or something?"

Welles laughed gently as he rested a hand on Fehrer's shoulder. "Nothing like that, sorry Nathan. But I've got a feeling Mister Fehrer will relax, right?"

Fehrer looked into the young man's pitch black eyes and found himself deciding, *Yes, I think I will relax.* Suddenly feeling much more at ease, he offered, "So do you want me to start the rituals, then? So you can see Kayla?"

Cord gave a *Can you believe this guy?* look to Welles, then answered, "No, it's okay. We're just gonna head out back to the usual spot, and Welles will take care of the rest. Just hang out in the kitchen or something, we won't be long."

"Sure," Fehrer agreed simply. "Kitchen sounds good." He wandered away, and Cord and Welles made their way to the rear of the house and opened the porch gate out to the expansive backyard.

Cord led Welles out to the yard, explaining, "We usually set up by the fire pit over there. Man, I was joking about that magic dope thing..."

"It seemed like a good idea," Welles defended. Then, as they got closer to the fire pit, "Ohhh. Okay, I see. Damn, that's pretty clever."

"What?" Cord asked.

"You need the eyeball in this particular location – that's why I couldn't get Fehrer's spell working on my own. Proprietary magic. Good business sense, I must admit."

Cord grabbed some wood from the stack and began to build a fire. "How long will this take?"

Welles pulled a bundle from his pocket, unwrapped it, and placed its contents on the ground. Cord's preserved eye. "Not long. Just finish your bonfire, I'll take care of the rest."

Just after Cord finished stacking the wood, Welles ended his chanting, and nodded that everything was ready. Cord pulled out a box of matches, struck one, and tossed it onto the leaves underneath the wood. A few minutes of prodding the flames went by, and finally the two men stood in the warming crackle of a bonfire.

"Ready when you are," Welles told Cord.

"Do it, please."

Welles began his final chants, sprinkled some kind of dust around the eye, then knelt down and offered it a gentle, life-giving breath. Then he stepped back.

The dust gravitated toward the fire, swirled around it, and started pulling the smoke away. The smoke began to reconstitute itself into the form of a human. A woman. A beautiful woman made of smoke.

"Hello, my love," Cord greeted the smoke, sweetly. Quietly.

The smoke spoke. "Nathan…"

Welles eyed it intently. A person made of smoke. There, but not quite. It was lovely. She was lovely. Welles said nothing.

Kayla drifted down to the ground, eye to eye with Cord. She looked at him. Her eyes, though gray like the rest of her, beamed with light and warmth. She lifted a hand up to touch his clean-shaven face. The fingers dissipated against his skin. "You look so nice. And you cut your hair!" Though her voice had an echoing quality to it, it still sounded so perfectly normal and human.

Cord chuckled self-consciously, and ruffled the back of his new haircut. "Yeah, thought it was time for a change." Then, remembering they weren't alone, he held a hand out toward Welles. "Honey, this is Wyatt Welles. He's a magician I've been working with lately. Welles, this is Kayla."

Welles wasn't exactly sure of proper etiquette in a situation like this. So he bowed. And immediately felt silly. "It's a pleasure to meet you, ma'am." Rising again, he looked at her proudly. "You're even more beautiful than Nate described you. And that's saying something."

Kayla smiled thoughtfully, then tossed a look at Cord. "Isn't he a polite one."

"Heh. He's nervous is all."

Kayla turned back to Welles and said, "You are very sweet, Mister Welles, thank you so much."

Welles wondered if he was blushing. "The pleasure's all mine, Mrs. Cord. I'll leave you two alone now. I have some things to discuss with Mr. Fehrer inside." He made a jerking half-bow sort of gesture, frowned at himself, and turned to head back inside.

When they were alone, Kayla giggled. "Oh, he's just the cutest thing!"

Cord laughed along. "Yeah, that's what Quinn tells me."

"Oh my…Quinn has a man in her life? Good for her!"

"Yeah…her mothers still hold out hope that she'll meet a nice Tree-bob to keep it in the family, but they work really well together. Welles is a good guy for her. Keeps her from getting too serious about things."

"That's good to hear. That girl always had the weight of the world on her. What is she doing now? Actually…" It was sometimes hard to read Kayla's expressions, but through the smoke, her hesitancy came through clear. "I don't note the passage of time the same way you do, but I feel like I didn't get to see you the last time I was supposed to, did I?"

Cord looked down at his feet. "No. I...missed that appointment. Some things happened. Lot of things, actually. But..." he stopped, not knowing what else to say.

"So what have you been up to?" Kayla asked casually. "I know usually we just sit here and you tell me how pretty I am and how much you miss me, but if you've been doing things, I'd love to hear about them."

The smoke image of Kayla turned around to face the fire, sat herself down on the ground, cross-legged. Cord looked down at her dumbly. So Kayla patted the ground next to her. Cord plopped down. But he still found the words hard to get out.

Kayla coached him. "It's a beautiful evening. Lovely sunset."

Cord looked up and saw the deep blue enveloping the day, the hints of yellow and red falling to the west. He looked at the fire. And then he looked into Kayla's lovely face. And the words came naturally. "Well, we set fire to the kingdom. So that was something."

Kayla raised an eyebrow at him. "Pleeease tell me it was for a good reason?"

Cord stifled a laugh. "A lot of good reasons. That asshole magician Grolev had managed to kill and reanimate most of the town. Quinn gathered her own folk, and me and Victor Mene, and Welles, to go save Allison."

Kayla put her hands to her chest in concern. "Our sweet girl, is she okay?"

Cord nodded proudly. "Our sweet girl is a woman now, hon. The queen, actually. She even asked that I refer to her like that in front of the people. She asked nicely. But now, whenever we're in a meeting, I always say, 'Excuse me, your highness,' or something like that, when I want to interrupt."

Kayla laughed. "Oh, that's too much!"

"Yeah, I don't mind, though. You should see her, Kay. She's on fire." He looked at his wife and immediately regretted his choice of words. He pressed on regardless. "When we got her out of there, brought her to Northern Sun...I don't think she waited a day before instituting all new policies. First thing she did was gather the northern elders together, tell them that she was there to serve their needs. Then she released Eastern Sun, sent the Fel we were working with home with the message that Beasts Old Throne could govern itself, and she would deal with them on a trade basis like the old days."

"How did the Fel take that?"

Cord thought back, and then answered by way of diplomacy, "Like they usually do. A lot of yelling and whooping, followed by a marathon drinking contest. Lasted two days. I had to bow out after a few hours."

"You must be getting old."

"Hey, I'd just destroyed a whole kingdom. A man's got his limits." He waited a moment, then added, "Victor didn't make it."

Barely above a whisper, Kayla told him, "I know. I'm sorry."

"Thanks." Cord didn't bother to ask how she knew that Mene had died. He knew he wouldn't understand most of the things she knew about now. "If you'd have asked me if I'd ever miss Victor Mene, I'd have laughed through the night, but now...But you know, he had a death he would have wanted. Protecting the queen." He opted to leave out the unsavory aspect of Mene's subsequent resurrection and dismemberment, and continued. "I think I'm gonna name a special team after him. Maybe get some of the young Pic girls together, call them the Mene Mothers or something like that. I dunno," he concluded, shrugging.

"So you're a soldier again?" A hint of concern in her voice.

Cord stared into the fire. "I thought about just going back to the bar. Or maybe just tending a ranch, like we always talked about. I even bought a plot just east of the city. But Allison asked me to stick with her."

"And?"

With a smile, Cord answered automatically. "And I serve at the pleasure of the Queen. You should see her, Kay. She's got Quinn inviting all the woodlanders out to open up their communities, exchange ideas. She's got Welles talking with all the mystics who left the region after Arius took power. And Welles isn't exactly a team player, but something about his dealings with Keegan and Grolev must've given him a broader perspective. He's been talking about instituting a set of mandates among magicians, make sure they're all working with the same goals in mind." He remembered Welles's ambivalence on the subject, and so on the magician's behalf, clarified, "Not laws, just some guidelines."

"Sounds big – like what?" Kayla asked. Her voice rang with enthusiasm. Cord was telling her things that were exciting and new. He knew she liked hearing it.

"Looking to the future. Making things better for everyone. He's still got that hippy streak in him, so there won't be any magic-police any time soon. But he's talking about opening up a school. We'll see how that goes."

She playfully tapped her shoulder into his, though neither of them could actually feel it. "Nate, you've made a new friend!"

"Guess I have." He thought for a moment, then added, "Wow. I have four whole friends. Go figure."

Kayla did the math. "Welles, Quinn obviously, Quentin, and...oh, your pirate buddy Udo. What's he up to?"

"It took a lot of cajoling, but I got him to buy me out of the bar. It was always his, really. He did all the real work, I just hung around there. I tried to make him change the name, make it his own, you know what he chose?"

"What?"

"Cord's Tavern."

Kayla gave another sweet smile, finding the whole thing so adorable, but she refrained from using those words again. "He loves you so much. I wish I'd gotten to meet him."

"Yeah, he would've fallen for you," he admitted, then added with a wry smile, "But then, who wouldn't?"

"Flatterer. Okay, so what about you, mister soldier man? Not a farmer, not a barman. What's next for Nathan Cord? Don't tell me you're the new Victor Mene…"

Cord brushed that off. "Nah. Not for me. Quentin's been put in charge of rebuilding the guard. All volunteers this time, Allie threw out the draft. I think that alone earned her a lot of love in Northern Sun. She asked me to be her protector, since the Blue Knives were compromised. So I'm working on putting together a new Coal Brigade. One mission only: protect the queen. It's good, honest work. I can be proud of it."

He couldn't find any more words, so he sat and looked at the fire. "Wow," he heard his wife say.

"What?"

"You're alive again."

Smiling, but a little nervous, he asked, "What do you mean?"

Kayla closed her eyes, and when she found the words, continued, "I haven't seen you so engaged, so interested in things since…"

"Since before you died?" Cord finished for her, fighting off the sadness that phrase carried with it.

"Further back than that. Even before I died, you were just so…crushed, by what you'd become, the things you'd been asked to do. Like you couldn't see any light in the tunnel. You'd given up hope that you could even get out of that tunnel. But you did it, baby. I am so happy for you."

Cord took in Kayla's words and thought about it. "It's a lot of hard work. Changing things. But Allison…it's funny, considering she's the daughter of the single greatest bastard I've ever met, but she had a lot of parents who raised her right. I know she's read up on her Uncle Lucius. Quinn taught her a lot. Mene looked out for her, in his own way. I did my part, I think. But I gotta admit, love. I see so much of you in her. Your brightness, your compassion. She did you proud."

If it was possible for a woman made of smoke to blush, Kayla pulled it off. "Oh, I wish I could see her."

Seeing his wife again had had the usual effect – it sent him soaring, weightless into a magical world where he and his wife were forever happy. But that sentiment brought Cord crashing back to reality. "I wish you could too, Kay. I really do. But you and I both know you shouldn't be here."

"Nate, don't talk like that."

"Honey, believe me, all I want is to sit here and talk with you until the stars burn out. But that's just me being selfish. I understand that now. I'm just sorry it took me so long to realize that. That I put you through that too, when I should have let you go a long time ago."

Kayla nodded slowly. "When you first called me here…you were so lost, so gone from anything that was you. I couldn't leave you by your lonesome. When you called me back…I wanted to be here for you."

Cord looked at her. And he felt a tear roll down his cheek. "That's why you're the most amazing woman I will ever know. I love you with all my heart, and I swear I always will. But if I really do love you, I need to let you move on to the next place. Wherever that is." He frowned. "I don't…do you know where that is, is it good?"

Kayla answered simply. "It's good."

He put his hand close to the side of her face and leaned in to kiss her. The smoke that made up her lips pressed against his. He felt a tingle and saw plumes of fog drifting up.

"I love you too," she whispered softly, "Goodbye, my love."

And then the smoke that made Kayla Cord began to drift away, until finally Cord was left alone with a warm fire.

He cried freely and didn't care who saw it.

Eventually, he collected himself, sat up, and walked back to Fehrer's house. When he reached the kitchen, he found Welles and Fehrer sitting cordially in the breakfast nook, drinking tea. Welles's book of ideas was spread out on the table.

Welles stood up. "So Fehrer and I have been talking, and he's agreed to join that little collective I've been putting together."

Cord wiped his eye of any remaining tears, then looked at Fehrer diplomatically. "Yeah? You want to be part of the new Northern Sun, Fehrer?"

Fehrer nodded happily. "Well, your friend Welles has been telling me a lot about what you guys are doing up there, and it sounds interesting, to say the least. I'm sorry, do you want some tea?"

Cord waved off the offer. "Appreciate it, but no, I think I'm gonna head out."

Welles stepped closer. With genuine concern, he asked, "Did everything go okay?"

"Yeah, as well as you could expect."

"You want some company on the ride back?"

Cord patted him kindly on the shoulder, but answered, "Nah, I'd just as soon be by myself for a while. Thanks, though. I'll see you back home." It hadn't been the first time over the last few months that he'd referred to Northern Sun as "home," but it still sounded strange in his ears. To talk about a place as a home, rather than a refuge. He had begun to warm to the idea.

Opening the door, walking out and unlashing his horse, Cord found that he was fully aware of the sun setting in the west, bathing him in the heartbreakingly beautiful orange and red hues reflecting off the ocean and through the trees. He turned to greet it, and smiled, still feeling some sadness in his heart. It was something he could live with. After all he'd faced over the last year, over the last lifetime, Nathan Cord knew he could survive anything.

He mounted his horse and began the ride up north, back to his new home. He found himself looking forward to tomorrow.

The End

Acknowledgments

This book started long, LONG ago, and somehow managed to survive a crashed hard-drive. And at that point, I might have chucked the whole endeavor, if not for a support crew of everyone I've ever met.

In particular, thanks go to: Tad Zawadzki and Jeff Skonier, for letting me live in their houses while I wrote, sitting on their porches as I muttered, cursed and pantomimed fight choreography. Megan, for being endlessly supportive of what's really just my only demonstrable skill. My niece Julia, who helped shape the Orphan in my mind. All my friends and family who didn't roll their eyes too much when I'd say things like "It's *Lord of the Rings* as a western with touches of Mamet!" as though that explained anything. And Chris Braak, my writing and publishing partner, for giving me the competition I needed to crack this thing open, and many, many instances of editing prowess.

Couldn't have done it without you guys. Which means, in a way, the monstrosity you hold in your hands is really all their fault if you think about it.

Cheers,
Jeff Holland
Phoenixville, Pennsylvania
July 2010

www.ingramcontent.com/pod-product-compliance
Lightning Source LLC
Chambersburg PA
CBHW031309170626
46807CB00001B/345